"Madeleine, now living in Paris, discovers a Europe unknown to the working class, she discovers the Europe peopled by the best classes. But she also discovers that the finest clothes cover the most twisted personalities of all."

Masquerade Books

THE FURTHER ADVENTURES OF MADELEINE

ANONYMOUS

MASQUERADE BOOKS, INC
801 SECOND AVENUE
NEW YORK, N.Y. 10017

Copyright © 1989 by Masquerade Books, Inc.
All Rights Reserved

No part of this book may be reproduced, stored in a retrieval system, or transmitted in any form, by any means, including mechanical, electronic, photocopying, recording or otherwise, without prior written permission of the publishers.

First Masquerade Book Edition 1990

First printing March 1990

ISBN 1-878320-04-1

Manufactured in the United States of America
Published by Masquerade Books, Inc.
801 Second Avenue
New York, N.Y. 10017

CHAPTER I

Paris in the month of May! No place on earth is lovlier. As the train had whisked me through Normandy I thirstily drank in the beauty; the carefully cultivated terraces, the orchards gay with the pink of cherry blossoms.

I obtained temporary lodgings at a quaint boarding-house on the Rue d'Anjou. That evening I took my first walk through Paris streets. Down the Boulevard Haussmann and the Rue Vignon, till suddenly I found myself alongside the beautiful Church of the Madeleine, its stately edifice so familiar to me from the many photographs I had seen in schoolbooks. I stopped and asked myself whether I was dreaming. A sign warning the public against urinating in that corner assured me that I was no longer in the land of hypocrites. To my left stretched the Boulevard de la Madeleine, and just ahead, drowned in a sea of gaslights, I recognized the magnificent Place de la Concorde.

"You are in Paris at last," I told myself, "and you have renounced the country of your birth to make this one your own. From this moment forward you are French, Louise." Louise... Satisfactory as my name had always been to me, I felt a deep distaste for everything that linked me to Plattsburg and the past. I decided I must adopt another at once. I glanced about. A street sign caught my attention. Boulevard de la Madeleine.

Madeleine! From now on, that would be my name.

I continued up the street of my namesake to the Boulevard des Italiens, past the Opera, and then to the Rue du Faubourgurg Montmartre. Here I seated myself before one of the innumerable street cafés and sipped a glass of claret while I watched the fascinating and interminable throng of pleasure-seekers go by. Never had I seen so cosmopolitan a parade; Syrians and Turks in red fezes, Indian rajahs in full turban and burnoose, dark-skinned Moroccans and Algerians, handsome French officers, easily recognizable English and American tourists...and women. These above all! Pert, blithesome little misses—prettily dressed, rouged and lipsticked—moved through the crowd, plucking an arm here and there to offer their luscious selves while the gendarmes looked on indifferently. Ca c'est Paris. All this, so familiar to my readers, was new and refreshing to me. I saw at once that I would have competition in my chosen profession; but to offset this, I gathered quickly that there would be little stigma and no criminality attached to it, and this meant much.

But I am ahead of myself. I must first mention my trip across from New York. It was by no means uneventful, as indeed, how can any fairly attractive and not too icy a lady travel alone without some interesting adventure?

On the second day out I was presented to the Captain, a handsome old rake of about fifty, retired from the British Navy and occupying his present sinecure in a social rather than a nautical capacity. His main duty seemed to be cosseting the wives of rich travellers and thus make them partial to his company's liners. He accosted me on deck as I stood alone at the rail, watching the wake of the ship, a vanishing trail over which I would never travel again. Seeing he was the captain, I could not very well ignore him. With pointed directness he complimented me on my beauty then asked if I was married. No? Going to meet a fiance? Travelling with parents? Friends? No? Alone then? Ah!

It's not the custom for conventional young ladies to cross the ocean alone, he reminded me.

Conventions don't faze me, I told him. It was not long before the gay old dog was inviting me to share his suite for the rest of the voyage. I refused him coldly.

"But you must have some company," he insisted, "else your trip will be blooming tiresome—and I'm here to see that such a thing does not happen. Would you prefer that I introduced you to some men younger than I?" I did not dare accept his offer—for fear that I would hurt his feelings. He misunderstood my silence. "Ah! I see. You don't care for *male* company. Oh well, I have just the thing; a very charming and interesting woman with whom you ought to get along very well."

That same afternoon he presented me to Madame Mona Lugini, a mysteriously beautiful Italian woman of about thirty, an opera singer, returning from an engagement in the United States to meet her husband at Cherbourg.

"Call me Mona," she insisted as soon as we were alone.

"It must be nice to be going home to your husband," I said inanely, just to make conversation.

"Oh, Men!" She snapped her fingers contemptuously, "I have to keep one just for appearances. But they do not understand us...as, say, you and I could understand each other, Carissima Louise." She took my arm in a most affectionate manner—unjustified, I thought, given our short acquaintance.

"Take that hairy old sea ape who just introduced us," she went on, "from the moment the ship left New York, he has been trying to make love to me, asking me to sleep with him. But men do not love women as women can love each other. They are just arrogant fools, out for another conquest. Don't mistake me. I don't mind men when there is something to be had for it, as when I favor my managers or a critic now and then. But to go through all that mess and pretend to enjoy it—ugh!" Her fine breasts quivered under her black satin bodice with the violence of her disgust, her breath causing her luscious bosom to fill out like sails before a wind. I had considerable difficulty getting away, so assiduous was she in her attentions.

Late that same evening my stateroom door quietly opened and there stood Mona in a most intoxicating negligeé.

"Can I come in for a few minutes, Louise?" she asked. I could not refuse her. She approached, shivering with excitement. She sat on my bed, her thin décolleté nightdress, falling away from her bosom, disclosing two full, glorious spheres of flesh as only the women of the Latin races can boast. She was so lonesome, she told me, and couldn't sleep, she just had to come in to see me. Her teeth chattered audibly as she spoke. There was a rather cool ocean breeze coming in through the open stateroom window, but nonetheless the violence of her shivering could not be explained by temperature alone, for she was a magnificent hot-blooded woman.

"I am so cold," she confessed pitifully, "If only you would let me get into bed beside you, Louise?"

I am naturally too aloof a creature to relish such intimacies with a stranger, but humanity compelled me to grant her request. She joined me under the covers. Instantly her shivering ceased. She took me in her arms compellingly, fondling and kissing my breasts with a hotness that belied her recent shivering.

"What on earth does this mean?" I demanded in confusion.

"It means that I love you!" she replied intensely, "With a love that transcends the mere lust of men—and yet a love that is persistently misunderstood."

I was considerably perturbed. It was all too sudden for me. But soon the pleasant, titillating warmth of her caresses overpowered my objections. Soon her hands sought the hem of my nightdress…gently raising it, caressing my thighs as she went along. Then, slipping entirely out of her own light negligeé, she pressed her burning body close to mine. Our respective breasts glided over each other with an indescribably smooth and soft sensation, till they came to rest dovetailed together, one of my bubbies nested deliciously between her two hot, gorgeous globes of flesh. At the same time, her belly writhed softly about, bestowing a glorious, satiny caress with which nothing can compare. The passionate heaving of her bosom kept our titties in a continual gentle palpitating turmoil against each other.

For a time she continued thus, caressing me only with her wondrous body, her hands employed all the time at my buttocks to hold me closer to her.

Suddenly, she threw the covers from off the bed and extinguished the light. When she returned, she leaned over me and forcibly separated my thighs. There was something so hypnotic in the intensity of her ardor that I could not resist her. Her desire was so palpably real, and my resistance was so tentative and weak, that it would have seemed a kind of blasphemy, a revolt against divine authority, for little me to try and stop her. Her panting breath ran before her moist kisses up my thighs like a hot windstorm before rain; the sirocco reached my cunny, which had by now gone some days without visitation. A moment later her tongue entered, her arms embraced my posteriors and raised my entire love-groove to her hungry mouth and she launched upon a divine gamahuching that, so far as mad intensity and passion was concerned, has never been equalled in my whole lifetime.

The strangest thing of all was that, unlike Nanette, she desired no reciprocal stimulation. Her sole joy was to devour my cunt with a delicious flurry of tonguing and biting. While thus unselfishly bestowing delight upon me, she raised her own hips up and down, writhing about as if she were herself experiencing my ecstasies again and again. I have never met another such exclusively active cunnilinguist. Most women will lap another only out of gratefulness for the same thing, or in exchange, or perhaps in hope of the reciprocal favor.

But perhaps because of her single-minded attention, the ensuing bout was the most intensely pleasurable such coupling I ever experienced. She varied her movements and her tempo until I was hitting a peak with overwhelming regularity. Again and again she would play me, bringing me right to the edge of the luscious precipice. Again and again I came. She didn't let up until I was screaming out with the unbearable sensitivity of my repeatedly stimulated cunt. Although no words passed between us, she knew each time when I could bear not one more swipe of her practiced tongue. Then she would rest her head on my thigh and use her slim fingers to gently calm my overworked cunny. As soon as the tension left that wondrous bud of flesh, she would again attack, mercilessly bringing me back to the heights of passion.

We slept together that night.

Next morning the captain accosted us after breakfast with the knowing smile of a satyr.

"I was searching for you two ladies late last night, don't you know? There was an extempore little party in my suite. The stewardess whom I sent reported that you, Signora Lugini, were not in your room. And as for you, Miss Louise, sounds so jolly strange were heard at your door that the stewardess was afraid to disturb you. Putting one blooming thing and another together, I jolly well needn't ask you two whether you slept well last night. Now what I'm aiming at is this: I'm the law on this ship, I suppose you know, and I'm not allowed to countenance such goings on. Now, tut, tut...I'm not proposing to put you two in the brig; but you might at least, out of common decency, ahem—declare me in on your party. What say, ladies?"

Angrily I walked away. I would have slapped him, had I not been restrained by the silly thought that to do so might constitute mutiny or lèse majesty of a sort. Mona remained behind to give him a piece of her mind—though it was a piece of another nature he sought.

When she rejoined me, it was to report that he had continued his indecent proposals in all seriousness, urging that he could give either or both of us a much better time than we could bestow upon each other. What British bluntness! After thinking it over, I decided it was all quite funny. "Let him pant," I said, but at the same time I made Mona promise not to join me again that night, in case there was any further eavesdropping.

Night came. Once more I lay abed reading. Again the door opened and there stood Mona, despite the promise I had exacted from her. I was very angry with her, and told her so; but so convincingly did she picture for me the tortures she suffered when sleeping alone, the nightmares and phantasms that beset her highly strung imagination, that once again I had to grant her admission to my bed. Immediately she took up her subtle caressing and mad rubbing. Soon she had stripped, doused the lights, and was between my thighs, quieting my fears with a repetition of the delights of the previous night.

I was just on the verge of an orgasm when I was frozen with horror by a sound at the door. It opened. Someone entered quickly and the door shut again. By the partial light that sifted in through the vents that opened onto the corridor, I made out the glistening uniform of the captain. Mona had her back to the door and was too absorbed in her dear task to note his entrance.

"Heave Ho, my hearties!" he spoke in a voice full of insolent assurance. "I was making my evening round of inspection and just stopped in to see how my two young charges were coming along. Ripping nice I should say from what I can make out in the dark. A pretty picture you do make—but what say to my finishing it up for you in the grand way intended by the good Lord Almighty?" I could only imagine that too-easy success with other women had made him so insufferably sure of himself.

Mona raised her mouth from its delicious

occupation and snarled, "Get out of here! We don't need your help, you beef-eating British bastard!" Like a tigress that cannot be lured off its prey, her mouth seized again upon my cunt and continued sucking and nibbling as if there had been no interruption.

The intruder whistled softly and came closer. "All right! All right! Come now Mona—I shan't interfere. But you might be a little more hospitable..."

He was silent for awhile. Mona continued her mad tonguing; but I now had some difficulty catching up to where we had been—what with that dim masculine form looming in the darkness.

He approached still closer. As what light there was came from behind him, I could make out his every move which I marked with an unearthly fear that was quite absurd, considering that neither of us had either maidenhead or chastity to lose.

His hand went down and felt the heaving white posteriors that projected over the foot of the bed.

"How nice! How nice!" he spoke, "Is this Mona or Louise?" Neither of us answered. Both of us were speechless, though for different reasons. There was a moment's silence, during which I could hear only the soft liquid lapping of Mona's tongue, the heavy breathing of the horrid intruder, and the slight rasp of his coarse hands upon the ivory-smooth buttocks that met his caress. He spoke again nervously: "I say... if no one is going to claim this, I'll take it myself."

I expected Mona to fly up and scratch his eyes out; but whether in consideration for me, or in oblivion to all but her sweet task, or perhaps from plain indifference, she said not a word—confining her mode of conversation to that dear language of love which held her so spellbound to my cunt.

In stark silhouette I could see the captain whip out a huge truncheon of a member...then, raising Mona's entire lower body with his easy strength, he forced her legs wide apart till each of her feet rested upon his shoulders. Mona groaned with rage but, like a leech, would not let her mouth be torn from me; her hands clasping my buttocks more fiercely, she dug her nails into me as if to anchor herself.

What a mad scene. By looking within the inverted angle of Mona's luscious thighs, white and almost phosphorescent in the semi-darkness, I caught another momentary glimpse of the captain's glistening bar as it slipped down between those widespread thighs and found the narrow place of origin.

I could hear his laboured breathing, I could picture his amorous fumbling as he sought the breach and lodged lip-deep in this madly ingenious position. I could not help but feel the fierce plunge that sent him gliding home into Mona's most intimate interior and brought him up with a dull fleshy thud, as his mount met her upturned arse, as her mount met his balls in this provocatively novel upside-down connection.

"Louise! Mona," he was gasping as he lunged in and out, his quavering accent testifying at once to the extreme delight he was experiencing and to the fact that he still did not know which of us he was raping! It was a situation to court madness. The worst having been accomplished, I yielded myself completely to Mona's titillations, to the whole unutterable lewdness and salacity of the scene. He was fucking me for all he knew, and though his prick was in Mona's cunt, I was experiencing all the exquisite stimulations of that heavenly act. By substitution, by transference—oh, how can I explain it, dear reader, so involved, so diabolical, so divine was it. I truly felt as if he were doing it to me. More—since his every thrust forced Mona's whole mouth closer to my cunt—I shared the identical rhythm of the act.

What a delicious complexity of movements, as I joined in with the other two, my hips screwing downward to Mona's mouth as he shoved her firmly toward me! It was his thrust that I was meeting. It seemed as if his monster organ had torn its way clear through her passion-tossed frame till, through her mouth, it had met my cunt. All in all, I could not have been fucked more effectively. To top this lascivious thought was the realization that I was being both fucked and cunt-lapped at the same time. One moment, Mona was a mere impersonal agency to my connection with that fierce fucking man, the next, she was my dear tender female lover, suffering herself to be raped rather than allow my pleasure to be interrupted.

Add to this indescribable commotion of our senses and bodies, the vibrations of the ship and the incessant rocking contributed by the waves, which now, whether in sympathy or by coincidence seemed to increase in wildness.

With such sights and sounds and thoughts and feelings lashing on my lustful senses, it did not take long for that earlier, fear-frozen discharge still stored within me to be melted and given release through the tingling of all my fibers and the ecstatic spasm of my limbs. So much stronger was my orgasm, no doubt due to the lasciviousness of our triple effect, my twitching womb poured a flow of love's secretions that even a man could not much outdo.

But Mona, gurgling in her throat with joy for my joy, did not stop but went right on administering stroke after stroke of love's exquisite dying fit. Soon my pleasures began anew. As for herself, she seemed to be coming continuously in a ceaseless spasm of spending. There are such women, who, at times of sexual excitement can bring themselves on at will again and again—and so it was with her.

The captain, not for one moment inactive during all this, but slow in reaching his climax because of his advanced years, now gasped, "Jove! What pleasure! Mona, Louise—whichever you are—I am coming! Push closer to me! Now! Ah! Ah gods! Ahhh." And with the furious short plunge that accompanied each violent exhalation, I could almost see and feel the great hot jets of sperm that were shot into Mona's cunt, inverted to receive and hold every drop of it—which yet, as I found later, overflowed bounteously over her belly and buttocks and dripped in great gobs, like tallow, on the floor at the foot of the bed.

Mona, as if nothing had happened, kept up the delicious caresses of her tireless tongue and the wild writhing of her hips.

"Stop! Stop!" the captain groaned, "Are you trying to pump my life's blood out of me?—or do you want to wrench my part off? Stop, I say, you insatiable siren, until I pull out at least!"

It chanced just then that the motion of the ship changed perceptibly and it seemed that the engines had gone dead from some cause or another. The captain withdrew his dripping rammer hurriedly, replaced Mona's thighs on the bed and dried himself.

"Sorry. Must leave you ladies. Navigation requires my attention," he muttered as he stumbled out of the dark stateroom.

When Mona had finished me a second time, she arose and turned on the light. Thick, creamy fluid was still trickling down her thighs. She made a move of distaste.

"Do you have a douching syringe, Louise?" she asked, "It would not be at all funny if I became pregnant by that beast. I guess he thinks I enjoyed that swollen piece of meat crammed into me; but if I came, Louise, it wasn't due to his efforts, but to that delicious cunt of yours." So she hadn't enjoyed his amateurish fucking after all!

Next day the captain accosted me once more while I stood alone on deck. I had decided to ignore him completely; but somehow my dreams of the night before had been entirely of being loved in that exotic wheelbarrow fashion.

"I say. Tell me." he asked, "Was it you or Mona I had so deliciously last night?" In fairness to my friend, I would not deny it. In honesty, could not claim credit for it—so I refused to say. He took it as an admission and there was no use telling him otherwise.

"By Jove, you were great," he said, "but we could do much better if we were by ourselves, don't you know. Tonight at my suite, aye what? And I'll have some bloomin' fine champagne."

Something compelled me to play up to his impression of me. "Supposing I did meet you—what's in it for me?" I queried provocatively. I decided that I might as well start right in to learning how to handle men if I was to make a success of my life.

"Ho! Ho!" he laughed, "What's in it for you? I say, that's quite funny. What's in it for you, eh? Why, if you don't mind my telling you, there'll be a fine stiff John Thomas and a good copious injection of the sap of life, by Jove!"

"By Jove!" I angrily mimicked his detestable self-assurance, "Your employers may pay you to amuse the old ladies on board in that way, but I'm attractive enough to take my pick of the youngest and handsomest men on board—if that's all I wanted."

"Oh, I see," he muttered, his vanity hurt despite his thick skin, "you want to be paid. Well, I've never done this before, but I suppose your kind have to live too. How much do you want me to pay you?"

"I don't want you to pay me anything," I answered, confused by the strangeness of being asked my price and utterly unprepared in the methods of bargaining, "But I don't like the idea of flattering you by being just another woman who has given you what you want. So let's not say anything more about it." And I walked away.

In my stateroom, I found a note to report at the purser's office. "You haven't turned over your passport for inspection yet, Miss..."

"Passport?" I said, frightened, "I have no passport. I intend becoming naturalized in France."

"But do you have a permit from the French immigration bureau? Without one or the other, I'm afraid you won't be able to get by the port officials at Cherbourg. Perhaps you'd better speak to the Captain."

In a frenzy I sought out the old satyr. As I entered his office, he came out of a corner where he had been squeezing a young Irish stewardess. She left hurriedly. I told him my predicament. In his best official manner he informed me that I would be deported immediately upon landing, and that he would probably have the pleasure of my company on the return voyage. I burst into tears.

"Well, well," he put in, "if you were a good friend of mine, I could vouch for you personally to the immigration authorities and everything would be spiffy. Only you've just refused to be nice to me, and so I suppose you'll have to ship for another voyage, till we do become acquainted."

I was sport enough to admit myself fairly beaten. My tears evaporated, and my prettiest smile adorned my features. "Dear Captain! Tonight in your suite, then?"

"No!" he roared, "Not tonight, and not in my suite, but right here and now, by Jove!"

He locked the office door. Of course there was a fine sofa in the room, but I shamelessly confessed that I wanted it done wheelbarrow fashion.

"So you liked it after all, last night, aye what?"

"No. It wasn't me."

That put an extra edge on his appetite. "I'll be able to tell in a minute. My dog has a better memory than I. He can always sense the difference where I can't." And he presented to my touch an instrument that completely defied my grasp.

He placed a sofa cushion on the richly rugged floor. I positioned myself upon it. With scarce an effort, my gallant grasped my thighs and placed them about his hips where I locked them firmly for the time. In a moment I became accustomed to the slight strain of the upside down position. My breasts, though not naturally pendulous, now swung back and caressed my chin. Looking backward between them, and under my belly, I could see what was being done. The strange topsy-turviness of the lewd pose served only to inflame me with impatient desire; to have the barrow hitched to the rider in that equivocal cart-before-the-horse gallop we were about to set out on.

His belaying pin lay ready, pressed up against my belly by its own tension. Loosening my thighs a little to allow himself to draw back somewhat from the breach which lay so fairly before him downside up, he lodged the thick swollen knob between the outer lips. Then, the proper direction determined, and his hands no longer needed for steering, he grasped my thighs and slowly drew my buttocks to him, as at the same time he steadily pushed down and inward to the crimson velvet-lined cavern of love. Moist and well-prepared as that part was for his reception, never had it entertained so bulky and exercise-strengthened a visitor. As he drew the sheath up over his majestically disproportionate weapon, I received so violent and painful a stretching that I burst out sobbing, regretting enough my over-adventurousness. I would have been split apart, had I not been favored by the generous lubrication afforded me by my excitement and by the natural elasticity and adaptability that healthy young women are blessed with in those parts.

"Don't cry, child," the Captain comforted me, "You'll be all right in just a minute. No...it wasn't you last night. I haven't been in one so nice and tight for as long as we both—Thomas and I—can remember." And he held still for a time, savoring and enjoying the unusual constriction of the tight—but moist and hot—sheath.

Then, as the wet folds adjusted themselves to the huge object that engorged them, he slowly withdrew and then he slid all the way home to the hilt, in the living, luscious, flesh-cylinder that gripped him so closely and deliciously. His succeeding motions gave him no more difficulty than what served to increase his enjoyment.

The great advantage of this unique position for

intercourse, dear reader, is this: the clitoris, ordinarily situated above the love grotto and receiving only the most glancing and momentary frictions of the lover's organ (unless he rides very high, and even this has its limitations), is in the reverse position immediately beneath the beloved male joy-giver, which, instead of sliding back and forth on the lower fornix of the cunt, rests and rides continually over the tender head of the clitty. Come what may, there can be no blundering missing stroke, and this, regardless of the shape, thickness, length or even stiffness of the masculine part. So much for the advantages accruing to the tenderer participant in the dear duel.

As for the man who is good enough to favor his lady-love with this delicious variation, there is this recompense. The underside of his penis being the most sensitive part of him, he can feel the spongy little nodule of the clitty stiffening and bounding up, and counter-stroking the delicate groove directly beneath the acorn-shaped head of his prick. As he shoves all the way home, the divine little female finger traces an exquisite tickling line straight down the shaft of his member to the very root, reversing and repeating the delightful titillation at every stroke; giving and receiving pleasure simultaneously.

What strain there might have been in sustaining our rather acrobatic position merely served to increase the lubricity of the act and the violence of the contrast when the final downpouring relief came. But between the beginning and the delicious end, there was an infinity of sensations that defy description. Firmly back and forth the captain drew and plunged his broad satisfying instrument, like the wielder of a bow on a bass-viol, never once losing contact with those strings that sent reverberating chords and harmonies of pleasure through me. Soon my eyes glazed over and became dim with the approaching ecstasy. I could no longer discern that red blood-gorged joy-dispenser as it plunged in and out. Then suddenly, I went stone blind.

The rich, hot, climactic flood of sensation went eddying and sizzling through my veins, contracting all my visceral organs, and causing me to faint away momentarily with the glowing overpowering sensations that inundated my brain.

I collapsed upon the cushion; but the Captain continued to sustain me, slowing up his motion to a gentle massage of my inner vagina and the mouth of my womb until I recovered. The entrance muscle of my cunt was so rigidly clamped about his member that he could scarcely move at all. But as the last waves of agonized pleasure passed away, my pussy relaxed once more from its attempt to hug its delicious intruder to death.

Now, gradually letting out sail and picking up speed, the Captain rode along at a spanking clip before the full blast of his own desires. But before his slow, majestic ship has entered the harbor of ecstasy, the seas of delight again rose to flood-tide levels within me and we shared the stormy motions of pleasure together: give, and take; back and forth, his pump working furiously and finally inundating me even further with his hot copious effusion as I drowned in bliss.

As he took a last farewell plunge into my flooded hold, his creamy sacrifice suddenly displaced, frothed over my outer cunt and hairs, sending a warm trickle across my arse and down the small of my back to my very shoulders—a generous oblation that was not, however, unmixed with some slight offering of my own, in the form of some pink and scarlet streaks of my cunt's intimate blood.

When I was dressed and taking my leave, he again assured me that everything would be arranged with the French officials.

"Now that there's no longer any need of hypocrisy between us, shall you come here tonight?" he asked.

"Mona might be suspicious," I told him. Jealous, is what I meant.

"Well, let's make it tomorrow afternoon again—between luncheon and tea."

I agreed, not unwillingly. Forty years of service in his Majesty's Navy hadn't been for nothing. In the five days that remained of our voyage, the Captain demonstrated upon me the essence of his experience. But when he had tried everything from the Argentinean to the Zulu method geographically and alphabetically inclusive, his fingers still fondled my tiny rear entrance rather longingly. A sailor will always be a sailor, I thought; but paid no further heed.

Our last afternoon together arrived. He was quite fatherly and most solicitous of my future welfare. I confessed my purpose of becoming an exclusive "vendeuse de l'amour" in Paris—in language blunt, of living by my cunt. He laughed and promised to give me letters of introduction to some wealthy prospects. "But," he went on, "not to seem discouraging, cunt is now out of fashion in Paris."

"What do you mean?" I asked anxiously, not believing him, but yet disturbed at the implied threat to my plans.

"They are a sophisticated people, the French. Naturally, with time and excess, a whole populace may become relatively jaded and blasé toward conventional sexual pastimes. Then begin the practice of various refinements—or 'perversions,' as the Anglo Saxon mind is apt to consider them. But don't you be frightened. There's nothing that a bright little girl like you can't learn in time."

"Oh? So you haven't taught me everything?"

"I'm afraid not. But there's still time for one more lesson."

"And that is…?"

"You understand French? Votre prochaine lecon, c'est faire l'amour en cul."

If I hadn't understood his words, his hand, creeping from my thigh where it had been resting, around to my coveted bum-hole, was explicit enough. I blushed. "Oh captain!" I exclaimed, "Do you mean that this huge thing (indicating the weapon that was generally in evidence whenever I was about) can be introduced into that tiny place where I cannot even insinuate a finger? Oh no! It would kill me."

"Darling child, you little understand the wonderful possibilities of the human body—especially of a woman's body. It is only at the very entrance that it is so tight—and even that is very stretchable. Beyond that, there is nothing to hurt." His knowledge of anatomy was correct. It is only the sphincter that seems so impenetrable. Within is the wide mucous-lined rectum or sigmoid, in size and shape very much like the vagina. He prevailed upon me to let him try it. I might more wisely have waited for a less monstrously sized lover to take this, my second maidenhead; but somehow, it seemed to me especially appropriate to have this operation, smacking as it does of male homosexuality, performed by an authoritative naval man. My literary and dramatic sense has betrayed me again and again; but all through life I have acted and chosen situations as if for an autobiography.

Gloatingly and dotingly, as usual, the Captain removed each article of my clothing, pausing at each stage to admire my disarray. When he could remove no more from me, he proceeded to doff his own clothes. Then, having me kneel on a soft cushion at the side of the couch, with my body leaning over it and my buttocks projecting at right angles, he went in search of some pomade—to ease his entrance, as he explained.

Like one condemned, with his head upon the block, I waited the executioner. I entertained but little expectation of pleasure. Indeed, I rather expected great pain; but a sort of wicked curiosity, the wish to see whether this unnatural thing could be done, kept me—as yet—from relenting. Anyhow, I told myself, I wanted to savor to the dregs every experience that life had to offer, and since I would be persuaded to do this sooner or later, why not at once?

He returned with a jar of scented Vaseline. Kneeling on the cushion behind me, he gently applied the soothing lubricant to the pink, puckered little exit that he so enterprisingly meant to employ as an entrance—the needle's eye through which he hoped to pass a camel—patiently dilating the little muscle with his middle finger and working in the Vaseline. At first I was miserably embarrassed by this intimate handling of that most personal part of me (I say 'personal' because, unlike my cunny, I could not think that it was meant for two). But soon, the caressing of that zone, more sensitive and erogenous than I had ever dreamt, became so pleasing that I was wriggling my hips with anxiety for him to get started.

At last, satisfied with these preliminaries, the Captain oiled his own part from head to root, which, as I glanced across my shoulder to watch the procedure, seemed—unless I was really seeing it for the first time—almost twice as large as it had been before. I buried my face in the sofa-cushions to see no more.

He brought the weapon to bear upon the tiny crinkled crevice. Two or three times it slipped down the groove of my buttocks toward that other cavity where it more rightfully belonged. He brought it into position once more. But this time it flew upward at his earliest pressure. Guiding it with his hand then, so as to restrain its merest slip, he brought just the tip of his huge arrow to the tiny aperture, and slowly, firmly, pressed inward. This time he succeeded in gaining the entry of half the head—this as I knew from the horrible, unendurable agony I suffered as that narrow passage was so cruelly distended. At the same time, the muscles of that part contracted rigidly—as if to force out the terrible foreign object that was now being crammed into such a disproportionately small entrance. But the Captain, expecting this, counteracted it with the pressure of his body, fully holding his own. "You must relax, Louise," he told me, "and not try to force it out."

"Oh no! I can't stand it! Captain, you hurt me

dreadfully! Oh! How you are torturing me!" I cried tearfully. "Please, please—stop. Oh, you are tearing me open! I'll do anything but this! Oh! Oh!"

"Now, now!" he comforted me, "As soon as the head gets by, the pain will not be so great. Come now, relax, and press toward me. Take it in as slowly as you like—or as quickly as you can endure it." And at the same time, to divert me from the agony which had me writhing and beating the cushions with pain, he put his arms about my waist and slipped a finger into my cunt. The dear clitty did not fail as universal anesthetic. As the pleasure from his light quick massaging increased, the pain faded, and soon my motions changed to a back-and-forth movement which, with his gentle pressure from behind, soon has his whole tool sheathed in my rectum to the very root. The Vaseline allowed its huge bulk to slide all the way in without bruising or further pain. I felt a most indescribably peculiar sensation of being full up...and a slight desire to evacuate, which quickly changed to a desire to hold that great bar of flesh within me indefinitely.

He withdrew half way and pressed in again, his movement easy and unobstructed. The caress to my soft inside passage was anything but unpleasant; only the entrance was still somewhat sore.

He took each stroke very slowly and with great relish. "Oh, how close and hot and soft and moist it is in there!" he said, "I confess, though it ordinarily takes me half an hour to come, when I do this, I come almost immediately." And he stopped his motion again, this time to keep the climax from overtaking him too soon. "Tell me when you are ready, Louise," he whispered, and, with his arms drawing me closer to him, he continued the rapid digital stimulation of my cunt.

"I am coming soon, Captain!" I gasped, as the divine dissolution approached. He fiercely resumed the full plunge and draw and thrust into my behind—the swelling fleshy curves of my buttocks alone protecting me against the violence of his contacts. "Now! Now!" I cried as the exquisite climax enthralled me. I felt innumerable jets of hot, thick sperm shooting out from his thick vibrating member, seeming to flood all my bowels, all the secret recesses of my body. We had come off simultaneously, and I knelt there bathed in thankful bliss as well as in his generous effusion, till the exquisite turmoil subsided.

His member was still hard and stiff. He began moving back and forth within me again. "If I pulled it out now," he explained, "the greater size of the head over that of the shaft would hurt you again—like drawing an arrow from a wound. It would be better to wait till I get soft. It won't take me long to come a second time." And he continued, more easily than ever now, what with the additional lubrication of his own generous ejaculation. True to his word, in scarcely more than twenty strokes I felt another, though less prolific, injection of his warm tingling love juices—and almost immediately his terrible engine began shrinking until, with no difficulty at all, he drew it out of my cream-gorged bottom. The deed was done—and I was now the proud possessor of two separate and distinct bodily cavities, each for the full and complete celebration of the rites of Venus. My newer cunt I even felt some predilection for, insofar as its use entailed no fear of pregnancy, no contraceptive precaution. As for after-effects, there were none. After bathing, I found my rear just as prettily puckered and chastely closed as ever. No sacrifice to love is long regretted.

CHAPTER II

Back in Paris now.

After a week or so I called upon one of the references the captain had given me. He was a handsome French-Jewish banker of about thirty-five, closely related to the famous Rothschilds. He carefully read the ambiguously worded note. Adjusting his monocle and caressing the ends of his carefully cultivated mustache, he looked me over with friendly deliberateness.

"A little American girl in need of a friend, I see." He spoke English carefully, though not faultlessly, with a decided French accent that I became fond of at once. "And not so bad. You have come at the right time. My last mistress has recently joined the Folies Bergère, thanks to my efforts, and now she is so much in demand that I cannot even get near her. And for a man of business responsibilities like myself, it is not advisable to stand waiting around stage doors. I must have my little woman always ready for me, whenever I can get—what you call it—the freedom. Do you mind if I ask you to remove your wrap and walk around the office for me to see—ah, pardon—the figure?"

Very much embarrassed, for such frank dealings were still beyond my experience, I complied. Very calmly and appraisingly he looked me up and down.

"Ravissante! Superbe!" he exclaimed in approval. "Now do you mind, mademoiselle...ah, forgive me, to bend over—as if to tie your shoestring?"

I began to assume the required posture until its purpose occurred to me. I stopped and burst into tears.

He sprang up and took me by the shoulders. "Mademoiselle! Ah, forgive me! How have I hurt you? Please! I cannot stand to hear a woman cry. I have the soft heart. What is it?"

And I spoke the lines, now so familiar as to weary the reader, but yet constituting one of the most valuable tricks in the whole of a woman's repertory.

"I am a good girl! (More sobs.) Of course I am willing to be nice to a kind man who will be good to me and protect me. But you parade me back and forth and examine me as if—as if I were a horse that you were going to purchase outright. Will you help me on with my coat, sir? I must be going..."

"What! Let you go out alone and unprotected in this wicked city—you who have no friends? Ah no, Mademoiselle! All my life I would feel responsible for your fate. I am sorry if I have offended you. Stay, I implore you."

He was a very fine gentleman, for all that his English seemed to derive from effete Victorian novels. I remained. We dined together. I drank just enough wine to make it seem logical for even the most well-behaved little girl to forget herself. He took me to a quiet hotel. I pretended to be horrified at the idea of being alone with a gentleman. As a matter of fact I was raring to go, but business first. Piece by piece, I let him undress me. I was discovering that pretended modesty is the one piquancy that the Frenchman doesn't get much of. It worked like a charm. When I snatched up my chemise, which he had just removed from me, and wrapped it across my bosom, he implored me on bended knees to uncover my charms for his admiration. When finally I did, he pounced upon them as if they were the first bubbies he had ever set eyes upon, fondling and squeezing them passionately with his hands, and deftly sucking and nibbling the tiny ruby sentinels that stood stiff guard upon each of my snowy mountains.

Then, to my surprise, he gently forced me upon my back, spread wide my legs, and placed a full gallant kiss upon my cunny at the very juncture of its lips.

"Oh, don't do that!" I cried.

"Every polite Frenchman will do as much for any attractive lady," he told me. "And what harm can there be in thus paying one's respects to the delicious little place that is soon to bestow so much pleasure?"

Drawing forth his weapon, which was of normal size and tolerable thickness, but lacking in the red cap or foreskin which it is the custom of his race to remove for hygienic purposes (my first kosher cock) he placed the unencumbered ruby head between the crimson lips of my cunt, still moist from his kiss.

In the preceding days I had prepared for just such an occasion by again and again bathing that part, so distended by the captain's frequent maunderings, with special solutions of alum and other restorative astringents—until by now all its folds were so contracted and tightly drawn together that there was no visible or even tangible opening. Consequently, his entrance met with every impediment that real virginity could afford. With the vanity that is natural to every man, my gallant was only too willing to credit me—and more especially himself—with my maidenhead. By the naive awkwardness of my movements I did everything to further this illusion and hinder his too easy progress, so successfully, that one of the minor folds of my vagina, bruised by the forcible entry of his part, yielded up that slight sacrifice of blood that no man is so unsadistic as not to enjoy. Luckily, these same men love their victims all the more because of it.

With our parts completely coupled at last, however, I had neither purpose nor inclination to overdo my role of innocent.

"My beloved ravisher!" I exclaimed, adopting his own dated English as the most convincing idiom. "How large and strong you are! Oh what fires you kindle in my blood! Oh! Oh! Stop—it feel's so good! No! Come into me further! Further!" and I wrapped my legs tightly about his back.

Out and in his throbbing member plunged in the tight quivering encasement of hot flesh that so hugged him, held him back, and always invited his return. Back and forth I writhed to add every conceivable counter-caress to his blood-gorged sensitive joy-distributor, as well as to give my avid clitty the maximum of furious action. So effectively did I do the latter that I came some moments before him. Then, as my own pleasure subsided, and I felt him stiffening all over and employ the short, panting jabs that heralded his climax, I slipped a hand down between us, arched up to meet his descending body, and just as he withdrew for what I can always judge infallibly as the final masterstroke, I seized his bursting weapon, wet with my own effusions, and drawing back my body, snatched it out from its warm nest, just as he ejaculated his hot torrent of creamy essence upon my white heaving abdomen, up to my very breasts.

Two thoughts had at the last moment led me to this expedient. First, that it would not be advisable to be entirely abandoned at the first engagement. A little girlish fear would go well with his present impression. Secondly, I had taken no precautions against impregnation and there was no use in taking needless chances when things could be finished satisfactorily enough this way.

After he recovered from the soft spasms of his pleasure, my monsieur took it all in good manner. I, on the other hand, pretended to be suffering deep remorse.

"It was the wine, monsieur, that betrayed me this way, I swear it. And now that you have had your will of me, I suppose you are through."

"Ma chérie! I should say not! If only you are willing, I shall take care of you. I shall be your good papa. You will want for nothing."

In a couple of days I was set up in a luxurious

apartment on the Avenue Wagram. Henri, though unmarried, warned me in advance that his business and his family claimed so much of his attention that he would be unable to spend as much time with me as he might like. On the very evening of our proposed 'Housewarming' he was two hours late. When at last he bustled in he smacked his lips at the array of delicacies and cold viands that I'd had sent up from a nearby café.

He embraced me tenderly. Then, immediately proceeding to take possession of my personal charms.

He asked (in French, for we had agreed that it would be best to use only that language): "What of our appetizer, dear Madeleine-Louise?" and seating himself in a soft armchair, he drew me down upon a hassock at his feet.

"Appetizer? Dear Henri, I'm afraid that I don't understand. Nous avons des hors d'oeuvres..."

"No. I don't mean anything like that."

"But I am anxious to please my kind protector."

"And I am always forgetting what a little innocent you are still. Well, if you love me, Madeleine, you will allow me the pleasure of teaching you." He opened his trousers and brought out his stiffening weapon. As I sat at his feet, it waved threateningly toward my face.

"Now, do you hate and fear this part of me?" he asked, smiling.

"No, monsieur. I love it. It has been so good to me these last few days, giving me pleasures I have never tasted before."

"Fine. Then you needn't shrink from it. Take it in your hand, fondle it, show it your appreciation." I complied, rubbing and stroking it timidly with my palm, closing both my hands about its shaft till only the scarlet head protruded, and squeezing it gently till a tiny drop of pre-coital fluid appeared at its mouth.

"Now, would you be very frightened if I asked you to kiss it?" A little hesitantly I complied, placing a quick kiss upon its beaming countenance. Its whole shaft tautened with a suddenness that nearly wrenched it from my hand.

"Now once more, darling Madeleine—only more like you kiss me."

I closed my lips moistly about the end and gave it a long kiss, during which my tongue played lightly back and forth across it.

"Ah! That is it, my divine woman. Look, I shut my eyes and leave it all to you. Imagine you were in my place. Do everything with your mouth and hands that you think you would like. And afterward I have a fine surprise for you." He lay back luxuriously in the chair. I felt that a great deal depended upon my ability to learn quickly.

Opening his trousers further to bare every part of his precious instrument, I reached in and brought out even his soft tender love-reservoirs, which I balanced upon my palm. Starting with the tip-top I dilated the little canal from which all blessings flow with the tiny tip of my tongue and then placed a series of the moistest conceivable kisses all the way down the shaft to its very root, then returned to the place whence I had started. I ran my tongue up its whole length to the very head. I repeated this again and again, sometimes varying it by running my wet tongue up along the sides or the top of the shaft instead of the underneath, sometimes encircling my tongue about its sensitive bulk in a subtle spiral that is difficult to describe, but which must have been intolerably exquisite to the owner of the part so caressed. Soon all my self-consciousness vanished, and I took an artist's pride in devising the utmost possible variations of caresses and titillations with my lips and tongue. When, from his flushed face, disturbed breathing, and troubled writhing I judged—and judged correctly—my Henri to be sufficiently charged, I took to licking exclusively the soft sensitive groove immediately under the acorn-shaped head, while I held the shaft tightly in my fist, much as a child handles a delicious lolly-pop, looking up to my lover's face for his approval.

Finally..."Take it in your mouth—all of it, ma chère Madeleine!" He gasped, yielding in his approaching extremity to the irresistible male impulse to sheath. With an effort, I opened my mouth wide enough to take in his bulky cylinder. He grasped my head with both his hands and drew me closer, closer to him, until his member, touching the rearmost part of my mouth, threatened to force its way down my very throat. I pulled away a little and took hold of his too-reckless member with my fist, grasping it tightly just beneath the point on the thick shaft that I considered would constitute a good mouthful. Alternately, I now sucked upon the fleshy morsel or stroked and rolled my soft tongue about its hot, throbbing head. The effect of this treatment, unbelievable as it may seem, was to swell that mouthful so prodigiously that there was no longer any room in my mouth for any further manipulation by my agile tongue. I was confined to sucking it and massaging the length of the staff with my hand.

As it swelled, preliminary to its final outburst, Henri shoved it forcibly back in my mouth once more, as if to drive it through my head. I tried in vain to clear my throat, so engorged was I with this tower of delicious living flesh.

Suddenly, with a few furious back and forth movements of his hips and a low triumphant cry of joy, Henri came, his organ stiffening into steel while a hot stream of his thick love balm spurted in soothing torrents down my throat, filling my mouth so that much of the creamy proofs of his enjoyment began dripping from the corners of my lips. Already much of it had gone down my throat. There was no point in being ridiculous. I swallowed the rest.

For a moment longer I continued sucking and tonguing gently, to make sure that his pleasure was all over. Another fitful little spurt of cream was my reward. It was delightful, wholly apart from the erotic element, this sucking of warm, polished, living flesh, this fruition of sweet human milk that came to me. I felt as happy and contented as a child at its mother's breast, and I could have gone on like this forever, giving great pleasure in return for a simpler one, had he not withdrawn himself, and taking me in his arms and covering me with ecstatic kisses. Then, in gratefulness for the incomparable pleasure I had bestowed upon him, he changed places with me and threw back the tangle of my skirts and chemise, his hot mouth, still panting with his own joy, sought out my cunny, which was in a state of excitement. His strong tongue separated the mossy folds and found the clitty—and he administered to me, to the great delight of all my senses, a divine gamahuching, so far superior in emotional and sensual strength to any I had yet experienced from women—so greater and more forceful is the passion and worship of the opposite sex—that I was left completely prostrated by the climactic joy, my breast rising and falling, my limbs twitching violently, my lips emitting low involuntary moans of pleasure, as I gasped inarticulate words of endearment.

CHAPTER III

Time passed. Henri was wonderfully good to me, showering me with jewels and clothes. Although not socially inclined, his influential connections frequently required his attendance at various salons, dinners, and balls. And on such occasions, as is the recognized custom among the French, he would openly present me as his "petite amie," or mistress, and nothing improper was thought of it. There was none of that snobbery that characterized my debut in New York, and I was able to meet ambassadors, dukes and even princes.

As for my excessive leisure, especially in the daytime, Henri, anxious to have me appear in the best possible light, engaged for me a tutor who, besides perfecting my French, gave me intensive daily lessons in German, Italian, and Russian. I discovered in myself a natural propensity for learning languages. I was spurred on by my deep desire to travel to distant lands, as well as my desire to be able to converse with the many fascinating literary and political figures from all over Europe that I was fortunate enough to meet.

For all his kindness however, it was not long before I began to tire of Henri—unfortunately, before he could tire of me. The monotony of always having the expected done to me in love-making was tiring even though beside the variations of copulation we stuck with most often, we also practiced the 'mimi' he had taught me, and gamahuching, and even 'L'amour in cul.' Still, all of it became dreadfully enervating. Women cannot generally admit to it but, if their desires are strong, they need variety in partners even more than men. Men can always get their pleasure from any old hole; but women, more subtly constructed, require a certain sympathetic harmony, a certain nervous tension, without which they begin missing thrills and become impervious to any but the most direct and prolonged frictionings.

It was inevitable then that, as other admirers, both young and old, whispered their compliments to me as we wheeled through the steps of a dance at some ball or another, I lent more and more favorable an ear, and became more and more susceptible to their proposals. Soon I was carrying on afternoon liaisons with other men, any of whom would have been glad to replace Henri as my protector altogether, but who had to content themselves with a bit of fruit now and then, stolen from someone else's orchard. Many a dress-shirt with diagonal silk band, glittering with military or diplomatic decorations, pressed against the tender charms of my bosom in the ensuing year. I had many an opportunity to employ languages other than English, or even French, the impassioned terminology of love. On my waiting list of men ready, willing, and able to pay the upkeep of the expensive-tasted young lady I had become, were no less than four marquises, two barons, two dukes (one Italian and one Russian) and a Prince—I'll not embarrass him by naming the country he rules. Quite a come-up from the naive little hayseed of Plattsburg, New York, U.S.A. What man, be he ever so talented, ambitious and fortunate could, in a whole lifetime, climb the distance that a woman can traverse in a few well-engineered nights? What, but cunt, can aspire to the beds of kings?

Such trouble with my conscience as I was still able to suffer during these numerous little infidelities was softened this way: Many of my lovers, anxious to allay Henri's suspicions, would overwhelm him with courtesies and favors of all sorts, so that I daresay the sums he spent upon me, generous as they were, were more than amply compensated for by the valuable business concessions that, without his knowledge, a beautiful woman was bringing to him. And I was—if I must say it myself—a delicious trick at this time. About twenty-one, five feet five inches in height, a hundred and twenty pounds in weight, hair a bit darker than chestnut, a faultless complexion, and above all—a good figure, with just the proper degree of both suavity and voluptuousness. My breasts, perfectly matured hemispheres by now, when held together by a low-cut close-fitting gown, displayed just that properly luscious hiatus or cleft between them, so alluring and provocative to men. My hips and thighs, too, had that quality of flowing line that so invites the hands of men to feel and verify their intoxicating curves. My ankles were slim, but with enough upward increase to assure all who looked that there was more generous plumpness above. Need I have been of royal birth or possessed of hereditary estates when such riches as these were mine?

For all my 'high-society' existence, my interest in the so-called demimonde did not forsake me during this time. At every opportunity I would induce Henri or his friends to take me to the wilder and more notorious of the Paris resorts. Of course there was the Moulin Rouge, with its swarms of expensive coquettes, the Bal Tabarin with its performances of the lewd 'can-can' and its female wrestlers—lasciviously dressed grisettes who pretended to go through the gestures of fighting merely for the purpose of striking various salacious poses and inflaming the more sadistic of the onlookers, which, when done, the little ladies, edible enough bits, would circulate among the crowd and arrange for more genuine combats in private whether with male or female. And so down the whole roster of cafés, some of them specializing in male perverts, some in female perverts, most of them generalizing in everything.

One week, while Henri was away in Amsterdam on business, I had a Duc, one of my amours, a fascinating young rake who knew the ropes, take me through some of the more obscure places of pleasure: the House of All Nations, the Crystal Palace, and so on, where 'circuses' exhibiting the practice of all the perversions under God's heaven were put on. Among the other and more usual things, a woman would allow herself to be lapped by a dog especially trained for that purpose (illuminating my mind as to the meaning of the term 'lap-dog' as applied to the pets some women are never without). Another woman, wearing a very logical rubber instrument strapped about her waist, would pierce the inners of another girl and perform the part of man. There were more complicated exhibitions too, employing as many as eight actors at once, as well as various mechanical implements, all to some lubricious purpose. I must admit, that even at the outset, I was more aroused than disgusted by all this—and in the aftermath, when I was at last alone with my companion, I acted like a nymphomaniac, fucking with mad tireless abandon.

It was on excursions like these that I gathered most of the inspirations that later I was to employ in a house of my own. I learned that there are certain postures, certain situations, that will whip up the most jaded or frozen senses and it is entirely in the proper plotting of such lustful scenes that the casual watcher is turned into a devoted habitué, a sincere worshipper of the voluptuous Venus. In the ultimate, it is as Wilde put it: "Life is the imitation of Art." Without all the exquisite stimulations of civilization's refinements, men would still be crude bestial back-scuttling creatures with only rare periodic ruts. Women would be graceless child-bearing drudges who never experienced the remotest glimpse of sensual delights.

Once—while the Duc and I watched a performance in which girls dressed as nuns were treated in a quite ungodly fashion by a number of handsomely proportioned men in cassocks whose bulging members almost convinced one that they were indeed of the

Carmelite order they portrayed—one of the girls approached as we sat cooling our fevered senses in iced champagne. She brazenly unbuttoned my escort, fell to her knees before his living symbol of Priapus and proceeded to do it homage with her mouth—though not at all verbally—and with such passionate zest that one might forget her calling and imagine that she hadn't had one in years. She was really quite good—and the Duc could scarcely be blamed for allowing his interest to be at once aroused. He looked at me helplessly and rather sheepishly said: "Do you mind, dear Madeleine?"

"Of course not, dear Duc. Enjoy yourself. And I shall turn my head away, lest my presence disturb you." As a matter of fact I was insanely envious of him. There was others about, but they seemed only mildly amused and ignored us for the most part—from which I surmised that this form of amusement was quite customarily served at this particular café. Out of the corner of my eye I could not help but watch the maddeningly lustful little tableau. The pretty cherry-lipped young lady between his knees was a veritable witch at surrounding his member with strange cabalistic circles and spirals with her tongue that soon set the cauldrons aboiling. And she was a vampire and succubus to boot when it came to the final stage of the 'aparash-tika'—as the Hindu's designate this delicious rite; viz, sucking the juice from the fruit—for she did this so effectively that he tipped her handsomely. When we returned home, the Duc was so exhausted that he could not raise even a little bone for my own relief. I sent him away, pretending to be ill, and roused a Baron, the Ambassador of yet another nameless country, in the middle of the night and had him come right up to extinguish the raging internal fires that the evening's entertainment had kindled in me.

On a few of these exciting excursions, I deemed it advisable to disguise my sex as I had done so successfully in New York that New Year's Eve two years ago. One night when Henri could not come with me, I dressed up in his best street-clothes (he was not much taller than I) and went alone to visit a notorious café on the rue Blondel that I had heard much of. Although it was a 'wide-open' place, facing directly on the street, and making no pretense at concealment, the *hostesses,* over sixty of them—and every one attractive, though of varying types and builds—were all stark nude. No sooner had I entered, but the whole mob of them, excepting the few that were already engaged in dancing or toying with the men, swarmed upon me, demanding that I pick one or more of them for an immediate round of drinks and loving. I waved them aside and seated myself at a table to collect my senses.

The large hall was entirely lined with mirrors, and heated to an almost stifling temperature—for the comfort of the unclad ladies if not for the temperaments of the male customers. I ordered a drink and looked about me. What an array of breasts and buttocks, ranging from the slim and petite through the pleasingly plump to the extra voluptuous! What a collection of pretty mottes, some entirely shaven, and showing as whitest ivory tinged with pink at their lower convergences, others richly begrown with every conceivable shade; from lightest blonde to gold, auburn, brown, and deepest sable black. They paraded about singly or in pairs to display their charms. It was a painting of an old pagan Greek scene come to life. As they passed me, some would wink, one would cup a luscious breast in her hand as if to offer it to me, another would roll her center about with a slow, sinuous, voluptuous movement and then throw it forward with spasmodic jerks as if in the very throes of spending. Others were demure and retiring so that every variety of taste was catered to. All in all, it was most arousing to anyone who found women pleasurable—and I am, I confess, though by no means exclusively, one of those.

Directly opposite me sat an elderly gentleman wearing a long beard and a high opera hat. He seemed a bit under his liquor, for he sat looking forward with a totally blank stare. At each side of him two comely naked sirens embraced and caressed him, trying to stir up in him some memory of his lost youth. "Ah, papa! Won't you come upstairs with us? We will be so good to you—ooh, la! la!" But all in vain. He sat there, puffing his cigar, unaffected. May you, kind friends and readers, never suffer such a fate!

Other grotesqueries were presented to my view by some of the cruder girls, who went about picking up coins from the edge of a table by means of contracting their cunnies, or actually puffing cigarettes placed between their nether lips by internal suctions. I did not relish this. Extraordinary muscle control it was, yes, but totally wasted and misdirected in clownings that deprived these parts of their natural dignity and beauty.

One of the quieter girls, unbelievably youthful and fresh in her appearance, attracted my attention. She sat not far from me, looking wearily and a trifle disgustedly at the noisy tomfooleries going on. Though her luscious, sensuous body was undoubtedly made for love, it was obvious that she was out of place amongst these public vulgarities.

Noting that I eyed her with interest, she came over and joined me. She was a dazzling, golden-haired blonde, nude like the others except for a flimsy bit of a silk scarf that hung around her neck and floated back and forth across her breasts and secret spot, lending her an air of intermittent modesty. Her skin was flawless, bright, and smooth as alabaster, her thighs, plump but daintily and perfectly turned, were close-meeting up to the very point where they melted into her hips and belly. Her delicious delta was shaded with dark silky hair, giving that promise of intensity and passion that her chaste blonde head seemed to deny.

She put her arms about me. I did likewise to her, running my hand—with a deftness that only a woman who knows what a woman likes can employ—down her side to where her soft, velvety buttocks were profaned by their contact with the leather seat.

"We are both young, monsieur," she said to me in an indescribably sweet voice, looking at me in an exceedingly friendly manner, "Neither of us, I fear, is very familiar with this sort of thing. You look so good and innocent that I would send you home to your mother if I dared. But if you must have a woman, I would very much like to be the one you choose." I said not a word. "I would be so much more kind to you than those more boisterous and hardened women. Do you wish to come with me?"

I nodded my head, afraid to speak and perhaps betray myself. Exactly as in my earlier adventure with Nanette we went upstairs together. Only this time I did not wait for her to discover my real sex. I disclosed it at once. When she had recovered from her surprise, she asked what I wanted of her.

"What is your name?" I asked.

"Fleurette," she replied. The name fell from her pretty lips like the petal of a flower—the 'r' flitted over with a tiny butterfly movement of the tip of her scarlet tongue that was flashingly visible through the slightly parted lines of her perfect white teeth.

"I want what men come for: a woman. Is there any reason why a woman should not be able to get company in the same way as a man?"

"Then mademoiselle wants a gigolo."

"No, Fleurette. It is you that I want. You are beautiful."

"I see, mademoiselle. Personally, I am not that kind. But we girls are here to please, one way or another. I am at your service."

I took my first purchased love into my arms and kissed her upon the mouth. Before long, my tender passion communicated itself to her. She responded in kind. Soon I was stripped, retaining nothing but my chemise. As she knelt between my knees, which I held widespread, she spoke in admiration.

"What a fresh, lovable 'little sister' you have

there, mademoiselle. It is like a fine fig, bursting open with ripeness." And her mouth went to my palpitating love-cleft with the unrestrained zest of a hungry person attacking a juicy piece of sweet fruit. She was a little awkward at first, but I helped her along with my own movements, and it did not take long for her to learn. My climax came soon. It was a soft, delicate, fleecy thrill, not intense or violent, but slow and long-lasting and ineffably pleasurable.

Fleurette was even younger than she appeared, but her wisdom as well as her lovely body was well beyond her years. She had taken to prostitution just a few months earlier, as a mere matter of course. Her sister was in the profession, and there had been nothing else open to her.

"It isn't that I don't like men, mademoiselle, for frequently they give me great pleasure; but I detest the idea of taking so many different men in my arms all in one night without the chance of becoming acquainted with any of them. I would like to be wooed, even if only for a day. And I would like to give myself in my own manner—not according to the passing whim of some stranger who pays me."

A bright idea occurred to me. "Fleurette," I said, "How would you like to come away from here with me? I am very rich. I have innumerable lovers—so many that you could help me to take care of them. You would pose sometimes as my maid, sometimes as a companion of equal social standing. I will pay you more than you can possibly earn here, you will have all the fine clothes you want, and I promise you that while you will have plenty of male company (and when not, you will have me) there will rarely be more than one a night."

"You are making fun!" Fleurette gasped, incredulous. She came away with me. She is with me still. And hardly ever, in the nine years that have since intervened, has she been for long outside the range of my voice. Faithful and unselfish, she has been my greatest single acquisition in life, my only really deep friendship. From the beginning she gave all of herself to me, in every possible capacity. As my sweetheart, her dear delicious body has always been mine in pre-emption of all others. As a confidante, she has always been trustworthy. When there have been little amorous intrigues to plot, ravelled situations to untangle, her advice has always helped. She has even doubled for me in bed on certain dark nights, though in more recent years there has developed enough disparity in our figures that such deceits are now impossible. And so self-effacing! Never has she controverted my word. And so much trust has she placed in me that, wishing always to be dependent upon my generosity, she has persistently refused to amass any money of her own, but has placed everything in my keeping.

In those earlier years of our association she was able to service me most valuably in this way: Whenever I tired of a master or protector, whenever the greater flares of an affair had died away—for me, at least—I would use Fleurette as a foil...Fully as beautiful as I, though in an almost diametrically opposite manner, less forceful, less compelling, I would bring her forward in the picture, giving her the high lights as it were, and allowing myself to sink into shadow. Almost invariably my man would fall for her, and the transfer of affections completed, my own severance could be made with pain to no one. Thus it is that I have never made an enemy. All of my ex-lovers are still friends. Sometimes I even allow them a return engagement. Always they have felt the guilt of our separation, and have been deeply grateful for my broad tolerance—which allowed them to carry on their liaison with my maid without subjecting them to the outbursts of jealousy they expected and deemed they deserved. Consequently, in leaving me, each has always left me well-provided for financially.

It was an ideal arrangement, a perfection of the technique I had used on Charley—and one which every other woman might well employ to advantage. There are no broken hearts and no jealousies. And there is not a man under the skies who is not susceptible to this drawing-off process. It requires only the maneuvering intelligence of a woman who is not so narrow as to play the dog in the manger and insist on keeping the fidelity of a man whose love she would well be rid of.

CHAPTER IV

Henri, of course, was the first to go by this method of painless seduction. I shall not be so conceited as to pity him. When I had approved his infidelity with Fleurette and had myself taken up with a handsome Italian duke, he paid her court openly for some months, before being entirely lured away by another. Soon the Italian went the way of the others. For another six months I shared my luxurious bed with a most persistent but extremely wealthy German diplomat. It was he who presented me with my gorgeous home facing the Bois, whither I repair whenever I feel the need of indulging myself in a quiet prolonged liaison—which is rarely.

During the winter that the German's blonde head lay upon my bosom or between my thighs on awakening every morning, I had to resort to the most arrant means to get away for a breath of another's passion, for he was a most jealous and possessive lover. At last, however, I succeeded in inducing my doctor (guess how!) to certify that I required a few weeks in the Alps for my hearth, and as my German's duties required his uninterrupted presence in Paris, I was free. I arranged with a romantic and wealthy young Spanish don who had been paying me court assiduously, to meet at St. Moritz in Switzerland in a few days. On the train going to my rendezvous, I had a thrilling little adventure that I am especially fond of recollecting as somehow it makes me feel as if I have paid off whatever debt I might once have owed to my native America.

I had left Fleurette behind to do her damnedest with the all-too-faithful German and I was travelling alone—impatient to get to my destination for an orgy of illegitimate fucking. Somehow I have always felt that as soon as I belonged to a man sufficiently for him to expect my favors as a matter of established economic right, it is as legitimate as being married. For me, such state soon become quite tiresome. I have learned too, that no man's prick is ever again quite as thick and upstanding as it is on its first unbelievably exquisite entrance into a particular woman.

The train was speeding through the French Savoy. It was night, but as yet too early to retire. Leaving my private compartment, I went out into the corridor—perhaps to seek an acquaintance. But the car was empty.

I went for a walk to stretch my legs, passing back through a number of cars until I found myself in the rearmost unit, a rough, unheated third-class carriage. This too, was empty save for two or three immigrants sprawled asleep and a lone young man who sat gloomily looking out of the window and shivering in his thin shabby overcoat. I don't know what it was that drew me to him—perhaps it was my own loneliness; but I sat down opposite him and ventured to address him—in French.

"Je ne comprend pas bien Francais," he replied apologetically, "Je suis Americain."

American!

I immediately disclosed my like origin. He brightened, and at once became very friendly. He was a poor student who had worked his way across to Europe late the preceding summer, thirsting for Old World culture. Now, nearly penniless, he was on his way to Geneva, in the hope of getting work as a waiter at the University so that he might attend some of its classes. He was handsome and genteel in appearance but

THE FURTHER ADVENTURES OF MADELEINE

seemed badly fed and shivered violently whenever a draft flew through the car.

"Do you sleep the whole night on these cold hard wooden benches?" I asked him. He nodded his head ruefully. I thought quickly, balloting my desires. I was not the one to hesitate over going forth to welcome adventure with open arms.

"Young man," I said, "I don't know your name; but you are a fellow being in distress. While you freeze to death here, there is a comfortably heated carriage up front that is more than half empty. You must come forward with me."

"But my ticket—my clothes—" he expostulated.

"I will stand responsible for that."

He accompanied me forward. I led him directly to my private compartment. When he saw my nightclothes laid out on the berth and the other personal articles of a woman's toilette strewn about, he hesitated to enter.

"Oh no. I cannot remain here and compromise you, madam," he said.

"But I wish to converse further with you," I replied, "and certainly you wouldn't have me catch my death of cold? You must remain here and thaw out." I removed my wrap—letting him glimpse my charms as I arranged the bosom of my dress.

For over an hour we conversed, most interestingly and impersonally. At last he arose to leave, shivering at the mere thought of the freezing car he was returning to. I took his arm.

"You are a clean, honorable fellow, Mark," I said, "and I judged you to be so from the first moment you spoke. I can't bear to think of you out in that cold box-car all night. If you will promise to be good, and not presume too much on my invitation, you can sleep right in here."

"But—but you have only one berth—"

"True—and I don't expect you to sleep on the floor or in the baggage rack."

He flushed, looked hungrily at my intoxicating silk-clad form and at the glowing hemispheres of my warm bosom which peeped over the edge of my bodice like a sunrise viewed by a man so drunk as to see double. Then he looked out the window at the cold, snow-wrapped landscape. He stayed.

While he went to the lavatory to wash up, I undressed and put on my very thinnest silk chemise. When he returned, looking clean and fresh and more handsome than ever, I was already snuggled expectantly under the covers. Since he was dreadfully self-conscious about himself undressing, I instructed him to do so in the dark. He put out the light. A moment later he slipped carefully between the sheets, keeping to the extreme edge of the berth so as not to touch me. But even at that, we were so close to each other as to be within the aura of each other's bodily heat—and I knew that as my bosom rose and fell my breasts just barely touched him. I smiled to myself.

An interminable period of time elapsed. Far from sleeping, my companion was vibrant with uncontrollable nervousness—at this no-doubt unaccustomed proximity to a woman. But still he kept his promise. Finally, as if by accident, I let my hand fall upon his shoulder. He shivered violently with the excitement set off by my contact. I confess that I felt almost as tense as he.

"You are cold," I whispered, "Would you like to lie closer to me?"

"How dare I?" he almost groaned. But I put my arms about him and drew him close to my hot body, nestling his head against my soft perfumed bosom, and bringing my abdomen gently up to his. He was wearing only underwear that left his arms and thighs entirely bare. Through its thin cotton texture I could feel the bulk, the hardness, and the heat of his member, which pressed against my thigh.

"Now you can go to sleep, dear boy," I said.

"Sleep!" he exclaimed, and crushing me

suddenly closer to him, he implanted a series of burning kisses on my neck and bosom. I pushed him away, pretending to be offended.

"Is this the way you keep your promise?" I chided. "If you can't lie here, nice and friendly, without getting insolent, we will simply have to part. Come now, and be good."

I cuddled close to him once more, forgivingly, but with some primness. "Good night, Mark," I said, "Sleep well and don't think of nasty things."

All of a half-hour passed. I knew that he was yet awake, though for fear of disturbing me, he lay very still. As for myself, I pretended to gradually fall asleep, regulating my breathing and the gentle rise and fall of my bosom. Would he be as 'honorable' while I was asleep? If so, I would be dreadfully disappointed.

The time passed, silent except for the slight clatter of the train over the rails and our respective deep breathing. Through my mind kept passing all the different pictures that I guessed must be troubling the thoughts of the young man beside me. At length I felt him stir.

"Madame—" he whispered.

I made no response.

Gently his hand came forward and felt tremblingly for my breast—which, left substantially bare by the loose droop of my nightgown, soon rewarded his search. His heart was beating so strongly that I could actually hear its loud thumping—and my own breathing was so disturbed by the tension of the situation that I had the greatest difficulty carrying on my pretense.

For a while his fingers fearfully traced the outlines of my provoking bosom, cupping each tender globe gently with his palm, and lightly stroking their little cherry tips till the usual firm erectness ensued.

Then, wandering lower, his hands felt my smooth substantial thighs, stroking gently around to my posteriors, returning to feel my polished belly and the soft silky clump that marked its base and hid the hot goal of love. In all of his caresses there was a furtiveness that whipped my senses to a frenzy of expectancy and anxiety.

For a time he contented himself with these contraband explorations and stolen touches; but reassured by my continued quiescence, he became more emboldened. His hands took hold of the hem of my gown and began pulling it up slowly from my knees as far as it would raise in front—which was only midway up my thighs. To the fine expanse thus uncovered, his hands went; but as if scalded by the heat of my flesh, he withdrew them—only to return after a moment's fumbling and lay upon me the even hotter throbbing bar of flesh that was his penis. Here he kept it, pressed between the blood-warmed ivory of my thighs, while with his hands he resumed the secretive fondling of my ineffably soft bubbies, which veritably melted beneath his hot touch. But his passion increased rather than satisfied by this expedient, and panting softly with leashed desires, he resumed once more the raising of my light negligeé now, however, finding it necessary to pull it up from under me.

I tried to aid him by imperceptibly stiffening my body and raising my buttocks from the bed a trifle, but the pressure of one of my hips pinned down the now detestable covering. As he continued to tug gently, still not recognizing the impossibility of what he sought to accomplish, I stirred, sighed deeply, and wriggled my buttocks about somewhat as if in a semi-waking state till I had slipped down and out of the imprisoning strain of the chemise. Frightened, he withdrew and lay quietly, his heart pounding away as if to burst; but when my regular breathing reassured him once more, he returned to his delicious burglary, and this time, his task eased by my own assistance, he soon had my dress well up on my belly.

I was lying on my side, facing him, and now, with the field at last clear before him, he brought his eager weapon to me, slipped it quietly up the groove of my thighs and forced it gently into the silky tangle of my mount. It slid in between easily enough, but, relax as much as I would, the contiguity of my legs kept the lips of the vital spot pressed close together, and his engine rested only on the outside of these essential soft parts.

Almost sobbing with impatience now, and yet forced to calculate and restrain every move to keep from waking me, he withdrew, and proceeded with gentle force to slip his knee between my thighs. This time when he approached his bursting member to me once more, the cleft was open and accessible. Carefully he placed it to the breach, quartering my cunt open with his fingers till he gained partial entrance, and then, releasing the hot soft lips of the vulva which closed hungrily about his shaft, he slipped his hands to my posteriors, and drawing himself closer, pushed the darling bolt all the way home, nailing us belly to belly.

For awhile he restrained his impatience to allow my sleeping body to accustom itself to this penetration of his hardened flesh, then slowly he began a rhythmic back and forth movement. It was lustfully maddening beyond the power of words to express. With every stroke, ungovernable impulses arose within me to give as well as to take, to heave, to writhe, to dance the immortal dance of love. Movement became as necessary to me as to him. I could no longer carry on my pretense of unconsciousness.

I stirred—awakened.

"Oh! What is this?" I exclaimed. "What are you doing to me? Go away, you—you base ravisher!" But I took care that my push did not dislodge him.

"Dear lady—I would have to be inhuman to be able to resist you. Please! Let me have you willingly—for if I hang for it, I must have you!" And goaded on by his urgent desires, he resumed his strong back and forth motion within my humid grotto.

"But what of my husband?" I lied, permitting myself a frantic little motion of the hips that was not at all meant to discourage him.

"Oh, oh! What will I do?" I cried—doing it. "And anyway, you are hurting my leg. You might at least lie over me in decent fashion!" He complied quickly, coming over me and between my thighs without losing his advantage. I aided him, but deprecatingly.

Once more he impatiently took up his divine movements. Now, being able to reach further within my sensitive sheath, his actions resulted so exquisitely that I felt compelled to second his motions. I laced my lithe thighs across his back. All my internal sources opened up to lubricate the path of his throbbing soul-prober.

Already I was on the verge of coming when there was a knock on the door of my compartment. My companion ceased his divine administrations, his stiff engine almost dying of fright within me. Could it be my jealous German, trailing me by any chance? The knocking became more insistent.

"Qui est la?" I asked fearfully.

"L'inspecteur Suisse, madame. Pardon de vous deranger—mais votre passeporte."

We were at the Swiss border. Greatly relieved, I told him that the car porter had my papers. He thanked me and moved on.

Mark was still within me—impotent with fright; but a few little squeezes of reminder from my well-controlled cunny soon brought him to. Just a few cooperative thrusts and he was back to the proper pitch, and then he went at it once again with redoubled vigor and zest.

The train had slowed down at the border, but was now picking up speed. Unconsciously my dear rider adopted the quickening tempo of the clattering wheels, compelling my own responsive heaves to be in kind. Soon we were going at a furious rate, and our orgasms, a bit tardy because of the interruption, but all the more intense for the same reason, came on at last. I swooned with unbearable delight as he poured hot jets of his thick fluid into my quivering receptacle, and lay upon me, overcome by delicious tremors, both of us simultaneously in the throes of indescribable bliss.

Exhausted now, not so much by love as by nights without rest, Mark slipped gently from my bosom and was immediately asleep. As for myself, sweet as was my languor, I lay awake almost an hour, revolving in my mind how I might aid the poor boy without hurting his pride. To give him money, even if unbeknownst to him, would make him feel as if he had been paid for the delight he had given me—and though I myself could accept money thus, as long as I could not afford to give away all of my love free, I had some regard for what I was sure were his more conventional standards. At last I hit upon it. At my destination I would write the University at Geneva and intercede for him. If necessary I would make some small endowment to the school.

And now, about to settle down to sleep, something else occurred to me. My American friend had, in effect, taken delicious advantage of me while I slept. What could possibly be nicer than to return the compliment?

Gently I reached out and felt for his part. It lay curled up, peaceful and soft upon him. I began to doubt the practicality of what I intended, for all that he was so deeply asleep. Changing my plans only partially however, I slipped noiselessly down lower in the bed until my head was opposite his middle. Carefully I took his recumbent organ between my lips, stroking it very gently with my tongue. Immediately it arose jerkily to approximately its former majesty. If I could get it stiff enough, I could climb stealthily over him, insert it in my ever-ready slot, and wake him with those same delicious rhythms that before had supposedly brought me from the Land of Nod to that of Prod. But due to his complete relaxation, as soon as I removed my lips, the organ began softening and I was compelled to resume my lingual titillations. Soon his light regular breathing become more labored and intense, his hips made little thrusts as if performing some role in a dream, and e'er I had sucked upon his sensitive part scarcely a minute, a long flood of his delicious, glutinous love sweets filled my mouth in slow spurts. He came thus quickly because of the utter lack of inhibitions during sleep. As my male readers know, the merest caress or pressure on their sex organs during sleep will generally suffice to bring on an immediate ejaculation accompanied by a pleasurable erotic dream.

With the climax, he began to stir and awaken; but before he had done so entirely, I was lying in my proper place beside him. In a whisper, he asked me whether I was awake. I replied that I was. "I had the most wonderful dream about you just now," he said, "I dreamt that you let me love you again. Only this time, you were upon me, our roles reversed—" and he went on to tell me all about it, little suspecting that his dream was the mere rationalization of a real enough stimulation, and that I had been the cause of it. Before many details of his picture had been sketched in, his John Henry was standing with interest—and perhaps anxiety to explain. My own clitty, with that subtle sympathy that exists in all sensitive women, arose likewise to the occasion.

"How beautifully you describe your dream, Mark," I said, "You almost make me long to try it in actuality."

"Will you—please?" he begged eagerly.

I did not require much coaxing. In a moment I was above him, spitting my tender but willing cunt upon his now fully wakened weapon. Fired by the lust that had been gathering in me from the moment I had first conceived my idea for raping his sleeping form, I fucked him with a mad lubricity that before long had us both writhing in the pleasurable frenzy of approaching dissolution. What a heat my internal organs were in! What long luscious strokes I bestowed upon his member—and of course, my joy-spot! When at last the suction from my wild, pumping cunt brought on the delicious fruition of my efforts, his fervent discharge was as a cooling lotion to my steaming, fevered membranes. I ground down close to the root of the noble gland that coupled us, crushing our mounts together furiously and then lay moaning and weeping upon his chest with unbearable pleasure.

But the best of things must end. As we lay in each other's embrace, the train pulled into a large, fully lighted station. Mark peeped through the curtains. It was Geneva. Hurriedly he sprang into his clothes. There was but a twelve minute stop here. Quickly he kissed me again and again, and begged me to disclose my identity. I had to refuse, in order to preserve intact the sweet mystery of this adventure. "I know where to write you in case I can ever see you again," I told him, and with this he had to be contented. He left the train just as it started, and running alongside the moving car, waved me a long loving farewell.

That was the last I ever saw of him, though I had the comfort of knowing that his desire to enter the University was indeed, through my efforts, realized.

CHAPTER V

At St. Moritz, I was met by my impatient friend and we spent three delightful weeks together, engaging for that purpose two adjoining rooms at the hotel, although only one was used.

There were the winter sports, which brought the color to my cheeks in the crisp, tingling cold, and there were the indoor sports, which my lazy Spanish lover much preferred, and which brought the color to all of my body with their delicious heat.

After a morning's thrilling round of skiing and tobogganing, from which my companion would generally beg off, I rejoined him at the hotel for an afternoon of delicious intimacies. Our amorousness was perpetual but it never got monotonous because my friend was of a poetic, romantic temperament—besides which, he was never averse as some men whom I have met are, to going down upon me for the celebration of those mystic rites brought to us from the isle of Lesbos. And I was becoming myself quite a devotee of the lush Paphian method—which, together, made sixty-nine.

"Your cunt, Madeleine," he would murmur from between my thighs "is a beautiful scarlet flower in full bloom, and its perfumed recesses are ripe with the drippings of sweetest honey." And his lips would avidly seize upon the object of his adoration with such grateful pleasure that I would almost long to taste and kiss it myself—just to find whether or not it was so much nicer than any others, as he told me so often. But having to satisfy myself with feasibilities, I would take his stiff, tanned instrument between my lips and play upon it those exquisite tunes with which the auletrides of old used to charm their lovers. And, of course, when finally he would favor my ardent mouth with the delicious proofs of his enjoyment, I would not think of insulting him—and depriving myself—of that dear essence of his virility.

Surely, one would think that some afternoons spent this way would soon satisfy even the most ardent woman. Yet, so increased by pleasures was my desire for pleasure, so ecstasy-provoking were my recollections of ecstasies just past—in brief, so incessant were my ever maturing passions becoming that if I were taking a warm bath alone, my finger would proceed at once to grant me the exquisite, slow, controlled relief that my pampered senses would not wait for, and that one would imagine I was the last woman in the world to need.

One morning, after as satisfying a night with my Hispanic lover as ever a woman could wish for, I went so far as to start a flirtation with a mysterious stranger in our skiing party. Without one word, he took my arm, and we skied off away from the crowd. He led me to a tiny emergency shelter on the mountain's ridge and silently laid me back upon the hard boards of the floor. As it was too cold to undress me, he deliberately ripped open a few inches of the inseam of my knickers with a tiny cigar-cutter, and through this narrow gun-slot, proceeded to open fire upon the tender target.

Throughout, no word was spoken by either of us. The silence of our meeting and our amorous combat made the eloquence of our gestures and motions all the more exquisite and keen. I wondered why he did not speak, but at the same time did not wish to break the peculiar spell that seemed to work so provocatively on both of us. When the lambent flames that spread from my fiercely embattled fortress had thawed away the last trace of coldness from my body and sent titillating liquid fires racing through my veins—even then I suppressed my sighs and murmurs and made no sound. Only a soft, liquid, sucking sound could be heard, made by the slow withdrawal and quick return of his firm flesh from my tight moist sheath. Outside the snow fell silently.

Suddenly, without any heralding by loving words, his supreme crisis overtook him and his seed spurted maddeningly into my yet unsatisfied cunt. When he saw, however, from my continued upward thrusts, that I had not yet had enough, he resumed his delicious fencing until I, too, surrendered the liquid tribute of my senses. But by this time, his own zest and libido re-aroused, he stood his ground for another round of the tender, silent struggle.

Though I at first resented his taking advantage of a lady combatant already completely prostrated and helpless with pleasure, my own spirit of sportsmanship revived and we continued our wrestling with full vigor until—this time better matched and timed—we both reached the ultimate divine discharge and collapsed together in a delicious 'draw' that cast no reflections upon the fighting qualities of either.

When at last we arose, there were some white stains on my knickers, though scarcely noticeable because of the pepper and salt shade of the material. The stranger silently strapped on my skis for me, I pulled my sweater well below my hips to conceal the tear in the crotch, and we went out into the snow again—our bodies pulsatingly warm and invigorated by our quiet little interlude. We rejoined the party of skiers on a lower slope, where he left me without a word.

That very night, I saw him in the hotel lobby. I was in a quandary whether to recognize him or no. In a moment when I was alone he approached me. I had scarcely noticed his features during the morning, what with the blinding glare of the snow and then my blinding passion. But I saw now that he was a refined, handsome Frenchman.

"Madame must have concluded this morning

that I was devoid of the power of speech. But no! Words obscure the true passions of the flesh and vitiate the ardent perfumes of desire. If I had spoken, it would have been to say 'I love you,' and yet who knows what 'love' means? How could I guess what connotations or qualifications, perhaps unpleasant, perhaps sentimental or conventional, you might attach to your conception of the word? The phrase is better left unsaid, though the gods know that what I felt toward you as a beautiful woman offering the divine gift of herself, was, if not love, something no whit inferior to it."

I was enthralled by the delicate precision of his speech.

"You have read Remy de Gourmont, madame?" he went on. Of course I had, this writer's books constituting, as they well deserve to, the very Bible of all sensualists. I nodded.

"Well, like him, I love passion for itself. What need is there to encumber it with base justifications, to obscure its iridescent colors and heady perfumes and exquisite tones—already ineffable beyond words—with a cloud of metaphysics? As he says, I love passion for itself, for that which it brings with it of movement, life, immediate sensation. And what sensation, pray, is more immediate, more genuine, more completely and directly experienced that that of love? To touch something exquisite, that is to experience a sensation emanating from something outside you. To see, to breathe, to taste exquisite things, even to perform a motion that is pleasing to the muscles, all these things are similar. But to love, ah, that is all of these things combined, plus something that transcends them all—that sensation originating within that does not submit to the measurement of any of the senses and hence defies all words."

I was fascinated.

"I would much like to meet you again," he said, "only in more civilized circumstances than the last. I do not often, I assure you, embrace fully clothed women."

THE FURTHER ADVENTURES OF MADELEINE

I arranged to join him in his room the very next morning, pretending to my lie-abed Spaniard to be out tobogganing. We had two hours of the most delicious and prolonged epicurean connection I have ever experienced.

With a peculiarly subtle intuition he would slow down and stop just as either of us approached a climax, which, delightful though it be is, alas, the end and not the beginning of pleasure. By thus stopping short we were able to slowly savor the delicious sensation without bringing it to a quick end. With uncanny insight and deftness he would add a timely stroke now and then just to keep the exquisite feeling from fading, or would grind into me with a rotating movement that increased the frenzy of my steaming wet cunny without actually bringing on the end. His control was marvellous.

For an hour he kept this up, till we were both bathed in inexpressible bliss, and, despite our pact of silence, I was writhing about with the unbearable burning ecstasies, uttering cries and moans for more, for relief, thrashing my arms about, my fevered head falling from side to side while he rode firmly upon me, flushed with pleasure and with the triumph of so killing me with joy. At last I could stand it no more—his prolonged teasing had me in a delirium—my heart seemed to be bursting with the excessive pleasure.

"Please—Andre—finish me—for god's sake!" I gasped, "Oh—please—you will kill me!"

Seeming to comply, he favored me with four or five furiously fast delicious strokes that carried me on toward that deeply needed conclusion. But then suddenly—oh how I hated him at the time and how I loved him for it afterward—just as I felt but one more stroke was needed to bring me down from that high precipice whose rarified atmosphere I could not longer endure, he stopped short, arresting the progress of my sensation at an intense pitch most unbearable of all.

I cried, I moaned, I begged. With all my power I tried by my own efforts to bring on the delicious climax;

but he pinned me down with his greater strength and rotated his stiff, teasing member within me in a reverse direction, stimulating me to further frenzy, though not in the required manner.

I screamed out.

Another such deceit and I would faint away. Andre brought his mouth to mine and took possession of my burning lips in a long, exquisite kiss that soothed me somehow by momentarily diverting my senses from my cunny. Our hot breaths intermingled: our souls dissolved together. Holding me thus, his strong loins withdrew the full length of his penis deliberately, pushed it back into my swimming lust-maddened sheath with exquisite slowness. He then repeated the motion a second time without haste. Every step of the intensification of my pleasure passed like slow cinema before my consciousness. A third, a fourth, a fifth! Oh gods! The dangerous peak of supreme agonizing pleasure was at hand! If he saw fit to forsake me now, I would perish.

But no! Another slow withdrawal that clamped my throat, intercepted my breath, and bade my heart stop beating while my cunny should decide my suspended fate—and he plunged home to the hilt, hurling me down at last toward the swift-flowing river of pleasure below that broke the fall from the great aethereal heights of the climax. Nor did he leave things to nature even then, but with lightning-like rapid short strokes followed up and intensified my delicious dissolution and brought on his own.

Oh what exquisite relief!

I shuddered, I twitched in the overpowering grip of pleasure as he shot into my already flooded cunt a stinging scalding load of his long-frustrated thick boiling sperm. For more than ten minutes I was completely hysterical. My lips, my breasts, and of course my cunny, were so supersensitive that any touch made me laugh and cry at the same time like an idiot. But it was a delicious hysteria, dear reader, and I would wish each and every one of you right now no worse than a similar experience.

As we rested from our labors of love, Andre broke the silence for the first time.

"How voluptuous your figure is, Madeleine," he said, "And voluptuousness alone is the quality that constitutes beauty—for to me beauty is no more than the promise of pleasure. And your body, every fold and nook and cranny, every smooth surface even—and all of it is finest alabaster—is meant only to give pleasure to men. Even your darling foot—" he bent to kiss my instep—"is as of genuine mother of pearl. What god would spurn to have you thrill him with that perfect little foot of yours?" And intrigued with the idea, he had me stroke his already stiff and upstanding love-organ with the soft, smooth sole of my foot.

With similar compliments I was induced to let him sample the possible pleasures of all the rest of my body: in the soft cup formed by the crook of my knee, in the rich folds that bordered my cunny, on the satiny surface of my belly, immediately over the depression of my navel, between the tender yielding mounds of my breasts, beneath my warm silk-lined armpits. Nor did I deny him a tiny caress with my full mouth and lips. Even from the silken tresses of my hair, garlanded about his sensitive phallus, he showed me how he could derive pleasure; and of course, there was the deep delicious groove between my plump buttocks, even apart from the tight cosy sheath it led into. In none of these places did he spend—only, as he told me, before he could even begin to tire of me, he would have to try them all. Hence I was assured of his ardent friendship for at least the balance of my little vacation.

After toying with me in my nudity awhile, he insisted that I don my transparent chemise of pale green chiffon. "To look at your white body too long is like looking at the sun," he said, "And anyway, art prefers that nude women should be adorned with some article of clothing to relieve the purity and frankness of their outlines—even if only a girdle or silk stockings—to accentuate the nudity by demarking it. A diaphanous veil or chemise add to the piquancy, suggestiveness, or mystery. They challenge the imagination and the keenness of vision."

When he lapsed into silence it was only to once more give all his senses to the worship of my body, which now burned to be possessed by this man who understood and appreciated it so exquisitely, I gave all of myself—making him promise only that he would not repeat his divine excessive teasing twice in the same morning. The approach of luncheon forbade too prolonged a connection anyway.

This time, he had me lie on my side with my back to him, my upper thigh raised and resting on his. From this position he inserted his dear self in the moist, well-padded slit that is as accessible—if not more so—from the rear as from the front. He slowly pushed in to the hilt, allowing me to bring my thighs together. Holding me close to him, his arms about my waist, his belly pressed pleasantly against my posteriors, he had me bend my trunk forward at right angles to himself, the better to facilitate his movements within me, and to bring my clitty in direct contact with his bar. In this snug position my cunt was able to engulf more of him even than is possible via the frontal method. My moist, downy lips kissed his very love purse—and more important still, since he was not upon me, I had as much freedom of movement as he.

Back and forth we both moved in unison, pressing toward each other: together, separating, together; his superb ivory pillar forcing its way through the moist resilient folds of my sheath, now so tightly clasped about him (because my legs were held so close together) that a most audible and sensible vacuum was created with each luscious withdrawal of his firm piston. At the same time his hot hands wandered wantonly over the whole front and back of my body and thighs, pressing my soft elastic breasts, my belly, my mount, and the snowy elevations of my buttocks that were placed so conveniently to his reach, at last coming to rest over the essential garden of delight with a finger slipped dow to pay additional court to my excited joy-spot.

Oh! the inexpressible happy delight of our wonderfully unencumbered rhythmic body heavings! Oh, the incomparable bliss of drawing the hot moist flesh of my now-fiery cavern over the full length of his satin-textured weapon and sitting back on to it again, letting it sink into me to the very handle, getting the utmost out of its exquisite dilatation.

Soon the approaching climax spurred us both on to an even more voluptuous abandon. The fast friction of his prick, its whole length traversed in double-quick time by our joint efforts, sent flaming tongues of titillating sensation up my abdomen and spine, his deft finger caressing my masterful little protuberance at such moments as it came away from its stroker making it additionally certain that the gathering intensity of sensation should not lapse for even a fraction of a second.

Panting and sobbing, I hurried on to my climax, aided in every way by my strong, silent lover. At last (what joy!) the supreme convulsion burst upon me, blinding me, dazzling me with its intensity. My womb contracted sharply, squeezing the liquid secretions into my quivering channel. All my glands gave up the last drops of their contents. It was like deliciously bleeding to death—and indeed, I nearly died of the blissful pain. Back into his lap I pressed with a madly oscillating movement, my cunny grasping his flesh convulsively in the desperation of its overpowering, agonized pleasure. I turned my head over my shoulder and met his hot mouth in a long kiss that completed the circuit of electrifying sensations that flowed through our bodies. His hands took each full heaving breast and with one final thrust that threatened to crash through my whole writhing body, he poured his burning blissful treasure into my quivering cunt, mingling our loving effusions in a sweet balm that soothed and extinguished the still-fitful fires that flared in that part. Through my kisses I uttered little gasping cries of joy. He strained me close, close, closer to his dear body, and here we swooned away with pleasurable relief.

Was I exhausted by this morning of delicious amorous combat, dear reader? I was not. After a bath and a hearty luncheon, I joined my Spaniard full of desire for a continuation of the morning's delights.

All in all, as you may gather, I spent a most enjoyable time in Switzerland.

CHAPTER VI

During the next few years I extended the circle of my acquaintances and lovers in Paris to include many fascinating literary and artistic denizens of the Left Bank, though all in all I still adhered to diplomats and financiers as being far more generous. It was not long before Fleurette alone was insufficient to take care of all my castoff lovers. It was then that a critical search of the city discovered for me pretty brunette Manon who was added to my staff. Before long a third, Suzanne, joined my forces. At this time, I must have it understood that I was not operating a 'house.'

Although Fleurette lived with me, Manon and Suzanne had separate apartments and our cooperation was merely social. We would meet frequently and I would contrive to put lovers within range of their charms, but beyond that our association was secret.

It was in 1923, I believe, over three years after I left New York, that my next great adventure took place. A Count, a Russian diplomat, had been madly infatuated with me. An unfortunate, though not unusual, arrangement of circumstances had kept him from gaining my bed for a long time. When at last the obstacle was disposed of and he was just about to attain my embraces he was recalled to Petrograd by his Imperial Government. Distracted by this added stroke of ill fortune, the Count threatened everything from suicide to disobeying his Tzar's command in order to remain with me. Since I had been considering a tour of Eastern Europe anyway, I saved the day by offering to accompany him if he would return. Thus it was that I came to spend some months in the Russian capital.

The two days travelling on the train, needless to say, was an almost uninterrupted round of fucking. The atmosphere of our private compartment was actually musky with the heavy odors of perfumes and of repeated seminal discharges, and its stimulation alone was enough to bring us back to venereal delights again and again.

The Russian capital was not a very festive place. So far as royal entertainment was concerned, there was none. The Tzar himself, a haughty, sullen and suspicious nincompoop, was almost impossible to meet. Like every other wearer of the Russian purple, his sole concern, apart from his private vices, was the dodging of imaginary bombs and the extirpation of all free thought in minorities. The Tzaritsa, an attractive enough piece from the glimpse I caught of her once, was a similar snob. As the Count told me, ever since her affair with General Orlov (the undoubted real father of the little crown prince) had leaked out, she did not dare to appear in public.

All our social contacts then were made through the salons we visited, such as Prince Andronnikov's. Here I met most of the really important figures in Russian politics. The unpopularity of the Tzaritsa was unanimous, and the favorite topic of scandal was her brazen goings on with the dissolute monk Rasputin, who seemed to be the real man of the hour and the man behind the Russian throne. Madame Alexander von Pistolkors, the sister of the Tzaritsa's lady-in-waiting, who became quite a good friend of mine, told me that she had it from the Monk himself (who had no compunctions about bragging of his royal connections) that the Empress of all the Russias would devoutly spread her thighs for him at any time. And what's more, so completely did the Monk have the Tzar under his thumb that the latter would have to stand by and like it.

Whether all this was truth or merely malicious scandal, I could not judge at the time. But I could not help but become interested in this strange figure of Rasputin, the crude Russian moujik who controlled a nation, to whom all sorts of strange hypnotic powers were attributed, and of whom it was said that the most beautiful and desirable women in all the land would travel thousands of miles, trade away their jewels, and betray their husbands to spend one night with him, although it was also said that he was so fed up with the adulation of princesses and countesses that he showed a marked preference for actresses, courtesans and foreign woman. I could not consider leaving Russia without meeting, by any means possible, this unusual character.

The closest I could come to him for some time, however, was some weeks later, when I induced a young revolutionary student whom I had met informally at the public art gallery in Petersburg to take me to hear the monk deliver a sermon at one of the churches in the lower part of the city. It was a snowy night, and as we rode across town in a hired droshky, Alexei, who was a peculiar feverish sort of a fellow whom I could not fathom at all, sat silently wrapped in his great fur-coat at the opposite end of the seat, paying not the least heed to my coquettish attentions. He was frankly anarchistic, and hated the Russian Orthodox Church bitterly, so our excursion was scarcely to his taste, and it had only been with considerable coaxing that I had induced him to undertake it at all.

The church was a gloomy edifice dating no doubt from the middle ages. Situated though it was in a poor quarter of the town, there were among the miserable congregation a great number of richly gowned and bejewelled ladies. They seemed to be waiting with as much expectancy as I for the advent of the great and holy Rasputin.

At last, heralded by shouts of admiration and awe, the famous man appeared in the pulpit. I recognized him at once from the many descriptions I had heard. He wore a long black caftan and was fully bearded; but his face was remarkably sweet, youthful, and disarming.

When he blessed the assembly everyone fell to their knees. I was about to follow suit, but was restrained by the example of Alexei who remained standing beside me. As the gaze of the holy monk wandered over the heads of the hundreds in attendance, he discovered us standing defiantly. Instantly his face darkened demonically, his forehead furrowed by a deep frown, and his strange pale blue eyes glittered violently. A moment later though, noting that one of the sinners was an attractive woman, his face again lit up and he favored me with an insolent leer, even as he spoke the words of his benediction.

In those few moments the whole multiplicity of the man was disclosed to me. First, the sincere, kindly peasant-preacher, then, in a flash, the baleful, vengeful antagonist, and finally and above all, the lewd lascivious libertine to whom women were of far greater a concern than God.

He went on with his sermon while all listened attentively. His voice was rich, soothing and caressing; but beneath its unctuousness there was a suggestion of sneering irony which, to the unblinded listener, proclaimed that he was above himself believing the nonsense he preached. As he spoke slowly and simply, I had no great difficulty following his Russian, though now and then I had to call upon Alexei to interpret an unfamiliar word or expression.

Only through repentance and humility could salvation be attained, he told us. But how can one sincerely repent if one has not first sinned? Virtue itself brings arrogance, and the arrogant cannot win heaven. Only through sin can one drive out evil, fighting fire with fire. So long as you bear sinful desires secretly within you, you are a hypocrite and odious to the Lord. So out with the desires. Sin and have it done with! A splendid piece of sophistry which meant in effect, "It is sinful to want to fuck; but the only way to stop wanting it is to do it." In a flash I saw the reason for his tremendous popularity. People—ignorant women especially—have always wanted a moral justification for their carnal lusts. It would not do to come right out and admit fucking is divine. Oh, no, that would be against the Bible. But to say that fucking is filthy and sinful, but it's divine to get that sin out of your system—that's religion.

After his brief but enthusiastically received sermon, all joined in the singing of weird hymns and folk-songs, during which the monk circulated among the crowd, touching the women here and there with gestures whose sanctimoniousness could scarce conceal their lasciviousness. Usually he contented himself with touching merely their shoulders or their foreheads; but sometimes he would "heal their hearts" by stroking the full breast that intervened. It was a great racket to get away with in the name of God; but monks have, under the auspices of the Almighty, done far worse things than 'feel' women.

With the distribution of his caresses, the singing became more enlivened; then there was dancing, wild and abandoned. The religious fervor—or mob fury, to designate it more honestly—kept mounting higher and higher. It was almost as bad as a Holy Roller meeting back in the good old civilized United States.

Before long, frantic, hysterical women, who could not all of them share in the embraces of the holy monk, threw themselves into the arms of strange men—who, nothing loathe, and their senses similarly whipped up by this exquisite religion, were soon ripping open well-filled bodices and raising skirts, uncovering monster Tartar pricks and shoving their 'devils' into hells while they proceeded with lust-maddened motions to rid themselves of their burdens of sin and attain the ecstasy of repentance. I could scarcely believe my eyes. Two 'politzia' entered to investigate the uproar. A gesture from the monk and they left immediately. So contagious indeed was the spirit of the mad orgy, that even my own heart began beating excitedly—and Alexei, carried away, put his hand on my bosom and crushed me close to him. "Not here!" I whispered, "Later, if you must." He accepted the postponement.

A moment later, a strange panting red-faced Russian pounced upon me and proceeded without ado to lay me onto a bench. Alexei struck him a strong blow behind the ear that felled him like an ox and gathering me up, dragging me out of the turbulent mob. Back at my hotel, I did not violate my promise: Alexei came up to my suite with me. Lying at my feet on a fur hearth-rug before a roaring log fire, he began making love to me. I had changed into a light, flowing negligeé of a diaphanous material which, as I passed before the fire, had permitted the full silhouette of my form to be glimpsed.

"You are so majestically beautiful!" he softly murmured, embracing my knees, "You are like a queen—so cold and unapproachable in your beauty."

Cold and unapproachable? Why I was just dying for him to hurry and get started....

"I would give my life now, merely to kiss you—but to even raise myself to the level of your lips would seem a sacrilege, so far above me are you, my divinity!"

"But Alexei," I protested, shocked by his words, "I am not a goddess, I am flesh and blood, a woman hungry for companionship—for love even."

"You do not understand, dear Madeleine," he spoke moodily, "Your sunny Western temperament cannot fathom the dark abysses of the Russian soul. We are an accursed people, a nation made up of cruelly mistreated slaves. My bitterness, my moroseness comes from the brooding melancholy of long winter days and nights behind the stove, spent in soul-clawing introspection, in impotent raging against injustices of every sort."

He paused and gazed into the fire. From the ballroom of the hotel below could be heard strains from one of Tschaikowsky's symphonies, played by a moody balalaika orchestra: Its gloomy music telling of perpetual snow over the Siberian steppes, of an old man weeping over the corpse of his son, just struck down by the tzar's cruel cossacks, while the snow falls and falls.

"We Russians are an abnormal people," he went on, breaking into my revery, "It comes from too frequent use of the 'knout.' The Tzar, accursed be his name, beats his ministers; the ministers beat their subordinates; officers beat their soldiers, and soldiers beat the populace. My father always whipped my mother, at the slightest pretext, or with none at all: Both of them would whip me.

Only I had no one to abuse in turn, and I had to endure—and in time learn to like it. I loved my mother for her cruelty; yet I hated my father for his. Perhaps it was because he beat her, too. When, while I was yet but fifteen years old, he was shot down by the Tzar's soldiers in some peasant uprising, I was so happy that I got drunk and remained away from home for over three nights. Later, mother, who was still young and attractive—she had married when scarcely twelve, as is the barbaric practice among us—would let me, her only child, sleep with her. She meant no harm, Russian nights are cold and we were too poor to heat our room, but my thoughts became incestuously lustful. As she slept, I would more and more boldly caress and investigate her soft female form... Maddened by prurient desires I would try to satisfy myself with my hand, imagining myself in possession of that delicious body whence I came. One night, when in my furtive caresses I had dared to stroke her widowed sex parts, she suddenly awoke, took me fiercely in her arms, and bursting into tears, she told me she had just had a wonderful dream of father... You don't mind my telling you all this, do you, dear Madeleine?"

"Oh no, Alexei," I said, stroking his hair with tender encouragement. In truth, I was considerably aroused by his lewd, incestuous picture. If most of my readers find the idea repulsive, I must opine bluntly that it is for the reason that most of our parents are too elderly to be sexually attractive to us. His, as in the case of the mother of Baudelaire, was obviously an exception. He went on.

"At last, one night, unable to contain myself further, I raped the sleeping form of my mother. She awoke. She screamed and protested. But I know she enjoyed it, too. When finally I threw my burning seed into her womb—the same womb that sheltered me in my gestation—the fierce joy of executing this criminal proscribed act of incest was so great that I knew from that moment that no other woman could ever give me a comparable pleasure. As I thus desecrated the body of this woman whose sole misfortune was to both my genetrix and a beautiful, desirable woman besides, it seemed that, once and for all, I was avenging the suffering her husband, my own father, had inflicted upon me.

"When at length she broke from my boyish but brutal embrace, she was furious with shame and remorse—and leaving the bed, fetched immediately the very 'knout' that father had so often used on us. With this cruel instrument she vented upon me all her moral indignation, whipping me with all her strength upon my bare body. But as the stinging thongs of the leather cut across my flesh, I experienced only a divine, martyred pleasure. With every stroke I loved that woman more and more. The orgasm which I had scarcely had time to finish upon her soft, white, body, now resumed, as was evidenced by the repeated liquid phenomenon at my parts. I fainted away in torment and rapture, and my mother exhausted by her efforts, desisted and carried me back to bed, comforting me with her kisses and caresses, weeping and begging me to forgive her. Slyly I took advantage of her present state, and soon I was within her again, committing once more the delicious crime against nature—this time with her full cooperation. It was not long before I had established my right to this incestuous connection at will, only always I would insist that she whip me before its consummation. Oh, if you could only imagine the delight of being maltreated by a woman whom one loves, the tormenting bliss of being her complete slave, her plaything, subject to her every whim—to be beaten fiercely and then perhaps to be taken back into her forgiving arms for a moment.

"Mother is dead to me now. Betraying doubly our own delicious relationship—perhaps her sense of sin conquered after all—she married a wealthy landowner scarcely a year after father's demise. As for me, I was sent away to school. During my military service, I would frequently violate some trifling regulation solely for the pleasure of being reprimanded, or better still, cuffed or whipped. Much as my mind and pride would resent the punishment, my body would tingle and glow in a strange way. I would suffer pain, but I would enjoy it."

He fell silent again. I continued fondling his hair, a little awed by the amazing intricacy of his character—a little impatient, too, at his seeming obliviousness of me. But no, it was only to make himself better understood before he could love me for now he again began caressing my legs, murmuring words of endearment, of worship and self-debasement.

"I want to be your slave, oh gorgeous Madeleine. Here, in token of my vanquishment, I place my neck beneath your tiny foot." He did so. "Now, kick me spurn me—only let me be your slave. I will execute the most menial tasks you can find for me.

Reward me only with blows. But let me belong to you—let me be near you always."

"Alexei!" I spoke sharply, "Put an end to all this talk of slavery and mistreatment. You are my equal—if you were not, I would not have you here. We are not living in the days of Roman autocrats, with slaves over whom we have the right of life or death!"

"Alas that we are not!" he went one, "That is why my life is so miserable and unfulfilled. I have sought everywhere a woman who would love me a little and chastise me often. But in Russia, the women themselves wish to be beaten and cannot be induced to lift the knout. Oh mother, mother!"

For a time we were both silent. Alexei, completely prostrated at my feet and gazing up at me from the rug with a mad, worshipful humility, deigned only to remove my slippers and kiss my bare toes, running his burning cheeks across the cool soles of my feet. Sympathetic as I felt for his malady I could not quite reconcile his avowed slavishness with the role of a man.

I lost patience with him. In wrestling my foot from his embrace I kicked him viciously. His eyes lit up almost ecstatically as he gazed into my now flushed and angry face.

"Ah! what a beautiful, cruel tyrant you would make! And how I would love you!"

"Alexei! You ought to have your foolish delusions beaten out of you! You deserve to be whipped!"

"Whipped?!" He sprang to his feet eagerly. From his fur coat he fetched a long heavy whip, a knout I presumed the symbol of Russian autocracy. He laid it upon my lap, and divesting himself of his shirt in a moment, threw himself once more at my feet.

"Now!" he whispered hoarsely, "Whip me! Kill me! Beat me, please!"

I fingered the whip fearfully. Its wicked thongs were heavy and knotted. In a civilized country it would not be used even on a horse. I shuddered.

"Alexei," I said, "I forgive you without a whipping. You can stay. And look—I am all your's." I opened my negligeé and offered my nude body temptingly.

He shut his eyes with insane resolution. "I cannot love you," he said, "unless you torture me first. You are an indifferent stranger to me if you will not accept my slavery and establish your right to my body by the knout."

"Can't there be love without suffering?" I pleaded, "Pleasure without pain?"

"No, all pleasure is sin, inextricably bound up with humility and pain. "But Alexei," I protested, "it doesn't have to be that way. Men and women both have needs and desires. I don't want to be your master, just your partner in pleasure. Why can't you accept me as an equal?"

"I can't," he groaned, "There are no equals in Russia. Everyone preys or is preyed upon. But why do we talk? Beat me..."

"No, Alexei," I said, "I can't. I am not Russian."

We were silent. He lay at my feet like a dog, only unlike even a dog, he begged for punishment. It was getting late. I arose. "I must retire now Alexei," I said, "I am sorry for you, but I do not twice offer myself to the same man—or any man. You may go." He clung to my feet. "Go Alexei," I pronounced firmly. He made no move other than to kiss my feet passionately.

"Go, Alexei!" I repeated for the third time, exasperated, and with menace in my voice; but he only clung to me more desperately. I was genuinely angered. And granting his point of view theoretically as much as I would, I still could not endure the actuality of his abjectness. What sort of game was he playing with me? I had offered myself, and he, like a worm, had refused me. Perhaps a little taste of the medicine he begged for would soon convince him that blows are not so sweet as kisses...I picked up the knout. Its weight, its pliancy, its whole unaccustomed feel—gave me a strange sense of power.

"Will you go, Alexei?" I asked for the last time.

"Beat me, kill me, dearest woman!" he cried, "But do not force me to leave your divine presence!"

Enough! Through the air I swung the whip and brought it down upon his bare back... The leather snapped about his shoulders, leaving a scarlet line across his dark skin. That should do, I thought, but he made no move to go or to plead for mercy. I struck him again—more vigorously. Stubbornly, he made no sound. Once more I brought the knout down upon him with all my strength. I would make him relent! Again and again I struck him, till his back was a criss-cross of red welts. If he had said one word, I would have gladly desisted; but his obstinacy aroused undreamt of powers of cruelty within me although it seemed to faze him so little. It was a quite exhilarating sport, this whip swinging, and I was becoming momentarily more expert at it. I was soon breathless and flushed with my cruel exertions.

"Remove the rest of your clothes, Alexei!" I commanded. I was determined to give him the whipping of his life. He complied and in a minute lay on the floor with his entire back nude to me. I resumed with vicious strength, striking now his thighs and buttocks. Only by breaking his will could I re-establish my self-respect. I lashed with all the force and swing in my body, furiously discarding my negligeé when its flimsy stuff hampered my movements. My breasts, my whole form, vibrated vigorously. I was the very incarnation of Fury—and every moment increased the brutality of my passion. Now impatient even of the time required to draw back the whip for each blow, I struck back and forth from side to side, getting in two blows for every one before.

Soon there was no inch of his back on which I had not scrawled with the writing of my hatred.

"Have you had enough now, dog?" I panted. He made no reply. With my foot I turned his body upward. Tears were streaming from his eyes, but his expression was ecstatic and martyred. "More," he whispered, "Divine woman; I will crawl after you through the public streets, your slave! More!"

More! Were all my efforts indeed nothing to him so far? Murderously, insanely, I redoubled my blows—striking till I could strike no more—upon his head, his face, anywhere. At last, exhausted, I sank upon the rug beside him. A thin stream of blood ran from his lip. At the sight I was overcome by remorse. I took him into the soft shelter of my arms and kissed him. For the first time he was responsive and hugged me tenderly. My blood was heated by the violence of my exercise. Imperceptibly almost, my boiling hatred changed to burning desire. Alexei must have been similarly affected, for his love organ now stood out erect and stiff from his pain-striped body.

"Forgive me, Alexei," I murmured passionately, "Forgive me! What can I do to make amends for my cruelty?"

"I want you...now!" he spoke tensely but he made no move. "Love me," he whispered, "I am your slave. Use me, then trample me underfoot again."

My lasciviousness was too much aroused, my desire too far gone, for me to stop at nice details. Panting with urgent lust I straddled his body and eagerly spitted my now swimming cunt upon his upstanding part, slowly sinking down upon it till I had engulfed it to the hilt, till his reservoirs of love pressed close against my buttocks. Even as I sat for a moment in this delicious position, I could feel his member swelling further within me, giving me that incomparably exquisite sensation that comes only when one's warm sensitive sheath fits its dear cylindrical visitor like a tight glove. With what hungry delight I relished the superb impalement! Slowly I raised my crouching body, my feet upon the floor, my hands supporting me against his ribs, until all but the very head of his turgid instrument had left my hot humid nest; then quickly and with a single continuous motion sitting down upon it again, I felt his hard smooth flesh flow over my soft clinging membranes till it penetrated to the utmost within my quivering belly. I pressed down upon him with all my might, till I could feel his stiff shaft distending the uppermost end of my hungry vagina, clamoring for entrance into my very womb.

Now panting with hot desire, I began my movements in deadly earnest, rising up and then down and around, caressing his bursting organ with the subtle spiral strokes of my tight clasping cunny. Electrified with pleasure at last, my pain-loving masochistic companion, so divinely linked to my hot flesh, pressed up to meet my thrusts, while his hands reached out to fondle and mold my palpitating breasts. But alas! This exquisite connection was too good to last! Already worked up close to the melting point, a few of my delicious pumping strokes was all he could stand. Seizing my buttocks fiercely to intensify our close conjunction, he let out a low cry and yielded to his climax, shooting upward into my pulsating body a spurting generous flood of his hot tantalizing seed.

I rolled and heaved desperately upon him to bring on my own highest pleasure, but his vigor was not up to the task. As my efforts became less and less availing, my urgent desires gave way to angry disappointment. Coming from off his futile impotent body I kicked his still quivering prostrate form with vicious exasperation. After all these hours of dawdling and exertion, after fulfilling his every desire, here was I, completely stranded and unsatisfied.

I took up the whip again. Perhaps a few cuts of the knout and he would be useful again. But no, I had pumped him dry.

Slipping into my negligeé again, I seated myself by the fireplace—a most inauspicious place to cool my fevered senses. A malicious idea came to me. "Alexei!" I said, "Come over here." Painfully he dragged his nude, tortured body over the floor to my feet. Opening my negligeé in front, I spread my knees apart. My cunny was still dripping from the generous results of his consummation.

"Alexei, I want you to thrill me with your lips—with your mouth and with your tongue."

He looked up in horror. "But madame—you may practice that vice in your France, but here in Russia, it is unheard of! Wives may be forced to do the equivalent to their husbands, but for a man to do it to a woman—oh no! Command anything, but not that!"

His obvious repugnance made me all the more determined to have him do it. The very element of compulsion would give me an added lascivious pleasure—as if I were a man, cruelly raping and defiling a young and unwilling girl. I reached for the whip and struck him brutally across the shoulder with its heavy butt. "You miserable ungrateful wretch!" I hissed, taxing my Russian vocabulary to the utmost, "You disgusting, detestable pervert, you—you will balk at what I ask you, after I have satisfied your own base cravings!" I punctuated each word with a blow of the knout. Never before in my life had I felt so majestically, so ruthlessly, cruel.

In his eyes pride struggled with abject slavish admiration. I dropped the whip and sent my hand out in a stinging slap across his cheek. Tangling my fingers in his thick disheveled hair, I dragged his head up to the level of my thighs, and then with both my hands forced his face against my spew-bathed cunt. "Now slave!" I screamed hysterically, "Wallow in your own vile exudations! Drink up that essence of your detestable self with which you dared to defile me!" Locking my soft thighs tightly about his neck, I viciously rubbed my dripping furrow over his whole face, bringing my most sensitive parts against his lips. For a time he did nothing. His frame shook with deep sobs. But in my passionate lust I was far beyond pitying him. Furiously I punched and pulled at his head.

"Your tongue! Lick! Lap! Suck! You hound!"

Reluctantly, gingerly, his tongue came out and felt timidly the upper part of my slit. Impatient of his hesitancy, however, I forced him down to the deepest wettest part of the groove—to accustom him all at once. Soon he was following the directions I gasped to him, now licking up and down, now across, now stopping his tongue to suck the erect hypersensitive clitty.

Soon the delirious climax approached. I was blind with the fury of my passion, panting, writhing, as I crushed his lips, his mouth, his whole face, into my wet, turbulent center.

"Now quickly! More! More, or I'll kill you!" I cried.

The supreme orgasm burst upon me in a sadistic frenzy of pleasurable agony. My thighs were locked rigidly still about his head, and as the waves of sensation convulsed my whole body I beat and tore at the agent of my delirium. The same rending delights that ordinarily express the supreme intensification of love now evoked paroxysms of inexpressible hatred, of desire only to debase further the unwilling victim of my orgiastic passions. My only regret was that I couldn't increase his discomfort with a flood of the results of pleasure, such as a man who defiles a woman's mouth can do! My body was once again wracked with pleasureable shudders.

"Circe! Divine enchantress!" he murmured, "Look how you make swine of men!" I wrenched myself free.

I had the greatest difficulty driving him away, for of course I could not have endured him for the rest of the night. He loved me more devotedly than ever, he told me; he would sleep at my door. I threatened to call the police. He went at last. When I had bathed and returned to my boudoir, I found that, he had left his knout behind. I have treasured it since as a memento of the madness that had overtaken me.

Some days later, despite the admonition of the Count, my protector, I called upon the monk Rasputin. Here was a man who would doubtless make history, of whom so many strange tales were told that I could not resist the desire to meet him and see for myself.

When I seated myself in his waiting-room there were at least twenty other people ahead of me; but when the monk emerged, he picked me out immediately as the most attractive woman present and led me within. Seating me on the edge of a leather covered sofa, Grigori Efimovitch Rasputin drew up a chair and sat opposite, facing me. Boldly as he, I returned his close scrutiny. His great head was covered with unkempt brown hair, parted in the middle and hanging in damp strands over his forehead and neck. His whole face was overgrown by a heavy brown beard. His skin was pock-marked and scarred. All in all, he seemed quite as unattractive and disappointing a sight as any other Russian moujik might present. But his eyes were fascinating and irresistible. They were pale blue and watery, yet they seemed to pierce and penetrate to one's depths.

As we sat, he pressed my knees between his—an affront which I overlooked for the time. A lewd sensual grin hovered about his lips.

"What brings you here, my daughter?" he spoke sanctimoniously, "I can see that you come from afar."

"I have come for your blessing, father." I lied.

"Have you been to communion yet, my daughter?" I hesitated.

"No, father."

"It is first necessary, my daughter, that you have part of Christ's divine body within you. It is only then, when you feel His holy flesh mingling with yours that you can experience the efficacy of prayer." He leered suggestively, and took one of my hands within his, tickling my palm with his thick coarse fingers. "But since you have journeyed so far for my blessing, I will not send you away empty. I am the vicar of Christ. His essence flows in my veins. I can grant you communion such as will make you feel His divine presence within you, more certainly, more ecstatically than if you had swallowed all the sacred wafers in Christendom." He pressed my knees more closely and put his hand on my bosom. I moved away. He went on speaking as if he had not noticed my rebuff.

"I can see, little daughter, that you are truly tormented by the desire to sin—else you would not have come here." He laughed vulgarly. "Well, why not? So long as you repent. And what could find more favor in the eyes of the Lord than that you should sin with a holy man, and thus sinning, rid him as well as yourself of burdening lusts? What do you say, my daughter? You will thank me, nay, you will bless me when it is over."

I was frightened. The massive proportions, the general hideousness of the man, all revolted me. And his strange, compelling manner aroused all my most innate oppositions.

"No, father," I spoke nervously, "I have no desire to sin, really I don't. I will go to communion tomorrow—that is, the ordinary communion—and return for your blessing some other day." I arose to go. He laid his heavy hands on my shoulders and pressed me back to my seat. His peculiar eyes turned from light to darkest blue, glittering with sensual desire.

"It is the will of God!" he rasped, "And I must enforce it! Would you dare to match your foolish youth against my matured wisdom?" Then his voice became soft and insinuating again. He spoke in a low passionate whisper murmuring strange voluptuous words that seemed to weaken all my body and weigh down my limbs. I felt his hot, heavy breath upon my face. His devouring eyes roved over my body. His hands followed.

"What opulent curves! Yes, I will administer the holy sacrament! I will fuck you!" He employed the ugly word for it, "yebotch."

I was on the verge of yielding; but with a supreme effort of will shook him off.

"No! no!" I cried, "Let me go! I hate you!"

He threw me back upon the couch and leaned over me, transfixing me with his burning eyes. All my powers of resistance ebbed away.

"Now, now," he murmured, mesmerizing me. "Everything will be all right. You do not hate me, my daughter—and you will love me afterwards. If you refuse me, you will regret it all your days. You will dream of me nights, and long for me. But see, you no longer resist me. I do not force you, you want me. You want this—" and laughing lewdly once more, he whipped out his brutal moujik truncheon. I shuddered. All my intellect and senses revolted against being the victim of this demon; but my body was paralyzed, pinned down by the man's hypnotic powers.

Now I could see only his gleaming, mysterious eyes, with their crafty lustful expression. I could feel his hands raising my dress to my waist, I could feel him pulling my silk step-ins down toward my knees. I wanted to scream. I couldn't. I wanted to resist, to spring up and escape. I could make no move. If only I could wrench my gaze away from his—but I could not so much as close my eyelids or turn away my head.

His huge bar of flesh lay on my cold ivory thighs, groping its way blindly upward toward their culmination. In a moment he would be rending my tenderest tissues.

Just then someone started banging on the door. He paused for a moment, but went on with his rape, unwilling to abandon his advantage. The pounding became more insistent. Angrily he cursed in Russian; but the noisy distraction continued. He rose and went to the door. In that moment his spell was broken. I recovered control of my limbs and sprang quickly to my feet but it took me some time to readjust my clothes. A moment later he was by my side.

"Never mind, little daughter," he spoke, laughing good-naturedly, "That was a servant from Tzarskoje Tselo—the imperial palace. Even as you were resisting me, the Princess Olga was summoning me to join her for some of the divine administration that you so foolishly refuse. So I might as well save it for her. Yes, I have fucked not only the beautiful Princess Olga, but also her sisters Maria and Tatyana, and Anastasia. The Tzarina herself has never refused me—and know you that the impotent Nicholas himself is pleased to have me do it for him. Ha, ha, little foreigner, if you remain in Petrograd long enough, you will soon learn that this—" and he brandished proudly his still stiff and rampant limb "—is the divine scepter that rules all of Holy Russia!"

He replaced the sacred rod in his trousers and led me politely to the door.

"Show mademoiselle to a droshky," he directed his plump, fuckable maid Dunia. Unbeknownst to me at the time, he had one of many secret agents follow me to my hotel to learn my address.

The next afternoon as I sat alone in my boudoir, reading with some slight difficulty a Russian edition of the secret memoirs of Catherine the Great, inflaming myself with the pictures of mad Tartar lasciviousness, the door opened, and in walked Rasputin, unannounced.

Whether of my own volition, or because of some inexplicable posthypnotic influence he had cast over me, I had been thinking of him all night and all day. What exactly could be the nature of this power he was accredited with? Something told me that I must yield to him and discover for myself.

I received him calmly, picking up one of my dainty garters that were strewn about, and laying it between the pages of my book to keep my place. He was quite friendly and apologetic.

"Do you still think of me so harshly as you did yesterday?" he asked. It was useless to contest his purpose. I knew his power, the futility of further resistance. I might as well save the situation by making the best of it.

"No, father," I spoke coyly, "You were right. I have regretted my foolish refusal."

"Ah, that is much better," he said, and proceeding immediately to remove his caftan and boots, he sat down beside me and opened my negligeé a trifle to appraise the texture and solidity of my breasts. When his will was not crossed, it was obvious that Grigori could be a most charming gentleman. He removed my negligeé and pushed my naked form back on the couch while he hastily stripped off his own clothing. His body was spare, but massively and muscularly built. His organ—despite, or perhaps because of, its no doubt frequent usage—was colossal, frightening, and was surrounded by a profusion of crisp black hair. His huge love purse resembled a pair of young coconuts, and promised an unprecedented quantity of love's elixir.

As he lowered himself upon me, his thickly begrown hairy chest tickled the erect upstanding nipples of my tenderer charms. A moment his fearful equipment imprinted itself on my belly, then, sliding it lower down over my silky mount, he brought the monstrous blood-gorged head to bear upon my quaking crimson tidbit. Tried as my parts were by many encounters with other not insignificant Muscovite weapons, my sensitive little recess seemed but a sorry match for his unwieldy bludgeon.

Against the delicate mossy gates his assaulting engine pressed firmly; but scarcely more than half the diameter of his giant cylinder could my nether mouth encompass, even with the best of its intentions. With my own fingers hastened to the specific scene of the fray, I stretched wide first one side of the moist excited folds and then the other; but even at this he was in only lip deep. Firmly he continued pressing inward. Anxious now as my cunny was to receive him, the disproportion was so great that I blanched and winced with the pain of the distention. He noted my suffering.

"Now little daughter," the monk spoke in a soothing tone, "I can see that you are not accustomed to the virile members of holy Russia. But forget that part of you which aches. Look into my eyes. See— there is now no more pain for you. All hurt is gone. You can experience only pleasure hence-forth."

And surely enough, as if an anesthetic had been introduced into my throbbing parts, the pain vanished, and now, though the membranes of my sheath were partially numbed by his hypnotism, I could sense his monstrous wedge sliding slowly into the grateful scabbard until it was entirely receiving into my body, clasped tightly in the hot moist flesh.

"Now you can feel me once more," he spoke, "your womb clutches the head of my member. You are ready to enjoy." I was. With the lifting of the spell, my organ awoke to a delicious state of pleasurable sensitivity, all its glands opening to add lubrication for the delightful movements to come.

"Fuck me now, father!" I moaned, beginning to writhe impatiently under the impalement of his soul-satisfying shaft. He did...and oh, as that solid stuffing of velvety flesh moved in and out of my hot voluptuous channel, I bounded frantically up to meet him with a violence that would have at once unseated any less expert a rider than he.

With such divine treatment, it could not take long for me to reach the acme of bliss—which I did, with a wail of rapture, my hips continuing to pump madly up and down to bring forth the easing balm of his discharge. But staunch and self controlled, he held on within me, requiring even further fires to melt the rampant rivet that sustained the tight conjunction of our heaving bodies. For all my efforts to bring him on, I merely worked myself into a second frenzy. Now I lost all voluntary ability for coordinated movement; but the exudations of my first orgasm had oiled his stiff stake so superbly that he was able, despite my wild fitful motions, to fuck back and forth with fierce full strokes. A few dispatching thrusts from his strong loins sent me again to the heights of ecstasy, and my womb poured forth a second oblation to the god of love.

But still his huge joy-giving assailant continued thrusting, fully potent, within my enspasmed cunt, uncompromisingly withholding its own creamy offering of surrender. A triumphant smile adorned Grigori's face when I opened my fevered eyes to look at him. I begged him to finish off quickly and let me rest from the already excessive pleasure he had bestowed upon me.

"No, no, my daughter!" he spoke hoarsely, still pounding fiercely away, "I must completely drain you of your sin!"

My over-sensitive membranes protested; the muscles of my cunt closed with steely desperation about his bar to restrain his maddening frictions; but it was useless. His strong engine rode down all the delicate resistance that the wet warm folds could offer, and soon another climax was spurting its fitful fires through my veins and nerves leaving my whole body stiff and rigid with wild lustful pleasure, choking my screams of ecstasy in my very throat.

And still he fucked me! Vigorously, unceasingly. The combination that nature has set over the treasure-source of woman's pleasure, the exact number of turns and twists and pushes that ordinarily are required to induce the nervous-system to open its joy-valves and pour out the amount of voluptuousness that it determines the woman can endure—all these judicious restraints were suspended, and my womb, my glands, never before so continuously and violently called upon, yielded up the keys as it were, opened wide their ducts, and poured out their ecstatic emulsions in an almost ceaseless spasm of spending.

For over an hour and a half he kept up the divine—I could as well say diabolical—workings of his august tireless tool. Long before this time I was completely overcome with pleasure, more dead than alive—unconscious except for the sense of his continual plunging in and out of me, my involuntarily responsive thrusts, and ever and again the stinging flare of sensation that tokened another orgasm. I must have come no less than twelve distinct times, not counting the numerous partial thrills that I was too fargone to keep track of and the final frenzy of unintermittent sensual titillation that kept me helplessly hysterical in the last half hour of his erect yard's relentless application.

For a time, as I have said, I fainted entirely away into a state of flaming lubricity that was now soothing and now torturing. When I came to, yet another tremendous orgasm was climbing to my brain. My congested cunt was brimming over with joys still exclusively its own, the whole tender passage still plugged up by the volume of his immense limb.

"Mother of God!" Rasputin roared suddenly, "I am coming! Sacred Virgin, receive my offering!" Grasping my buttocks to draw my wildly heaving body closer, he pushed and drove and tore within my overstimulated membranes more fiercely than ever. His face was livid with lust. His breath whistled sharply between his teeth and down his beard. My own breathing had long since ceased except for some spasmodic gasps now and then.

Suddenly his whole body stiffened. His bursting member swelled perceptibly within me and I came again. With one final crushing thrust he poured into my irritated vitals a hot flood, or rather a long series of spurning jets (like a quick fusillade of shots), of his copious thick manly creme that soothed the burning tender convolutions of my cunt and left me squirming and wriggling and screaming with the divine relief.

For whole minutes he continued ejaculating his

warm glutinous stream into me. My parts overflowed, my thighs and anus were inundated as never before or since.

At last he withdrew his huge lolling member which, even as seen through my joy-clouded eyes, made me shudder with the reminiscence of yet tingling sensations. I was still moaning and panting and beating my arms and legs about like a person possessed—for the hypersensitivity of my body, indescribable, ticklish, convulsing at the least touch, did not pass easily.

The monk, himself entirely recovered, gave me a drink of some strong vodka from a flask and gradually I revived. Now I knew the secret of his fame. His was an accomplishment that any man might be proud of; the ability not only to satisfy the most ardent of women, but to give her more than she has ever dared dream was possible.

Seated beside me now, Grigori chatted on in a pleasant manner, helping himself frequently to the contents of his flask and becoming more and more confiding and boastful.

"You don't believe that this has pushed within the Empress of Russia, do you? Well, she has even kissed it. And I know her so well that I could tell you the exact number of wrinkles in her cunt. When first I met her, she had fitted up a private subterranean chapel outside the palace, especially for me, where none were allowed to intrude. Here, while the Tzar thought his dear spouse was at prayer, we would fuck for hours. I—Grigori Efimovitch Rasputin, simple abused little moujik of Povroskoe—fucking the Empress of Russia!

"But Olga, the eldest daughter—she's a sweet piece! And Princess Maria, too. And the Tzaritza's younger sister, the beautiful nun. I've driven the devil out of all of them. And all the attractive ladies in and out of court. Why their husbands consider it an honor to have me hallow their wives' cunts with this!"

Such bragging soon put the temporarily wilted

subject of his discussion in boasting mood again. Feeling sinful once more, the monk began making application for additional salvation. But I was still so sensitive in the requisite sanctuary that I had to induce him to consent to the substitute I offered.

So I tried to get the head of his monster bar into my mouth. But I had to confine myself to external stimulations. Seated on a cushion on the floor between his knees, I did my best, rolling my tongue over the huge ruby knob, stroking the delicate grove of the underside, inserting the tip of my tongue into the scarlet sensitive urethra, and sucking on it when I could. Rasputin watched with voluptuous interest. Myself, I attended earnestly to business. The enormity of my task, the honor of sucking this master prober that had plumbed and fucked all the choicest and most aristocratic cunts of Russia, all made me strive to make this the finest lingual fuck I had ever administered.

It was.

"Ah, God! What have I been missing! I must teach the Princess!" he murmured as my agile tongue made spirals about the swollen flesh and my soft practiced hands stroked the long shaft.

It took a long time, perhaps all of fifteen minutes, of this delicious expert titillation to bring him on; but at last I could judge from his heavy breathing as well as by other unmistakable symptoms that the supreme moment approached. I knew what to expect from his oversized reservoirs, and just as he stiffened in the final throes of pleasurable ejaculation, I placed my fingers firmly about his spouting member, allowing only as much to spring past my lips as my mouth could at one time hold, clamping off the rest by pressure upon the delicate canal.

The intensity of his prolonged and intercepted pleasure caused him to roar with agonized delight. When I released the pressure on his bursting pego the damned up torrent of thick hot sperm shot out with inconceivable force, flooding my mouth again and overflowing to my breasts and abdomen.

"Bless you, oh bless you, my daughter!" he exclaimed, overwhelmed, "I am just beginning to appreciate the French!"

"And I have only this afternoon learned to appreciate the Russian," I returned in kind, swallowing the last benefits of the melee.

When the Holy Monk at last was about to leave, he in gratefulness wished me to take a heap of currency that he drew carelessly from his pockets. I refused. In its stead he forced me to accept a beautiful signet ring bearing the imperial Russian double eagle that he had received from the Tzaritsa. I cherish it still.

CHAPTER VII

After a few more weeks I had my fill of the Russian capital, and I travelled to Moscow for a few days with the Count and some friends. But soon I tired even of this more lively metropolis—though I couldn't decide whether to return to Paris or to do some further globe-trotting.

Then I received a strange proposal that fired my imagination and set my footsteps southward to encounter the most dangerous adventure of my life.

Ivan Rudschenko, a wealthy land speculator from Rostovnadanu, first told me of a Baron Grigor Feodorov, who in this modern day and age still ruled a huge plantation located in the South of Russia (the Zaparuzhti) with slaves, a harem, and all the insignia of medieval autocracy. A harem could mean only one thing to me: Fucking—and lots of it—perhaps some strong spicy competition. I became interested. Ivan confessed that the Baron was a friend and neighbor of his, and that he had been commissioned to recruit additional wives or concubines for him. He was returning home soon. If I were interested in joining him, I would be well paid for my time—10,000 roubles in advance. Somehow, I was developing great confidence in my ability to get along, or to handle even the strangest of men. And my curiosity and adventurousness tempted me further. After all, I thought, what else has a woman to lose after her maidenhead, especially when she is willing to be fucked, sucked and even buggered? I little dreamt what lay in store for me.

Whether, during the arduous trip, my relations with Ivan were platonic or not, I leave to my astute readers to judge.

As our intimacy deepened, he seemed to show more and more regret for my undertaking. He even intimated that I could still return to Moscow without forfeiting his deposit. Since it was not the money that had lured me hither so I refused to abandon the enterprise; but by the time we reached the end of our journey, some of his ill-concealed uneasiness had communicated itself to me, and I was especially disquieted by the somberness of the ancient godforsaken castle that finally turned out to be our destination.

I was led into a great medieval hall, and here I made the acquaintance of the Baron. Typically enough, in my first glimpse of him, he wore heavy iron-shod boots and a high shaggy fur hat, and with whip in hand was in instigating two huge ferocious wolf-hounds to do bloody battle upon each other.

He paused in his occupation and approaching, greeted me with a sort of sneering supercilious politeness that, in externalities at least, proclaimed him fairly civilized. He even addressed some words in French when he learned of my supposed nationality. As he spoke, his deep bass voice, his dark menacing eyes and ugly beard, all struck me with a conviction that I had met him somewhere before. Yet reason told me that such was impossible. I had never been to Russia before—and certainly my own span of life thus far hadn't been so extensive as to make it likely that I had met him elsewhere and forgotten. Nor could I think of any other person of my acquaintance that I might be confusing him with. This strong sense of recognition was doubtless the phenomenon of déjà vu that psychologists write of; the mere fantasy of a tired mind. But yet, for the life of me, I could not cease racking my brain to place him—and the more I worried, the further from a satisfactory solution I seemed to get.

I was shown into the library. Here I was left alone while the Baron and Ivan retired to settle some business between themselves. To occupy the time I glanced curiously over the many cases of books. There were hundreds of volumes on flagellation in every conceivable language. There were numerous volumes devoted to the cruelties of the Roman Caesars and of the Christian Inquisitors, and any number of histories of the bloody perverted exploits of the Marshal Gille de Rais, the Bluebeard of the Middle Ages, who, as I remember, inspired by reading Suetonius' descriptions of the orgies of Tiberius, Caligula and Nero, had defiled, mutilated and killed thousands of girls and young children in his lifetime.

Over the fireplace hung a horribly realistic portrayal of "The Slaughter of the Innocents." In the corner stood a huge couch equipped with steel manacles. On the desk, lying on an open volume of the Sade's bloody book "Justine," was an odd diabolical little thumb-screw affair that was obviously an instrument of torture. My anxiety quickly grew to horror. I must rejoin Ivan and get away from here. I rushed out of the door into the hall—full into the arms of Baron Feodorov. He held me firmly.

"What is the matter?" he demanded sternly. As he spoke, his dark shaggy eyebrows twitched nervously up and down like fluttering bat-wings.

"Ivan...I want Ivan!" I gasped.

"Too late," he told me, "Ivan has gone. What did you want him for?"

"Nothing...only...only I don't like this place. I don't wish to stay here."

"Indeed! You are all bought and paid for. You must stay." He leered horribly and reached insolently for my bosom.

"Let me go!" I exclaimed, "or I'll scream!"

He was convulsed with laughter.

"Scream!" He pinched my arm viciously. "By all means scream! A woman's screams are music to my ears. But if you think to scream for anything other than my pleasure, you are unfortunately wrong. Even if this building were not sound-proof—which it is—everyone within a radius of fifty versts belongs to me, and far from daring to come to your aid, they would return you to me in short order if you tried to escape. Moreover, the entrance to this castle is never unguarded. Now, scream again!"

I forgot my horror in the fascination of my growing conviction of familiarity. His very words, I seemed to have heard before—even the cruel grip of his hands was an experience that seemed linked with him in some vague irreducible past.

He dragged me back into the library and threw me upon the couch.

"Woman!" he pronounced ominously, "I am going to strip your clothes from your body, chain you down to this torture rack, and rape you! Now, what do you think of that?"

I decided to make the best of it.

"Nothing," I replied, as serenely as I could, "except that you needn't trouble either to remove my clothes forcibly or to strap me down. I know what I'm here for—and I like it. If I didn't, I wouldn't be here. So why talk of rape? You can't take away from me anything that I'm not just as anxious to give as you are to receive. Shall I undress?"

This speech, though it cost me some effort, was meant to mollify him. But no. As if aggravated by my suggestion of complicity, he turned red with anger, the veins of his forehead and neck stood out like whipcords, and without another word, he dealt me a blow to the face that brought tears to my eyes.

The sight of my pain enlivened him. His hands felt of all my parts brutally, then suddenly he tore my gown from me with a single ripping movement. Where had I seen that bearded, diabolically leering face before? Where in my lifetime had this very same scene been enacted? Another tearing sound and my silk slip lay in shreds at my feet. I stood before him now clad only in short-silk panties and a narrow satin brassiere from which the flesh of my breasts overflowed alluringly. To forestall him, I reached behind me to open the confining band. He tore my hand away and ripped it off forcibly. Once he had them freed, he squeezed and molded my breasts till I was sick with pain. But even this, it seemed, had happened to me before.

Throwing me back upon the couch, he locked my ankles and wrists with manacles, holding all my limbs widespread perforce, and keeping me in every way completely subject to his whim. For a moment he pried about my intimate charms with words of cynical admiration, working himself into a frenzy of lust and anger. Nor could he forego the villainous pleasure of threatening me with his slender vicious knife that he drew from his belt.

"Look upon this!" he roared, "As soon as I grow tired of your vile cunt, I will slice you to ribbons, piece by piece!"

His tones—his words! Where, where, had I heard them? His attitude... The strange sense of familiarity that troubled me overshadowed even the fears I might have felt at his deadly threats. I had lived through just such an experience before—so why be frightened by it?

He drew out his member. It was huge and fierce, vein-knotted and blunt-headed. He fell upon me, brought the truncheon approximately to the breach, and without troubling to entrench or open the way, lunged brutally inward. If he had exercised the conventional firm gentleness of any other lover, if he had properly stimulated in me the necessary secretions to lubricate my vulva, I would even then have experienced trouble sufficiently coping with his monstrous engine. But as it was, the rending pain, the agony of his single-plunged onslaught was so sharp, so unbearable, that I screamed out and nearly fainted dead away.

Never before had I experienced such horrible suffering. It must be just an awful nightmare, I told myself. Never before? Nightmare? In the short moment that he crashed into my body's tenderest parts, in the moment of my most excruciating agony, the strange sense of reliving a scene reached its most unendurable, insanity-courting intensity. "Put the great key—in the lock—" And turned it! Finally I remembered the strange nightmare of my childhood. The scene which was so inextricably linked with my own awakening sensuality. But sensuality had little to do with my present circumstances.

The Baron, obtaining complete insertion of his huge cruel probe, had ground it about within the lacerated folds of my cunny. With the infinitely redoubled pain, more of the nightmare scene flashed upon my tortured consciousness: Front de Boeuf, the great key, that horrible dream of years before! Only this was reality: The nightmare seeking its fulfillment in waking life. And this overwhelming sensation of yielding to an annihilating torture: That too was in the dream. Only from this reality there could be no escape, no awakening.

I struggled against the impulse to faint, desperately clinging to consciousness, refusing the insidious invitation of oblivion and death. I would laugh at the pain! And surely enough, echoing my thought, I heard, as from a great distance, a hysterical female laugh that I recognized as my own.

I continued, laughing, though my teeth were clenched. My determination and my laughter brought me fresh vitality and resistance. My mind cleared, my emotions subsided.

My assailant continued plunging back and forth

within me. There was now no question of pleasure for me. Indeed, as he raised his body and withdrew his engine between strokes, I could see it covered with a rich crimson that was my blood. Whether naturally or perversely, despite the passionate fury which ordinarily hastens a man's climax in direct proportion to its heat, the Baron showed no signs of coming. To shorten the agonizing alliance of our bodies, to at least deprive his weapon of a share of its cruel excessive stiffness by bringing on the unstarching, I attempted one of woman's most ancient devices—that to date I had had but little necessity for simulating... Within the limitations of my manacles, I set about to employ all the means, all the possible subtleties of cooperative movement—counterfeiting, so far as I was able, the symptoms of approaching pleasure myself.

Instantly, he realized my intention and stopped me with a blow, withdrawing his encarnadined weapon.

"I take my pleasure!" he growled, "I do not share it. Your enjoyment, whether real or pretended, subtracts from mine and distracts me. Later I will cut away your clitoris—to ensure that it is I who use you, and not you me! And meanwhile..." He adjusted the chains that held me so that my legs and thighs were high in the air. In this way both my front and rear were equally visible and accessible to him. Without turning me over, without troubling to employ any easing lubricant, he brought his part against the lower and more tightly puckered gateway to my body, and rammed it fiercely inward.

How fortunate it was that someone more gentle than he had already opened that path, how thankful I was for the moistness on his monstrous tool even of my cunt's blood—else, surely, I would have been burst asunder. Even as it was, he hurt me cruelly. But happily, in this tight unnatural sheath of mine, it did not take him long to consummate. As his crisis approached however, the bloodthirsty baron sank his teeth sharply in my bare shoulder—a moment later flooding my bowels with the thick spurts of his fiery essence.

His fierce growl faded into a low moan as the pleasure melted his over-tensed body. When he withdrew from my dripping anus, he was a changed man—a bit cold perhaps, but rational and dignified. Chastened, if anything, by his cruel orgiastic outburst. With the deft hands of a surgeon he dressed my bleeding shoulder.

"Till next time," he said, "I do not require that you should suffer at such times as I am not with you. In the intervals between my pleasures, my women are well treated—fattened up, if you will, for the tortures I subject them to. Ultimately of course, you all go to the bone-heap."

I took this opportunity to ask him whether he really meant to execute his murderous threats. "Why not?" he laughed, "if it suits my pleasures?"

"But have you no fear of being held accountable by the law?"

"In this part of Russia, I am the law."

"But I have friends—influential friends—" I told him, "in Moscow, in Petrograd—and of course in Paris. You cannot keep me here long before there will be an investigation. Count—"

He interrupted.

"Does anyone beside Ivan know you came here?" he asked, seemingly perturbed.

"Yes!" I lied, "I was about to tell you that my friends, the Count and the Baron, tried to dissuade me. They asked me not to remain away long."

He fell silent. I knew my ruse had succeeded. My captor now, it was obvious, would think twice before inflicting any serious injury upon me.

I was taken away to the women's apartments. I shall not record the details of all that followed. Nor shall I give the accounts of the eight women who were for two long horrible months my companions. Suffice it that their tales of our master's bloody practices were replete with horror—and worthy of comparison with the worst in the Marquis de Sade's writings—so much so, indeed, and so similar to them, that I shall omit all but the very latter part of this nightmare, referring the reader to the annals of psychopathology for fuller descriptions of what such monsters are capable of.

One of the number of prisoners, a beautiful young girl of sixteen, I was horrified to learn, was the legitimate daughter of our captor by one of his earlier wives, now long since deceased as a result of his criminal mistreatment—and for this delicate flower of maidenhood the incestuous villain showed especial preference in his cruel sadistic orgies. In one of his more rational moments, I ventured to question him. Without morals as I was myself, I could not comprehend any justification for his thus torturing what was in effect his own flesh and blood.

"On the contrary, mademoiselle," he told me, with a supercilious smile, "the fact that she is my own flesh and blood, as you put it so quaintly, the fact that she is forbidden to me by all the laws of man and church, makes the use of her body all the more interesting and pleasurable. And since she is so closely a part of me, since she is in truth beholden to me for bestowing life upon her, who should more justly be entitled to the benefits of her body than I, her father, her creator?"

"I pity you your inhumanity," I whispered, shocked.

A frightful spasm seized upon his features. His eyes and forehead and cheek muscles twisted fearfully—as if torn between the two struggling aspects of his character, the Dr. Jekyll and Mr. Hyde of it. I watched with bated breath. But suddenly the battle was determined. The Baron's jaw shot out into a hideous rigidity, he drew back his arm, and with the knuckles of his open hand struck me full across the mouth.

"Why, you presumptuous little French bitch!"

he hissed deliberately, "You pity your omnipotent master, eh? You pity me? Ha, ha, ha! I—who could crush you like a worm—if crushing weren't too short and easy an end for a female so brazen as you. I suppose you were going to reform me, weren't you—you big-hearted, tight-cunted foreign hussy! Well, to show you how close I am to resuming the narrow path of virtue, I shall stage for your benefit an orgy such as you have never witnessed before and may not live to witness again. But meanwhile, down on your knees, bitch. Take this prick between your pretty bleeding lips, and suck for the life of you—for I give you just three minutes by this clock in which to make me spend. If I don't, may your God help you, I won't wait till tonight but will throttle you here and now!"

His fury was truly insane, it brooked no protest. I complied—sucking with all my strength and breath as I had never sucked before—sucked and lipped and tongued, though my mouth bled profusely from his inhuman blow. Sucked and sucked with all my might though hot scalding tears ran down my cheeks, tears not of mere pain be it understood, but bitter tears of deepest despair, of forlorn hopelessness. Oh, how I wanted to sob and cry out loud and rail at fate's injustices, but that great detestable prick of his choked back my cries.

And all the time this beast laughed and laughed at me. Laughed—while with both his hands he rained blows upon my head, pulled my hair, pinched and twisted my ears, my breasts, or anything he could lay hands on.

He had allowed his watch to dangle on the front of his vest within my full view, to tantalize and distract me further from this task which so demanded my highest concentration. And now, as the second hand relentlessly traversed, all too quickly, for the second time its short circular path, denoting the elapse of two-thirds of my allotted time—and that towering master of my fate still showed not the least signs of coming, a cold horror swamped all my being. My jaws and throat were aching unendurably with the strain of my desperate sucking, yet as that mocking indicator rounded its second lap, and without even pausing, started chopping off the fragments of what was to be the last minute of my life—that leering clock face seemed to rush forward like the head of an oncoming railroad engine, filling my entire consciousness. A fad impulse seized me—to arrest at any cost of the cruel working of that chronometer—but I seemed no longer to have any volitional control over my body. Louder and louder became the ticking of the clock, more and more urgent, seeming to shriek at me 'Quick! Quick! Quick!' Each time more stridently, more metrically, until it resembled the clang of a sledge-hammer, measuring out my doom.

Fifteen! twenty! thirty! forty of the sixtieths of my last minute passed by while that fateful clock-dial became shrouded in blackness—only the remaining segment to be traversed remained, which glowed with an increasing fiery brilliance that seared into my soul. Quick! quick! The strand of remaining brightness became narrower and narrower as it was submerged by the tides of oblivion. Quick! quick! But I can do nothing. I am vaguely aware that my head is still transfixed by that unrelenting bar of demonic flesh. Five! Four! Three seconds remain—and now the clamor of time is earsplitting. Two! The executioner's axe is lifted... A sharp convulsing tremor seized my body...My muscles tensed for that final moment. Involuntarily my teeth closed, without regard for what was between them...A roar of agony from the Baron broke my spell of horror, drowned out the awaited final clang, rocketing me instantly into full consciousness. With his great bestial hands locked about my head he held me from him, pulling his part sharply from my mouth as a thick shower of his hot sperm spurted onto my face and bosom, announcing his climax, the villain demonstrated the intensity of his sensations by viciously digging his thumbs into the sensitive nerve-center that exists just above my eyes. I fainted away, blinded with the excrutiating pain, but soothed by the realization that I am saved—veritably, in the nick of time. Apparently, it was my accidental bite that brought on his orgasm.

In the evening, the Baron did not break his promise. All eight of us were summoned to suffer for his pleasure, and horror reigned supreme at Feodorovskoe that night. I shiver to think of that night even now. Far be it for me to try to arouse the reader's pity or incredulity. Similarly distant from my plan is it to mar the general tone and purpose of my book by playing up this unpleasant aspect of my Russian adventures. Yet, not to be accused of concealing too much, and judging that a few pages given over to the abnormal side of sex will not amiss, convincing the reader as I trust it will, that he can never be too thankful for the normalcy of his instinct, even if it be qualified by a few personal foibles, so long as they are this side criminality—I shall describe that typically horrible night as impersonally as possible.

When we were all assembled, nude of course, our dread master appeared wearing over his usual clothes a coat of thin mesh-steel studded with numerous small metal projections—obviously calculated to make any of us whom he should so honor, painfully aware of his embrace. In his hands he carried a varied assortment of knouts and switches—the least dangerous of his devices.

For all of half an hour he amused himself by merely milling us around the room in a circle, like beasts in a cage, while he stood in the centre, keeping us on the alert with blows on the thighs or buttocks from one or another of the weapons in his armory. Next he compelled us to jump over stools or chairs at the crack of his whip, helping one of the less agile of us over the hurdles with a vicious kick in the backside, tripping up another with his foot so that she fell face forward to the floor.

But even these spectacles were all too tame for his over-stimulated, jaded senses—and to help work himself into a proper frenzy he would, at frequent intervals, take great lusty swigs of various liquors. Suddenly he spoke, "Well, you whores. I think I want to piss."

Instantly all gathered about him and fell to their knees, offering their mouths. Only I, not yet acquainted with the procedure, held back in indignation. Noting this, he kicked aside the others and strode toward me.

"Quite obstinate still, eh?" he muttered, "You have a lot to learn yet around here." And throwing me on my back onto the bare floor, he drew out his genito-urinary apparatus, now flaccid and obviously employable only in the latter of its hyphenated capacities, and brought it close to my face.

"But wait—" he suddenly changed his purpose. "I'll show you a different trick." And reaching for a bottle of spirits, he took a long drink and then poured the rest over my cunt and pubic hairs, soaking the latter thoroughly. Then, igniting a match, he briefly explained his purpose in sneering, cynical tones.

"I am going to set fire to your bush," he says fiendishly, "that dear silky clump that lends such a false air of mystery to that pubic slot of yours. Then I will extinguish the fire with this," indicating his dropping member. "But if the sight of your distress moves or arouses me too much, then of course, I won't be able to come to your aid with the liquid that you just spurned. Do you understand?"

I was horrified—but had to conceal the fact—for I knew only too well that if he should be favored with an erection he would be utterly unable to urinate—and I knew, too, that my visible suffering would excite him.

He held the burning match to my spirit-soaked pubic delta. Immediately it caught fire. But to my surprise and relief I felt no pain. At least, not yet. The alcohol he had poured over me burned with a bright blue flame; but somehow, the considerable residue of water from the spirits protected my skin from the conflagration, and even the hairs themselves were scarcely singed. A miracle indeed, and one comparable to any of those marvels described in the Bible; say those of the prophets who went through fire unscathed, or that of Moses and the burning bush that would not consume itself. But the Baron, disappointed at my failure to evince any pain, and realizing that the fire would soon expire of itself, brought his part to bear upon me, and with a good deal of satisfaction, extinguished the conflagration with a copious stream of his urine.

This last procedure seemed to bring a flush of interest to his blood, and soon he was in fine enough fettle to demand and execute more active and direct satisfactions. Not at all flattered or overjoyed was I, however, to be again chosen as his maid of honor, and the recipient of his now monstrous cock—especially since, before wedging himself into my cunt, he took the precaution of slipping a little metal guard over the upper juncture of the lips and clitoris to ensure that I derived no pleasure from his contact.

But even with this inhuman limitation he was not yet satisfied. No sooner was he properly in the saddle than he had his daughter Sonya approach and squat over my bosom, offering her cunt to his mouth. He had four more of the girls lie, two on each side of me. They were parallel but reverse to each other. Their nude figures were within easy reach of both his hands choice of either breasts or cunts to caress or torture. The two remaining women, their buttocks raised in the air, had candles inserted in the anus of each. The tapers were lit, and these human candelabra crouched nearby to give additional light to his nefarious procedures.

Then and only then did he start fucking me.

And how he fucked me. With full, fierce, bone-breaking shoves he drilled deep into my innards with his brutal bar, deeper and deeper, till its dull head battered heavily against the entrance of my very womb. But he was not entirely into me yet. I could feel that he has inches still to spare. He continued feeding in his cock. It strained and tore at the mouth of my uterus—for my cunt proper was already filled to capacity. If only his fiendish device I weren't now prohibiting me from enjoyment, the pain would not be so unendurable. But pain alone is my lot—and at last, to the accompaniment of internal physical pangs comparable only to those of child-birth, the thick head of his seemingly endless prick forced its way through the tiny aperture into the very throbbing womb itself! A third maidenhead indeed is this now taken. Here I had been thinking that all that could arouse the envy and violence of the male sex had been taken from me—or at least made painlessly accessible and here was yet another atrocity—and if anything, the most excruciating of all, inflicted upon me.

As the climatic frenzy of his criminal pleasures approached and the pain that he caused me alone was insufficient to satisfy the fury of his destructive lust, he scratched and tore at the breasts and privates of the human sacrifices that lay on each side of me. At the same time he bit ferociously and unrestrainedly at the cunt of his beautiful daughter, who was squatting over my face, as I have said.

At last the prayed for ending came. I could not have held out much longer. The huge head of his prick, insinuated into my very womb like a burrowing serpent, cast out its prolific load of venom, flooding all of that dangerously susceptible female organ that it had always been my chief care to protect from insemination.

Unceremoniously the Baron withdrew from my torn, distended body and went on to the execution of other brutalities—brutalities in which, fortunately, I played no further part other than that of unwilling spectator. Brutalities which I have not the heart to describe, and which were repeated night after night in our captor's den.

On this same evening though, something occurred to give me a ray of hope—that suggested that there might yet be some interference from the outside world to put an end to our imprisonment. For just as the Baron was about to immolate one of our number, Illena, in the fires of his bestiality, there were sounds of a struggle at the door, and despite the two guards that tried to hold him back, in rushed a huge elderly peasant who turned out to be none other than than Illena's father, come to wrest her from the suspicious employment that had kept her away from home for some weeks.

Our elation was short-lived however. He was no match for the Baron and his men. Soon he was overcome, and with strong ropes, trussed up against a pillar. Our master, with the consummate cruelty he was distinguished for, proceeded to rape the peasant's daughter before his very eyes. The old man strained desperately on his bonds to get at the villain, actually frothing at the mouth because of his helplessness and uttering inconceivable oaths and threats. But the Baron went right on fucking the pretty Illena, making all sorts of cynical taunting remarks to the father, and finally transferring his attention from her cunt to her backside—to torture the father even more with this vicious demonstration upon the tender body of his beloved daughter. From threats the helpless parent turned to entreaties and prayers, calling upon all the saints and the Virgin Mary to aid him. This seemed only to increase the Baron's unholy delight.

"Stop your sanctimonious mouthing, old man," he said, "If you knew what fine fucking your daughter makes, how tight her cunt and how warm and tighter still her rear sheath is, you would want to try her yourself. I could prove to you, if I wished, that your loud words are the ravings, not of injured innocence, but of envy—and of a lust deeper than mine in that it considers itself thwarted by the restrictions of man and church. If I were to release you now on condition that you carnally possess the body of your charming offspring, you would be glad of the excuse to commit the incest."

"If you were to release me now," the great moujik roared through his clenched teeth, "I would tear you limb from limb, even if it took my last bit of strength to do it!"

The Baron paused in his occupation. A smile of cynical confidence was on his face. He withdrew his still-randy member from the tight illicit channel to which it had been paying homage.

"Illena," he ordered, "Go and see what you can do with those pretty hands and lips of yours to put your father in a better humor. Many times as a child you have no doubt coveted that which you saw bestowed only on your mother. Here is your chance to get it and satisfy those same desires."

"Sir..." Illena stammered through her tears with every determination, "you have compelled me to do many things since I have been here, but I would rather you killed me than force me thus to shame my respected father. Ask anything, but not that...."

The Baron scowled. From a nearby cupboard he fetched a revolver and leveled it at the breast of the moujik.

"I hate to do this Illena," he spoke with frigid calm, "But you leave me no alternative. If I can't make your father one of us by sealing his lips with a sin of his own, then I must insure that he does not leave here alive."

"Oh no!" Illena screamed, "Don't shoot...I'll do as you command, sir." And falling to her knees before her father, she tearfully and hesitantly opened his shirt and brought out the instrument of her creation, caressing it, while the Baron, whenever her actions lagged, egged her on with pitiless threats. If the mere vision of his daughter's nude beauty had not been enough to make the poor moujik forget the taboos of his relationship, certainly he would need have been more or less than human to withstand the inescapable seduction of her soft hands and luscious lips.

"No! no! Let him kill us both!" he had cried at her first overtures; but now he was sobbing and moaning, "Oh, my dear daughter! My sweet, loving daughter! Oh—you wonderful, beautiful woman!" And with each progression of his locution and her manipulation, it became more and more apparent that in the struggle between the ethicological and the biological, the latter and more fundamental power would soon triumph. Nor was my prediction a mere empty hypothesis: it was substantiated momentarily by the visibly increasing bulk and hardness of the moujik's great tartar cock.

The contrition with which the lovely Illena executed the Baron's commands could not mitigate their effectiveness. Soon the paternal bludgeon reached that bursting maximum of magnitude which insured that any insurrection of vestigial moral-conscience would be summarily repulsed, and the Baron, beckoning to two of the girls, had them raise the form of the tearfully protesting Illena to the level of her father and forcibly join his quivering member to her unwilling cunt.

The Baron stepped behind the post to which the moujik was tied, and with a single slash of his knife severed the ropes that bound him.

"Now, old man—" he sneered, "You are free to execute your threat of tearing me limb from limb—that is, if you can bring yourself to leave that delicious warm cunt." The moujik looked around him with wild eyes that mirrored his confusion and perplexity. Then he looked down at the pretty tear-streaked face of his daughter, framed in her flowing black hair, looked at her soft undulating bosom, shaken by her frightened sobs, and then lower still over her bare white belly to the dark shaded mount of love where her body was connected to his. He groaned; and in that groan was epitomized all his horror, despair, resignation, desire—and yes, pleasure. Then he slipped his now-free hands to the white luxuriousness of his daughter's buttocks and drew her whole body fiercely to him to keep from getting dislodged. He rammed himself further up into her tender body, and sank down with her to the floor. Negotiating the fall without losing an inch or a moment's contact with her exquisite female flesh, he proceeded at once to fuck her with a fury and lust that was, if anything, only augmented by the illicit incestuousness of their carnal connection.

"Father! father! Are you mad?" the horrified Illena screamed, struggling to get away; but he pinned her down with his mass, and soon it became obvious that she was being vanquished by that inescapable potent charmer of his.

"Think of mother...oh!" she gasped, in a last appeal to his conscience. But if he thought of mother, it was no doubt to decide how much nicer daughter was. And if she thought of mother, it was now probably to think of what mother was missing—for her desperate wrigglings were now becoming heaves of passionate cooperation. For all of its inevitability, I was horrified. Rape was bad enough. But to have the daughter thus revel in the incest was too much. Whatever remaining belief I may have had in the efficacy of man's laws and arrangements, I lost it then. Only this remained: that prick is prick and cunt is cunt, and ever the twain shall meet.

And so father and daughter continued their lustful, maddened mingling of flesh and blood with own flesh and blood, of kind with kind, the daughter wrapping her little but richly developed white thighs and shapely calves tensely about her father's loins, her bottom working wildly—the parent plunging back and forth into the hot moist flesh of the cunt he had fathered—both of them gasping words of pleasure and endearment that were not at all the usual expressions of filial and paternal respect that one might expect between such close relations. It was soon over—that most proscribed of all prohibitions, the insertion of a father's seed into the womb of his offspring—with no bolts from heaven to evidence the Divine wrath—only sighs and moans of ecstasy, wild quivering of lustful pleasure, and then the final orgasmic transports, the crucial stiffening, the relaxation.

For a time they lay together. I could picture the tragic turmoil that must have existed in the mind of each. At last they shuddered, guiltily avoiding each other's eyes. The father slunk off into a corner as if to hide himself from all the world, his head hung low in shame. Even the Baron must have realized, if not been touched by, his anguish—for he came out of his cynical gloating for a moment to slap him on the back and say:

"Cheer up, old man. Cunt is cunt—so don't let the accident of your relationship trouble you. I'll give you a crack at my own daughter if you wish: Just to even accounts. But first I'll fuck her myself—to show you that you're not the only father in this district who doesn't allow the law to frighten him off the cunt he's most entitled to. What do you say, eh?"

The moujik did not reply. The Baron shrugged his shoulders indifferently and left him, impatient to himself again execute the crime he had just spoken of.

A moment later was the deafening report of a gun being fired. Even before the dense smoke lifted, we saw the bleeding form of Illena's father crumpling to the floor. He had taken the revolver which the Baron had earlier left carelessly on the sideboard and had shot himself through the heart.

"Old fool!" the Baron muttered, and resumed his interrupted sexual calisthenics.

A few weeks after this tragic incident, as I was walking along a corridor that led past the Baron's private study, I was arrested by the sounds of an altercation within. My curiosity was further peaked when I heard my own name was unmistakably mentioned.

"So you're not going to give me even a single crack at that little French Madeleine of yours?" I recognized the voice of Ivan, the man who had brought me to this hateful place.

"No!" the Baron answered definitely with an oath, "Here's one female that I like well enough to keep to myself. Why her tight oily slot milks me in half the time the others take. No! I've paid you for her, she's mine!"

"A fine friend you are. Getting exclusive, aren't you?"

"No, Ivan. But why have it stretched any more than necessary? I've offered you the pick of all my other women. You can even have my daughter if you wish."

"Damn you, Grigor. I don't go in for children—and least of all could I copulate with the spawn of any cursed devil like you!"

The Baron laughed complacently, while Ivan angrily continued.

"I brought you the French girl, didn't I—the nicest piece of flesh you ever had. If I hadn't, you wouldn't have her. It may have been your money, but it was my personality, my time and effort that got her here. If you can't treat me honestly, you can go out and trap your own cunt hereafter. I'm through!" And he came stalking out the door.

"Don't forget tonight, Ivan," the Baron called after him good-naturedly, "You're still invited, you know. And if you don't want Sonya, there's still Olga, and Gruschenka, and—" Ivan slammed the door, scowling fiercely. But when he spied me, his face lighted up. He drew me aside into a little alcove and reached hungrily within my dressing gown for the opulent curves of my nude body, of which he no doubt still had pleasant recollections.

"With or without his consent—" he muttered, as if speaking only to himself, "I'll fuck her anyway."

"Don't I have anything to say about that?" I whispered coquettishly, narrowing my eyes as if amorously and running my fingertips lightly up his thighs. Silently he crushed me in his arms. Then, slipping one hand between our bodies and pinching the full lips of vagina as if to reassure himself that they were still there after his two months absence, he proceeded to bring out his stiffened love-part. Against my smooth bare skin I could feel the delicious heat emanating from his smouldering boulders.

"Listen to me, Ivan!" I whispered hurriedly, replacing his thick hot organ within his trousers and rebuttoning them with some difficulty, "It would be madness to take me now. The Baron is likely to come upon us at any moment. You must wait—and you will have everything. I want it as badly as you: the Baron has been giving me nothing but pain. Do you want more such nights of love as we spent together on the train? Then get me away from this horrible madhouse. No!—No, Ivan—please don't take it out again... There, now he'll stay put. Listen, this is neither the time nor the place for it Ivan. Get me out of here and you may have me for as long as you wish—a whole month even—and I'll refuse you nothing."

His obvious reluctance to forego the present gradually gave way to eager anticipation of the future that I pictured for him so glowingly.

"Agreed!" he finally said hoarsely, squeezing both the cheeks of my posteriors in friendly renunciation, "This very night it shall be! Leave everything to me." And he hurried away, chuckling to himself at the thought of how he would avenge the Baron's parsimoniousness.

I awaited the evening's orgy with great anxiety. Would he be there or not? He was—and the Baron, pleased to have his invaluable recruiting officer still with him, was in extraordinary good humor tossing off glass after glass of vodka, and entertaining his friend with loud vulgar jokes. I watched Ivan closely. He seemed to have forgotten all about me and was diddling around with one of the other girls. But during a moment's diversion, I saw him stealthily empty a powder into the Baron's glass. The Baron went on drinking. Soon he declared he was getting sleepy. Then he complained of dizziness. A moment later, he collapsed to the floor in a sodden stupor.

Ivan was equal to the occasion.

"You—Madeleine," he called to me in a loud voice, "Run and send the doormen in here! Tell them their master's ill. Call the outside guard, too." And in a whisper (in French so that only I might understand), "Wait for me behind the cart out there—"

"And all you other chattering females—" he roared masterfully, "get back to your rooms at once!"

I rushed out and did as I had been directed. The guards did not think to doubt my errand, but left their posts hurriedly to go to their master. I had some difficulty finding the cart, but succeeded finally, and hid under a quantity of straw and some robes. A few minutes later I was joined by Ivan who had left ostensibly to fetch a doctor. My absence had not been noted yet.

All night long we drove in our slow vehicle, my anxiety gradually subsiding as the mileage between ourselves and the castle increased and no pursuers came after us. No doubt it must have been well into the next day before my flight was discovered.

Suffice it that we escaped—although I was actually without even a chemise—having had nothing but my kimono on my back when I made my escape. Need I record too, that as soon as we were a safe number of hours away from my prison and before the dawn broke, Ivan joined me in the straw for a half-hour of relaxation? And must I remind the inquisitive reader that it had been over two months since I had really had a piece—to convince him of the glorious fuck my saviour gave me and the superb belly-bumping I returned, pouring out at last the pent-up passions of months?

With this supremely satisfying spend—in the straw of a cart in the south of Russia—with the dawn breaking over the yellow hills of the Caucassus—let me draw the curtain and bring to an end this longest and perhaps most trying episode in my life and in my book.

CHAPTER VIII

Let me pass rapidly over the succeeding weeks. Of course, when we reached Ekatrinodar, the rail terminus, Ivan had my wardrobe temporarily replenished with some quaint but becoming Russian costumes. My first act, as soon as I was able to appear upon the streets was to hasten to the post-office, where, at the "poste restante" I found many anxious letters from Fleurette and others awaiting me. I immediately telegraphed messages of reassurance to Paris and requisitions for more sophisticated apparel.

From here, Ivan and I journeyed to Yalta, a fashionable Russian resort in the semi-tropical Crimea, near Sebastopol. Here we spent three delightful weeks together that were for me vacation, dissipation, and recuperation—all rolled into one. Most of it was taken in bed.

Apart from Ivan, nothing particular transpired, except a brief affair with a handsome young army officer that covered just two stolen afternoons. Come to think of it, there was one other; with a charmingly impatient young bellboy at the hotel, who discovering my infidelity to my registered protector, exacted from me some pleasant enough blackmail in the form of two or three wee little pushes—the price of his silence.

Once my promised dalliance with Ivan was completed, I returned to Paris. The entire nightmare of my Russian adventures was soon forgotten in one continual round of pleasure. My absence had, if such a thing were possible, increased my popularity ten-fold.

All my past lovers, it seemed, came back for re-engagements—as if they had all been saving their passion for me—which was, of course, not very likely. As usual, I would skim or sip a bit of the top cream and pass them right on to my assistants for the more arduous and prolonged milking. But now my faithful little squad of Fleurette, Suzanne, and Manon was far too small to cope with the vigorous platoon of pricks that presented themselves nightly at our private parties for immediate immersion in soft flesh. With all the calculation in the world, temporal, physiological, geometrical, equational and fractional, we couldn't accommodate them all. All we succeeded in doing was cluttering our books with future engagements that we could never catch up with, or postponing an admirer so injudiciously that he finally required triple our time to assuage him.

There was but one way to relieve the increasing congestion and that was to strengthen our ranks with fresh enlistments. This I did—carefully and critically, having the finest flesh marts of all the world from which to choose.

Unwillingly I was being drawn, by force of irresistible circumstance, into becoming a professional "entremetteuse." Much as I struggled against the commercialization of a "metier" which, I assure the reader, I had chosen only because it embodied my cardinal success, how one friend always insists on bringing another friend, how impossible it is to refuse one's hospitality to a stranger when he has charm, wealth, and all other attributes that obtain admission to our house for so many others. How in brief, the moving snowball gathers size and weight till it is, an avalanche that cannot be stayed.

Before long there were fourteen of us. Because of the liberality of my terms and the generosity of my patrons, there were always scores of girls from all walks of life on my waiting list, anxious to fight under my aegis in the tender tournaments of love. Again and again I was assured that never had Paris been honored by a "maison de plaisir" quite so nice, refined and discreet as mine since the days of Madame Giordan (who, operating an establishment for princes and bishops back in the previous century, could scarcely be considered serious competition.) Only in this respect did I differ from that other famous Madame: I never accepted the service of genuine virgins. The applicant could go home and snip her maidenhead with her mother's sewing scissors, she could try sliding violently down the banisters (as so many respectable women manage to have done by the time they reach their nuptial bed), or more sensibly still, entrust the delicate operation to some worthy stiff-pronged boyfriend; but always and absolutely I refused to be instrumental in actually launching the career of a virgin. Frequently too, I would make them undergo a sort of non-committal apprenticeship, during which they would serve as waitresses or maids. Since the rules of my house strictly forbade patrons molesting the help in any way, they were given every decent opportunity to watch everything that went on, themselves untouched, before they decided whether or not they really wished to enter my services as true dispensers of joy. Because of this particular conscientiousness of mine, I was rewarded by a congratulatory letter from the Prefect of Police, which he authorized me to frame and exhibit as testimony to the fact that my house did not countenance that one sexual offense forbidden by French law—the seduction of virgins and minors.

Frequent medical examinations under my personal supervision were, even at the beginning, a strict part of our regimen. Should a girl be found infected, which due to our hygienic precautions was nigh impossible and happened to only two of my girls in all the years of our association, she was immediately retired until she could present a totally negative

Wasserman reaction and a perfectly clear bill of health. I take greatest pride in boasting that, inconceivable as it may seem to those fearful prudes who are ignorant of the aseptic immaculacy that reigns in the high-class Parisians house of accommodation today, I can truthfully say that my establishment and my girls have never even once been instrumental in the transmission of any venereal disease.

It follows without exaggeration then that mine was the kind of place where no patron need hesitate to go down on—or even drink our health from—the cunny of any one of us, which was at all times as kissable and clean as the lips of his wife or sweetheart. If not considerably more so.

From the foregoing prospectus I must pray the reader not to conclude two things: First, that we did all the fucking in Paris. We did not. Paris is a big place, and fucking, thank god, is not restricted by law here, or by patent or copyright anywhere. Secondly, I would not have the reader think for one moment that I allowed the increasing burdens of my generalship to interfere with my own active participation in the delights of Venus—for when indeed has wholesaling prevented a profitable 'retailing' on the side? Fleurette made a competent second in command—and whenever my cunt called me into the thick of battle or into some private hand-to-hand duel, whenever I was exhausted by some too furious engagement, she was always there to uphold the standard in my stead, as gracious and well-poised a hostess as I, with the advantage, if anything, of a cool prepossession which was not always mine when in the presence of prick. Never more than once in a night did she allow her white shoulder to go to the mat in the delicious wrestle of love—and so, must I confess it, she had more time to attend to my routine affairs than I was willing to afford them myself.

Another problem that I was confronted with at this time: The expensiveness of our usual champagne dinners and parties of necessity barred many friends who while eminently worthy were somewhat limited in purse. Many fascinating young artists and writers were comprised in this category. I did not like to forego the benefit of their company. There was but one thing to do. I opened a branch establishment of more modest pretensions on the Left Bank, and divided my time between the two places, riding to and fro in the luxurious Hispana-Suiza that I had recently acquired. Indeed, more frequently than not, I gave the greater part of my time (and not time only) to the stimulating long-haired Bohemians who gathered at my less-expensive resort.

Times without number I would generously spread my thighs for no other stipend than the gift of a canvas or a small sketch by some than unknown post-impressionist painter, and soon every available inch of wall-space in my Latin Quarter house was covered with some such offering. Surprisingly and gratifyingly, many of these apparently meaningless and worthless pictures, earned by a few ungrudging motions of my hips years ago, have since become much sought after masterpieces that have netted me thousands of francs.

One must not think however, that with the increasing systemization of my love-life all adventure came to an end. Not at all. The life of a courtesan in itself is the most varied and interesting occupation, indisputably, that a woman is capable of following. Add to this my natural curiosity, my intellectual interests and my financial independence, and you will agree that whenever things threatened to become at all tiresome, I could very well vary the routine.

Thus, on warm summer evenings, we would sometimes transfer our activities to the shaded groves of the Bois du Boulogne or to one of the other suburban parks. Here, under the moon's indulgent beams and on the soft carpet of the grass we would, with a select group from our clientele, celebrate Priapic rites in the classic manner of the ancient Greeks and Romans. It is really inconceivable how the beauties of the night and the freedom of the open air can make even of the most commonplace fucking an entirely new and dazzling aesthetic experience. What gorgeous dances and lascivious exhibitions my girls, stripped to the nude, would stage for us within the circle of our automobile headlights! And then, the delicious personal relief from all this appetizing stimulation when we scattered in pairs into the woods for the next, but not necessarily the final act of our wondrous drama of the sexes!

At about this time I met a wealthy motion picture producer who insisted on immortalizing me, as he put it, in some erotic films to be made privately at his Neuilly studios. I had never considered acting as one of my abilities; but if the only acting were fucking, I thought, I certainly had every right to deem myself capable. It was not all quite as simple as that.

At the studio, I was introduced to a handsome fellow who was to play the masculine lead opposite (or atop of me) and after some scanty instructions from the director, we got right down to business. Beneath the glare of the Klieg lights and with the loud clicking of the cameras for accompaniment, my partner proceeded to the preliminaries of courtship with such unhurried finesse and artistry that soon I forgot completely that we were making movies, and became so aroused that I was on the verge of taking the initiative myself. When he had at last finished undressing me deliberately, piece by piece, and with all the provocativeness in the world, he stretched me on the sofa and spent at least ten minutes more and 500 feet of film in placing long, deft, searching kisses in all the tender depressions of my body.

"Fine! Fine!" the director was muttering, hopping excitedly from one leg to the other, "Hurry up! No, no,! I mean take it slow and easy. We'll be able to make a ten reeler out of it. Fine! Fine! Now come over her easy now... That's it, that's right. Be very gentle. Remember—in the script she's supposed to be a virgin—so make believe you're trying not to frighten her. That's it! Now—produce the pin. Slide it up her thighs slowly. No! no! Sacre dieu! Over to the other side more! How do you expect the cameraman to get her cunt with your big arse blocking the whole set! That's better. Now, hold yourself high—separate the lips of her twat—bring up just the head—rub it around the vulva awhile.... Now! Ride those cameras in closer. Good. Now, start shoving in. But slowly! You're going to take her cherry. It's blocked! It's tight! You shove, you push! But remember—you can't get in!"

"That's a damned lie!" I wanted to scream: My hot cunt could have swallowed him in a single quicksand suction of its own, if my partner had not been so bent on teasing me. Millimeter by millimeter, with a stinginess that was scarcely human, he fed his part into my hungry cavity. It seemed to be taking him years; but at last he was all of half-way in. I would have shoved up to meet him—instructions to lie still be damned—had he not held my hips down with his hands and the weight of his body. What a conceited fool of a man, I thought, to be able to subordinate his instincts for his acting. As for me, I have already recorded how in the presence of prick I lose all presence of mind.

He was half way in, as I have said, and I was all tensed with dreams of pleasurable possibilities, when suddenly the voice of the director broke in again.

"Now you can't get any further. It's too tight! It hurts her, it's killing her. Now withdraw and take some Vaseline from that jar beside you!"

As if Vaseline were necessary! I don't know what restrained me from quitting there and then. And now the whole rigmarole had to be gone through again... But don't let me torture the reader as my partner tortured me. At last he got it substantially all the way in, the full torrid length of my oily sheath.

"Now rest awhile—as if from a terrific task. Lie still—both of you. Now pull out a little. In again. Very, very slowly! It's too tight still to go any faster."

The teasing was more than I could bear. "If this is entirely for the movies," I muttered sarcastically to my partner, "I guess it'll have to be all right. But if any of this is for me, I wish you'd go just a little bit faster."

"But madame! The director?" he whispered dutifully.

"Oh, fuck the director!" I replied, forgetting myself entirely, "I have my own ideas of the way this should be done!" And dislodging his hands by sheer force from my insatiate hips I began fucking him, fast and furiously.

"Sacre Sainte Ciboire!" came from the direction, "Slow down! Nom de Di'eu! You'll register nothing but a blur on the film!" But by now neither of us was in a state to pay much heed. My hips were moving at the rate of a hundred oscillations a minute: my leading man was plunging his piston at least seventy a minute making a combined frequency of one hundred and seventy per. Perhaps we did spoil the Film; but thank god, we didn't spoil the Fuck.

As I washed up and rested prior to taking the next scene, the director, somewhat appeased by now, approached me.

"Not so bad after all" he grumbled, "but why didn't you at least keep your face toward the cameras and smile when I told you to?"

"I couldn't keep my head still in any one position," I explained simply, "and as for smiling to the cameras, I didn't know where they were, for I went stone blind toward the end. And anyway, I didn't hear a word you shouted."

For the next scene, I was supposed to be alone in my boudoir, examining some erotic postcards and playing with myself, when another male character, who has been secretly watching me through the keyhole, is supposed to burst in and rape me. I carried off my solitary role to perfection, lazily titillating the proud nipple of my right breast, gradually working my hand downward to my mount of love, and finally spreading wide the lips of my cunt to have them photograph to best advantage.

During all this, the rest of the company stood on the sidelines, watching my performance with tense interest. The dapper mustachioed little gentleman who was to come in next waited eagerly for his cue.

Action was halted a moment for some further instructions, and then the director, with a signal to my next partner to rush in on the set, yelled, "All ready? Shoot!" This last was of course for the cameraman; but my partner must have misunderstood. He shot his load instead—prematurely and all over my thighs. I had played my part all too effectively: the delay had been more than he could withstand. The director, in a fury, ordered the film to be chopped and came downstage to give him a good round word-dressing. This only confused the poor fellow further and made it additionally difficult for him to get in shape to continue the action.

"Come now!" roared the director, "Suppose you show us whether or not you can get it in properly before we waste any more film on you."

All flustered, and blushing furiously, the young man climbed over me and awkwardly brought himself down between the accommodating luxuriousness of my separated thighs.

"Par dieu! That's no way to dot it!" groaned the director, tearing his hair in despair.

"Well, supposing you do it yourself!" sighed the martyred thespian with some exasperation.

"I won't do it," roared the director, putting aside his megaphone and unbuttoning himself, "but I can show you how it ought to be done!" And bringing out a lusciously large piece of love equipment that immediately increased my respect for the man, he angrily took his position and shoved himself into me with demonstrative unhesitancy.

"There you are!" he spoke, "Do it that way, and not as if you were a damn fool fumbling around in the dark." And immediately he started withdrawing to reassume his directorial role. With a little clasp of my moist velvety sheath I tried to hold him back. So absorbed was he in his work however, he didn't seem to notice it, didn't even relax his frown to favor me with an appreciative smile.

"And what am I to do in this part?" I queried sweetly.

"Just what you're doing right now: nothing."

"I'm afraid I don't have it straight yet. Do you mind showing me again?"

Grudgingly he complied, returning his loving rigidity to my internal custody once more.

"Don't you think I ought to do this?" I asked, giving a brief back and forth movement to my hips.

"No!" he replied sternly.

"Or this?" I gave a little sideways twist to my buttocks. "Or this?" and I gave a slow sinuous spiral movement to my whole lower body that bestowed upon his flexible rod a membranous caress that immediately seemed to deprive him of all his aloof impersonality.

"Well, maybe," he muttered confusedly.

"And wouldn't you like to play the masculine lead to me hereafter?" I cooed coquettishly, playing my cunt muscles deftly up and down the full length of his instrument.

He squirmed uncomfortably, then squirmed once more—this time with reluctant pleasure. Then, suddenly remembering the numerous people who stood by, he glanced officiously at his wrist watch: "It's time to quit—" he shouted irritably, "Company's dismissed. We film again at 10 a.m. tomorrow. And I'll fire anybody who's late!"

As the group of players and employees filed out of the studio and the director turned his attention fiercely and resentfully to me once more, a funny little cameraman wearing a cap with the visor behind his neck winked to me significantly. I winked back.

When our little tête à tête was over (alas that it was not filmed, for the real thing was much more convincing than any mere acting could be) and I stood in my flimsy chemise slipping my dress over my head preparatory to leaving, I asked him whether I would be satisfactory.

"No!" he rumbled, "You were awful. You'll have to do it all over again. I want you to come in at 9 o'clock tomorrow for some preliminary rehearsal!"

"Will my leading man be on hand that early?" I asked sweetly.

He slapped my buttocks in mock anger—an intimacy that ordinary I greatly resent—and for the first time yet, laughed heartily.

I was telling the reader how interesting my life was even at this comparatively sedentary period of my career. In the spring of 1914, a Monsignor, a Papal legate to Paris whom I had met on a number of occasions and who had expressed himself extremely well pleased with my discretion, approached me with a mysterious proposition. The events which followed I now divulge for the very first time. I was to select four of my most trustworthy and attractive girls, and, under a pledge of secrecy, accompany them to Rome on a mission of whose exact nature we were, for the time, to remain ignorant. Wholly apart from the generous stipend involved, I accepted immediately. Within a short time we were transported to the Eternal City and put up at a rather shabby 'albergo' facing the muddy River Tiber. As it happed to turn out, we were the sole occupants.

On the second evening after our arrival, our conductor appeared, and taking us down to the cellar of our hotel, led us into a long subterranean tunnel. The damp dripping walls immediately suggested to me the hypothesis that we were passing under the River to the nearby Castle Angelo, the island strong-hold of the Pope. I have since learned definitely that this Island, known as the Isola Sacra, is connected by passages under the River with the Vatican Palace on the opposite bank, and is supposed to be resorted to by the Vatican inmates as a kind of fort In case of military or counter-inquisitional stress.

After passing innumerable ancient doors by dint of much unbolting of bars and rattling of chains—all of which lent to our adventure a most authentically medieval flavor—we climbed a steep stone stairway and found ourselves suddenly in a sumptuously furnished apartment brightly illuminated by hundreds of candles.

As our eyes became better accustomed to the light we were confronted by a group of middle-aged, important-looking men, clad in clerical garb. They seemed to be awaiting us impatiently. The centre of the group, and the particular object of their respect, seemed to be an elderly gentleman who of them all alone remained seated on a regally cushioned dais. Irreligious as I was, I could not help but tremble at the exciting and flattering supposition that flashed through my mind...

My girls and I were soon put at our ease, though. Introductions, obviously false, were made all around: "This is Cardinal Aquaviva, Bishop Cacambo, meet Miss Cunnegonde. Here we have Monsignor Farniente and so on.

As a civilized preliminary to what we had every right to expect, we all retired to an adjoining chamber where a regal repast was spread for us. Each gentleman chose for himself a companion to his taste, and as I was the mistress of my party, I was delegated to the attentions of the elderly gentleman, beside whom I took my place at table. There was a surplus of males present, but these proceeded to make themselves pleasant and useful in whatever way; they could.

As bottle after bottle of the rarest old Chianti, muscatel, and lacrimae Christi bubbled forth into our glasses and was tossed under the board to make room for other wines, our merry group warmed up more and more while the conversation becoming less and less delicate. My priestly companion alone ate and drank with great moderation, and while he made no contribution to the general levity, he would smile indulgently at each lewd sally.

"It is well that they enjoy the relaxations of the earth occasionally, my daughter," he addressed me in his soft kindly voice, "for tomorrow they go forth again to shoulder the cares of both this world and the next." And as if to keep our conversation on a level different from that which went on about us, he spoke to me, not in the bad French which the others employed as an excuse for license, but in a musical crystal-clear Italian that made me glad I had studied enough of this beautiful language to enable me to hold conversations with this great man.

But at this point we were distracted by a great burst of laughter which acclaimed the exploit of one of the cardinals, who, unlacing Fleurette's bodice and releasing her luscious little pent up breasts, placed a kiss deep down between them. Immediately the Monsignor jumped up, and snatching a dainty slipper from one of her tiny feet, filled it with champagne and gallantly proceeded to drink a toast to her quivering charms. Forthwith all the cavaliers followed suit, first undoing the waists and brassieres of their lady-partners till the table seemed surrounded by a flock of snow-white doves arrested in flight, and then pledging flattering toasts all around.

Not even I was spared—for one of the clerics who was without a partner, seeing my bosom in a state of veiled mystery, came toward me exclaiming: "What manner of heresy is this, mademoiselle that you are permitted to still profane your God-given charms with sinful trappings? With your permission, Reverend Sir, I will strip the applicant of her earthly vestments and prepare her for the communion to come."

Blushing helplessly I looked toward my august partner. He nodded his head, smiling. "You may proceed, Your Eminence." In a moment my bosom too was bared to the excited gaze of all present—and each nipple, in unison no doubt with all the other erectile tissue in that gathering, arose and hardened into a delectable little strawberry. The prelate could not resist the temptation to run his hand over the soft intoxicating curves of my flesh; but the further savoring of them he had to leave to another. Apologizing to my partner, he withdrew for the time.

The earlier awe that my girls and I may have felt at our introduction to this august assembly was by this time, it is needless to state, entirely dissipated. And why not? For whatever our hosts may have been at all other times, it was obvious that tonight they were to be merely human. And their priestly vestments while perhaps still a restraint upon some of us, would not, I now felt certain, remain in evidence much longer.

We all waited expectantly for something further to be done to crack what little ice may have been unthawed by now. Suddenly, one of the gentlemen, more flushed with drink than the rest, leaping on to the table and dragging my sweet little Gisele after him, proceeded to strip her of her remaining clothes. At his request, a deep armchair was passed up to him, and upon this Gisele threw herself. Reclining far back and spreading wide her adorable richly developed thighs, she awaited her lord's pleasure. Snatching up a bottle of champagne and falling to his knees within the grateful haven of her shapely limbs, he with one hand gently parted the luscious silk-grown lips of her cunt—which for all the world resembled the inside of a rich casket of dark soft velvet lined with rose-colored satin—and pouring the bubbling contents of the bottle over her mount of Venus, drank it up as it flowed from the lower end of the channel formed by her widespread vulva.

We all applauded heartily. But when, having sucked up the last drop of the effervescent liquid, he still continued with his mouth at her cunt, and it became clear to us that they intended going through a gamahuching, our enfevered senses broke all bounds of patience. Leaving these two to their devices, we trailed into the other room, some of the gills hopping along in but a single slipper and dragging some already discarded bit of clothing after them, the men with flushed faces and eager mien fingering great threatening (or should I say promising) bulges in the front of their cassocks and pontifical robes.

Then the fierce fun began in real earnest. Manon, with wild sparkling eyes, made a rush for one of the divans, tearing off her remaining clothes. Throwing herself upon the springy furniture, she bounced her superbly rounded buttocks impatiently up and down, screaming "Come on—anybody—fuck me quick!" I was both proud and a little ashamed of her.

Spreading her legs and opening the lips of her luscious slit, she invited the immediate onslaught of the first comer—and had not long to wait.

In a moment my other girls too were stripped to their skins. Couples sought divans or chairs, or simply sank to the heavy rugs on the floors. Cassocks were thrown back over shoulders or furled up hastily, and monster members that had not tasted female flesh for lord knew how long came into evidence—only to be quickly hidden away in the hot rosy depths of the clefts that their stiff bursting strength rudely divided.

All this happened ere I was scarcely seated on the platform beside my distinguished consort. The lustful fury that pervaded the room reached even to our little Olympus. Breathing a bit feverishly, I looked inquiringly at my partner. He smiled benignly and made a timid gesture toward my nerve-tautened, swelling breasts; but it was only to cover them with the waist that I still had partially about my shoulders. He was saying something, but I did not hear him, for my attention was now everywhere else: on the moist seething state of my own cunt among other things. However, though a number of the unoccupied men were casting longing eyes at me, none made any move to rescue me from their superior. So I tried to make the best of it. Uncovering my bosom once more. I cupped one of my swelling white globes alluringly in one hand, and slipped my other hand under the folds of the reverend sir's robe, in search of the proofs of his manhood. He arrested me gently but firmly, and with a sad smile said: "Whether happily or unhappily, I am, and have for a long time been, beyond the tyrannical claims of the flesh. If I am here tonight, it is, strangely enough, to cooperate not actually but morally with my brethren of the stole. I would rather share in their sin, if sin it be and if sin they must, than have them sin without my knowledge and behind my back. In the great and holy task that we are about, it is of all things most essential that there be complete harmony, frankness and understanding between my colleagues in the Lord and myself—else all would indeed be impossible. One lie, one concealment, and they would be forever lost to me and to our cause

"Perhaps you are wondering how we dare to bring in women from the outside world on such occasions as this. No doubt you share the misconception of so many others that we monastics resort to the women of our convents for such purposes. That is entirely false. What may have been in the earlier days of the church is, of course, beyond our knowledge and control; but in all sincerity I can assure you that we laborers in the Lord's vineyard value too highly the soul that is dedicated to Christ to dare lead it astray. The Lord in His boundless grace can well forgive the sins of you women who have never been His, who have never seen the Light. But of those already pledged to Him, He is majestically jealous. We have more than enough as it is to prevent immorality in the convents—much less do we consider launching them upon the paths of sensuality. And so, whenever the need forces us, and I fear that the very nature of our work by its peculiar necessity of repression makes it all too frequent, we call upon women of the more worldly kind, and thus despoil Heaven of no soul.

"As to possible reflections upon the clergy, we have no fear. So deeply entrenched is the universal respect of our power and integrity, that if you were ever to recount the events of this night to all the world, none would believe you anything but mad.

"Does it follow then that we vicars of the Lord are walking in the ways of hypocrisy? No, my daughter. It is merely that we have been compelled to adopt a deep sense of expediency in addition to our sense of duty. As shepherds of the people, we have a very important task to fulfill. Marriage and the family—these are the institutions that are absolutely essential to the stability of society and its perpetuation; hence we must foster them. But yet, as Plato has pointed out, the narrowness of these same institutions, their self-seeking, is inconsistent with the idea of broader social service, such as that of the church. If we were to have wives and children, our first concern would in the nature of things be for them and not for the millions that we must lead. That we forego these is at once the proof of our sincerity and our altruism. Hence arises the concept of celibacy for the clergy, and we do all in our power to follow it by living simply and thinking purely. But while all of us may be spiritually fitted to our task, yet there are many of us who physically are still attached to the earth—and this is a thing beyond our personal dispensation: it is in the hands of the Lord. If we must satisfy our flesh, then in all humility we must. And since to do so openly would countenance a profligacy in the people that would soon destroy society, since to admit our weakness would deprive us of the prestige that is necessary—not for our own good, mind you, but for the welfare of mankind—we deem such expedients as these the best compromise between our heavenly and our earthly heritage."

As he concluded, my gaze leapt to the varied tableaux being staged all about us. What a maze of heaving joy-contorted loins and feverish thighs! And Manon, finished her first fuck while I sat talking, and having started on her second, with a lechery that I had never dreamt she possessed was shouting at the top of her voice "Come on, you stiff-pricked stags! Come on, I'll fuck you all! Come on! I'll take everyone of you on at once!" And surely enough, as those heretofore nonparticipating eagerly approached, she received one in the delicious enclosure of her cunt, another in the no-less delightful haven of her pretty luscious mouth, and she was still able to accommodate two others by manipulating their impatient scarlet cocks in each of her soft well-groomed hands, while all her many lovers in turn squabbled for possession of her pert firm breasts. It was more than I could stand in continued inactivity.

"Pardon me, father," I spoke with some embarrassment, "I feel deeply honored at your deeming me worthy of your words—and I shall not soon forget them. But would you mind if I jumped in just for a little while? Don't you see how unfair it is to my little Manon for me to sit idly here while she is being torn to bits by four of your voracious pontiffs?"

"Go, my daughter, with my blessings," he replied kindly, and drawing a little volume of sacred meditations from his sleeve, he settled back to fortify himself against what must have been for him a very wearisome situation indeed.

And now—to the rescue!—true to rescue form, discarding my clothes as I went. I was nearly too late, for Manon's dextrous fingers were just bringing on the supreme surrender of the man to her right, who, just as I approached, yielded up his creamy tribute in thick copious jets every drop of which reminded me of the pleasures I had been missing. And the two who occupied her lower and upper mouths respectively, excited by the sight of this triumph, joined him in ejaculation almost immediately after, flooding both of her warm caressing orifices with their prolific love juices simultaneously, even ere the last spurt had shot from the turgid gland of the first, past her supple milking hand and onto her wildly heaving bosom. Only the remaining gentleman, whether due to the weaker manipulative power of her left hand or to greater staying qualities of his own, still withheld his final offering. I slipped alongside him and gently released his bursting crimson bone from her soft perspiring grasp. Manon, trembling in the throes of her own dizzy climax with eyes tensely shut, and inundated with these triple sacrifices, scarcely noticed the deprivation of a fourth, but continued wildly pumping both her hands, working her transfixed cunt in mad jerks, and sucking away for dear life at the spouting prick that filled her mouth.

Leading the cock that I had captured to a nearby heap of cushions without so much as glancing at the face of its owner, I threw myself on my back and stuffed it into my swimming cunt, praying only that it would not go off too soon, imploring only that it would not lose its stiff stamina before I could manage to catch up with it.

"Fuck me!" I panted, consumed with lechery. And lest my rider should fail to understand me, I inaugurated the essential movements by my own initiative. The hungry lips of my feverish cunt ran up and down the solid morsel of flesh that distended me, as if seeking a point at which it might bite it off satisfactorily without getting too little and at the same time finding that all was too much for it.

Such greedy maneuvering soon had the expected result. Before my partner could even well adopt the intricate rhythm of my lustful abandoned motions, we both came off together in a climax of nerve dazzling splendor. But men who live in the monasteries, as I had learned before, are a single round of love's soft ammunition. Without pausing to reload or even to allow the breech to cool, he continued pounding away. Ram for ram I responded, and when the next tally was taken, I was one ahead of him—though completely exhausted. Only then did we rest for a moment, his organ still stiff and soaking in my seething cunt. He introduced himself.

"I'm not even a cardinal," he said, "Just secretary to one of the archbishops. That's why I was the last to be taken care of. But if I am the last to get started—and by the Madonna I've scarcely begun—I'll be the last to finish. Ready for another yet?"

I wanted a few more moments of respite; but he was raring to go. So I varied the routine a bit, first washing his blood-gorged dripping member with some fresh champagne, drying it with a napkin, and then giving him my best in the french manner.

When he had finished filling my mouth with the proofs of his still unabated potency, he immediately demanded another.

"What a man!" I exclaimed, "But I'm not going to let you be so selfish this time. Do you know the sixty-nine?"

"Yes," he responded, "though I've never tried it myself."

"Well, there's no time like the present to start in learning. If you don't object to doing it—after your coming in me—"

"Why should I?" he put in unhesitantly, "It's my own, isn't it? If you can stand it, I suppose I can. Let's get started."

And we did: I above him to restrain him from shoving his still menacing member too far down my throat, he with his head smothered between my thighs as I crouched over him in the ingenious reversed position. That he liked it was evidenced by the quickness with which he learned his part and the passionate eagerness with which he drew my buttocks down toward him and crushed his face into my cunt as I gave down spending after spending of pleasure into his avid mouth.

At this stage we declared time out and paused for some refreshments. While my partner was getting me a glass of wine, a slightly tipsy bishop with flushed eager mien rushed me and took hold of me.

"Why here's one I haven't screwed yet!" he exclaimed, "Down you must go mam'zelle. I'm passing nothing up tonight. For who knows when I'll get another woman. Do you take it 'a la garcon, too?'"

I was anxious to please. But still— "Do you have any pomade? Vaseline? Cold cream?" I queried, regarding his huge member a bit doubtfully, "The path you choose to follow has no lubrication of its own, as I suppose you know well enough." He laughed heartily at my innuendo, and reaching over to a sideboard where there was an array of fancy foods, he flicked some whipped cream off the top of a pastry— "This will do in a pinch, my daughter," he said as he spread it over the expansive head of his crimson cock.

"Why that looks good enough to eat." I sallied.

"Oh you French girls!" the bishop guffawed "Always looking for something to eat."

But the first sight of my shapely jutting posteriors as I leaned over a chair expectantly soon put my ecclesiastic in a more serious frame of mind. I felt the bulging badge of his manhood pry asunder the two firm hemispheres of my buttocks and—suffice it that whipped cream will do in a pinch, dear reader, and suffice it that my man did his work with the easy skill of an old pilot seasoned to back channels and thoroughly acquainted with the navigation of the narrow and illicit but nonetheless delicious rear canal.

Other couples, noting our happy example, soon followed suit.

"Why this feels just like home!" shouted one of the less discreet cardinals, as with arms wrapped about Yvette's soft naked waist he drove fiercely up into her tight rosy rear enclosure. And two of the 'stags,' having no women, for lack of better and released from their final restraint, uncovered themselves and proceeded forthwith to commit the detestable crime of buggery, the one of them forcing his prick up into that passage of the other which is alas common to both sexes. Lightly as we might talk of such vice when far removed from it, to be confronted with its actual perpetration so shamelessly was enough to revolt the senses.

The old man on the platform, glancing up from the perusal of his livret, and for the first time noting what went on, arose in indignation.

"Gentlemen!" he cried, "We have been lenient enough with you, we think. But we cannot countenance this vile recreation of the sinful city of Sodom—and before our very eyes! We are leaving your gathering at once and wish to have it understood that we strongly decry and disapprove of your conduct." An attendant rushed to his aid and he left the room.

"That means we all have to do penance with an extra mass tomorrow," my partner confided to me, "But it's worth it!" he went on, as he resumed a vigorous movement that soon flooded my bowels with a generous load of his boiling sperm.

"And now my dear mademoiselle," my bishop remarked as soon as he had recovered enough of his breath to speak, "you are in too well oiled a condition to even consider withdrawing. May I come?"

I was beginning to feel a bit tired: many of the others were dropping out of the lists too, what with the exhaustion of love and the final triumph of wine. But I kept my posteriors arched and let him go on.

By the time the last drop of his juice had been pumped up from his capacious reservoirs as they swung back and forth against my tightly distended anus, and had been catapulted into my entrails by his powerful male duct, everyone had called quits except for ourselves and one other couple.

My rider, vanquished at last, retrieved his spent arrow and we went over to watch the sole survivors of this long amorous marathon. They were, as the reader may have guessed, Manon, who had got it first and wanted it still, and the slighted secretary who had given me four rounds of his shot and lord knows how many to others since then. He was still at it, pounding away—in the proper spot, I might add—as if it were his first. Manon was returning tit for tat with a vengeance. But oh, what a flushed and bedraggled sight she was, her hair wildly dishevelled, her palpitating bubbies bruised from much handling, her shapely thighs streaked with perspiration and spend. She was moaning and moving about uneasily as yet another pleasurable climax approached, her milk-white belly heaving, her feverish buttocks writhing passionately as she pressed up to meet the impact of her assailant. How he was giving it to her! Fatigued as I was, I felt my pulses awakening with envious desire.

"Enough!" panted Manon, when, having poured down her maiden joy-flow, he still continued his mad prodding.

"No! no! Another! I'm not finished yet!" groaned her vanquisher as she squirmed to get out from under his relentless drill. He fucked her all the more vigorously and determinedly. Manon emitted a pitiful quivering scream as his bar brushed her sensitive insides anew. That cry pierced to my heart.

"Man!" I expostulated, seizing the assaulter by the shoulder, "Haven't you enough decency to leave off when the lady says she can't stand anymore? Do you want to make her hysterical?"

"Well," protested the insatiable fuckster as he withdrew two-thirds of his scarlet probe from the soaking rosy depths of her twitching swollen snatch, "what am I to do with this stubborn unsatisfied beast? If I stop halfway while it's so stiff, it won't go down for weeks!"

"All right, then," I replied only half-reluctantly, "let up on my little Manon and I'll let you stable it with me."

He made the transfer with alacrity, and I, his fresher steed, enlivened by my short rest and the vision of his earlier performances, leaped and twisted under him to give him the maximum of action in the minimum of time. And though I had scarcely expected it, I twice gave down a discharge of womanly bliss before his soft substance had shot from him to soothe my irritated membranes.

But heaven! the satyr was still stiff—and demanded yet another encounter. I pushed him from me in despair, turning a deaf ear to his pleadings. Two of my other girls, however, had come up to watch this male marvel's last bout—all the others had fallen asleep in various undignified postures about the room—and they agreed to take him in hand.

"Remember your own advice, Mademoiselle Madeleine," Giselle said to me laughingly as she proceeded to give his unbending member its second champagne bath of the evening prior to taking it in her mouth, "there's nothing like a fully satisfied customer." And while Yvette furnished some auxiliary titillations, putting one of her soft chubby breasts in the subject's mouth, Giselle went down on him in a fashion to make me proud of her, and calculated to soon deprive this hard customer of his obstinacy. If any of my male readers happen to doubt the possibility of this man's virility as I picture it, I can only suggest that he live celibately in a monastery for a few months and then set to with as attractive a group of girls as my company presented.

Considerably exhausted myself by now, I drew up an armchair to sit and watch—drying my dripping vagina with a soft silk handkerchief that I had held clenched in my fist through thick and thin. For all the exquisite treatment he was receiving at their hands and lips, our "last stand" was a long time in finishing. The show was becoming monotonous. I grew sleepy. In the candelabra the candles were guttering and flicking and going out altogether. Beside the soft liquid sound of Giselle's practiced lips, nothing could be heard but the snores of these combatants long since vanquished.

I must have dozed off for a time, for when I opened my eyes next, it was Yvette who was tonguing that troublesome shaft, while Giselle stood by nursing her aching jaws.

"How is it coming, dearie?" I asked her.

"Oh. we're on a second now," she replied, "But we expect to reach bottom soon. There wasn't but a drop or two that came out last time."

Even as we discussed the problem, the conclusion drew nigh. Our gentleman, stiffening with the approach of his terrific pleasure, was plunging his part desperately in and out of Yvette's lovely mouth, his hand fiercely straining her head to him as he wrapped his fingers in the silken strands of her beautiful blonde hair. Suddenly, with a sharp cry, half of ecstasy, half of anguish, he pushed her violently away from him. A tiny spurt of creamy white shot from his enspasmed urethra, and in its wake a few drops of fresh scarlet blood. We had indeed drained him. The stubborn tool now at last drooped its head and retired, completely beaten. It's owner fell into a fitful exhausted slumber almost immediately after.

The three of us who alone remained awake, surveyed the battlefield triumphantly. While everyone lay with his intimate nudity fully exposed, the reader may accept my assurance that there wasn't a cock left standing. Our job was done, and gloriously well-done. A decided chillness in the air told us that it would soon be morning. Gently we awakened Manon and Henriette, retrieved our scattered clothes and dressed ourselves hurriedly. Shaking up our reluctant sleepy conductor, we set him aright and left the orgy behind us just as the first rays of a cold dawn broke through the curtained windows and just as the bells of Saint

Peter's nearby began ringing out their resonant matutinal call to early mass.

"Must we stop at this dump hotel another day?" complained Manon when we got back to our forbidding albergo, "I wish I were back in Paris, snoozing right now in my nice broad bed."

"There is a train deluxe with sleepers that leaves for Paris at 7:20—in exactly one hour," suggested the monsignor, "You could just make it."

"We will!" shouted the girls in unison, "Who wants to hang around this fearful graveyard? Home and Paris it is!"

I gave my consent, although I myself was still determined to remain in Rome a few days longer to do some sightseeing. While our host hurried ahead to reserve places on the express, we packed our belongings and then followed to the station. I saw my girls off, each of them kissing me dutifully and then, with Monsignor, I took a taxi to transfer to some more luxurious hotel.

In the cab my partner raised an unexpected complaint.

"I was so busy seeing to things," he said "that I scarcely had a chance to get anything for myself. No more than two—or three at most. Here, just feel that hard-on if you don't believe me."

I felt of his proffered tool. Surely enough, it was as hard as iron. I breathed a sigh of resignation.

"All right, monsignor," I assented, "I'll let you come to bed with me at the hotel. But do remember that I'm terribly tired and do need some sleep."

And so it goes, dear reader. Our work is never done. Like the warriors who sprang up again and again when Cadmus sowed the dragon's teeth, so for every erection we conquer, another—or perhaps two or three—rise up in its stead to beset our pleasant but arduous path.

CHAPTER IX

A day or two later in my peregrinations about the Eternal City, I took a 'carozza' and rode out to the suburbs to examine the famed Baths of Caracalla. It being a week-day, the neighborhood was entirely deserted, except for a rather handsome young Italian guide of olive hue who approached and offered to show me through the ruins and explain them in any one of four or five languages—none of which he spoke very well. I accepted his services—and thanks to his information, I for the first time learned the real former character of the place. It had been nothing less than a colossal house of pleasure—with numerous finely tiled bathing pools and steam-rooms, true, but also with scores of private cubicles and larger orgy chambers in which were satisfied those needs naturally aroused in the course of bathing.

The thought of the purpose this ancient building had performed, as well as the hot Italian sun, heated my blood and put my ever-ready libido to the fore. I stepped up onto a fragment of a broken marble cornice—ostensibly to get a better view—but actually to give my swarthy handsome guide a glimpse of my legs and figure and test his reaction to them. A smouldering glint came into his eyes. The Latin temperament is indeed easily ignited. It soon became obvious that at the slightest further provocation he would rape me.

A soft warm wind played about my dress, moulding the diaphanous material to the voluptuous contours of my body. I bent over to tighten my shoestrings. Without actually raising my dress, I pulled up my silk stockings, snapping my garter with a luscious 'smack' as I did so. My companion took a threatening step closer, his eyes narrowing, his face flushing hotly. Blithely grabbing his hand, I jumped off my low pedestal, landing close up to his tensed body and looking smilingly into his face.

A struggle seemed to be going on within him. He was obviously at a loss to interpret my foreign ways of coquettishness. I settled his mind by boldly leading his hand to my bosom. His countenance lighted up joyfully as he pressed my bubbies for a moment, then, immediately after, he returned the compliment by leading my hand to a part of his own anatomy that resembled far less flesh than bone. My soft caressing hand encompassed the bulk of its circumference with difficulty, and once or twice gently peeled back the foreskin from the dull crimson head. That object, in this moment of my soft rich desire, represented to me not merely the symbol, but the veritable essence, the god-head of maleness.

I would have enjoyed holding on to that firm, reassuring, velvety limb of flesh a while longer; but my companion, with a perhaps excusable impatience, wrenched it from my grasp and proceeded to force me to the ground.

"Nolete, mio amice!" I whispered, "Don't! The ground is dirty. We can do it standing—this way."

And as his urgent hands ran down my body, I helped him raise my dress up above my waist, where I held it from slipping with my chin. As late May in southern Italy is as hot as Paris in midsummer, I of course had on no underthings to impede him further. Thus uncovered, my rich silky brown pubic triangle made a most pleasing contrast in the bright sun against the dazzling white of my belly and of my shapely thighs—now still close-meeting but in a moment to kiss each other adieu to make way for the lovely intruder. Still holding up my skirts, I raised my right leg sideways and rested it on a convenient block of stone. My cunt was thus brought forward and my legs held apart as effectively as if I were on my back with a well-stuffed cushion beneath my posteriors.

My partner caught on to the idea immediately. Bracing me with one of his hands behind my soft buttocks, he bent his knees a trifle, and bringing the point of his fine instrument up between the gaping lips of my expectant cunny, he sent the thing up and home to the hilt with a single motion as sudden and impetuous as the thrust of a stiletto. I winced with pain and delight as the broad bull-dog like head forcibly clove asunder the adhering membranes to the maximum and came up full against the 'cul de sac' of my cunt. It seemed as if my whole body and being were upheld by the length and strength and thickness of the firm shaft that impaled me.

My Italian, too hot-blooded by nature to brook much dallying, now with both his hands on my posteriors, was withdrawing part way to shove home once more. I joined him with an oscillating spiral motion of my cunt that was especially facilitated by my unimpeded standing position.

It was superb! The full horizontal strokes that his bar bestowed upon my clitty were all that I could possibly have wished. Only, indeed, as the taller waves of sensation began washing over me and I grew faint with pleasure, it required a decided effort to keep my feet when all my impulses now were to sink to the ground. His wand continued working its magic, running up and down the tight torrid length of my clasping sheath. My skirts still furled up on to my heaving bosom, my bare belly palpitating with excitement and with the reflex action of my pumping cunny, I continued madly gyrating my middle upon the firm axis he furnished. I took a last glance downwards:

through a hot misty maze I could see his proud penis plunging rapidly in and out of the glistening box beneath my brown pubic thatch. Then my head fell back as I abandoned myself to the quick overpowering augmentation of sensation that his operations were affording me.

"Viene?" (Are you coming?) my partner soon gasped to me, betraying by his uncontrolled breathing that he too was approaching the final extremity.

"Vengo...preste.... Mi aspetti!" (I am coming soon. Wait for me!) I managed to reply falteringly.

"Allora pronto!" (Then be quick!) he groaned brokenly, clutching wildly at the soft flesh of my buttocks. Desperately, my body all atremble, I fucked back for the life of me in short tense jabs that gave my clitty hell. At last! I felt it coming!

"Now!" I veritably screamed, forgetting myself, and speaking not Italian and not French but my native English: "Now! Give it to me! Oh, you dear damned garlic-eater! Give it to me!"

He did. Two or three vicious bone-breaking shoves were my reward, our bodies tensed, and just as I reached the dizzy climax of bliss, I felt spouting up within the seething crater of my cunt, the thick burning lava of his own enjoyment. My head lay on his shoulder as we both continued fitfully moving. The explosion of delicious sensation within me, unbearable in its intensity, had me sobbing and moaning and beating my partner with my fists and crying "Oh! oh! Wop, you fucking bastard, I love you!"

Even as the good feeling ended, my turbulent centre continued twitching spasmodically back and forth, to make our paradise last as long as possible. Only the common necessity to sit down or lean on something compelled our separation. The huge flesh pole that had worked such turmoil in my senses slipped from me with a moist audible 'cluck.' Immediately, the quantity of our mutual spendings, released by this sudden unplugging of my cunt, gushed out and began dribbling down the soft inner sides of my thighs toward the tops of my silk stockings. With my frail gossamer handkerchief I tried to staunch the flow; but of course its capacity of absorption was far too limited to avail me much, and in a moment was soaked beyond all usefulness. My partner however, noting my predicament, with native gallantry whipped his brightly colored bandana from about his neck, and after wiping his own dripping part, passed it to me with a polite bow. I mopped up the rest of the sticky fluid and handed him back his handkerchief. He shook it out carefully and hung it on a stone ledge in the sun to dry, explaining that he would get it on his next trip.

Straightening my clothes as well as I could, we continued our inspection of the ruins; but now so halfheartedly, that soon I decided to give it up. Anyway, it was quite obvious that my guide wanted to talk cunt and not history, while I as a matter of fact was so exhausted by my unusually straining fuck that I wasn't much in the mood to appreciate either subject.

"Perhaps I hurt you, signorina?" he asked with timid solicitude when he noticed my apparent distraction, "Was I too big for you?"

"Ah no, my dear man," I reassured him, "I like them big. In fact, the bigger the better."

"Oh! Then the signorina should meet my friend Luigi. He is gifted with an equipment alongside of which mine is as nothing!"

"Indeed?" I put in, somewhat infected by his enthusiasm.

"Ah, yes! And how all the girls are crazy about him! He takes them all away from me."

"Really? I should like to meet your marvellous friend."

"If the signorina will but leave her address and say when she will be disposed..."

I wrote out for him the name of the hotel at which I was stopping, and suggested 2 o'clock the next afternoon as a convenient hour. His friend, like most

Italians apparently, managed to live without working.

As we parted at the entrance to the ruins, a huge sightseeing bus drove up, crowed with rubbering robots from my own, my native land—America. I paused to watch the queer chattering cargo. One of their number, a rather prim looking young lady of about 25 whom I sized up at once as a school-teacher, wearing clothes of a decidedly masculine cut, seemed especially familiar to me. She too was looking at me rather intently. As the passengers filed off the bus, I suddenly recognized her. It was my old classmate Sylvia Watson, she of the dubious high-school-lavatory incident over eight years ago. Putting two and two together there was no mistaking the line of development that she had followed. I approached her. She too recognized and greeted me; but there was a snooty constraint about her manner a sort of sneery condescension and leering curiosity that cut me deeply. I thought of the circumstances under which I had left home, the impression that must have been made on my narrow-minded Plattsburg friends. I couldn't let the matter rest thus. Sylvia was to me the representative of that past. I wanted to justify myself in her eyes. Or failing that, I wished to wipe out her detestable air of superiority by telling her just how thoroughly I saw through her soured homosexuality.

I invited her to visit me at my hotel.

"Oh, I don't know, Louise. I'm so busy. There are so many things to see here in Rome. Tomorrow we're going to the Diocletan, and the day after... But I would like to hear what you've been doing all these years. . Maybe I will get a chance to drop in on you."

"Yes, do, Sylvia," I replied in the hypocritical saccharine manner which women find so necessary in their social intercourse; but which, thank god, I was generally able to get along without. In truth, I would have liked to scratch her eyes out.

"But if I do come," the creature smirked, "there won't be any men with you, will there?"

THE FURTHER ADVENTURES OF MADELEINE

I reassured her, intimating even for my purpose—though she seemed skeptical—that I too disliked the male sex and was a sympathizer with the 'great sisterhood' of which she was no doubt a member. She left me to rejoin her party while I returned to my hotel for a much needed bath.

Next afternoon, at 2 o'clock sharp, the desk clerk sent up to my suite to notify me that two-rough-looking natives were asking for me. I explained that they were to do some work for me on a villa that I had just purchased and asked that they be ushered up.

My friend Benito of the day before entered, dragging behind him a great hulking companion whom he introduced as Luigi. Both of them were crudely, but neatly dressed, and their skins shone with perhaps unaccustomed ablutions.

I offered them some wine and tried to make them feel more at ease by striking up a conversation; but it soon became apparent that both of them were hopelessly uneducated and stupid, and Benito's glib explanation of the Baths the day proceeding had no doubt been a memorized spiel, delivered parrot-like. I felt a little ashamed of myself for having made an engagement with such lowly characters; but there was no thought in my mind of disappointing them when they had taken such pains to prepare for the occasion.

Leading them to my boudoir, which they entered with awe, hat in hand, as if visiting a cathedral, I drew the blinds to shut out the glare of the sun and got right down to business.

"Where is his marvellous equipment you told me of yesterday, Benito?" I asked. He addressed his friend in some to me incomprehensible dialect. Luigi seemed to be protesting, but finally at his companion's insistence, nervously unbuttoned his trousers and brought out the subject of our discussion. Unexpected as had been the order to 'present arms,' and extinguished as was the simple-minded Italian by the luxury of his surroundings, yet his semi-stiff organ was of a size and bulk to make me burningly curious to see it at its best. With my soft tapering fingers I laid hold of the bent sword. Under my cunning caresses it took but a moment to make the yard as straight and august as any I had ever handled. Luigi nearly fainted with embarrassment at my unexpectedly direct procedure, but a grateful grin illumined his features as he stood, awkward and submissively awaiting the end of my inspection. Lowering his trousers to see the rest of his attributes, I weighed on the palm of my hand his heavy bag of love's elixir, estimating in my mind how many cuntfuls its spacious chambers could afford me.

Satisfied with my investigation, and my further interest aroused, I added at least another inch each way to the size of his member by slowly and provocatively removing, first my dressing-gown, then each of my silk stockings, and lastly my alluring crepe chemise. I then had both Luigi and Benito strip to the skin—and let me record that, relieved of their cheap vulgar clothing they were a pair of bronze heroes out of some classic Greek frieze—with this one important qualification: While the ancient sculptors invariably presented their male figures with insignificant flaccid sex parts such as would cast doubt on their gender of even a child, these two before me had their forms completed by a pair of handle-bars eligible for consideration as major limbs of the human body.

Climbing up on my high sumptuous double-bed, allowing my well-rounded buttocks to jut out maddeningly, I called to Luigi to follow. He held back.

"What is it?" I inquired impatiently.

"E troppo bello." he stammered, pointing to the silk and lace counterpanes. The bed was too luxurious for the simple-hearted Italian to dare muss. I suppose he wanted to do it on the floor. But we compromised thusly. Seating him in a comfortable chair, I mounted astride his lap facing him. As much to get my own lubrications working prior to undertaking the invagination of his monstrous cock as also to make him lose all self-consciousness, I coaxed a stiff-nippled tit between his lips and wrapping my legs tightly about his brawny waist, held him in the tender clutch of my soft white thighs while I rubbed my silky mount up and down his belly and chest, till the lips of my cunt became tingly and moist.

Soon he caught the spirit of the thing; but it was only when the upstanding stiffness of his organ became such as to threaten crashing through me at one point if not at another that I decided to let it in where it belonged. What a rich and randy delight as I sat down slowly upon the erect shaft, letting it feed into me with exquisite deliberateness! The usually oval shape of my cunt was for once, I could plainly see, stretched into a distended O-shape by the bulk and circumference of the welcome intruder. So on my plump dewy nether lips were clinging to the very root of it, our pubic bushes interwoven, while at the other end the swollen head battered against the mouth of my avid womb.

Thus deliciously skewered upon his prodder, I contented myself with minor wrigglings for awhile to give my muscles and glands a chance to adapt themselves to the truncheon distender and better oil the now open road to voluptuousness. Then—slowly at first and then more rapidly—I began the full oscillation of my agile buttocks, giving the utmost play to my throbbing quivering cunt, and rubbing the hard slippery little lump of flesh that is my clitty against the broad velvety bulk of his prick. That magical little touchstone soon had me weltering in enjoyment. My soft clinging sheath was yielding up its secretions so generously, that I could feel the soft mucous dribbling down over the root of his prick and balls. Slow long thrusts and short digs succeeded each other in turn. Sometimes we would pause for a moment to leisurely savor the close carnal conjunction of our bodies. My partner, competent as he might have been, no doubt had but little left to do that I did not take care of in his stead. Just as we were about to settle down to the steady concupiscent canter that would carry us to our goal, however, Benito, who had been till now standing by watching us jealously, his rod held sheepishly in his hands, approached and demanded some part in the activities. Impatient, to avoid delay, I took his prick in my mouth while he stood in front of me behind the chair on which Luigi and I were engaged. Only a little hampered by this second prick to take care of and the necessity to keep it between my lips despite all the jolting I should give and receive, we resumed our delicious game of peg in the hole after only a nominal interruption.

With the approach of the final celestial rapture, my bounds became so frantic as to have unseated me, had not Luigi's rampant weapon held me well transfixed. What vigorous writhings and oscillating motions ensued, as, urged on by the tormenting pleasure we separated our feverish mounts only to shove them together again with mad violence. My partner's hands were still holding on to my buttocks, pressing and pulling on them, handling the plump cheeks like a pair of cymbals, tightening and relaxing the stricture of my cunt upon his cock by this outside pressure. By inserting one his fingers into my anus—which was now twitching spasmodically in unison with my cunny—he bestowed upon me an even further bawdy lustful joy....

All this time I sucked faithfully and desperately on Benito's by no means negligible penis—to keep him apace with us if possible. But now, with the uncontrollable floods of sensation gathering in me, with cords of fiery pleasure knotting all my fibres, I found it increasingly difficult to coordinate the sucking action of my lips and tongue with the necessary movements of my hips, loins and cunt. Blindly, feverishly, uttering spasmodic sobs and stifled cries, I took the to me superfluous and distracting roll of flesh in my hand, removed it from my mouth and pushed it far away from me. Then, burying my burning face in

Luigi's shoulder and wrapping my legs more tightly about his back, I gave myself up entirely and selfishly to the attainment of the delicious end.

A few more wild tense movements of my hips—dictated by some deep impulse within me rather than by any conscious volition of my own—and as his large soul-satisfying staff of life glided quickly up and down my quivering channel, the ultimate acme of bliss burst upon me in veritable sheets of flame. My salacious cunt took one last sweep around his engine with a tense spiral motion, then my whole body stiffened with convulsive rigidity as a long low wail of rapture was torn from me. Luigi, gasping explosively, himself intercepted at the very apex of pleasure, and finding my up to now active cunt suddenly paralyzed, raised my body with his hands till his bursting prick had retreated to the very mouth of my cunt, then with a single crushing motion rammed it back into me to the hilt. A moment later he poured into my lust-maddened body his burning priceless treasure of liquefied pearl. My twitching cunt muscles would not release him until, in their sweet agony, they had pressed the last drop of that soothing spermatic joy from him, then I collapsed in a soft breathless hysteria of relief.

Even before I could entirely recover myself, Benito was at my side demanding his next. I was not a bit averse to more of the erect yard's steady application, but I did want a breathing spell. Just than there was a knock at the door. Climbing quickly off Luigi's lap, and slipping into a kimono, I hastened to answer it, with the effusions of my just happily ended encounter still trickling down my thighs. It was the hotel-boy, to tell me that there was a Signorina Watson below to see me.

"Send her up" I said. On the instant a malicious idea had come to me. Hastening back to my male guests, I explained that I was to have a visitor, bundled them into the bathroom with their clothes and an album of erotic photographs—I had recently wheedled it from one of the cardinals—to keep them in form, and then locked the door on them until I should have further need of their services. I dried my cunny superficially and went to admit Sylvia.

"Oh what a beautiful room you have here Louise!" was her first exclamation as she entered.

"There are two more to the suite, my dear Sylvia," I made sure to add.

"But how can you afford such expensive accommodations? Where do you get the money?"

"Oh, I've held various positions. And I still work hard on occasion. But tell me about yourself—about the folks at home."

We chatted for awhile, sitting close together. The way she had of putting her hands on my thighs as she spoke, while certainly permissible between members of the same sex, further confirmed my suspicions about her tastes. I played it up further by allowing my peignoir to droop open, letting her see one of my ripe luscious breasts entirely bare. Her eyes glistened.

"What a gorgeous kimono you have, Louise" she spoke stiltedly, reaching over to feel the material, and incidentally brushing my soft flesh.

"Yes, I'll tell you where you can buy one just like it. Look how well-made it is. Look at this hand embroidered hem and the satin lining on the inside." and deliberately, I raised the whole lower part of the gown, uncovering my bare thighs up to my dark 'accent circumflexe.' Her face flushed excitedly. She was really quite pretty, I had to admit against my will, except for the ridiculous masculine costume that she affected and for a certain virgin primness about her that struck me disagreeably.

Allowing my gown still to sag open, I took her hand in mine, resting it in my warm bare lap, and spoke confidentially: "Do you remember that afternoon in the school lavatory, Sylvia, when I caught you and Miriam Smith together? I have often wondered what you two were doing to each other. Come, tell me. I'll understand."

"Well," Sylvia spoke in a hoarse low tone, "We had been fingering each other."

"Is that all?"

"There was more—but we didn't know about it at that time." As she spoke I could feel her fingers burrowing gently between my close-meeting thighs, trying to gain access to my cunt. I kept my legs close together—and she could proceed no further. There was a long silence.

"Let's play with each other, Louise," she finally managed to utter in a prurient broken whisper. I made no reply.

"You don't like me?" she asked pathetically.

"Not in those horrible clothes you are wearing."

"I'll take them off."

"All right—and then we shall see."

Anxious to please me, Sylvia sprang to her feet and removed her hat and coat, and then her waist and skirt. She was still fully covered with underthings of plain white linen, spotlessly clean indeed, but in the most god-awful taste. I helped her undo the string of her petticoat: she pulled it down and stepped out of it. Now I could discern that her legs were quite passable, with fine shapely calves.

Hesitantly and blushing, she pulled up her linen chemise and slipped it off over her head. A bare dimpled belly came into view, and then a pair of dainty little breasts, each tipped with a tiny scarlet rose. With the removal of each article of her ugly clothing, she was becoming more and more attractive. As I aided her in pulling down her bloomers, baring the spare but shapely columns of her thighs and the undulation of her neat posteriors, I could see that she was in fact quite beautiful—in every sense of the word meant for good honest fucking, but by some misarrangement of circumstances curbing her charms and saving them for the barren embraces of other females.

Seating herself for a moment and crossing her legs to remove her stocking, with the ankle of one leg over the knee of the other, I could see at the juncture of her thighs her rosy garden of delight, bowered in thick dusky foliage and differing from any other adorable cunt only in that it had probably never been pilfered by man, and that the little elf-like clitty that dwells therein and is usually out of sight was in her case a bit overdeveloped by handling or suction, and was peeping insolently out from between the plump pink casements of its delightful palace.

I led her into the bedroom and insisted on her trying on one of my flimsy silk combinations that had nothing but a frail ribbon across the crotch.

"Don't you like yourself much better this way?" I asked. She was indeed indisputably alluring now.

"Oh, I don't know—" she said, throwing her arms about me, "It makes me feel so—so frivolous. Let me take it off." I did not insist.

She joined me on the bed, where I allowed her to caress me as she would. First timidly, then more boldly, her hands made the whole circuit of my body. Soon her lips followed. On my own part, I acted noncommittally. As she reached my cunt with her lips, she looked up and said.

"Let's do it together, Louise. It's not fair that I should do it for you and you not for me."

"I don't like it that way, Sylvia," I lied, "I like to concentrate on what I'm doing, wether it's enjoying the thrill myself or making someone else enjoy it. Anyway, you can't do it so well with the thing upside down. Your tongue doesn't go in so far. You do it to me first, then I will do you."

"But if I do it first, you may not want to do it for me after," she objected shrewdly, "You lick mine."

"It works either way, Sylvia. But you started it, I didn't. Either take it or leave it. It's all the same to me," and I pretended to be leaving the bed.

Looking stricken, she held me back.

"All right," she grumbled, "spread your legs; but Louise, if you refuse to lick mine later, I'll never speak to you again."

I would have liked to wring the little vixen's neck; but I had my own plans. What a shame, I thought, that such a delicious piece should possess so detestable a temperament, so small a character. Perhaps, I myself might have become that way too if I had remained in Plattsburg's cramping atmosphere all my life.

With none of the passion or impetuousness that might have excused the act, but with only a venal surreptitiousness that seemed to proclaim, "I know I oughtn't be doing this, I know it's wrong; but you won't tell on me," she started tonguing my cunt. The unaccustomed moistness and creamy content that had so recently been injected into that part made her pause.

"I'd hate to think, Louise," she spoke liquidly from between my thighs, "that I was putting my mouth where a man had just been."

"Don't be such a fool, Sylvia," I said rather impatiently, "Do you think I'd be satisfied with your awkward little tongue if I could have a big stiff dolly in me right now?"

"Louise!" she exclaimed sharply, "How can you talk that way to me? I won't do another thing for you!"

"Little hypocrite!" I retorted, "Do you mean that you've never longed to have a man's long velvety thing sliding in and out of your tight little hole?"

"No, Louise, honor bright! It makes me sick to even think of their long ugly snaky things."

"Do you mean to say that you've never used a candle on yourself?"

"Well, supposing I have? A candle's different. There are no germs shooting into you to put you in a family way and get you all diseased up. I know all about it."

That was, without a doubt, the crux of the whole situation, as most any girl who has never dared savor a prick will admit.

"Well, we'll have more to say about that later Sylvia," I put in, "How about finishing up what you've started?"

She went down on me once more, in a more businesslike manner this time, separating and then sucking and tonguing the soaking lips. I derived a keen salacious pleasure from the thought that she was unknowingly filling her mouth with that much-feared semen which she wouldn't ordinarily touch with a ten-foot pole, much less allow to be introduced into her cunt on a ten-inch prick. Even when my touchy clitty had been fully aroused by her perverted tonguing and I felt my climax coming on, I held back the gathering flood of pleasure as long as I possibly could—just to keep her working longer. When I came finally, my contracting muscles wrung into her mouth the remains of the emission which she had not already swallowed in her diligent sucking.

"Now it's my turn, Louise," she said, wiping her brimming mouth with the back of her hand, and settling herself comfortably on her back with her white thighs thrown wide apart with expectant abandon. Her cunt, with its fresh pouting vulva certainly looked good enough even for me to eat; but I had something more substantial in store for her.

"Wait a minute, Sylvia" I said, hopping suddenly from the bed, "I have a surprise for you. You know what a dildo is, don't you?—one of those rubber things shaped just like a man? Well, I'm going to try it on you."

"It won't hurt, will it,"

"No; but to make sure, slip this piece of cocoa-butter into your cunny. It will soften and lubricate you." I handed her a medicated vaginal suppository and she slipped it up between the scarlet inner lips of her cunt.

Hastening to the bathroom, I released my two ravening lions. Thanks to the warming influence of the picture album I had left with them, not to mention the condition I had left poor Benito in, they were so far gone that they were about to bugger each other. I separated them by sheer force and led them into the bedroom. Sylvia, glancing up from her loving occupation, uttered a horrified scream and dived under the covers to hide her nakedness as well as to escape the sight of the two menacing pricks that could not have failed to meet her gaze.

I approached the bed and tore the cover from off her. She lay there cowering and sobbing.

"Listen Sylvia," I spoke determinedly, "another such cream and I'll either gag you or chloroform you. Not that anyone outside this apartment could hear you, but my nerves can't stand such screeching. You think that you can sneer superciliously at me, and perhaps carry tales home about my relations with men... Well, you'll have to tell them a few things about yourself, too. Because, whether you like it or not, you're going to get fucked—and right now. And if you don't know what getting fucked means, you're going to learn in just a minute. Benito! Luigi! Come here! Which of you is the hardest? Let me feel..."

Again Luigi was the chosen one. I gave him his instructions. Benito and I would each hold her thighs apart while he was to perform the operation with relentless rapidity. "Remember," I said, "in deflowering a woman, gentleness is no mercy."

"Louise!" screamed Sylvia, choking with horror, "You can't actually mean to have them do that to me? Why it's a crime! It's rape! I'll—I'll—"

Luigi during this speech had brought his affair to her central mark, thanks to the advantageous position in which Benito and I held her for him. A single furious thrust and his staunch scalpel had severed so much of her maidenhead as was left from her lifetime's fingerings and candle-masturbations.

Another plunge, and the rest of his throbbing cock sank from sight. As he withdrew for another stab, I was frightened by the sight of the blood upon his weapon. What if he should do her some harm? I would have to answer for it... But Sylvia's threatening voice reassured me.

"Louise Smith!" she cried, "I'll have you arrested for this! Oh! oh! Please take him away! He is killing me! Oh, you beastly man! Get off of me! You are tearing me apart with that dreadful thing of yours! Oh, oh! my whole stomach is split open!"

"Take it and don't complain, Sylvia" I said, unconsciously forming a rhyme, "—for if you want the pleasure, you must have the pain."

But she kept right on yelling.

"Will you keep quiet!" I exclaimed impatiently, as I became more and more aroused at the fine sight of Luigi's superb tool, hard and polished as Carrara marble, its veins swelling with an abundance of hot blood, plunging in and out of the juicy folds of her cunt, right before my eyes and I began to decide that I would have done better to keep that fine morsel for myself, "This is the best thing that could ever have happened to you. Here—" I released her thigh and signaled Benito to do like-wise, "wrap your legs about the man's back and put a little action into that leaden backside of yours. And one more word out of you and I'll put Benito's prick in your mouth to shut you up!"

She stopped crying, but continued moaning softly, regarding me with infinite hatred in her eyes... the ungrateful wretch.

"Come, Benito!" I said, throwing myself accommodatingly on my back beside the raped Sylvia, "You now to get your's at last—and we'll show them how to do it. I'm sorry I have no more maidenheads to offer, but we'll manage all right without."

The eager young Italian mounted between the firm white flesh of my thighs; but only a moment after he had penetrated into the soft quivering channel of my body, he went off in a premature spasmodic frenzy, deluging my excited crack with his warm creamy spend. However, without pausing, he set off on a second and more prolonged course, during which I came twice. From the corner of my eye I had seen Sylvia watching us with an interest that was increasing as her pain decreased. From disgust her expression soon changed to understanding, as Luigi's various frictionings stirred in her the first echoings of a delight she had never tasted before.

Just as she was apparently beginning to enjoy it though, Luigi, unable to withstand the overpowering sensations fostered by her tight gripping cunt, reached his climax. As his hot prolific sperm deluged her wounded quim, and the realization of the danger she was being subjected to dawned upon her, Sylvia gave a scream of horror and renewed all her tearful complaints. But Luigi kept right on raping her, this time moving more easily in her well lubricated sheath, and as luckily at this moment Benito was spilling his second load into me, I let him finish, pushed him from me, and mounting over Sylvia's tearful face, smothered her cowardly wailings with my dripping cunt. She sobbed with hatred and disgust as she choked on the plentiful spendings that dripped down her throat; but as the continued administration of Luigi's peerless prick began to take effect upon her, her lower body began writhing pleasurably, and she was so carried away with lecherous feelings as to begin sucking zestfully upon my spew-bathed joy-pouch. Thus does generosity come to even the meanest creatures during the approach of the supreme enjoyment in fornication—that great humanizer.

When I had given down my own rapturous effusion, I climbed from off her to better watch the superb sight of the finish. Our blushing, protesting maiden had twisted her legs tightly about her assaulter's loins, her arms clinging convulsively to his neck. Her bottom was heaving up to meet his thrusts with passionate abandon, her whole body vibrating in a frenzy of mad desire.

"S'arrete, Luigi!" I cried at this point, "Stop a moment!"

Luigi obeyed with extreme reluctance.

"Now, Miss Watson" I addressed the quivering bit of humanity nailed to my bed by Luigi's stiff cock, "I am beginning to regret my taking advantage of you. I shall have your torturer desist at once."

But such a reproachful and appealing glance came from her feverish joy-clouded eyes, that cruel as I felt, I could not bring myself to deprive her of that rod, that staff, which comforted her.

"Go ahead, Luigi," I directed resignedly, "Give it to her." And as Benito was by now presenting himself with an entirely resurrected hard-on, I stretched myself face down on the wide bed, and to shock my initiate rather than anything else, let him force his way into my narrow rear crevice and revel in my tightly fitting fundament.

The best of things must end, and before long we all had had—not enough, but all that we could stand. I dismissed the two men immediately, and leading Sylvia to the bathroom, loaned her my douching syringe to make her vaginal toilette.

When she came out, I offered her my hand cordially.

"No ill feelings I hope, Sylvia" I said, "It's really all for the best."

She turned her back sullenly—and quickly putting on her ugly clothes once more, the ungrateful wretch left me without a word.

The very next day however, she paid me an unexpected visit at my hotel rooms.

"Those men aren't around, are they?" she asked, peering into my bedroom.

"No" I reassured her.

She was visibly disappointed. She had come to get the name and address of the man who had violated her, she told me rather curtly.

"And what do you want that for, my dear Sylvia?" I asked.

"Oh, don't be a fool, Louise!" she snapped, "If I should be in a family way, I suppose I have the right to know the name of the father of my child, haven't I?"

I laughed and told her of the contraceptive suppository that she had unknowingly used. "If you want to try it again though, here's Benito's business card. I suppose he can lead you to Luigi—or take pretty good care of you himself."

She took the card and stalked out haughtily without so much as thanking me.

Some months later it came to my ears that when she returned to the United States, the great well-equipped Italian went with her—undoubtedly, at her own expense. Such can be the irresistible allure of a strong cock even to one who, before its proper introduction to her, couldn't even think of one without turning sick.

CHAPTER X

After a few more days in Rome I started north, stopping over at Florence for awhile—where, to but indicate it hastily, I was deliciously back-scuttled by moonlight on the Ponte Vecchio, that same bridge over the Arno where Dante would meet his Beatrice—and, if history may be disregarded a bit, probably did the same for her as was done for me.

From here I proceeded to Venice, the lovely watery stamping grounds of that full-testicled Casanova whose female reincarnation I sometimes like to think myself. Did I try fucking in a gondola? the eager reader asks. I did—and let me say, there's nothing like it. The gentle graceful motion of the boat seems to be intended just for the rhythms of coition, the gondoliers are the very embodiment of discretion, and if one can't get in enough rogering by night, there are always deserted canals and fully enclosed gondolas that permit action at any time of day. To lie in love's delicious lethargy while floating on some lazy lagoon, to the accompaniment of the gondolier's sensuous intoning of some Neapolitan tune—ah, this was paradise!

Then further north into Germany, with a stop at Munich for a few days. And here let me disappoint the friendly reader as I was disappointed. Munich is the only city on the continent which I have visited without getting pushed. There the bellies of the populace are so distended with beer-drinking that fucking is, if not impossible, at least a most discouraging thing to contemplate.

Then to Berlin—a visit that I had postponed for some time. One of my first acts was to look up my old friend Bob, who, you will remember, had been dragged away to Germany just about the time when he might have had my maiden flower. He was pretty much the same now as I remembered him—only now he was more romantic and impractical than ever. If anything, I was the only one of us who had matured.

He was not living with his wealthy parents any longer, he told me, preferring to act out the part of the impecunious bohemian suffering for his 'art,' knocking around, painting a little, writing bad poetry on occasion and playing the violin to soothe his anguished soul. We did not hit it off so well together—although he professed to still be madly in love with me. Sentimentality was what I had outgrown and he had yielded completely.

One gorgeous June evening we went together to the Tiergarten, Berlin's beautiful public park. We drank beer and listened to music for awhile. In the intervals he read to me some Baudelaire from a volume which he always carried with him now in place of the Keats of former days. I know my Baudelaire perfectly in French and in English: in the German it sounded nothing less than barbarous.

After awhile, we wandered off into the dark wooded groves where the atmosphere was heavy with the redolent perfumes of roses and honey-suckles. He made love to me. To his naive poetic soul, I was still a virgin. He regretted those past days he told me, when he had taken unfair advantage of my inexperience; yet it became clear that with his increasing amorousness he would sue for a renewal of those privileges. I liked him and of course it would have been the easiest thing in the world for me to give him all that he craved and then some. But there was a beautiful hopelessness in his voice, a poetic aura in which he enwrapped me, that made me feel it would be sacrilegious to allow it to be resolved down to 'mere' fornication.

Standing under the trees, I allowed him to put his arms about me and kiss me. But when he dropped to his knees before me and began caressing my thighs and buttocks, I shook him off and ran back a few steps to avoid him, feeling foolish enough in this unaccustomed prude behaviour and yet feeling that it was the thing expected of me.

He followed me on his knees until the brambles of a bush catching in my dress arrested my further retreat.

He disentangled me, and still on his knees, passed his feverish hands up under my perfumed skirts. I wore no underthings and stood in a momentary quandary. Pushing up my dress, he buried his hot face high on my bare thighs, holding me to him with his hands on my naked posteriors.

I could feel his panting breath on the damp gates of my cunny. My mind went back for a moment to that day in the woods when I had first met him, when he had buried his head in my lap just so... A feeling of tenderness pervaded me. I rested my hand upon his curly hair. I experienced that same excitement of having him so close to my cunny—and yet knowing that to tongue it would doubtless be the last thing on earth that would enter his mind.

But to my surprise—and yes, horror—for I was still transported back to those virginal days—he pressed his mouth to the very quick, and inserting his tongue between the full luscious lips, began lapping me. I tried to push him away, but he held on desperately. Soon I found my thighs unconsciously relaxing and easing apart to allow his velvety tongue to get into me further.

"So!" I thought to myself resignedly, "the rogue knows what he's doing after all. He'll excite me so much with his tongue that I just won't be able to refuse him when he offers to finish up with his prick." But if that had been his original intention, he overstepped it, for even when the success of his manoeuvre became apparent by my wildly quivering body and low voluptuous cries, he kept right on lapping me—till the climax came and passed. Weak and trembling, I let him draw me down beside him on the grass.

"Did you like it?" he panted—a bit foolishly, I thought.

"Yes—of course—it was nice."

"Then my darling, my goddess, let me love you! Yield your divine body to me entirely!" He brought out his stiff part, no considerable affair in the light of the many others I'd encountered since last I had seen it. There still seemed to be a note of uncertainty in his voice. It did not flatter me—at least not in my physical being—and I wasn't going to make up his mind for him. And the thought of all his poetic ideals, his exaggerated estimate of my chastity and my worth—all made me ashamed to yield to him—unwilling to destroy his illusions with the carnal earthiness of a fuck. Surely, I reasoned, after all his dreams, my cunt, nice as it might be, could only be a disappointment. And anyway, I was quite sated, what with his injudicious gamahuching of me and with the nice tussle I had had that same afternoon with a hotel bellboy who had come up to deliver a telegram and found me in my bath.

I drew my skirts down and pushed him gently from me.

"Please!" he begged, approaching me once more and nestling his excited part in my hand.

"No, Bob" I expostulated softly, unconsciously stroking the velvety warm cylinder of flesh, "I couldn't possibly give myself to you. Yes—as you said before we were young and foolish when we played with each other years ago the way we did. I am trying to forget that now, and you must help me. No—the man I give myself to will be the man I chose over all other men—the man I marry." And silently I continued stroking his stiff smooth instrument, as if lost in revery.

The expected climax was not long in coming. Suddenly he threw his arms about my neck, sobbing "Oh, you pure, unattainable woman!"

I drew my skirt discreetly out of danger, and turned his spouting weapon downward to the grass—feeling only then a slight qualm of regret at the waste of the dear warm fluid that I can never get enough of. With faked ingenuousness I pretended that what had happened was entirely accidental: nevertheless he was profoundly grateful.

As he ushered me back to my hotel later that evening, we noticed a considerable crowd gathered in front of the French embassy making some hostile demonstration. The relations between Germany and France, according to the newspapers, had been becoming daily more and more strained. I decided to curtail my stay in Berlin and returned to my beloved Paris the very next day.

* * * * *

Paris from July 1934 onward, with sombre war clouds hovering over all Europe, was a place of rather forced and unnatural gaiety. The shadow of possible death hung over the head of almost every man that sought our arms. But we did 'our bit' in our own way—exerting all our powers to make our friends and patrons forget the morrow and yet when that morrow came to have them look back on our day with the satisfaction of having lived life to its fullest.

The pressing demand upon us became greater and greater. There was no one now whom we could turn away from our doors in clear conscience. More and more recruits became necessary to fill our lists, more space, more houses. Before long I found myself, entirely against my will, all too well known as a wholesale trafficker in female flesh. When the government sent out a call for an organized group of women for the complaisance of the men at the front, my friends in the official bureaus veritably forced the contract upon me, and I was compelled to nearly kill myself rounding up scores of healthy women to send to the towns behind the lines to keep our boys happy and fit. Without needing or desiring it, I was becoming wealthy hand over fist—with money pouring in from more branch houses, public or private enterprises, than Fleurette and I could keep track of.

Borne aloft on a wave of patriotism, I was, for a time earlier in the war, actually induced to undertake a commission for the secret intelligence division which took me into Belgium and the enemy territory. Only the recentness of the great conflict prevents me from divulging the exact nature of my errand. But suffice it to say—and to dispel any budding romantic notion on the part of the reader—that as a spy I was a total failure. Falling into the hands of a company of German soldiers while masquerading as a simple Belgium maid, I was raped, or rather gang-fucked, for I did not put up any very strenuous resistance, by eighteen privates in succession. Had not two officers returned from a prolonged absence to disperse the men—but not before becoming the nineteenth and twentieth—lord knows what might have happened to me. As it was, when they finished, my cunt was almost in a pulp. For the reader may take my word for it, that while the first four or five were very nice and the next two or three were bearable the rest were decidedly unpleasant. For once in my life I had had more than enough.

Having learned only that Teutonic pricks are on the whole bigger and thicker than Gallic ones, and this being a discovery of no particular value to my country in winning the war, I resigned my commission and returned to Paris where I could do much more good, I thought, being fucked by our allies rather than by our enemies.

But let me hasten on to the end of the war, and

with the approach of the date of my present writing, the end of my story.

With the armistice, Paris became once more the joyous centre of the world of pleasure, with people pouring in from every country of the globe to celebrate the awakening from the four year nightmare that had been ours. Wine flowed and joy reigned supreme once more. Gladly I closed down or sold out my subsidiary houses and concentrated all my lavishness and attention on the one that I occupy now, making it the most exclusive and desirable house of rendezvous in this most desirable city of the world.

With the Peace Conference, which was only about six months ago, when I first began penning these fond foolish lines, the greatest men of every nation gathered here in Paris. There was scarcely one that I did not have the honor of entertaining intimately during that period here in my luxurious establishment. When I first began these memoirs I must confess it was in the boastful mood of telling of my relations with all these celebrities. But my tale even in its simpler aspects has been—I hope—so interesting, and yes, I fear, so lengthy that I have decided to awake no regrets in the hearts of generous thighs, to cause no embarrassment to any who have shared my hospitality—no, not to them, not to their friends, decedents or co-patriots, for I realize that the world that exists outside the walls of my bounteous mansion on the Boulevard Haussmann is not the same unashamed world as exists within.

* * * * *

Dear reader, the parting of our ways draws nigh. But before you leave these pages, before you leave me, perhaps never to return, I would have you spend just one more joyous evening with me at the Maison Madeleine. Any evening, a typical evening, in fact just yesterday evening will do.

I come from my (private) boudoir where I have just enjoyed a long refreshing nap and a cool bath to prime me for the evening's pleasant exertions. I am already thirty the reader will remember, and a bit plump from my luxurious living; but my years sit lightly on my shoulders—my admirers swear that I look no more than twenty-six at most.

I greet my many friends who are already assembled and have a kiss for each of my faithful girls, every one of whom is bright and smiling and at her very best tonight. They are wearing—not slovenly kimonos, as one might expect—but the very finest evening gowns that the studios of Poiret can afford.

Monsieur 'Quatrefois' an elderly but wealthy patron of ours, so named by us because while he has the greatest difficulty raising hard for even a single round of love's battle, is continually entertaining us with accounts of how in his younger days he never hit less than four times running—calls me aside to tell me a new smutty story that he has already regaled to all present. Also he brings me good news of an investment in some South American bonds he has made for me

A light luncheon with many sparkling wines and stimulating liqueurs is being served by two of my most attractive maids, both of them dressed in maddeningly prim dresses that make them appear, though desirable, as severe as cloistered nuns—and as unattainable. One of them is to be admitted to our ranks as a fully commissioned dispenser of pleasure this very night; but this feature of the evening is reserved for later.

My good wine soon banishes that slight restraint that can exist at the very outset even in such a place as ours. The conversation becomes more lively; but without taking too loose or vulgar a turn. The genuine Sybarite knows better than to evaporate the imagination of words in advance of action and thus secularize the secret mysteries of love. Here and there a breast or thigh is uncovered to be kissed or fondled;

but the radical instruments of amorous warfare are by both sexes kept discreetly out of sight until the actual tender hostilities should begin. By thus concealing the exact extent of their armament, an element of conjecture and suspense is added to the number of other pleasant emotions that charge the perfumed atmosphere.

Our spacious drawing-room, I might say for the benefit of those readers who have never visited my maison, is brightly illuminated by concealed non-glaring electric lights. The furniture is luxuriously adapted to meet the demand of the most precise and specialized voluptuary. On the floor is spread an extraordinarily thick and expensive Persian rug that in itself makes a couching place as soft and comfortable as anyone could wish—and in addition there are innumerable cushions and hassocks of varying sizes and consistencies strewn about, making possible any arrangement, any elevation that might be desired. In the centre of the floor there is a huge cushioned dais, all of fifteen feet long and ten feet wide, and so much of the available wall-space as is not occupied by my well-stocked buffet is lined with large sofas and ingenious reclining chairs. Doors lead off to the dining-room, two dressing rooms with baths, and three retiring rooms. In the luxurious reception hall, where we sometimes hold dances or special functions, there are ascenders leading to the upper stories, our numerous private chambers, and our living quarters.

Someone remarks that it is time the concert should begin for, he adds laughingly, he fancies all the instruments are in tune. I give the signal to begin, for I have a most delightful novelty to present to my guests tonight. Yesterday we played a new game called 'Put and Take,' employing a large dice-top, marked 'Put one,' 'Take one,' 'Put two,' 'Take two,' 'Take all,' and so on. Everybody would spin in turn, alternating according to sex.

For each 'put,' a male player would be allowed

just one intimate stroke within the cunny of his partner. A 'take' gave him the privilege of planting just one sucking kiss at the same place. A female player would win corresponding privileges over her male partner. A 'take all,' authorized the player to do just that, retiring from the game with any partner of his or her choice and collecting his winnings within sight of everyone; but as a 'take all' occurred only at long intervals in the game, the reader can imagine to what a pitch of excitement the players were worked up, forced to content themselves with one or two sucks at a time. Ultimately of course, every player makes a 'take all,' but picture the feverish plight of the last few players after almost two hours of gambling. One couple makes enough 'puts' and 'takes' to reach a complete orgasm by instalments—and when the last two survivors spun again and again without making the desired 'take all,' we who had long since expended our winnings, were favored with the ludicrous sight of the interlocked couple spinning the top, taking a shove or two, spinning once more, and so on to the end. The game was an uproarious success.

But for tonight, as I have said, I have invented something different. I call it 'Cunt Polo.' A wide spotless sheet is spread over the centre dais, and Manon and Rosa, undressing quickly, lie nude on their backs with their legs wide apart and the soles of their feet pressed together—thus forming a fascinating diamond of plump shapely limbs. Now I called for four male volunteers. A number of American college boys, wealthy and devilish, who are with us tonight, come forward immediately. I ask them to strip, which they do unhesitantly, bringing to light fine weapons that are just raring for adventure of any sort.

Two of them, under my direction, take their places in reverse or '69' positions over my two pretty assistants respectively lodging their members in the mouth of the girls, who however make no active move until I give the signal for the game to start. The pretty cunts that crown each apex of this charming double triangle are the goals. The vigorous young men lying with their mouths conveniently near are to be the guards. The other two men are to be the opposing field players, and a large brandied maraschino cherry is to be the ball or chukker.

The players choose their sides for the first quarter as I explain the rules to them. With tongues as the only implements of play, each is to attempt to get the ball between the glistening posts of his opponent's goal. The guards are of course to protect their goals with their tongues. But what complicates the game is the fact that the two girls are meanwhile to suck upon the instruments of their riders, and the quarter is to end whenever any one of the players should go off, whether voluntarily or involuntarily.

The game starts amid the encouraging shouts of the numerous spectators. Mock bets are being placed. But I shall not describe the game in too great detail. Suffice it that there is much bumping of heads on the part of the two men fighting for the ball in the field and much frenzied cunt-tonguing on the part of the respective guards whenever the ball shows any signs of approaching the fleshy goals. The first quarter ends most unexpectedly With one of the 'goals' going off—that is, my passionate Manon—and a heated discussion ensues as to whether this is to end the quarter or not. I rule that the game cannot continue so long as anyone is in the throes of pleasure.

The goals are changed and the game proceeds. Within the very first few minutes of play, one of the guards becomes so distracted with the naughty little love-bites with which Rosa favors his organ that he allows two goals to be made against him; but just at this moment Manon does as much for her superincumbent. His panting mouth is unable to protect his goal, the score is evened and the quarter ends as Manon proudly pulls a spouting cock from her mouth.

Now we observe a short intermission in which

refreshing drinks are passed around. Before proceeding with the second half we find it necessary to put two new guards in the game. All the girls want to be goal-posts, but I decide to keep the same ones in. The play resumes, but suddenly comes to a stand still in the third quarter. Where is the ball? As referee I intervene and search between the lips of the two darling goals. No sign of it. Then one of the field-men confesses shamefacedly that in the excitement of the game he swallowed it! I fetch another cherry and put it into play. But something is the matter with this same blundering player. He muffs the ball and allows his rival the entire field. Were it not for some remarkable play on the part of his goal-keeper his team would be heavily scored against. But the reason comes out and the quarter comes to an end when we find the pathetic young man has come off in his trousers—what with the Unaccustomed proximity of all this luscious cunt.

    The last quarter starts off with some rapid field play. The score being tied so far, everyone is anxious to see the final result. The ball is now heading for Manon's goal... That was almost a touchdown, but her guard repulses the bit of fruit nobly. It caroms against her white thigh and goes shooting across the field toward Rosa's cunt. The two field men rush to the spot and dribble the ball back and forth against her satiny flesh, dangerously close to the goal, battling for the possession of it. Closer and closer to the gaping scarlet goalposts it comes, every inch of territory desperately contested. It all depends on the goal-keeper now! But he is panting with the excitement not only of the game but of the lovely concentrated assault that he is receiving at the lips of Rosa at his other end—and though he is moving his tongue bravely back and forth, he is doing it blindly; he is too far outfield, high up over the clitty, and not over the lower part of the goal. The breathless spectators lean over watching anxiously. The cherry is maneuvered to the very lips of the cunt. It is a certain touchdown. But no—just as the

THE FURTHER ADVENTURES OF MADELEINE

powerful tongue of the opponent presses the cherry for a straight-away to the goal over the infinitesimal remaining distance, Rosa suddenly doubles up in the delicious agony of spending, throws up her legs and wraps them about her lover's neck. The field of battle is wiped out, and the player headed with the ball for her cunny, meets up only with her tiny wrinkled anus. The game is over in a riot of hearty laughter as both Rosa and her cunt's guardian finish off the superb sixty-nine in each other's mouths.

While we stand about refreshing ourselves with cocktails and more liqueurs, Janet and some handsome young man who is a frequent applicant for her favors regale us with a gracious and voluptuous exhibition waltz. One of the girls plays the piano, and as they dance slowly about the room her partner undoes her dress, disclosing to our view a pair of finely molded delicious twin-orbs. Then, without interrupting the dance, he removes her gown altogether. Her shoes are loosened and kicked off without one false move and now the whole company is dazzled and delighted at the sight of her exquisitely fashioned thighs and buttocks, which, disclosed to us so rhythmically, and with the accompaniment of the sensuous music, can not help but be doubly effective. As the number draws to a close, her gallant whips out a master member whose eminent size and goodly shape at once proclaims the owner a true hero among women, and as with the final chords of the selection, the accomplished Janet springs up into his arms and wraps her lithe legs about his waist, he catches her ready cunt upon the upstanding head of his part and carries her gracefully to a nearby couch where he falls upon her and concludes and augments the pleasure of the dance with a vigorous to and fro motion that soon brings on the ultimate melting dissolution for both of them.

But there is yet the important business of the evening to attend to. I introduce our most recent enlistment, Mimi, to the assembled company and offer her choice between a public and a private initiation.

"In wishing to enter your service, madame," she replies modestly, "I wish to please the greatest number of people in the greatest possible number of ways. My only fear is that my comparative inexperience will make me appear at a disadvantage among all these beautiful girls."

"Well spoken, my darling," I say, kissing her reassuringly, "Your inexperience is what will delight us most."

The lucky man who has been chosen in advance as her liberator steps forward and, with extreme relish, deprives her piece by piece of her convent-like habiliments which heretofore she has worn as a contrast for the more desirable impudicity of we others whom soon she is to join. To the charms of her flashing eyes, pouting mouth and little retrouse nose are now added those of her bare shoulders, the curves floating away into her shapely arms and soft tapering fingers—digits made especially for the delicious manipulation of the sensitive phalluses of hot-blooded men. Then with the removal of her chemise comes into view two dazzling white opulent globes of firm flesh, each topped with a dainty rose, and a soft polished belly, sweeping down in a majestic curve like a broad plateau and relieved in its centre by a maddeningly coquettish little dimple of a navel. Then the majestic columns of her matchless thighs, adorned at their sweet intersection with the delicious rosy cleft of flesh, the spring of love, bowered in dark silky foliage.

In accordance with a rather strange procedure of initiation, insisted upon by some of more imaginative and sentimental clients, I, as the mother superior of this temple dedicated to the worship of pleasure, must hold the initiate upon my lap during the whole inaugural ceremony. Changing into a light negligeé, I take my place upon the couch in a semi-reclining position with a number of silk cushions beneath me. Mimi lies on her back upon my soft generous body, and as I have taken care to open my peignoir all the way up the front, I can feel her bare satiny skin upon my naked lap and bosom.

We both spread wide our thighs, her somewhat slim but perfect, mine decidedly more voluptuous and ample. The celebrant approaches, wearing a dressing robe which he hurriedly removes, displaying to us the proud proof of his manhood, stiff and upstanding, threatening the very skies with its pleasing power, its kingly acorn-shaped (but by no means acorn-sized!) head, broad and shelving, purple and distended with the blood pressure of his vigorous state. As he comes between our out-stretched thighs, he compliments me prettily by confessing that between the two fine cunts before him he is in a quandary which to choose.

"Who told you you were to choose at all, young man!" I chided him with mock severity, "Attend to your business!" And from my position of supreme vantage, I pass my hands down over that smoothest, whitest, roundest belly to that soft groove which kind nature has stamped there between two crimson fleshy ridges for the mutual delectation of man and woman. Gently spreading the lips of that luscious nether mouth with one hand, I with my other lay hold of the staunch velvety officiator and approach that dear idol so worshipped by women to its true and proper niche. Forcefully he shoves it in. While Mimi, according to the rules of the house, comes to us without her maidenhead, it is obvious that she has disposed of it with her finger or a candle, and that this is her very first penetration by man. With all the delicious difficulty of a defloration, we see his tumescent part sink into the tight scarlet crack inch by inch until it is entirely out of sight sunk in the tight moist folds of her lush laboratory of love. The poor dear winces at first, but with the hypnotizing effect of her master's slow to and fro movement, she is soon roused to active participation. Then, under the stinging lash of pleasure, she is unable to contain herself. Throwing her arms and legs about wildly, she heaves to meet his eager thrusts, twists and writhes upon her stiff fleshy axis—at that moment indeed the very centre of her world. The breathing of both is now swift and laborious, the tumult of their senses, as evidenced by the tumult of their bodies, keeps rising to a higher and higher pitch. To save myself from his, to me, useless pounding, and to give them more freedom of movement, I slip out from under Mimi's quivering form. A moment later, with sudden stiffening, she stretches out and a delicious little shudder runs through her pleasure-convulsed frame, and they both lay motionless, dying with that dear delight, and occasional spasmodic movement or a soulful melting sigh being the only signs of life they show.

By this time, it is needless to say, all my friends and clients—and not excluding myself—are sufficiently wound up by the spectacles of the evening to themselves wish to participate. Some of them indeed accustomed to the privileges of my house, have not waited for the last act, but have taken possession of sofas—and girls—to themselves stage their own little tableaux and dramas. But there are other more dignified and self-conscious patrons present, who, while enjoying the sight of the others' enjoyments would not think of taking their own pleasure in public. And so, though my strongest urge is to grab a man and hurry off into some corner, I must pair them off with my girls for private tête à têtes, like the captain of a burning ship at sea, saving myself the last. And then, when I finally get to the end of my roster of guests, I find that there are two men remaining, with room for only one in my lifeboat.

"Baron, you will come with me. Now Monsieur, I am sorry, but if you will wait just a few minutes, Henriette will soon be down to take care of you."

"But Madame! It is with you that I wish to be. Perhaps the Baron, if he has no especial preference, will be willing to cede priority to me."

THE FURTHER ADVENTURES OF MADELEINE

"Mais non, monsieur!" the Baron bristles, "I am leaving Paris in a few hours, and this my last opportunity, my farewell, with Madame!"

"But Madame!" Monsieur expostulates, "Did you not give me your solemn promise last week that the very next time—"

"Gentlemen, gentlemen! Please!" I exclaim distraughtly, "What can I do? Must you resort to something like duelling or cutting a pack of cards to determine which of you is to have me?"

"Sacre, non!" the Baron puts in, "I'll tell you what. We are both gentlemen. We shall be friends. If Madame Madeleine has no objections, and if you are willing, monsieur, we shall all retire together—a trois, comprenez-vous?"

"Oh, gentlemen!" I cry, overwhelmed, but nevertheless pleased by this friendly solution.

We repair to one of the most luxurious of my private chambers. When I turn around after switching on the lights, I am confronted with two stiff peters, levelled at me by my two guests respectively.

"Hands up!" the Baron exclaims in laughable English.

"Your cunny or your life!" shouts Monsieur, catching the spirit. They make for me—both on burglary bent. (Yes, I said burglary.)

"Now gentlemen, no squabbling," I urge as we tumble upon the spacious bed and they rifle my secret treasures and charms, "Let us all undress and then we'll divide the swag evenly." They comply, and I, too, divest myself hurriedly at the same time both of my clothes and my dignity. By now I am hot enough to want to be raped by the Eiffel Tower.

"You, Baron," I say to this personage as he turns to me stripped of everything but his monocle, "lie back here near the edge of the bed."

He does so.

I climb over him and bringing the head of his stiff tool to the dewy lips of my furry, satin-lined muff,

I let it sink into me to the utmost extent of its delicious powers of penetration.

Monsieur stands by with disappointment written on all his features, wondering no doubt where his share is to come from. I set his mind at rest immediately however and find 'penal' servitude for the naked symbol of his manhood by having him oil it first with some scented pomade, and then, as I lie forward over the Baron, allowing him to step up behind and slip it in between the jutting cheeks of my posterior and into my tight but willing cul.

As his erect staff slides into that part of me, made additionally narrow by the close proximity of the other bulky distender just to the other side of the thin membrane, I can feel their two members rub against each other in friendly fashion through the negligible intervening partition. Exalting not only in the delicious well-stuffed sensation, but also in the unusual lasciviousness of my doubly spitted position, gorged with a double share of the 'dearest morsel of the earth,' I feel like some high goddess, uniting in the mystic bond of my body, two men, a nobleman and a commoner, who but for me would not know each other.

However, it is not the metaphysical overtones of my salacious, truly two-horned 'dilemma' that long engrosses me. My itching clitty clamors for its tribute. And so, our bodies linked together in this position, all the more delightful because of its difficulty, stretched almost to breaking on this double rack of joy, I start giving them the proper motion. How can I convey to you, dear reader, the incomparable feeling as that local over-fullness spread through all my body, putting me almost entirely out of my mind with a furious lust that my two partners might perhaps equal, but certainly not surpass. As back and forth I fuck, as the one of them rams fiercely into my rear while I rise up on the stiff sensitive staff of the other only to come down on it again, both of the favorite parts of my ravenous body are in turn engorged or partially evacuated in an indescribable feverish alternation of attacks and caresses.

Now they crush me mercilessly between them, timing their lunging strokes together instead of in succession, their active loins quivering with the violence of their super-heavenly conflict (for indeed heaven could hold no bliss like this!) I feel the waves of pleasure surging, foaming, raging to a height, inundating all my senses, all my faculties. That critical delirium of supreme felicity that all the pages of my volume have not, I fear, even begun to do justice to, is almost at hand. In wild transports I throw myself about, sob, moan, protest against the extreme pleasure. My stiff-mettled partners drive all the more tempestuously, batter me more cruelly in the blind lust of their own approaching orgasms. Yet it is not mercy that I desire—oh, no! I sob and cry because I would want this divine ecstasy of the senses to last forever, yes forever, this tremendous cataclysmic pleasure which, if at its height, it lasted five minutes instead of five seconds, would kill even the sturdiest of humans!

Lifted then by the mounting waves of delirious sensation to the highest pitch of joy that life can bear, I am poised for a moment at the sweet terrific critical point—and then suddenly, all the juices of my body are opened up, all my being, all my soul is dissolved in bliss and poured down into that sensitive passage where escape luckily is denied it by reason of that part being so effectively and deliciously plugged up. And almost simultaneously, with savage cries of triumph, my two riders cram into me the utmost fraction of their flesh that I can engulf and with ungovernable impetuosity feel the hot pearly elixir spurt from both sides, into me their joint loads of scalding love fluid, flooding both my orifices, spreading into my joy-knotted bowels, mingling with my own pleasurable effusions. Some few more moments of tremulous, convulsive shuddering, the delicious conjunction of our bodies is ended, and we collapse upon the bed, spent, drenched with pleasure, gasping for breath, completely vanquished by love's bounty, and yet resting only so that we may recover strength to resume the stirring of those exquisite vibrations of sensation that tremble still on the strings of delight...

That was yesterday, dear reader, and tonight is another night. But though we can go on loving so long as there is life and health in us and still find ever renewed delights in the exercise of that divine function, we cannot go on writing about it indefinitely.

I have, I believe, kept my promise to tell about myself, even more thoroughly than I had originally intended. Perhaps I have even succeeded in somehow justifying myself—although, I hasten to add, it has been my purpose throughout to vindicate not myself but the human body, enchained through centuries by hypocrisy and false modesty.

It was just half a year a go that I began confiding my life to these sympathetic incensorious pages. It was then early spring. It is now late summer. I am seated in the spacious garden behind my house basking in the sunlight which in Paris is of a brighter gold than anywhere else in the world—and feeling once more that exuberance which begot this arduous scriptural enterprise of mine. I glance along the high walls that surround my garden, the arbors and nooks that have witnessed so many delightful fetes during the past summer. I drink in my surroundings with a happy sense of possession. I have brought my record at last down to this very living moment. I need only one final thought with which to close these pages, a send-off for the kind and tolerant reader who has lived through so much with me, who has endured the many deficiencies of my unpracticed writing.

From within the house I hear the happy chatter of my girls, and the blithesome voice of Fleurette singing some haunting ballad of her native Province as she goes about her work of social secretary. Would it

THE FURTHER ADVENTURES OF MADELEINE

be too much a cliché to say that we are all one big happy family? Well, it must stand—for we are just that.

But as I grope for my farewell words, I see an interruption coming. A little street urchin has climbed to the top of our wall and is regarding me curiously. My writing can wait: life can not. I will call him, and perhaps he will furnish me with the ending for my book.....

* * * * *

I am back again, dear reader, all out of breath and still without that closing thought. Life moves on apace. Things happen more rapidly than I can record them. Shall I tell you what happened? I needn't of course; but I will not leave the reader's curiosity unassuaged.

I called the gamin down from the wall. He came to me timidly. He was young and possessed that bright insolence characteristic of his kind. I like little boys and I was in a state of especial good will. I asked him to name to me anything at all that would make him happy.

"To touch your pretty titties, mamzelle," he replied brazenly, pointing to where my loose peignoir drooped open a bit.

I was vastly amused, and anxious to measure the extent of his precocity.

"Mechant! Naughty boy!" I laughed; but I granted his request.

"Ces-ci sont trest jolis, tres interessante," (These are very pretty, very interesting words he murmured importantly as he fondled my luxurious curves, rather roughly.)

"And have you anything interesting to show me?" I asked.

"Certainly," he replied, "I'll show you my great big 'little brother.'"

I agreed, and with a swaggering air he brought

out his youthful organ—the merest plaything of a boy.

"Why that—that isn't very interesting," I told him teasingly, "I'd call that rather small."

"Small, hell!" he retorted bellicosely, "Just play with it awhile and see how big it gets. I'll bet if you'd let me shove it into you, you'd say it was big!"

"Come then, you young braggart," I put in, "I'll call your bluff." And leading him to a sheltered arbor where we would be unseen, I threw myself in a hammock and opened my negligeé. He was frightened at first and confessed that though he had once tried it on his elder sister, he had never really done it before. I took him upon my bosom and bestowed upon him the first and sweetest joys of his coming manhood.

And now I really must bid the reader adieu—ere something else occurs to demand inclusion in this book of life and to stretch it out indefinitely.

Often times I have wondered—have even been rather pleasantly appalled at the thought of the great number of fucks that have fallen to my happy lot. At such times I have regretted not having kept some tally of the exact number of passengers of every age and estate that have travelled to paradise on my heaving body.

Twelve centuries before Christ cast his dark stigma of impotence upon the world, Cheops, an Egyptian monarch, ordered his beautiful daughter to take to prostitution to replenish his dwindling treasury. She, wishing to leave a monument to herself, besought each of her numerous lovers to present her with a single stone to be employed for that purpose. Her pyramid still stands outside of Cairo—only all the resources of modern science have failed to estimate even the approximate number of stones in that immense pile. So inexhaustible is the marvellous joy-giving power of woman...

As for myself, dear reader, I desire no such immortality. To be remembered pleasantly for awhile by all those many who have tasted of joy between my thighs in one way or another is all that I would ask. And as for all you who know me only through the medium of these pages, I can but conclude at last by saying that every hard-on raised during the reading of this book, (even if it be only temporarily, even if it be doused immediately in soft female flesh or destroyed by hand) will be, of the noblest sort, a monument erected to my memory.

Title	Book#	Price
—MEMOIRS OF MADELEINE	017	$4.75
—THE YELLOW ROOM	025	$4.75
—SECRETS OF THE CITY	033	$4.75
—FURTHER ADVENTURES OF MADELEINE	041	$4.75
—FRUITS OF PASSION	05X	$4.75
—LOVE'S ILLUSION	068	$4.75
—ANNABELLE FANE	084	$4.75
—PAULINE	025	$4.95
—TRUMP, THE MAN, THE MYTH,		
—THE SCANDAL	173	$4.95
—THE METAMORPHOSIS OF LISETTE JOUAUX	106	$4.75
—THE AUTOBIOGRAPHY OF A FLEA	076	$4.75

Ordering is easy; MC/VISA orders can be placed by calling our toll free number 1-800-458-9640, Dept. M, or mail in the coupon below:

Please send me the following books

QTY	TITLE	BOOK#	PRICE	TOTAL
			SUBTOTAL	
NY STATE RESIDENTS ADD 8 1/4% SALES TAX				
Add $1.00 P&H for first book and .50 for each additional book. Outside USA, add $2.00 for first book, $1.00 for each additional book.				
			TOTAL (U.S. FUNDS)	

MAIL TO: MASQUERADE BOOKS, 801 SECOND AVENUE
16TH FLOOR, NEW YORK, N.Y. 10017

PRINT NAME_____

ADDRESS_____APT #_____

STATE_____ZIP_____TEL( )_____

PAYMENT ❑ CHECK ❑ VISA ❑ MC ❑ MONEY ORDER
CARD#_____EXP_____
Please allow 4-6 weeks delivery; No COD orders.
Please make all checks payable to MASQUERADE BOOKS
PAYABLE IN U.S. FUNDS ONLY

SHELTER

#22
FAST-DRAW FILLY

BY
PAUL LEDD

ZEBRA BOOKS
KENSINGTON PUBLISHING CORP.

ZEBRA BOOKS

are published by

Kensington Publishing Corp.
475 Park Avenue South
New York, NY 10016

Copyright © 1985 by Kensington Publishing Corp.

All rights reserved. No part of this book may be reproduced in any form or by any means without the prior written consent of the Publisher, excepting brief quotes used in reviews.

First printing: June 1985

Printed in the United States of America

1.

The black, greasy water slid past, winding around the rotting piles of the riverside piers. Across the Missouri River port somewhere a bell clanged and a man yelled indistinctly. There was drunken laughter drifting across the water from the St. Joseph saloons. It was the dead of night but the western town was still awake, still moving.

The man in the shadows of the warehouse crates was silent, crouched, waiting. He had a Colt revolver in his hand, and he had come prepared to use it.

Waiting, watching. These weren't new to Shelter Morgan, nor was the use of a gun. He had walked a long trail since war's end, and there had been blood all the way. He let his eyes flicker from the dock to the black water below. Something squealed, drawing his attention. A water rat drifting downriver.

Shelter looked down the dock again, waiting, watching, listening.

Cord Levitt was the name of the man he wanted. Cord Levitt. He was a coward, a killer, a traitor, a bastard. Tonight was his night to pay for all of it.

Morgan stiffened. A coach with lighted sidelamps moved past along the cobbled road, the horses' hoofs clattering on stone. A sailor in a striped shirt and peacoat staggered along the quay, working his way through the damp, twisting river fog which rose now off the Missouri.

Then he saw the other man and he stiffened, drawing back a little.

"Come on, Cord. Walk right out here, nothing's gone wrong," Morgan was thinking. His hand was cramped around the butt of the big blue Colt in his hand. The man had hesitated. Now he walked forward.

He was the right height. He carried a cane and wore a top hat. A cape was draped around his wide shoulders. He paused again, out of decent range, looking around. That was all right. There was supposed to be another man here tonight.

"Cord and a man named James Maxwell," the one-eyed sailor had told Shelter over a cup of rum in a sleazy riverport saloon. Smoke had wreathed the man's head, rising from his stubby, brown cob pipe.

"Who's Maxwell?"

"He's a merchant, you might say," the sailor had said, choking on a cough.

"Stolen goods?" Shelter had poured the man a little more rum.

"Everything. You want it, you get it from Maxwell. Mostly he's been doing guns lately, though he's sold whiskey to the Indians—caused a damned bloody Kiowa massacre, he did."

"I can't see Cord Levitt dealing with Indians," Shelter had commented.

"Why not? They all get into it once or twice. There's a big money to be had. An Indian wants whiskey and he don't have money—" the sailor shrugged— "he'll go get you some. And I don't mean," he added with a wink, "by trapping no furs. No, sir, hits the first farmer he sees over the head and lifts his watch. Don't sound like much, but multiply that by a hundred Indians all willing to rob and kill for trade goods, and you got you something."

"It still doesn't seem like Levitt's line."

"Maybe not. You know your man better than me, I'm just telling you what Maxwell's done—among other things a sight too numerous to mention."

"You're sure they're going to meet tonight?"

"I saw 'em, heard 'em. If the man you told me to look out for is the same one. They didn't mention names, mister. He was dressed fancy, like one of these new-rich planters we got around here now. He had black eyes, real black, and black hair slicked back. His cheeks was scooped out, you know. And the bones beneath the eyes kind of bulged out, knobby like."

"That's Cord. There couldn't be two men that fit that description in St. Jo."

"There you are then." He had looked hopefully at Shell and Morgan had given him the bottle. Putting five dollars down he had gotten up and gone out into the heat of the Missouri summer. Trail's end. Time had just caught up with Cord Levitt.

Now, crouched in the shadows by the warehouse, his nostrils filled with the scents of tar and stagnant water, effluent and rotting wood, he waited. Waited for Cord Levitt to come a little nearer, near enough so that Morgan could be absolutely sure.

Someone else was coming. Long-striding. Slender and very tall. Maxwell, by the descriptions. Morgan's upper lip curled back involuntarily into a sort of rictus which showed his teeth wolfishly. It was Levitt then. If Maxwell was here.

The two shadowy figures met as the river fog swirled around them. They drew together, spoke briefly and then turned directly toward Morgan's hiding place.

Shell's breath caught. His eyes narrowed and grew hard, bright in the darkness. This was going to be an easy one. Step out and level that Peacemaker at them and haul Levitt off. If he ran, well that was too bad for Levitt, as it had been for those good men he had killed.

He could hear voices now.

"Delivery before the first of the month or it doesn't do me a damned bit of good." That was Levitt. Maxwell answered calmly.

"I know what I'm about, you'll get it on schedule. You've paid, haven't you?"

Levitt growled an answer. "Yeah, in advance. Don't be forgetting that, will you."

"If you want to go somewhere else and conduct your business . . ." Maxwell's voice was a little tighter now. The two men had halted not twenty feet from where Shell hid.

"No." Levitt waved a hand. "Sorry if I got a little hot. We've a deal."

The challenging voice came from around the side of the warehouse, from the alley between it and a boat repair shop. It was a commanding voice, narrow and thin.

"Cord Levitt, stand where you are!"

Morgan smothered a curse and leaped up. Cord Levitt took three running steps and leaped into the dark water of the Missouri River.

Shelter fired a warning shot over the bastard's head. A narrow tongue of flame scored the night. Maxwell screwed it up then.

The arms dealer turned, his hand dipping into his

waistband. He came up with a little chrome pistol which he fired toward the person in the alleyway. His shot was a thin, whining, almost tinny report. The answering gun was a big .44 and it spat lead and flame.

"Jesus!" Maxwell screamed in pain, clutching his belly as the gunshot echoed across the docks, bringing people out of doorways—or into them. The .44 fired again and Maxwell was slammed back into a tarred pile where a rotting noose of heavy line was draped. He hit it hard and then sat down easy, going slack against the dock, going slack and very dead.

Shelter Morgan stepped back, his own pistol ready. His eyes were on the mouth of the alleyway where the gunman had been hidden. Now the shadowy figure strode toward him, bootheels clicking on sodden wood.

"You can come out now," Morgan was told.

"Holster that damned Colt and I will." Shell was mad and his anger showed in his voice. He came forward, scowling bitterly.

She was young and dark-haired, wearing a man's gray suit and a black shirt which did something but not much to conceal a set of very womanly breasts. Morgan felt like backhanding her, but he didn't.

"Any sign of him?" she asked, looking down at the water which flowed past unruffled, dark. The rat was still squealing somewhere beneath the dock.

"What the hell did you do that for! Do you know how long I've been looking for that man?"

"This one?" She toed James Maxwell's body.

"No. The other."

"You got paper on him?" She brushed back a strand of dark hair and stood with her thumbs hooked into her belt.

"Have I got what?"

9

"Paper."

"I don't know what you mean."

The woman unfolded a wanted poster and handed it to Morgan to glance at by the light of a match he thumbed to life. The picture was old, blurred. It was definitely James Maxwell. There had been five hundred dollars in it for the woman. More than a year's wages for a lot of men.

"A bounty hunter? You?"

"Yeah. Me." She turned at the sound of approaching footsteps. Someone had gotten the local law out of bed or out of a saloon. Either guess could have been it. He was red-faced and sloppy, wearing trousers and longjohn shirt, floppy hat. His badge was pinned to his galluses.

"What in the bloody hell is going on here? Stand still there, mister," the lawman cautioned.

"She's not a mister," Morgan said.

All that earned him was a warning glance. A deputy took Shelter's gun from him and lifted the Colt from the woman's holster.

"This one's warm," the deputy said. "This one ain't been fired."

"All right. Let's go on down to my office and talk it over," he said.

"You heard the man say my gun wasn't fired," Morgan tried.

"That don't matter. You were here together, weren't you? You and this dude—" he finally got a better look— "damn it, she is a woman." He pushed his hat back on his head in wonder.

The deputy who was crouched over the dead man reported, "It's James Maxwell, chief."

"Son of a bloody whore bitch," the police chief of St. Joseph, Missouri said solemnly. "You know who that is you killed?"

"Yes," the woman said with a shrug. "A thief and a snake."

"You don't know Mr. Maxwell. He supports—"

"All he's supporting now is that post and all he's going to support from now on is a few inches of dirt for them to plant daisies in."

Morgan shook his head in wonder. He had known some women, but he hadn't run across a hard case like this one before. The police chief was working his way through an even more elaborate oath. He got to the end without stumbling and then told Shelter and the woman, "I said we're going to my office. Let's move that way, shall we." He snarled at the small dockside crowd. "Get out of here, the rest of you. Got no homes? Tom, get Mr. Maxwell tucked away somewhere until the undertaker can do what needs to be done."

They started walking single-file down the cobbled street toward the heart of town. The police chief first, then a deputy, the girl, Shelter Morgan and another deputy. This one carried a scatter gun and an expression which seemed to indicate a wish to use it.

Morgan didn't give him any reason to think hard about it. He only glanced back once, toward the black river where Cord Levitt had made good his escape.

The office was a two-story brick building. The sheriff was upstairs; downstairs was the courthouse and jail. A few drunken jailbirds were singing off-key in the cells there. The deputies prodded Shelter and the girl into the lighted office, and while the police chief sagged into a leather chair behind a scarred desk, they flanked the doorway and stood throttling their weapons with sweaty little hands.

"What the hell happened?" the chief asked. He was simmering. Maxwell had meant something in this town. Probably the chief had just lost a good chunk of his under-the-table pay. For if Maxwell was an honored citizen of St. Jo and environs, he was also a well-known crook. The girl's poster proved that. She tossed it onto the police chief's desk. He let it lay.

"What's that prove?"

"It proves he was a wanted man. There's a reward on his head. I'm collecting," she answered, and there wasn't any backdown in her voice. The chief turned his head and spat, missing the cuspidor.

"Go ahead and collect."

"I guess you'll vouch for this?"

"Maybe. What is it with you? You don't do this for a living." The police chief began a grin which didn't go anywhere.

"The hell I don't. The name's Andy Rice. Maybe you've heard of me. Even you," she added with a touch of nastiness.

"*Andy* Rice!" The chief spat again, missing again. "Yeah, I've heard of him."

"It's not *him*, it's me. Parents hung me with the name Adeline. I didn't take to it. I'm Andy Rice."

"The bounty hunter."

"Bounty killer," one of the deputies spoke up.

Andy Rice, if that was really her name, shot him a hard look. He looked away, recalling that she knew what that Colt she wore was for.

"I never heard of nothing like this," the chief sputtered. "I don't believe it."

"Good," she said. "You don't have to believe it. I don't give a damn if you do or not. Just vouch for the kill on Maxwell, have the name Andy Rice put down on the forms, and when the money comes I'll bank it. The rest doesn't matter."

"Did Maxwell draw on you or something, little lady?" The chief leaned across his desk, biting at his upper lip.

"It doesn't matter if he did or not."

"Murder matters."

"The poster says dead or alive."

"Listen, lady . . ."

Shelter Morgan spoke up. "He started for his gun, chief. I saw him. You want me to testify, I will."

"You will, will you? And just where do you fit in? You her partner or something?"

"No."

"Just another bounty hunter."

"I didn't want Maxwell. I wanted the man he was with, but not for a bounty."

"No? You carry a star then?" the chief asked. Then he got a look at something he didn't like in those icy blue eyes of Shelter Morgan and he backed down a little. "What did you want him for?" he asked, gathering himself again.

"A little matter of a bad debt," Shelter Morgan said. He noticed that the chief had started to tire a little. He had reached for a whiskey bottle in his desk drawer to try to prime himself back to life.

"What kind of debt—didn't get your name either."

"Morgan, Shelter Morgan."

"What kind of debt?"

"The usual kind."

"That means you won't tell me, is that it?"

Shell smiled softly. The chief wasn't all that stupid. They all waited while the lawman had a deep drink of whiskey. When he was through, he shook his head and said, "There'll be hell to pay for this. If you two got any sense at all, get out of St. Jo. Tonight. You understand me?"

"Sure," Andy Rice said. "Maxwell's got friends and you're not going to bother yourself to stop them if they want to kill me. I don't give a damn, chief. I

13

want that money. You tell them Andy Rice took him down, you see that the cash is available in the St. Jo bank. You keep your oily hands off it as well, or I'll be back to skin you." She rose, looked at the deputies scornfully and started out. "Tell your dogs to move aside."

The chief started working on his most grandiloquent curse of the night, gave it up out of exhaustion and said, "Let her go, boys," instead.

He poured out another glass of smoky whiskey and turned again to Morgan. "Well, want to tell me your part in this?"

"I already did."

"A bad debt, yeah," the chief said, looking the lean, dark-haired man up and down before polishing off his drink. "You want to sing, or spend the night in my jail?"

"He is a bastard, that one, that's all. It goes back a long way."

"You came here to kill a man in my jurisdiction. I don't like it."

"I wouldn't have killed him unless he went for a gun."

"But he would have."

Morgan thought about it for a moment. He smiled before he answered. "Yes, he would have gone for a gun."

He just hadn't had the time because the bounty woman had leaped out of the alley and started filling James Maxwell full of bullets. But he would have. He had always been a man to start shooting, Cord Levitt.

"Well?" The police chief, leaned back in his chair, bottle and whiskey glass in hand, was waiting.

"I guess you were in the war."

"I don't know anyone who wasn't."

"I take it you were Confederate, although that

doesn't much matter to the story," Morgan said. The chief gave him the bottle and a second glass, dusty as sin. Shelter wiped it on his shirt tail. He poured a short drink and began his story.

"It seems a long ways back now, the war. But I recall it well enough. I guess you do." The chief nodded. "It was a hard time, the hardest. Friends dying, suffering. The damned Yankees coming, telling us we had to live their way, to think the way President Lincoln thought, to follow the laws of the infallible United States government, the rights of the states and the citizens be damned." Shelter waved a hand, he was getting off the track.

"There was some gold, a hell of a lot of it. It was supposed to go for boots and blankets, food and bullets. It didn't. It went to Cord Levitt and a gang of his friends, officers and men I was serving with. They took that gold and left those that were hungry, those that were cold and suffering because we had no medicine. They took off with that gold and left a lot of my friends dead. Some of them they had plugged themselves. They tried to plug me but I was too lucky, I guess. So lucky the Union army caught me in civilian clothes and locked me away as a spy. That was a death penalty but—again I was lucky—" Shelter made a wry face—" and they commuted it to seven years in prison."

"Tough."

"Yeah, it made a long war out of it."

"You talk like your war's not over," the chief said.

"I just told you it wasn't. Not until every one of those robbing, killing bastards is behind bars or buried and moldering."

"All right." The chief took a deep, noisy breath. "I don't see any point in holding you. You'll be leaving town, I suppose," he said hopefully.

"If Cord Levitt's gone, I'm gone."

"I'd recommend you go anyway, Mr. Shelter Morgan."

Shell nodded. "I'm not here to bring trouble into your life. That crazy woman ruined my night as much as she ruined yours."

The chief stood. "You don't know her?"

"Never saw her before tonight."

"Lucky," the chief said, "damned lucky."

He led Morgan to the door. "You are clearing out of St. Jo." It wasn't a question.

"Sure," Shelter answered.

"I really would. It's not healthy for you. I don't like having my sleep disturbed. If you're seen wandering around tomorrow—well, you won't be."

"No," Morgan agreed, "I won't be."

Not unless Cord Levitt was there. If he was, then nothing on God's earth was going to stop Shelter Morgan from exacting retribution. Not a police chief or fumbling deputies with shotguns, riverfront thugs with their clubs and sudden knives—and not a female bounty hunter. Shelter Morgan went out of the building and into the foggy night.

2.

The hotel room wasn't much. A narrow, oily window overlooking the river, a squeaky, sagging bed, a dark, chipped mirror on the wall. The woman greatly improved the looks of the place but she didn't make it seem much more homey. Not with the big Colt on her lap where Morgan would have liked to rest his head.

She had her coat off and the black shirt she wore was open three buttons at the top. By tilting his head properly to the right, Shelter could create a good view of soft, curving cleavage. It was beautiful and alluring, completely contradicted by the scowl on the woman's face.

"One of those, are you?" she snapped.

"One of what?"

"I read your eyes."

"Oh—one of the masculine gender," Morgan said. He sailed his hat to his bed, crossed to the basin on the bureau and filled it, rinsing his face.

"Don't underestimate me, Morgan," she said.

He turned, drying his hands on a stained towel. He looked her over and said, "I'm not even estimating you, lady. You look pretty, but you've got something poisonous about you. Why don't you lift your shapely posterior out of my chair and get on out of here—unless you think we could get together and rub each other right."

"One of those," she said sourly. Her hat was off now, hanging down her back on a rawhide lace. Her dark hair was clipped short. It wasn't exactly manly—there wasn't much but her clothes manly about Andy Rice—but from the right angle you assumed she was a man. Shell had. It was a bad assumption he saw now as he sagged onto the bed next to her and studied her more closely. She lifted the blue Colt she carried, the gun that had already killed one man that night, and shoved it toward him, muzzle first.

"Put that goddamned thing down," Morgan growled.

"Forgetting your manners now?"

"I don't care if you're male or female now, no. You point that gun at me and I'll force you to use it or get your wrist broken."

"Then I'll use it," she purred.

"Then you'll hang, Andy. There's no price on my head."

Slowly she lowered the pistol. "Don't get excited, Morgan. Have you got a cigar?"

"No."

"No matter." She rose and walked to the window, looking out at the empty night. He had been right—she had a nice posterior. "Where's Cord Levitt?"

"Now you want him, too?"

"Now I recall who he is. El Paso. Three years back. Murder during a bank robbery. It didn't click at first. I think it's three hundred dollars."

"You do it for the money or the thrill of blowing

men up?" Shelter asked.

"I don't like that."

"I don't give a damn, lady. I don't know where he is," he said flatly.

"But you've got a good idea." She came toward him a step. Morgan got a whiff of some delicate powder you don't associate with bounty hunters.

"If I had an idea, I'd be there—I want the man badly."

"For what?"

"For a good reason—it's not important to you, killer."

"No, you're right." She wiped at her dark hair with the back of her hand. "It's not important to me. You just stay out of my way if we end up travelling in the same direction."

"You smoke opium or something?" Shelter asked. He crossed to the bed and lay back, putting his boots up while the lady tried and failed to come up with a clever answer.

"Why?" She walked toward him and stood, hands on hips, staring down, measuring him.

"If you think I push, it's a pipe dream. If you think you've got what it takes to move a real hard man, the same. You can walk up and shoot somebody, but you haven't got the size or the muscle to back down a tough man in a tough spot."

"You're tough?"

"What do you think?" Shelter asked. "Lady, I've spent the last three years hunting. I've been hit and stabbed and shot and had people try to blow me up. Yes, it makes me hard. At least when it comes to two-fisted, gun-toting little girls who want to play Jesse James. I don't believe in hard women—I've never seen one yet outside of a dime novel. Another thing I don't believe in is a woman who has nice looks and a good body walking around playing man. Nature wanted you to be a man, you would've had the right equipment hung on you."

"I'm really starting to dislike you, Morgan," she said in a nasty little voice. He was looking at her breasts through the gap in her black shirt, liking the soft rise and fall of them as her temper increased.

"Don't waste the effort. I'm not worth it. Besides, getting mad might shake your aim."

"Listen, Morgan." She turned toward the window and stood looking out. "Why don't we go after this Cord Levitt together? He can't have gotten far."

"Nope."

"Afraid I won't split?"

"No. I just don't need a travelling companion—what's on your mind anyway? Hate me one minute, want to share night camp with me the next."

"Night camp? You figure he's left St. Jo?" she asked.

"I figure, yes."

"You have reasons."

Shelter didn't answer for a minute. "I have my reasons." He shrugged. "Maxwell deals—dealt—in stolen goods and guns. Cord had already paid for his goods, whatever they are. Why pay *before* he had what he ordered unless he wasn't going to be around to pay later? Besides, after that shooting he'll cut and run."

"Run where? If you're right, he's got a load of guns—we'll call the goods guns as if we knew—going somewhere. Where?"

Morgan shook his head. He didn't mind sharing a little specious reasoning, but he didn't want to give his good guesses away. Nor did he want to be travelling in the same direction as Miss Calamity when he left St. Jo.

"Maybe the men that work for Maxwell would know."

Shelter nodded. "Could be."

"You don't think they'd talk, do you?"

"Why don't you go and ask them. If you find out anything, write me a letter. General delivery."

"What town?"

"Any town, Andy Rice, any town at all."

"You bastard," she said. "I hope you lose that damned precious 'equipment' of yours."

Then she picked up her coat and stomped out. Andy Rice wasn't easy to get along with. Morgan didn't bother to lock the door or turn down the lamp. He closed his eyes and went to sleep, dreaming of a lot of Cord Levitt-face rats swimming in the dark Missouri River.

The police chief wasn't in when Morgan strolled down the dusty, busy street to the jailhouse. The deputy told Shelter they hadn't picked up Cord Levitt and didn't expect to. It wasn't a real friendly interview either. All over St. Jo people were coming to dislike him.

He grinned at himself in a store window, seeing a tall, dark-haired, blue-eyed man with a lean jaw. He was wearing a dark twill suit and a white shirt, black string tie and black, flat-crowned hat. A hell of a fine-looking fellow, he told himself. "*I* like you, you bastard."

Morgan turned into the restaurant he had eaten at each of the four days since blowing into St. Jo. The waitress asked, "Find your Uncle Ned yet?"

"Funny thing. I found him but he fell in the river and drowned."

She wasn't sure he was kidding. "Steak and eggs, potatoes and coffee?"

"Thanks." Shell put his hat beside him on the

empty chair and leaned back to wait.

The door opened and she came in, wearing a little yellow bonnet, carrying a little yellow parasol in one hand, a little yellow purse in the other. She had bouncy chestnut hair and wide green eyes with huge lashes, a little button of a nose and a little bow-shaped mouth. Very pretty. Someone was very lucky. If she had a man—and if she didn't then the world had gone crazy.

Her eyes searched the restaurant, blinking a little from time to time as if in astonishment that she was actually there. Those green eyes met Shelter's and she started across the room, waving her parasol. Morgan looked around behind him to see who the girl could be looking at, signalling.

"Yoo-hoo," she said, bringing his head around again. He touched his lapel questioningly.

"I know you have to eat," she said as if she had just run up the street to meet him. "But, please, please hurry." She had a nice little breathless voice. She hadn't been running, she just talked like that. She had her hands together now, wringing them imploringly.

"Lady . . ."

"Please hurry, because I don't know what we shall do if we don't have at least one man with us that we can count on. With this much gold at stake, God knows what Jake Stoddard will do. He and his thugs . . ." she shuddered. "With only grandfather and myself—well, there's Harry, but he's not much help, I'm afraid. You'll meet him soon enough."

Morgan held up a hand and she sort of skittered to a stop, her eyes going wider, her breathless voice fighting through the last few words.

"Wrong man, lady."

"William C. Sterling?"

"No."

"But they said . . ." she looked around. "Where is William C. Sterling?" she asked in amazement.

"I don't know. A little advice, though, don't go talking about gold if you don't know who you're talking to."

"Did I mention the gold?" Two little gloved hands went to her lips. "Oh, no. Please just forget what I said."

"Sure." Morgan was agreeable. The waitress arrived with his breakfast and still the girl stood watching him as if he knew the secrets of William C. Sterling. That name did ring a bell, but Morgan couldn't place it. Nor at the moment did he care to try. What he wanted out of life just then was to pop the yolks on those steaming eggs and let them run all over the golden brown fried potatoes on his plate and then put it all where it would do the most good.

She seemed to suddenly realize she had no reason for standing there, spun around and walked out, yellow bustle bouncing. Morgan settled in to eat.

When he was through he had an extra cup of coffee and sat meditating. Cord would have blown town. How? When last seen he had been riding the river south. Odds were he had made the bank easily enough once he was out of gunshot range, found himself a place to hole up and dry off. This morning he would have had to make arrangements to leave St. Jo. The police wanted him, Shelter Morgan wanted him, Andy Rice wanted him.

"Not the stagecoach. Train? Best way'd be by horse, but once west of here, a man travelling alone takes his life in his hands. Could be he could hook up with a wagon train, but that's damned slow for Cord Levitt."

Shell finished the coffee, slapped down a silver

dollar, rose and walked out of the restaurant. The big man with the black leather gloves and black silk scarf was waiting on the boardwalk outside.

"Sterling?" he growled.

Shelter looked him up and down, not liking the way he was put together, big and mean and stupid. "No," he said, and he started past the big man. The man with the black gloves and black silk scarf made a mistake then, he put his hand on Morgan. He grabbed Shell's shoulder and started to turn him.

"Damn you," he said, "I'll tell you when I'm through talking to you."

He was through all right. He turned Morgan and Morgan instinctively ducked away, pulling his head back as the fist the big man threw grazed his jaw. If it had landed flush it would have done a lot of damage. There was power behind the blow and an inexplicable rage.

But the blow missed and it wasn't any more dangerous than a puff of wind. Shell came around with a left of his own which landed solidly on the big man's ear. Blood flowed from the side of his face and trickled down on his nice silk scarf. Morgan saw that as he stuck another left into the big man's face. This one flattened his nose out and sent blood exploding from the nostrils. The man was already partly out on his feet when Shell winged in the following right-hand shot.

It landed on his neck below the left ear and it should have rung a bell or won Morgan a cigar, but all it did was fold up the big man's legs at the knees and send him staggering back to tumble over the hitching rail, do a little face-first dive into the dust of the road and lie there, his booted feet twitching a little.

Morgan hovered over him a minute and then went

on his way, knowing he had done the community a service. Anybody that wore silk scarves needed a kick in the ass from time to time.

The police chief looked up at Shell with swollen red eyes as he entered the station. The lawman started to say something, shut his mouth again and then muttered, "Thought I told you to get out of town."

"You know a man called William C. Sterling?" Morgan asked.

"Yeah, don't you?"

"No." Morgan shrugged. "I've heard the name, but I can't recall where."

"Why do you want him?" the chief asked. The red eyes were narrow and hard now.

"I don't know if I do. It's just that somebody mistook me for him, and I was curious."

"They won't mistake you anymore."

"No?" Shell's eyes narrowed to match the police chief's. "Why's that?"

The chief rose, crooked a finger at Morgan and led him to a small room off the office. It was warm and close in there and smelling of decay. The dead man lay on a door placed across two sawhorses.

"William C. Sterling?" Morgan asked.

"That's right."

"Who got him?"

"You tell me," the chief said a little savagely.

Morgan shrugged. "How the hell would I know?"

"You came asking for him. Maybe your little friend with the big cannon did this?"

"Andy Rice? No. She'd be asking for a reward."

"Recall him now, do you?" the chief asked as they went out of the room.

"I've never set eyes on the man," Shelter said, "but, yeah, I've heard of him. Some sort of gunfighter, wasn't he?"

"So he thought." The chief took up his place behind his desk. The whiskey bottle had found its way into his hand again. "It didn't do him much good to be handy with a gun. The one that got him was in the back. Arnold at the livery found him outside his door when he opened up this morning. You don't know anything, is that it?"

"Nothing at all."

The police chief drummed his fingers on his desk, glowering at Morgan. "Do you know what you are going to do, my friend?"

"Sure," Shell answered cheerfully. "Get out of town like you told me to do."

"Now?" The chief wasn't smiling.

"Right now."

Shell nodded and went out. The day was bright. Boats along the river nudged each other passing up and down the Missouri. It was a dusty, dirty town. Morgan wasn't sorry to shed it and head west again. He was only sorry that he had missed Cord Levitt, blown the deal or had it blown by Andy Rice. Who knew how long it would be now before he caught up with Levitt.

But he would catch up. He owed it to the dead. They called out in the night to Shelter Morgan, asking him to send Levitt along to join them.

Shell checked out of his hotel, made a stop at the stage depot to see if anyone resembling Levitt had bought a ticket that morning, was told no, and ambled along to the train station—his best guess as to Levitt's choice of travel. The train was fast, easy and there were ways of concealing yourself on one.

Morgan walked up and down the tracks, peered into the open boxcars, rattled the doors of the locked ones and drew a lot of challenging glances from railroad employees.

Hell—maybe the bastard had drowned after all.

The man who sold the tickets thought not.

"That one—sure, I seen him. He didn't buy no ticket, though. He flagged the through freight down. I told him not to, but he did it anyway. If they hadn't had a mail sack he never would have made it. But he hopped her."

"You're sure it was him?"

"I'm sure of nothing. He looked like a drowned rat, fits your description well enough."

"Where's that freight going?"

"West. Springfield, Wichita, Santa Fe."

"I want a ticket through to Santa Fe then."

"Not today." The man shrugged. "No trains out today."

"Not today? What's that sitting in front of the station?"

"I guess you know what it is, but it's a private train. All other traffic's held up until this one's cleared through."

"Must be a hell of a big man to swing something like that."

"I wouldn't know."

"What's it waiting for now?"

"I wouldn't know that either," the trainman said.

"No," Morgan said, "I guess you wouldn't."

"What's that mean?" he bristled.

"I wouldn't know. Look, can you find out when this train is leaving, what it's waiting for?"

"Stationmaster knows," the ticket seller said dubiously. A little silver changed hands and the dubiousness became a more or less confident smile.

"I'll see what I can wring out of him."

"Do that."

Shell stood rocking on his heels, looking out along the straight twin rails which ran away to the distance like silver arrows. Levitt had done himself proud flagging that freight. There was a whole lot of land out there, half a continent, and by now Cord Levitt must be figuring he was free and clear. He wasn't. There were only so many places to get off the train, and if Morgan didn't find him at the first stop, he'd find him at the second or third.

"Santa Fe," a too-familiar voice at Shell's elbow said.

"What?"

There was Andy Rice, looking cute, pert, deadly in her black suit. One hip was cocked challengingly toward Shelter. "Santa Fe," she said, "is where Cord Levitt is going."

"How the hell do you know that?"

She smiled thinly and handed Shelter a folded newspaper which he knew without opening would have a Santa Fe banner on it.

"So?"

"I found it in his hotel room. Several articles cut out of it. Whatever he's up to, he's up to it in Santa Fe."

"Well, that leaves him to me, doesn't it?" Shelter removed his hat and wiped out the sweat band. It was getting hot. The locomotive to their backs let out a whoosh of steam.

"Why does he get left to you?" the lady with the big Colt asked.

"That's a long way to go for three hundred dollars. I didn't figure it's worth your time."

"Maybe not." She looked Morgan deliberately up and down. "But then maybe it is."

"Christ, she's joined my legion of admirers."

The dark eyes twinkled. "Maybe I have, at that."

The ticket seller had reappeared. He was behind Andy Rice, looking across her shoulder at Shell who gave him the slightest flicker of the eyes. The ticket seller nodded. He didn't know what was up, but he knew who was handing out the silver dollars.

"No train today then?" Shell asked. Andy, a slight smile pursing her lips, turned toward the ticket seller.

"Not today." The railroad man was a lousy liar. "Have to come back in the morning. There's a six-fifteen out to the West."

"Too bad. Sorry, Andy."

"I'll bet you are." She looked at the ticket seller's eyes and then at Shelter's. "What's with this train here? Broke down?"

"That's right," the railroad man agreed happily.

"Tomorrow is the best you got? Six-fifteen?"

"Sorry, yes . . . ma'am." He hesitated a little and then flushed.

Morgan told him: "That's all right, bud. A lady that goes around wearing men's clothes shouldn't get mad if you get a little confused as to what she is."

"Are you confused, Morgan?" Andy asked, and her finger touched his chin as she looked into his eyes even more deeply.

"I'm mostly confused about everything most of the time," Shelter Morgan said.

"Yeah," she muttered vaguely and then wandered off toward town with a last warning over her shoulders. "Better not be lying to me, ticket man!"

The man took off his blue cap and mopped his head. "Say—that dame carries a gun. She's not dangerous or anything, is she? I mean she wasn't too happy."

"She's as harmless as a little butterfly," Shelter answered. "What'd you find out?"

The railroad man looked around cautiously and leaned a little nearer. "They're just waiting for the last few passengers. Should be along in the next half hour. The name of the man who runs the train is Colonel Jesse Hart. I don't know what he does except to make money."

"What're the names of the people they're waiting for?"

The trainman scratched his head and Shelter figured that meant he needed more silver to weight his pockets. Two more dollars passed between them.

"If I recall . . ." the trainman hesitated, but there was no more silver forthcoming. "A man named Channing, his son and daughter. A man named Stoddard and another named William C. Sterling." Shelter was smiling and the ticket seller leaned nearer yet, peering intently at him. "Something wrong?"

"Nothing at all."

"Well, all right. That's all I can tell you. I don't have the time to talk any more anyway. I got to get to work. Glad we could do business, Mr. . . ."

"Sterling," Shelter told him. "William C. Sterling."

3.

There was a wooden bench in a ribbon of shade, and if you slid down on your spine you could prop your boots up on the hitchrail before it. Morgan did just that, waiting for the guests of Col. Jesse Hart to arrive.

He would have had time to go back to the hotel and get his belongings, but he didn't know it at the time. He didn't intend to miss that train for the sake of a few dirty shirts and a worn-out saddle.

They came rolling up the street something like an hour later. In a buggy with a fringed top was the old man with the chin whiskers, the girl in yellow—now in green—and a heavy-shouldered, dull-looking kid. If that was Harry it was no wonder the lady hadn't much confidence in him.

Shelter rose, tugging his hat lower against the harsh glare of the sun as he leaned a shoulder against the porch rail. Behind the buggy a good hundred feet rode four men. One of them seemed to have on black gloves and a black silk scarf. His face also looked a little puffy.

The buggy halted nearly in front of Shell, and he stepped down, taking the small trunk riding on the back of the buggy nearly from beneath the big kid's hands.

"Who the hell are you?" he asked and his voice was as dull as a glance at his face had promised.

"Are you Harry Channing?"

The kid seemed to have to think it over for a minute before he answered. "Yeah, who are you?" He had a thin, reddish mustache sketched on his upper lip, freckles across his nose and a brand new Smith & Wesson .38 in a brand new holster. He looked like he would like to shoot someone if that was the local custom.

"I'm Bill Sterling. *Wild Bill* Sterling," he added maliciously. The kid's hand drifted away from his belted gun.

The old man with the chin whiskers, the ramrod bearing and the sharp green eyes exactly like his daughter's had come back to see what was happening. He overheard the last of the conversation.

"You're Sterling, are you! And where the hell have you been? Didn't you get my letter and the money?"

"I got them. Sorry. I got held up on another job." Sterling, Shelter thought, had definitely gotten held up. He was lying cold and stiff in the back of the police station.

"Well, at least you're here." The old man patted at his brow with a folded cotton handkerchief he carried inside his hat, riding on his balding head.

"You told me . . ." It was the girl. Her eyes looked as puzzled as ever. "Yesterday you said you weren't William C. Sterling, our man."

"I couldn't talk just then, miss," Morgan said. "It might have meant my life."

"Oh." She blinked and nodded as if he had said

something with some meaning.

"We can stand around here in the sun all day," the kid complained.

"No. Get the bags on board, son," his father said. "Mr. Sterling, you have your baggage?"

"I'm wearing it, I'm afraid."

The old man looked him up and down, shaking his head as if it was a shame the depths some people could sink to. The men who had been riding up to the station now had swung down. They stood watching Shell with unmoving eyes.

Jake Stoddard broke away from the group and swaggered over to where Morgan stood with the Channings. The other men led their horses away toward the freight car where a ramp had been put up for loading their stock.

"Morning," Stoddard said. No one answered him. The girl looked frightened. Her little cupid's-bow mouth twitched. The old man spat to settle the dust. "Who's this?"

"Our guide. I've a right to hire a guide," Channing said.

"You got a name?" he asked Shelter.

"It's Sterling," the girl said, gathering her pique. None of them seemed to like Stoddard. Shelter figured he was on the right side of things. He didn't like the big man either. "Wild Bill Sterling. Perhaps you have heard of him, Mr. Stoddard?"

"I guess I might have." It was Stoddard's turn to spit. "Going all the way to Santa Fe with us, Mr. Sterling?"

"Of course."

"Hope so," Stoddard said with just a hint of a smile. Shelter took his words for a threat. Everything Stoddard said seemed to be a threat. What Morgan couldn't tell was if Stoddard still thought he was

Sterling. Maybe he knew damn well by now that he wasn't. Maybe it was Stoddard who had drilled the gunman in the back.

The whistle on the train blew angrily just as two black men in red jackets appeared to snatch up the equipment Stoddard's men had left scattered on the ground and hustle it away toward the train. Odd-looking men appearing ill at ease in those pretty jackets, they weren't American blacks, at least Shell didn't think so. They looked to be out of the heart of Africa. One of them had a double row of raised scars across his forehead. Shell frowned. Whoever Col. Jesse Hart was, he appeared to have his own ways.

Morgan didn't care who he was just then. He wanted to get to Santa Fe and this was the only way to get there. He would be Wild Bill Sterling all the way to New Mexico if he had to be, then make his confession and bow out. His business was with Cord Levitt and not with the Channings and their gold. They could find plenty of men willing to take their side in Santa Fe, plenty who would fight for a good payday.

The train whistled again angrily and they started that way. The girl had a little hatbox with her and Shelter carried it for her, receiving a slightly confused smile for a reward.

"Where's Colonel Hart?" Shell asked.

"In his private car, I imagine."

"You're not all together then?"

"The colonel is kindly allowing us to travel with him. I believe he is only accommodating Father. They have common friends, I think."

Shelter helped her up the steps and into the Pullman. There were only a dozen scattered plush seats in the car, two glassed-in compartments, a card table, a dining table already set with silver and a lace cloth.

Glasses couldn't be left unattended and so there were none. The carpeting on the floor brushed Shell's ankles as he helped the lady to her seat. There was a rack overhead and he started to put the hatbox there.

"Please. I'd rather have it under my seat."

Shelter shrugged and gave it to her. Touching his hat brim he started up the aisle to select a seat for himself, but Beth Channing called him back.

"What is it?"

"Won't you sit by me?" Her green eyes were wistful and very young.

"Your father might not like it, or Harry."

"Father won't mind. He mostly lets me do what I want. And Harry doesn't matter."

"I'll be happy to sit with you then," Shell said, swinging in.

A few minutes later, a silent, surly Jake Stoddard came past, trailed by his hirelings. They glanced at Morgan but said nothing, taking up places at the card table. They started a game as the train whistle blew twice and the engineer eased the throttle out. The drive wheels spun, gears clanked and then the private train of Col. Jesse Hart was on its way out of St. Jo and off across the wide plains toward the Southwest.

"It's nice to have someone we can trust," Beth said. She was near and soft and she smelled very good. She smiled up at Shell and blinked her eyes.

"It's nice to be with you."

"I'm glad you turned out to be Bill Sterling," she said. "I was afraid he'd be some old man with a tobacco-stained mustache and a dirty mouth."

"I'm glad too." There was a lot Morgan wondered about this setup, but maybe it had all been explained in the letter to the real William C. Sterling. "Why can't you trust Jake Stoddard?" Shelter asked.

"Just look at him," she said, laughing behind her hand. "Who could trust him? Did you beat him up?" Her dainty little gloved hand rested on Shell's knee briefly and then slid away.

"We had a short conversation. Nothing much." He was trying to figure out a way to word his question without being suspicious when Beth volunteered a lot of it.

"Colonel Hart suggested Stoddard and his men, God knows why, and so Father was practically forced to hire them—after all, it's the colonel's train, isn't it, and we're only travelling on it out of his sufferance."

"Yes." Shell looked out the window at the small farms rushing past, at the distant river. "It makes you wonder why Hart would run with someone like Stoddard."

"Yes, it does. Well, it's a charity thing, Father guesses."

"The colonel giving a job to Stoddard and his men?"

"Yes. Although he ought to have considered . . ." She paused. Her lips parted, revealing white, even teeth; her breath held. Shelter helped her with the sentence.

"The gold?"

"Yes." She squeezed his hand and looked around secretively.

"How did your father hear about me?"

"Well, you know. Through Dutch Schmidt."

"Yes, that's right," Shelter said quickly, knowing he'd stumbled. He decided to try keeping his mouth shut for a while. The only trouble was, he was in on this deal temporarily at least and it would have been nice to know what was happening.

The way he got it now Bo Channing, his daughter and son were going west to pick up—or try to find—

some gold. They had confided in this Colonel Hart who had urged them to hire on Stoddard and his thugs. Channing trusted the colonel, but not Stoddard so he'd also hired a little insurance in the body of William C. Sterling, deceased, who he knew by reputation but not by face through a man called Dutch Schmidt.

"Very good," Morgan said beneath his breath. He knew all of that. He knew absolutely nothing. All he could do was keep his mouth shut, watch out for the girl and her father until Santa Fe and relax while he could.

The door to the compartment opened. They heard the puffing of steam, the hiss of wind, the clacking of the wheels and then the door closed again.

"Colonel Hart," the black man who stood there said, "wishes to see the Channing family, please. No one else," he added as Stoddard started to fold his cards and saunter along. "Only the Channings."

"You're going, too," Beth said, and again she rested her hand confidingly on his leg, and again Morgan found he liked it resting there.

"Come along, Beth," Bo Channing said. Harry had found his way up too and they stood waiting for her.

"Mr. Sterling is coming."

"You heard the man," Harry squeaked. He looked into Shell's eyes, had enough of that quickly, and let his gaze slide away. "Just us."

"Father, if Mr. Sterling is going to be able to help us, he should know everything that is going on."

"We can inform him later, Beth."

"I want him to go," she said like a pouty little kid. She folded her arms, tossed back her body in the seat and sat with her lip thrust out. Like a pouty little kid, she got her way.

"All right, damnit," Bo Channing grumbled. "You come along, Sterling. I guess the colonel can't object that much."

Beth brightened up. She reached under the seat for her striped hatbox and stood up, taking it with her. Shell let her go first, then he followed her to the front of the car, past the poker-playing Stoddard.

"Didn't you hear the smoky?" Stoddard drawled. "Family only."

"Why, didn't you know I was related?" Morgan answered.

"I know a sight more about you than you think, *Mr. Sterling*," Jake Stoddard snapped.

"Do you? And how do you come to know so much, Stoddard?" Shell glanced at the cards the man beside him was holding. "Those three tens aren't good enough."

Shell grinned and started out of the car after the Channings. He heard the curses, saw the cards thrown down in anger. Another enemy. Good, it kept him on his toes. Not that he needed any special motivation. Trying to stay alive had been a full-time job for the past ten years with Shelter Morgan. The political war shaded into the personal war almost without a break. He fought and kept on fighting, and one of these days he would lose the last battle and they'd leave him out here for the coyotes. Maybe in Santa Fe.

The railroad car he entered while the African in scarlet held the door was agleam with silver and crystal. A chandelier hung from a polished mahogany ceiling. There were a half dozen huge green leather chairs, overstuffed and inviting, a long table set for dinner, leaded windows in place of the usual plate glass, silver brackets supporting the lamps on the walls where deep red, heavy draperies with gold cords flanked the windows. In the other car there had been a few blue bottle flies buzzing around. No fly would dare enter this sanctum. If he did a dozen black servants would leap on it, tearing it to bits. Whatever the colonel did do, he seemed to do it well and profitably.

He was already there, waiting. Shell had been expecting a tall, slender man with a silver mustache. What he found was a Colonel Hart with twinkling eyes, ruddy cheeks, thinning reddish hair and a belt line that had kind of gotten away from him over the years. If it hadn't been for the impeccably tailored dinner jacket, Morgan might have mistaken him for a travelling drummer.

"Hello, Bo. Glad you all finally made it," he said, using two hands to wring Bo Channing's. He shook Harry's hand as well, hugged Beth briefly, avuncularly, and then settled his dark, merry eyes on Morgan. "How are you, my name's Jesse Hart."

"Bill Sterling," Shell answered. The colonel's shake was dry and strong, his hand comfortable as if he spent a lot of time glad-handing.

"Glad to meet you."

"I brought Bill along," Bo Channing said, "on account of he's our guide. He ought to know what's what."

"Your guide?" The colonel sucked at his lower lip. "You don't take to Jake Stoddard then."

"It's not exactly that, sir."

"Well, no need to explain to me, Bo. I was just trying to help. They told me they knew Santa Fe and all the territory south to the border. And they were willing to travel. I took them on. Maybe it'll be up to me to dismiss them at Springfield." The colonel sucked on his lip some more, rocked on the balls of his feet and nodded.

"I don't think that'll be necessary, sir," Bo said.

"I want to do what's right, Bo."

"So long as they know who's in charge."

"Yes," the colonel agreed, "that's the main thing. Shall we eat? Fill our stomachs and then we can talk, all right?" He called to one of the servants in a language which wasn't English, and another table setting was brought for Morgan.

It wasn't much of a meal. Duck, roast beef, smoked pork and wild rice, scalloped potatoes in cheese sauce with new green peas and pearl onions, spiced peaches and cheesecake with cherry sauce, a couple of kinds of wine and brandy with coffee to follow. Morgan figured he knew what had happened to the colonel's waistline.

The man talked as they ate. "Me, I came up out of Georgia, just a barefoot country boy." The colonel smiled, reflecting. "I went to sea, worked my way up to mate, then to captain. Three years later I had sixteen ships, all clippers on the Orient route. I did some profitable trading in Africa, picked up these men—" he gestured to the servants—"in a battle with some slavers. Saved their hash and they took up with me. Can't get rid of 'em if I wanted to, and I don't. Faithful as a good dog. Bambo there—" he pointed with his fork at a giant of a man who stood silently to one side— "he drinks a little too much, and he's a brawler. But he wouldn't touch me if I went up to him and started to cut his fingers off one by one."

Beth blanched a little and hiccuped. The colonel apologized, "Sorry, dear. I get a little graphic."

"How'd you get into the railroad business?" Morgan asked. "Or is it your business?"

"It is. I own forty-one percent of the line we're riding on. Traded up from my clippers. Started to get weary of the sea and the salt pork, the hard weather.

Got old, I guess." He smiled. "Got me a job now where I dine like a king, ride the rails in the comfort of my own castle. When I want company, why there's always plenty to be found."

He didn't specify what sort of company he had in mind. Maybe that was a secret between him and Bambo who stood stock still, glaring, a mahogany statue.

Later they sat at an oval table with a lace cloth and sipped champagne while the train raced on across the wide land.

"How much does Mr. Sterling know about this project?" the colonel asked. He had loosened his cummerbund and was leaning back comfortably, his face satisfied and glowing.

"Not much."

"Just what was in the letter," Morgan said.

"That's all he needs to know," Harry said. Harry wasn't growing any fonder of Shelter. His big, dull face was unhappy. "He can wait till we get to Santa Fe. If you ask me, he don't need to know."

"Nonsense," Beth said. Her eyes sparkled as they lifted to Morgan's.

"The man's got a right to know. He might even want to pull out after he hears what we want to do," Bo Channing said. He smoothed his gray chin whiskers a little and leaned back, lighting a pipe after a nod from the colonel permitted it.

Channing got his pipe going good and then he waved out the match, watching the trailing smoke for a moment. "Gold in the ground is one thing. Gold already mined and smelted, some minted, is another. This ain't a wild goose hunt, Sterling."

"I didn't think it was."

"There's something like a half million there. Some coin, a lot of goldware, some jewelry, a few bars."

41

"A nice hoard. Whose is it?" Shelter asked.

"Why, it's mine!" Bo Channing said in surprise. "If I can get there first, that is."

"What I meant was, how did it come to be yours?"

"Pa . . ." Harry shook his head in warning.

"Settle down, boy. The man is with us or against us. I'm judging Mr. Sterling is with us.

"It came about in this way," he began, puffing contentedly on his pipe as he spoke. "In the old days—and not very damned long ago—all of Mexico, most of the southwestern United States was broken up into Spanish land grants. Grants given to families in favor with the king of Spain, those who had been warriors or relations or simply politicians." Morgan nodded. "Oftentimes these grants would run up to the thousands of square miles. Why not? Anybody crazy enough to want to come over to the New World and live out in those deserts might as well feel like a rich man even if some never were to be."

"Some of those grants proved amazingly rich though," Shelter put in.

"Sure they did. Take the Ybarra grant in Chihuahua. There was so much silver in the hills there that the king himself snatched the land back from Ybarra who'd been working the silver with Indian slaves at an enormous profit. Most grants didn't prove out like that one. Generally they built their haciendas and ran cattle over their huge parcels, selling the steers for leather and tallow when the Spanish ships came in. Those long-horned Spanish cattle bred tough—same stock as the Texas longhorns—they liked the dry land, thrived on the sagebrush and cactus diet. A lot of people got rich without half trying."

"But not the *Indios*."

"No, not the poor *Indios*. Times changed in Mexico. The hungry many rebelled against the wealthy few. Well, you know all of that. I'm talking now of one particular family, the Castillo y Cortes family that had a huge rancho just the other side of the border, south of Santa Fe."

"What happened to them?"

"Time and lack of fertility pared them away, Mr. Sterling. Finally there was only the grandfather and his son's young daughter left. Young—well, Beth's age. She upped and married a Yankee. With grandfather's faint approval. There weren't any good men with noble blood around the place anyway. Everyone had run out or been pushed out, returning to Spain before some of that blood the rebels were spilling down south could touch them."

"But the young couple stuck it out."

"They did. Rebels under that Ramon Chavez all across the country were tearing down the old haciendas, driving people out. The government is still new in Mexico, Sterling, bandits run the territories in the mountains and the north, way down south, anyplace far from Mexico City. Finally the old man died and the woman, Donna Elena, and her husband looked at each other one day and decided to get out. Not back to Spain but to the United States where her man had people.

"They gathered up the gold and silver, everything valuable, and started toward the border with twenty servants carrying the goods, driving donkeys before them. They didn't make it."

Bo looked up and shook his head. "Wasn't Chavez or the revolutionaries that got them in the end. It was Yaqui Indians. Heard of them, have you? Fierce little devils, like sand rattlers. Tough, determined, merciless. They got the entire party and killed them— apparently. There was never any word from a survivor."

"Then they got the gold."

"No. No, they didn't. The American had hidden the stuff when he saw how it was going to be. Travel was too slow with it and he wanted to get out fast, get his Donna Elena to safety. He didn't go fast enough."

"This is the gold you're after?" Shelter asked.

"That's it. I have a map and it's a good one. Shows every ridge and gully in that area."

"Mr. Channing," Shell said reluctantly. "I hate like hell to crush a man's dreams, but you know how it goes with these treasure maps. How could you know it was authentic?"

Bo Channing sucked at his pipe and squinted at Morgan. "How could I know? Why—didn't I tell you?—that American husband of Donna Elena's was my brother."

4.

Shelter sat there feeling a little vacant. "Wasn't that mentioned in Father's letters?" Beth asked. "I was sure he told you that it was his brother Abe who married the Spanish woman."

"I'm not thinking straight," Shelter said. He wasn't doing a very good job of playing William C. Sterling. "I just wondered how you knew no one else had found it."

"Man, that's bad country. Yaquis and rebels. No one goes down there without a reason. No one is going to stumble over it by accident."

"How did the map get out?" Colonel Hart asked, and Shelter was grateful to him for inquiring. He wondered that himself.

"Nothing to it. The day before the massacre, he sent a lone rider on ahead. Just on the chance. The man, an Indian, happened to choose the right direction and get out. He posted it in a border town called Chadwick and eight weeks later I got it."

There was a little more chatter and a little more wine, but Morgan didn't pay much attention to it. He was happy to get back to his comfortable seat in the rear car and watch the countryside race past while Beth, still holding that hatbox, dozed.

It began to grow dark early although they were racing with the sun. Bambo came through lighting the lanterns in the car, and on his way back he stopped and spoke to Shelter and Beth.

"Your compartments. Come, I show you." And he smiled very nicely, showing a lot of white teeth behind his thick lips. Somehow Shell wasn't able to smile back.

He rose anyway and walked behind Beth. The Stoddard gang was still playing cards. No one so much as glanced at Shelter as he walked past.

The sleeping car was forward. Bambo showed Beth her compartment first, opening the door with a little flourish, stepping back with a bow that brought his head almost down to Shelter's level. Damn, he was a big man.

"Goodnight, Mr. Sterling," Beth said in that breathless way of hers and Shell smiled.

"Goodnight. Lock your door and sleep well."

"And your compartment," Bambo was saying as they walked on, "is the blue. Every door, you will see, has on it a different color. So. Green, yellow, blue."

Shelter was fascinated. He almost listened. The big African opened the door and Morgan went in, the way lighted by the brilliance of Bambo's smile. He closed the door and looked around. Wide, four-poster bed, bureau with oval mirror, two chairs of some gold material with oval backs. A carpeted floor, a built-in basin. And no lock on the door.

It didn't matter. Morgan took off his gunbelt and sagged onto the bed, staring at the door as the train clacked on through the settling dusk.

"You've got yourself into a place where you're not wanted," he told himself. There was gold at stake, and plenty of it. Stoddard advertised greed with his eyes. The colonel might have plenty of his own, but maybe a man didn't get too much gold. Everyone but Beth and her father would be happy to see Morgan blow away. Maybe he ought to just tell them right now that he was only a stowaway. What would they do? Stop the train and put him off in the middle of nowhere?

Maybe.

He couldn't chance that. He had to get to Santa Fe. There was a man there who needed killing. Shell got up, propped a chair under the knob—it didn't fit real well, but it would at least give him a warning—pulled off his boots and sat down on the bed again.

After a while he lay back, closing his eyes while the lantern on the wall burned low and the train raced the rising moon across the plains.

His eyes blinked open. Somehow he had fallen asleep. The lantern had depleted its fuel and flickered out. It was dark and cool. It took Shelter a moment to remember where he was, another longer moment to discover what had awakened him.

There was a tapping in the corridor outside his compartment. A tapping he had had trouble distinguishing above the constant clatter and clacking of the train. There it was again.

And again. Like the slapping of a shutter in the wind. Except there were no shutters on this railroad car. Shelter slipped from the bed, filling his hand with his Colt. He crossed to the door, listened for a while and then quietly slid the chair from beneath the knob.

The powerful hand shot out and latched onto Morgan's wrist as he opened the door and he was yanked into the empty corridor, his pistol dropping free as his wrist was bent under, forcing his fingers open.

Stupid.

There was time for Shelter to curse his own stupidity. He had been drawn out by his own curiosity and the waiting man had been quick and strong. Very quick, very strong.

Morgan threw a forearm into his assailant's face and produced a small grunt of pain. The train swayed around a bend and both men were bumped toward the wall.

Shell's attacker had him by the throat now, shaking him, powerful thumbs digging into the carotid arteries, shutting off blood to the brain as Shell clawed at the fingers.

"Bambo . . ." Was it Bambo? Morgan tried to grab a handful of hair and from the result knew it was one of the Africans with close-cropped wooly hair. He also knew the man was very big. He had pried one of the fingers loose from around his neck now—the little finger of the left hand—and Morgan bent it back, hard.

Bone snapped and the African grunted again—a little more loudly this time. Meanwhile Morgan was driving his knee up at the black man's groin. Once, twice, three times, his kneecap bouncing off hard thigh muscle.

Morgan stamped down. His leather bootheel smashed painfully against the African's toe and there was still another grunt. Morgan wanted more than a grunt. His own head was filled with flashing colored light. He was going out and still the powerful, strangling hands gripped his throat.

Shell drove his fist into the African's crotch, and with a howl of pain he fell back, his hands falling from Shell's neck. Morgan followed up the brief advantage. Two hard right hooks smashed into the African's face. They didn't have a lot of effect.

Bambo—if that was who it was—dove for the Colt revolver which showed only as a thin, bluish glint against the floor of the darkened corridor. Shell swung his boot out hard, catching Bambo in the face and the African rolled away, angry, panting hoarsely, blood trickling from his nostrils.

He came in quick and grabbed Shell by the shirt sleeve, spinning him around. A black fist slammed into Morgan's forehead as he tried to duck a roundhouse punch and Shell was staggered backward toward the Pullman's door. He tried to stop himself, but the black man charged ahead, head down, bulling him through the door and onto the platform.

Morgan's back came up hard against the iron railing. The noise outside the car was startlingly loud. The land beyond the train was dark as the railroad locomotive and its string of toy cars rushed past. Below, iron wheels slashed against iron rails.

Below was where the African meant to put Shelter.

A straight left hook backed the black man away momentarily and Shelter had a chance to get set before the next wild onslaught. The African had no science to his fighting, but he was damned determined. He threw an overhand right which grazed Shell's temple before he could get his guard up. A following left would have taken Shell's head off if he hadn't ducked.

Morgan got off a good solid right which snapped the African's head back. The train swayed and he lost his balance briefly again, but so had the black man so there was no harm done. The big man came in again and Shelter peppered his face with three lefts. The blood still flowed from his flaring nostrils, but he seemed unhurt, unstoppable.

Shelter kicked out at the big man's kneecap, wanting to break it, but the kick was blocked. The moon shone now on the black face, scarred, tattooed, bloodied, on the white eyes which stared out almost without intelligence, but with plenty of malice.

Bambo yelled—a terrible, primitive yell which even the racketing of the train could not cover—and he threw himself bodily at Morgan.

And then he was gone.

Morgan ducked, shouldered up as he felt the solid body collide with his, and flipped the African over the rail, where the whirling iron teeth of the railway cars devoured the flesh and bones of Bambo. There was a terrible, guttural cry which filled Shell's ears for a brief second and then was cut off sharply. The night was silent after that, silent but for the racketing, the squeaking and chanting of the train.

It wasn't until Morgan got back inside the car and closed the door with his back that he could hear his own ragged breathing. He stayed there for a while, his back against the door, shutting out the ghost of Bambo, letting his heart slow, his breathing quiet. Then he walked forward along the carpeted corridor and picked up the big Colt.

Staggering a little, he made his compartment, went in and shut the door. Crossing to the basin he filled it with water, undressing to rinse off by the faint light of the moon which now peered through his compartment window.

At the tap on his door he spun, snatching the Colt up. The door handle moved a little and then the door swung open. The hammer of the Colt in Morgan's hand ratcheted back.

"Mr. Sterling? Oh!"

It was Beth, standing in a wrapper, her blond hair loose around her shoulders, staring open-mouthed at the naked warrior before her.

"I'm sorry," she said, turning half away. "I heard noises. I thought something had happened."

"No." Morgan put the Colt down and wrapped a towel around his hips. "Nothing has happened."

"Maybe it was a nightmare." She had closed the door behind her and now she was leaning against the wall, her voice becoming very breathy indeed. "I sometimes have nightmares. I really don't like sleeping alone."

"No?" Shell was wary. Was this another game, another trap? If it was, it was a damned good one. Beth Channing came forward in three quick little steps and took hold of Shell's forearms.

"Kiss goodnight?" she asked, looking up at him, the moonlight in her eyes. Her lips were parted, moist and full.

It was a little kiss goodnight that turned into something stormy when Shell pulled her into his arms. Her mouth searched his, her tongue tasting his lips, her body sagging heavily against his, so that her pelvis met Shell's.

"You said a kiss goodnight."

"I'll make it a good night," she said in that breathy little way. Her wrapper had fallen open and beneath it Shelter could see her full, young breasts straining at the sheer fabric of her white nightdress.

"I'll bet you would." His hands slid up over her hips to cup her breasts and she stood, her head tilted back, her eyes cool and sparkling, watching.

"You act as if you don't trust me."

He didn't. "I hardly know you," was what he said.

Her hands reached up, took his and pressed them firmly to her breasts. His thumbs toyed with the nipples and she made a small pleasured sound deep in her throat.

Morgan stepped back, looked her up and down and dropped the towel from around his waist. Beth's tongue darted out and touched her upper lip nervously.

He turned his back to her and walked to his bed to sit, watching out of the darkness. Beth shrugged her shoulders slightly, holding her arms behind her, and the wrapper she was wearing slipped from her back, landing silently against the floor. She stood there in that sheer white garment, the moon revealing every stunning inch of her: long, tapered thighs; full, buoyant breasts, round and pink-nippled; long golden hair fanning down across her back and shoulders; full lips pouting and smiling at once; eyes inviting; arms outstretched in a summoning gesture.

"No? You don't want to come to me?" she teased.

"You come here."

"How about now?" As if by magic the white gossamer that had sheathed her body in that flimsy cocoon slid away and Beth Channing stood naked and proud before Morgan.

"Now, yes." He stood and walked to her. Her hands found him and wrapped around him, feeling the slow pulsing of his erection. She leaned against him with a shudder, her soft breasts flattening against his hard-muscled chest. Her right hand slipped behind Shell, clenching his buttock, a finger trailing up the narrow crevice there as her other hand slowly stroked his shaft, the thumb teasing the head of it.

"Now," she puffed, "I've changed my mind. I want to go with you. To the bed."

He led her there. She still held onto his erection as if afraid of losing it. That was one thing Beth Channing didn't have to worry about on that night. Morgan didn't mean to take it away from her. He meant to give it to her again and again.

Shelter sat on the bed and she went to her knees, her eyes bright with interest as she studied the maleness of Shelter Morgan, hefting his sac gently, lovingly, running a teasing finger up along the warm length of his shaft.

Her tongue followed the inner surface of his thigh and she suddenly bit him there, an impulsive, hungry act.

"Easy, woman, I can't afford any damage there."

"Don't worry," she said and she stood to hover over Shell, to step nearer so that her soft abdomen was before his lips. "I won't do anything to hurt you."

Morgan let his hands run up her thighs, find the soft

blond bush flourishing between her legs. A finger darted inside, finding Beth warm, moist, ready for him, the firm tab of flesh there swollen with need.

She spread her legs a little and sat down on his lap facing him, her fingers guiding Shelter inside of her. She hovered there for just a second, with only the head of his erection inside her heated body, and then with a shudder, she lowered herself, taking him in to the hilt.

"Any good?" Shell asked. She smiled and kissed him.

"Very good." A hand slid behind her buttocks and touched Shell where he entered her, pressing his sac up against the wet flesh. "You're so big . . . very big."

Morgan lay back, his hands reaching up to find Beth's breasts. He lay there kneading them while she shifted and experimentally lifted her hips, nudging her pelvis against him.

Morgan could feel the loosening of her inner muscles, the soft trickling warmth. He could smell her close and near, and looking up he could see her head thrown back, looking into the distance, her jaw clamped shut, her upper lip peeled back to allow the moonlight to glint on her white, even teeth, damp and sharp.

"Don't move," Beth said, but she was moving. She began with a tremor and then she suddenly thrust against him, rolling, pitching, swaying, her body giving forth small liquid sounds as she gasped deep in her throat. "Oh, God," she cried out and Shelter reached up to hook her neck and pull her down. His mouth pressed against hers, bruising her lips. He reached behind her and gripped her ass with both hands, spreading her, drawing her against him as he arched his back, swept along by his own needs. She gasped again, nearly choking on the exclamation as Morgan drove it in to the hilt again and again, his rhythm as mechanical and solid as the driving of the locomotive's wheels.

He came suddenly, copiously and Beth stifled a cry by

biting on a knuckle as he completed the act, lifting her to a frenzied second climax.

They lay back on Shell's bed, her breathing close and childlike, her fingers toying with the dark hair on his chest, still joined together.

"I don't want you to get in trouble," Morgan said, kissing the top of her head. "Won't your father wonder about you if he wakes up?"

"He won't. He always sleeps like a log if he's had anything to drink. That wine at dinner will keep him deeply asleep."

"And Harry?" The finger stopped its search of Morgan's chest briefly.

"Harry doesn't matter," she said. She turned her head and looked up at him. "Do you know what I wish?"

"What?" he asked through a yawn.

"I wish Father would give up this idea, just forget about searching for that gold."

"You do?"

"Sure," she said in a voice that had gotten rather squeaky, "I don't want to ride out in the desert with all those Indians, all those *bandidos* around! They might kill us, all of us."

"Maybe you can stay in a hotel in Santa Fe," Morgan suggested.

"I'd like that—especially if you'd stay with me. But I'd still worry about Father and Harry—and you have to go along, don't you? I know you're a man of your word, Bill Sterling, and you promised to go."

"Yes," Morgan said a little uncomfortably, "I agreed."

"It won't be so bad out there with you, I suppose, but still . . ." Her thought faded away and she shivered a little. Not from the cold, but from fear. Well, she had a right to be afraid, Shelter thought.

He held her tightly and after a while she fell asleep,

54

breathing quietly in his arms. Morgan must have dozed off as well, but if he did it was unintentional and for a brief period. He spent a lot of the night watching that compartment door, waiting for another surprise.

In the morning he rolled out and stood looking down at Beth. It was still gray outside the compartment window. No one seemed to be stirring in the corridor. The train clanked and rattled on.

"William C. Sterling," she yawned.

"Yes." Morgan stood looking down at her sleepy figure, at the full breast, pale and smooth, the rosebud nipple peering up at him. Her ass was full and round too, engaging.

"Do it again."

"What again?" he asked teasingly.

"Shove it in me. I'm warm and ready."

She was all of that. She scooted forward a little, face-down, and then drew her knees up under her. Shelter saw her hand reach back and grope for him. The pink cleft hidden among the golden down between her legs was inviting, eager. Shell eased up behind her.

"I'll put it in," Beth said.

"Whatever appeals to you," Morgan said. Her hand closed around his erection eagerly and she drew him forward, rubbing the head of his shaft in small circles across the erect tab of flesh between her own legs. It was maddening.

"In a little. Just a little," she puffed.

It went in just a little. The head of his erection disappeared into the soft pink flesh. Beth's thighs were quivering. Her mouth gaped open as if she couldn't catch her breath. Shelter leaned far forward and kissed the soft mound of her ass.

"A little more . . . just a little," she said in what was nearly a whimper. Morgan obliged. Another inch. Outside the sun was dawning. The scattered rays of light which fell through the window highlighted her golden hair.

"A little . . . oh, goodness!" she said and the little more became all of his length as her hands reached between her thighs and groped for him, pulling him in as a liquid sound, a soft shudder, let Morgan know he had touched a deep well within Beth Channing.

She rocked forward and back now, rubbing her face against the sheets of Morgan's bed, lifting her tail higher and higher, her face contorted with concentration as Morgan drove it in time and again until she was sobbing with joy. With a final twisting thrust Morgan came to his own climax and stood behind her, slowly letting his need ebb away.

In the corridor now they could hear one of the Africans ringing a little triangle, calling them to breakfast.

"Oh, dear," Beth said. She drew away and sat up, rubbing her eyes as if she had just awakened from a dream. She blinked at Shelter and smiled wanly. "You make me tired, Mr. Sterling."

"That's all?"

"Tired and very happy."

"Good." Morgan bent over and kissed her head once. "You'd better get dressed. You'll be lucky to make it back to your compartment without getting caught."

"I don't care if I am caught," she pouted.

"I do." Shell stepped into his trousers. "Your father might not be too thrilled to have me along if he knows you've slept with me. I'd be out of a job."

"You would, wouldn't you?" Her fingers went to her lips. "And I'd have no one—we'd have no one to watch out for our interests." Beth scampered from the bed then and picked up her nightgown. Lifting her arms overhead she shimmied into it, then slipped into the wrapper. "Goodbye. No, good morning is better, isn't it? Good morning, Bill Sterling. I'll see you at breakfast. I'll try very hard to ignore you."

She came to him on quick little feet, kissed him with warm, parted lips and then went to the door, peering out cautiously for a moment before, with one glance back, she slipped out. Morgan stood smiling, watching the closed door.

He dressed and shaved and went out just as the African with the triangle came by for the second time. He strode along in his wake toward the dining car.

Colonel Hart was there, sipping coffee from a china cup, and so was Harry Channing. Bo arrived a minute later with Beth on his heels. She did a good job of ignoring him.

Bambo never did show up.

5.

"It doesn't really surprise me," Colonel Hart was saying as they finished off their huge breakfast. The colonel's cheeks were glowing and Morgan thought that the rosy little man was a morning drinker. "I have had trouble with Bambo in the past. He's not like the other boys. So when I saw that someone had been into my liquor stock, I suspected Bambo."

"But you couldn't find him on the train?"

"No. Nowhere. Every inch of the train has been searched—excepting the freight cars. There's really no way to get back to them while the train is rolling."

"What do you think could have happened?" Harry Channing asked around a last mouthful of omelet.

"I am afraid that poor Bambo filled himself with my liquor and somehow fell off the train. What do you think, Mr. Sterling?" the colonel asked, shifting his gaze suddenly to Morgan.

"I wouldn't have any idea," Shell said.

"No. Of course you wouldn't. By the way, Mr. Sterling, we do have a man who's very good with leeches and carbolic. I notice you have a rather large bruise on your

58

forehead."

"It's all right," Morgan said, putting his linen napkin on the table. "I generally stumble around when I'm sleeping in a strange place. I did last night and walked into the door."

"It happens."

"More than people think," Shell said. "In fact it's downright dangerous to go wandering around in the dark. A man ought to stay in bed."

No one answered. Bo and Harry exchanged a questioning glance, not understanding what was going on around them. If the colonel knew, Shell thought he did a damned fine job of acting. Maybe he didn't know. He seemed the same affable, red-cheeked man he had been the day before, hardly a murderer by proxy. Maybe Bambo had just had too much to drink and gone a little crazy.

Maybe the sun would go down at noon today.

When the train pulled into Springfield, Shelter was still thinking about Bambo without having come to any conclusion. He sat alone in the Pullman in back of the dining car watching a brooding Jake Stoddard and his gang play cards. Beth was with her father and brother, watching Springfield draw toward them through the window.

When it stopped they all got to their feet, wanting to get out and stretch their legs.

It was warm and sunny outside. A few waiting passengers crowded the platform, craning their necks toward the locomotive, then turning eyes down to their tickets, having it explained to them again and again by a railroad man that this was a private train.

Shelter strode up the sunny plankwalk and into the depot where he looked around aimlessly. He bought a Springfield newspaper and picked up some molasses candy in a paper sack.

By the time he returned to the platform the locomotive whistle had given a short blast. The engineer was ready to creep ahead to the water tank.

The kid with the thatch of yellow hair and torn overalls found Morgan just as he was about to step on the train.

"Mr. Sterling?"

"That's right."

"Lady said to give you this note."

The kid handed Shell a folded piece of paper and Morgan gave him a nickel. Frowning, he glanced up and down the platform. The note was written in a small, cramped hand.

"Mr. Sterling," it read, "Something of great importance has come up. Please meet me at the freight dock. Side entrance to depot, across from the grain store." It was signed, "Beth."

What the hell of "great importance" could have come up in Springfield? The answer was almost anything. Morgan didn't have a handle on this expedition of the Channings yet. He wasn't quite sure who he trusted, who he believed. But the Channings were paying his wages, or thought they were, and if the lady wanted him, he would go.

He started south along the plankwalk, stepped down where it ended and turned up the narrow alley beside the depot, following the sign that read Freight Office.

The shade beside the depot was cool and deep. He passed a water barrel and a pile of empty crates. A rat scuttled away. He could see the loading ramp ahead of him, but no Beth. She must be around the other side.

Maybe she was, maybe she wasn't. The big man with the shotgun was there, however—directly in front of Morgan, the twin muzzles of a big ten-gauge staring at his midsection.

"Hold it right there," the man commanded.

He was a wide-shouldered, thick-chested working man, someone hired for a simple job. Go out and cut this Bill Sterling in half with a shotgun.

But he wasn't a gunman.

Morgan threw himself to one side and the shotgun exploded in the close confines of the alley, the buckshot tearing long splinters from the weathered gray walls of the grain store next to the alley.

The big man had cut loose both barrels at once. The kick had lifted the muzzle of the ten-gauge into the air, and a cloud of black smoke rolled down the alley. The man with the shotgun turned around very slowly and dropped onto his face.

Firing from one knee, Shell's Colt, its thunder lost in the roar of the scattergun, had sent a .44-40 slug to its mark, stopping the big man's heart even before he hit the ground.

Morgan kept moving. He had been ambushed before. They never sent one man. Bushwhackers work in teams. Being cowards, they need the reassurance. Morgan rolled out of instinct. It was a good thing he did.

A rifle spoke from the roof of the depot and a bullet kicked up a spume of dust at Shell's heel. Morgan was flat on his back when he triggered off the big Colt again. It bucked in his hand and spat death and flame.

The man on the roof took it in the throat. A gaping, bloody wound was torn open there. His hands opened and the rifle fell from his hands, clattering to the roof, sliding off to the floor of the alley. The gunman followed, dropping in a shower of his own blood to land hard on his back against the oily earth.

Morgan looked ahead of him and then started back, moving in a crouch. The train had started ahead toward the water tank. The whistle shrilled again.

He rounded the corner of the depot, seeing the heads on the platform turned toward him, toward the alley where the noise of gunfire had sounded.

The shot from behind him took him by surprise. *Careless.* Damned careless. Morgan spun and drew his pistol, nearly sitting down in the process, waiting for the second shot, the one with his name on it, to slam into his body, ripping muscle and tendon, artery and bone apart, sending Shelter Morgan down to join those he had sent ahead to pave the way.

There was no second shot.

He squinted into the yellow sunlight, frowning. A little fine dust sifted down behind a waist-high porch attached to the back of the grain store. He started cautiously that way, Colt in hand, hammer thumbed back.

The dead man lay behind it, his eyes open wide, flies gathering already to walk across his face, in and out of bloody nostrils. Beside him was a Winchester. There was no one else around. Nothing stirred but the train on the tracks, the last of its freight cars just now passing Morgan, then the red caboose where a brakeman in a blue uniform clung to a rail, staring at Shelter and the crumpled body.

Shell holstered his gun. No one came running. The local law was apparently far away and slow in coming. No one at the depot could see the body for the porch. That kept a mob of onlookers from descending. Shell looked to the east once more, then stepped away from the dead man, walking along the tracks to catch up with the train at the water tower.

"Why, no," Beth said, "I never wrote this note. It's nothing like my handwriting."

She handed the letter back to Morgan who poked it away in his vest. He didn't think she'd written it, but he had to ask. Beth looked puzzled.

"What was it about?"

"Nothing. An old friend."

Morgan leaned back, shutting his eyes, and the train ran on. All right—who the hell had tried to gun him? Hart, Channing, Stoddard? Bambo's friends? And who had shot the third bushwhacker? That made no sense at all. People don't do something like that secretly. They make it known when they save your life.

The train lurched forward and refueled. Once its tank was full of water it was ready for the long run across the dry plains to the Southwest. The next stop was Wichita, but it was a long run. There wasn't much to do but lean back, take it easy and rest—with one eye open.

No one tried to knife Shell that night. No one came creeping around to spread her legs for him. The train rambled west.

Wichita was full of cows and cowboys and a mean marshal called Hickok. No one sent a note inviting Shelter into an alley. When they pulled out again on the last long leg it was hot and dry, and Morgan was soaked in his own perspiration. They all were—except Beth who was one of those women who knows the secret of appearing fresh and powdery all the time.

She sat close to him, but they hardly spoke. Morgan had the idea her daddy had given her the word. Her brother had taken up with Stoddard and his crowd, playing poker and losing steadily. Shell mentioned it to Bo Channing.

"What business is it of yours?" Channing asked. His attitude toward Morgan seemed to have gone a little sour.

"I'm along to watch out for your best interests, Mr. Channing. I thought you'd want to know that the kid's betting heavily and losing. He's paying with IOUs and Stoddard's taking them."

"Harry hasn't got any money."

"He must plan on having some shortly, wouldn't you say?"

Bo Channing looked a little worried now. "Yeah. He's got to be warned, I guess." He looked up at Shell. "Will you do it, Sterling?"

"Me? I thought we were on the outs."

"No. It's not that. It's the damned heat and nervousness. You haven't done anything to me. Look, I've never been real close to the kid. He'll resent anything I tell him. I thought maybe you could clue him in, man to man."

"Harry doesn't like me."

"But he'd listen to you. I know he would."

"Do you? Listen, Channing, I'll be frank. I think Harry's got himself a problem of some kind. He went and bought a gun and can't wait to use it. He's throwing away money he hasn't got at the poker table. He's asking for trouble down the line, and I don't think I'm the one to steer him away from it. More likely I'll be the start of it."

"You're right," Bo Channing said. He tugged at his gray chin whiskers. "I can't handle the kid. I'll admit it. His mother spoiled him and when she passed away, the kid took it personal—why, he acts as if I killed her," and the dry little laugh that followed was totally unconvincing. Bo was straddling a wire between anger and pity. Morgan began to wonder if Bo Channing was quite all right. What had he hired Sterling for anyway? Sterling was a known gunman with a few notches to show for his efforts. Was there someone Channing figured on having killed down the line?

Morgan was glad of one thing—at Santa Fe he was pulling up stakes and departing. He would rather ride out on the desert with a bunch of Yaquis than with this group.

"I'll talk to him," Shelter said at last, only because he figured Sterling would have, and he started off down the carpeted corridor toward the Pullman where the perpetual card game continued. He got there as Harry Channing was writing yet another IOU.

Stoddard looked up with dark, red-rimmed eyes, challenging Morgan silently. Shelter looked over Harry's shoulder and caught the amount. It was a thousand dollars.

"You take an IOU for that amount from someone with empty pockets?"

"What the hell do you care, Sterling?"

"I don't. I just thought I'd sit in if all you're playing for is paper. Hell, I can sign my name as often as the next man."

"I intend to pay," Harry Channing said coldly.

"How?"

"That's none of your damned business," Stoddard interrupted.

"Jake," another of the thugs said, "let's finish with this jasper once and for all. Let me throw him off the train."

The man was big enough to do it, and he seemed to think he was tough enough. He had a sagging, whiskered face, watery blue eyes and almost girlish lips which looked sinister somehow.

"Leave him be, Crabbe." Stoddard looked up from his cards. "A man like Mr. Sterling usually gets what he deserves in the end."

"Up some alley?" Morgan asked, but that didn't draw any blood apparently. Jake Stoddard shrugged as if he didn't know what Shell was talking about.

Morgan returned his attention to the kid. "How much have you lost, Harry?"

"What the hell do you care?" the kid asked, trying on a growl he must have learned from Stoddard. He leaned back in his chair, hooking his thumbs behind his belt.

"Your father asked me to talk to you."

"Tell him to screw himself."

"How much?"

"Fifteen thousand," he said casually, and Morgan just looked into the big red face with pity.

"Throwing a lot away, aren't you?"

"There'll be plenty."

"Supposing there isn't? Suppose the gold is gone? Suppose your father doesn't mean to cut you in? You think Jake is going to let you off the hook?"

Crabbe spoke up. "Leave the kid alone, Sterling. Or I'll throw you off this train with or without Jake's OK."

"It's been tried," Shelter said very softly. "The last man who tried it is a long way back now. He won't be riding any trains anymore."

"I don't know what the hell you're talking about," Crabbe grumbled. "I guess you're trying to scare me, eh, Santos?" he asked of the wiry Mexican across the table. Santos's black eyes flashed to Morgan but he said nothing.

"Deal," was all Stoddard said as Harry pushed the IOU across to him. The fourth thug, the bald one who hadn't spoken, started spreading the greasy cards around. Stoddard looked challengingly at Shell, but Morgan just walked away. Bo hadn't said anything about dragging the kid away by the collar. There was a little ripple of laughter behind Morgan. He didn't pay any more attention to that than to a hovering fly.

He went forward and walked to his compartment. It looked like hell. Someone had come in and ripped the place apart looking for something. Morgan cursed and looked around slowly, shaking his head.

"Wrong guess." He didn't have anything anyone would be anxious to find, but someone thought he might. He tossed the ripped mattress back on the bed and lay down on it, watching the ceiling until his eyes closed and he slept again.

Santa Fe was all adobe and yellow sunlight, red earth

and dust, dark faces, burros, old women in black, peasants in white wearing brightly colored striped serapes, smells of tortillas and beans, of dry, gritty lives. Peppers hung in bright red strings from porches, drying in the sun, ollas, holding water, precious in this country, hung beside them. All of this Morgan saw from the train window as they pulled into Santa Fe.

Stepping down into the brilliant sunlight, he could feel the heat through his boot soles, feel the waves of it rippling across his body. Dry, tugging, insistent. He squinted and walked ahead, Beth on his arm, looking cool and bouncy, very young. She carried only the hatbox.

"What about the rest of your luggage? Do you want me to get it?"

"The colonel's people will deliver it to the hotel. The Western Skies is the name of it. It's on—" she searched her memory—"Barcelona Avenue."

The locomotive gave a heaving gasp and a little steam escaped the relief valve. There were laborers already at work unloading the freight cars. Stoddard and his men were retrieving their gear, seeing to their horses, some of which looked a little sick after the long ride. Harry was hanging around with them, slouching like Stoddard, a cigarette in the corner of his mouth.

And, then, goddamnit, she appeared.

Morgan ground his teeth savagely. The ramp was placed onto the iron hooks which held it and the freight car door opened. The Mexican who had started to jump up and slide the door leaped back quickly.

The dark-haired woman in a man's suit came out, leading a tall buckskin horse. She squinted into the sunlight, tugged her hat lower and then, with everyone gaping, stepping back, Andy Rice came ahead. Some of the men asked her questions, but she brushed them aside and led her horse away from the train, not glancing at the tall man who stood on the platform, his eyes glowing like coals.

"Friend of yours?" Beth asked, squeezing Shell's arm.

"No."

"Who is he?"

"You wouldn't believe me." He patted her hand. "I've got to have a talk with him. You'll be all right?"

She looked a little put out, but she answered, "Yes, of course. The colonel is going to take us all over to the hotel in a carriage. You'll be along later?" she asked a little anxiously.

"Of course I will."

She squeezed his arm again meaningfully and Shell smiled. He stepped off the platform and started after Andy Rice, Beth watching him curiously.

His bootheels kicked up tiny, angry puffs of dust. He reached the side road Andy had taken and saw her, mounted now, riding away, coattails flapping. He hollered twice, but her head didn't turn. Shell stood hands on hips, watching for a minute, then he turned back toward the depot.

Beth was gone. He was losing all the way around.

He made up his mind not to worry about it. He was in Santa Fe for one reason and only one. Cord Levitt was here. Somewhere. And the women could wait. Cord Levitt had just reached the end of a long, long rope.

6.

Morgan found the Western Skies Hotel easily enough, but it was a long hot walk. He was drenched in perspiration by the time he got there, walked through the tiled, dark lobby to the small semicircular desk and asked for his room.

"We have no rooms," the slender Mexican with the narrow mustache said.

"I'm with Colonel Hart's party," Morgan said. "Mr. Sterling."

"Oh, yes!" The man brightened up. "Colonel Hart's party. Yes! A room for you on the second floor." He pointed toward the gallery above. "Room 206."

Shelter took the key and started up while the desk clerk sputtered something about luggage at his back. The stairs were carpeted. Upstairs the gallery, porticoed, set here and there with small round tables, ran around three sides of the hotel.

206 was to his right, the third room down. The door was locked and when he went in there was no one waiting. That suited Shelter fine. He had had

enough of games, of people ignoring the old custom of knocking on your door before entering.

He walked to the French window opposite, opened the latch and stepped out onto the sun-blasted balcony, peering up the street below, seeing nothing. It was siesta time, the middle of the day when all the intelligent citizens of Santa Fe dozed in the shade. To work out in the sun was very dangerous in the middle hours.

Morgan closed the door behind him, walked to the bed and sat there for a minute, thinking of nothing at all. Then he rose, stretched and, with some reluctance—and a regretful glance back at the soft bed—started out. Andy Rice wouldn't be having herself a siesta. She was after Cord Levitt and she would be working at it.

He walked to the lobby and started out the door. The familiar figure was lounged in a chair in the corner of the lobby, near a potted nopal cactus.

Her hat was tugged low. She was slumped far down in the chair, her legs crossed. Morgan knew she was watching him from beneath the hat. He walked to her and stood waiting.

The hat was tilted back. "Howdy, Mr. Morgan."

"Hello, Andy."

"Surprised to see me?" The smile was thrown in his face, a challenging expression which Shelter ignored.

"Not much. How'd you catch on?"

"You didn't think I'd take your word for anything, did you? I checked around myself and found out just when and where the 'broken down' train was going." She grew complacent, leaning back. "So here I am."

"All the way in a boxcar, couldn't have been much fun."

"Who says I was in the boxcar all the time?"

Shelter chewed on that for a while. "You were in it at Springfield," he said.

"Yes."

"Thanks." It was Andy who had killed the third ambusher, shot him from inside the freight car. If she hadn't, Morgan would still be in Springfield. Somewhere beneath it, rather.

"Who set you up?" she asked.

"I don't know—do you?"

"Search me." She stood, squaring her hat. "Maybe your little blond friend."

"Why?"

"How would I know? Maybe you're not stud enough," Andy said with a little venom. She looked him up and down and then studied his face to see if the needle had gotten to him. It hadn't. Morgan knew what he had and a remark like that didn't bother him a bit. "Let's talk somewhere," Andy said a little more softly.

"Why should we? Andy, maybe you don't realize how things stack up. You're in my way, and it looks like you have every intention of staying in my way. I don't need you around. If I had the chance, I'd lose you again."

"I don't stay lost," Andy said. "Cool down. I know something about Cord Levitt you'd like to know. Do we discuss it or do you want to run me off?"

Shelter considered. "Where?"

"I don't care. If you're not hungry, have a bottle sent up to your room. They don't let a lady into a saloon out here—and I don't feel salty enough to shoot up a place over it, but I could use some whiskey."

Morgan nodded slowly. "All right. This had better be good though, Andy. Whiskey and?"

"There ain't no 'whiskey and,' Morgan. Whiskey is

whiskey. It gets along fine by itself."

Morgan just shook his head and turned away. He caught a passing bellhop, a quick-eyed, tiny Mexican kid and told him what he wanted. Andy Rice, not being the shy type, had already gone up to his room. Morgan went after her, still feeling like an idiot, but she had dangled the right bait in front of him—whatever she knew about Cord Levitt he wanted to know.

He could have sworn he had locked the door, but when he got to his room, Andy Rice was inside, sitting in a chair, one leg slung over the arm, her coat and hat on his bed. It was like old times.

"What is it, Andy?" he asked sharply.

"Wait a minute, Morgan. Slow down! We haven't even had a drink. Not very damned sociable, are you?"

Shell sat on the bed and waited. It seemed an hour before the boy got there with a bottle and two glasses. Morgan gave him a dime and he went away whistling happily.

"Say when."

She never did say anything so Morgan stopped within an inch of the rim of the water glass. Andy thanked him and downed a good two fingers of bourbon without blinking.

"Now then." She wiped her mouth with the back of her hand. Always the lady, was Andy Rice. "What was it you had in mind?"

"No games, Andy. You know what I have in mind—if you know something, let's hear it. Otherwise, take the bourbon and go away."

"You really *don't* like me, do you?" she said with a mixture of amusement and surprise.

"I'm wild about you."

"You like them blond."

"I like them female."

"I'll bet I could show you a trick or two," she said, downing another two fingers of whiskey.

"I'd rather hear what you've got to say."

"All right." Andy's mouth tightened.

She slammed her whiskey glass down on the table at her elbow and told Shelter, "He's already left Santa Fe. I've been to the livery. He hired a horse and beat it out of here, riding south. Which would figure."

"What do you mean?"

"He's going home."

"I thought Santa Fe was home."

"It would be if he wasn't wanted here. He lives across the border—not that he isn't wanted there as well. But he can keep them off him down there."

"What do you mean?"

"He's got an army on his side."

"I still don't follow you."

"You would if you'd talked to the sheriff like I did. Cord Levitt is pretty well known. The sheriff could possibly have taken him yesterday if he'd had the nerve to try. He didn't. Levitt's got half a hundred badmen riding for him. He's the worst *bandido* in this territory, on either side of the border—unless it's his partner."

"And who's that?"

"A man named Ramon Chavez."

That one got to Shelter. She saw him start a little. "Chavez, is it?" he mused.

"I see you've heard of him."

"Yeah. I've heard of him."

The name had come up before. Ramon Chavez who had been or was a rebel leader south of the border, who had burned down a number of villas belonging to the old aristocracy, who had murdered some of the old landowners of Spanish blood, who had looted their houses. It was Ramon Chavez who had driven out the Castillo y Cortes family. Ramon Chavez who had chased Bo Channing's brother and his Spanish wife into the hands of the Yaqui Indians. Everything was coming together in a strange way. Long arms of coincidence gathered the whole thing into a bundle and placed it in Shelter's lap.

"You off dreaming or what?" Andy Rice asked.

"Maybe. I was just trying to recall what I knew of Chavez."

"What did you dredge up?"

"Nothing much."

"Thanks," she said acidly. "Look, Morgan, I'm helping you. Why don't you loosen up. Let's play together. I want Cord Levitt for the money involved. You just want him. I can't see the conflict there."

"No, there's no conflict."

"Then we're together on this?"

"No. I told you, I don't want you in my way."

"All right then, damn you! I'm going after him alone and it'll be a cold day in hell before I ever give you another tip or save your ass when some bushwhacker wants to gun you down."

"That I'm grateful for."

"Thanks a lot!" Andy had her hat on again. Shelter didn't try to stop her from leaving.

"You're crazy, you know, if you think you're going to cross that desert alone and find Cord Levitt."

"And what are you going to do?" Andy mocked.

"Go after him."

"You don't even know where he is."

"I'll find out," Morgan said. "I guess the sheriff will talk to me, too."

"Bastard—what do I see in you?"

"Andy," Morgan said, and he walked to her and

put his hands on her shoulders. She shrugged them off violently but he put them back. "Why don't you slow down? You are a woman, you know. You want to be one. Why don't you give up on Levitt."

"Leave him for you, you mean?"

"Sure."

"Like hell," she spat. She knocked his hands away again.

"Look, if I get him you can collect the reward."

"I don't need charity, Morgan."

"All right. I give up. Do what you want. Go ahead and get yourself killed."

The whiskey glass hit the floor and then she was gone again, a whirlwind of anger and emotion swirling out the hotel room, slamming the door behind her.

Shelter grinned, picked up his own hat and went out. He was just in time to see Andy Rice go out the front door of the Western Skies, shoving a puzzled-looking cowpuncher aside as she went.

Morgan went down and out onto the dry, dusty street. He found the sheriff's office down three blocks past a plaza where a little fountain bubbled water into a blue-tiled fountain. Three naked kids played in the water.

The sheriff's office was adobe, low and deep. Inside there were three desks. A Spanish or Mexican deputy sat at one. Hanging on the wall above him was a crucifix. The pale man with the straw hat, trimming his bunion with a pocket knife, was the sheriff of Santa Fe.

"Be with you in a minute. Damned boots. Had these all my life. Suffer from 'em, do you?"

"No."

"Lucky." The sheriff examined his foot, shook his head and put his pocket knife away. "What can I do for you?" he grunted as he tugged a floppy boot back on.

"I'm looking for Ramon Chavez. Where do I start?"

"First, answer me this—why would anyone in his right mind look for Ramon Chavez?"

The Mexican deputy had stopped his writing and he glanced around, measuring Shelter suspiciously.

"I hear that wherever he is, Cord Levitt is."

"Cord Levitt again? Hell, there was a young lady— guess it was a lady—in here not an hour ago, wasn't there, Miguel? What, if I ain't repeating myself, do you want to find Cord Levitt for?"

"I want his hide."

"Same thing this lady told me." The sheriff scratched his head and chuckled. "Well, I wish you could get him for me, save the world a lot of trouble. He's bad, Chavez is bad. They like to kill. They run with a gang of dogs that don't care what they do. Revolutionaries—" the sheriff spat on the floor— "damned filthy murderers, ain't they, Miguel?" The deputy didn't answer. The sheriff forged on. "You know the area south of here?"

"Some."

"*Some.*" The lawman shook his head. "Son, that ain't good enough. It's bad country, rattlers and scorpions, bad Injuns and bad water. Chavez and his cutthroats and a sun that'll eat you alive. I can't go down there legally, and nothing pleases me more. The army can't go down there. I think that pleases them. The Mexican army won't come up here. Nobody will."

"Is there a certain place where Ramon Chavez is known to hang out?" Shelter interrupted. He had the feeling that once the sheriff got wound up he could go on for a long while.

"Sure."

"May I ask where."

"The hacienda. The old house. The Castillo y Cortes house."

The deputy spoke for the first time. He didn't look at them, but talked to his desk. "No one live to come back. No one can take Chavez."

"You see! Now that's what I been trying to tell you, boy. Why don't you enjoy Santa Fe. We got a nice town here. One of the oldest in the United States, you know that? There's a lot to see. We got our share of cantinas, too, and here and there a willing lady— so they tell me. Being a lawman, I wouldn't know myself."

Shelter didn't hear the rest of it. He was already out the door, standing in the narrow band of shade beneath the awning of the sheriff's office, thinking. Thinking, that was all, and he didn't like what he was coming up with. He spent an hour walking around Santa Fe. It was too hot to enjoy it and he had too much on his mind for sight-seeing.

Back at the hotel dining room he ran into Beth and Bo Channing having a meal. Shelter pulled up a chair on invitation and ordered a beer from the dark, pleasant waitress in the striped skirt.

"Good thing you got back, Sterling," Bo Channing said around a mouthful of rice. "We're getting ready to move on, you know."

"No, I didn't know. Tonight? Now?"

"Yes, the colonel thought—"

"Hart's going along?"

"Yes, he decided to give us his assistance. We'll have a larger party this way. His blacks will go along as well, and—"

Shell broke in again. "Look, Channing, I don't think much of this idea. For one thing Beth ought to stay here. That's number one. Hart going along is number two. What do you want with him?"

"If it hadn't been for Hart we wouldn't have gotten this far."

"I know that, but it doesn't smell good."

"I can't go by your nose, Sterling. I didn't hire you to ask for your opinion. I'm going. Hart's going. Beth is going. Are you?"

Beth looked appealingly at Morgan. Bo Channing was waiting for his answer. Morgan swallowed a slow, bitter curse and said, "Yes, I guess I'm going."

"Good. Then as soon as Harry returns with the *señorita* Ramirez we can be on—"

"With who?" Morgan asked stiffly.

"Señorita Ramirez. Someone Harry met. She needs an escort south to her rancho. It's on our way. We couldn't very well refuse the lady. Besides, she seems taken with Harry." Channing interrupted himself this time. "Here they are, good!"

Shelter slowly turned his head toward the door. There was Harry Channing in a blue suit, wearing a white hat. On his arm was a young lady in Spanish dress, lace mantilla and long black skirt. She looked very lovely. Shelter thought Andy Rice made a hell of a fine looking Spanish beauty in fact.

78

7.

"What ever's the matter, Bill?" Beth Channing asked. "You act as if you know the lady."

Shelter didn't answer. He couldn't. The only option was to tell Channing that Andy Rice was a bounty hunter and not a Spanish *señorita*. Then Andy would tell them that he was Shelter Morgan and not William C. Sterling and they would both be out of the game. He clamped his jaw shut and waited while Harry Channing crossed the room, his head high, his trophy on his arm. If he knew what he had really hooked onto the kid would be in fast retreat right now.

"Hello, Father," Harry said, playing the gentleman for once in his life. "Sister. Mr. Sterling."

"Hello," Morgan grumbled.

"You haven't met the *señorita* Maria Ramirez, have you, Mr. Sterling?" Harry was going to be polite if it killed him.

"No. Howdy," Morgan growled without standing. Andy Rice managed to look vaguely offended. She hid her face briefly behind a lace fan. Shelter grumbled something inaudible and very dirty.

"The colonel has the wagons nearly loaded," Harry said. "As soon as we can change into travelling clothes, we'll be ready."

"Where's this rancho of yours, Señorita Ramirez?" Shelter asked.

"Please, you call me Maria. You all call me Maria," Andy said. "Not far. Not far south. Along your way, you shall see." Then, damn her, she tittered, hiding behind the fan again, just the coyest little thing this side of Laredo.

Shelter watched them walk away. Beth was keeping an eye on him. "She's lovely, isn't she?"

"Sure."

"You don't like her. Don't you like Spanish women?"

"Not her type," Morgan said.

Channing said, "You don't have to be impolite, Sterling. We all have our preferences, but if we're going to be travelling together, let's at least be polite to one another."

Morgan's mouth opened and clamped shut again without a word escaping. He left some money on the table and rose.

"May I come with you?" Beth asked.

"Don't you have to change?" She was wearing a dark blue dress with a huge bow on the bodice and a little blue hat.

"There's time for that."

"I don't mind," Morgan said.

"Father?"

"Go on," Channing said in a way that seemed to indicate he thought his daughter was asking for trouble. "I'll be down here or up in my room."

Outside it was hotter, if anything. Beth hooked onto Shelter's arm as they walked the plankwalk.

80

"Where are we going?"

"I need a few things. A horse, a rifle, canteens."

"The colonel could supply you with those."

"I'd rather have my own," Morgan said. "Why do you think the colonel is going along?"

"Why, to help, I suppose."

"Why not just outfit you and wait here? He's hardly the type to be running around all over the desert, is he?"

"Why, maybe it's just his sense of adventure, I don't know." She watched him silently, expecting him to say more, but he never did.

At the general store on the corner Shelter bought a blanket, two one-gallon canteens, a Winchester repeater and a box of .44s for it and his Colt.

At the livery he found a tall gray horse with one white ear. The hostler wanted an arm and a leg for it and ended up getting the leg. Shell wasn't in a position to bargain. That and a used Texas-rigged saddle depleted the few gold coins he had been carrying stitched into his belt. He had enough loose change left for a ham sandwich and a beer, but he wasn't hungry. He gave what he had to a Mexican kid who was to lead the horse back to the hotel. He would either come back from Mexico with a little pay in his pockets or he wouldn't come back. He didn't have much use for money right now.

He tried again on the way back. "Beth, I want you to stay here. Talk to your father. He won't argue with you if you tell him you're afraid."

"I'm not afraid as long as you're along."

"Well, you should be. It's a bad situation, no good for a woman."

"I see," she teased, "you've fallen for Maria Ramirez."

"Not likely," he muttered. "You won't stay?"

"Not unless you do."

"Don't tempt me," he said. "If I had any brains at all . . ." He supposed he didn't. There was also the dream. Last night it had come to him in the middle of the night. A nightmare filled with flame and gunfire. He had lived it all again, that ambush along the bloody Conasauga River. The guns opening up, horses rearing in fright. Welton Williams and Jeb Thornton going down as the traitors opened up, shooting their own men to bits for the gold they carried. The face of Cord Levitt was there as always, twisted by greed and blood lust. His gun firing into Shell's face, somehow missing a clean kill, wounding his arm so that Morgan had to get the hell out of there, leading a terrified Dink with him.

And then young Dink had died and they had searched for Shelter, wanting to finish off all the witnesses. And in some ironic twist the Yankees had captured Shelter then, taking him out of the hands of the Confederate traitors.

When the nightmare got to that point it always started over. Again and again, running through his mind until with a jerk Morgan sat up, bathed in sweat, his heart racing, his hands clenched angrily. Then he could not go back to sleep. He could only sit awake and look at the list he carried, a list of names with more than half of them crossed out in blood-red ink.

"I'll go with you," Morgan said. "I have to find him."

"Find who?" Beth asked innocently.

"Never mind." Although it was broad daylight and a lady would object, Beth didn't. He put his arm around her, turned her to him and kissed her. "We'll go. We'll both go south."

Behind the hotel the wagons had been formed up.

There were four of them, three covered, one an open freight wagon. A dozen horses stood, tails switching, hipshot in the sun. Flies droned up the alley. Two black men in cotton shirts finished loading the freight wagon.

"I've got to change," Beth said, and she hurried up to her room while Shelter found his horse, thanked the kid again and got his own gear organized, filling his canteens, making up a bedroll, adjusting stirrups and bridle.

Harry Channing walked past in range clothes; beside him was Andy Rice in a buckskin skirt, white blouse, flat crowned, black Spanish-style hat and riding gloves. Either she was wearing a wig or she had a hell of a lot more hair than Morgan had believed. It was to her shoulders, gathered in a red ribbon. She looked at him and spoke.

"And how are you, Señor Sterling. A ver' good day for the travelling, no?"

"Very good," Shell said through his teeth. She smiled brightly and went on, Harry slavering after her.

It was another hour and a half before they pulled out. Colonel Hart in a red checked shirt, new white hat, jeans and shiny boots appeared to sit in the front wagon with one of his blacks driving.

Jake Stoddard and his men came along shortly after that. They were moving a little unsteadily. They hadn't had any trouble finding a cantina apparently.

Channing was driving the second wagon with Beth beside him. The last rig was piloted by Harry. With him on the bench seat was Señorita Andy Rice.

They pulled out of Santa Fe three hours before dark, riding due south toward the border.

It was an uneasy feeling, knowing they were riding into the *bandidos'* stronghold, into the land of the

Yaquis and the rattler, where water was mile after long mile between. Still, it was good to be forking a good horse again, to be out of the confines of a hotel room, a railroad car, a town.

Shelter rode far to the flank, leaving the blacks and Stoddard's boys to ride close escort. He wanted to get away from them all for a time, to cross the red sand desert, to watch the far mesas, to weave his way through the thorny mesquite and stands of nopal cactus alone, without another human voice to break the silence.

The sun was coasting toward the far mountains now, but the day was as hot as ever. The heat rose in veils from the sand. The horse moved gingerly across the land. Shell was out of sight of the wagon train temporarily. He could see the low, chocolate-colored hills to the west, the glint of the late sunlight on something sinuous, bright, which had to be a distant stream. Beneath the tangled mesquite now the shadows grew long.

Here and there he saw ocotillo, their tips bright red with flower. Long, thorny coachwhips, they dominated the land where all else was small, shrivelled, shrunken. Barrel cactus with a frost of dangerous thorns studded the sand.

Nothing much lived here, or nothing that was immediately perceptible. But Morgan saw a roadrunner dart and then briefly fly across his path, saw sign in the soft sand of a coyote working the area, twice he saw jackrabbits sitting in the shade of a cactus waiting for the sun to drop a little lower.

Then there were the small things, the scorpions, the sidewinders, the gila monsters, all the deadly and virulent things that inhabited this place where to survive you needed thorns or fangs or poisonous stingers.

It was coming on to dusk when Shell rode up out of the little gulley he had been following and headed for the wagons which cut dark silhouettes against the eastern sky.

They already had a fire going, most of the horses unhitched when he rode in. Harry wasn't very happy.

"Damnit, where have you been! Who's going to unhitch my team? What do you think we're paying you for!"

"Not to unhitch your horses for you, Harry, that's for sure. I was out looking the area over—for one thing I wanted to see if we were being followed."

"Why would we be followed?" he asked belligerently.

"How about the gold as a reason." Shell was disgusted with the kid. He didn't need the aggravation. He turned away and Harry challenged him.

"You wait, Sterling! You're working for me. You unhitch that team of horses!"

"You jam it," Shelter said roughly.

He heard it; without having to look he knew what was happening. He heard the whisper of steel against leather, the ratcheting of a pistol hammer and he turned angrily, his boot coming up, kicking the gun out of Harry's hand. There was a crack of bone and a loud scream as Harry grabbed his wrist. Two blacks were coming on the run. Jake Stoddard and the bald man were sauntering over, grinning contentedly.

"What happened?" Andy Rice appeared. She had momentarily forgotten her accent. Now she put it on again. "What ees the troubles?"

"He pulled a gun on me," Morgan said, nodding toward it. "The next time that happens, Harry, I'll take it away from you and beat you with it."

"You broke my wrist," Harry whimpered. Morgan didn't have a lot of sympathy to spare for poor Harry

85

Channing.

"Good," he said, though he doubted it was broken.

"What is this!" Bo Channing was there suddenly, outraged. He knew his son wasn't much, but he had a father's protective instincts.

"He'll tell you," Morgan said, and he strode away, leading his horse toward the campfire where coffee was boiling. He could feel the eyes on his back, boring in, but he tried to ignore them. "You know how to make friends, Shell," he told himself tightly.

Beth was at the campfire, watching his approach with anxious eyes. "What happened?"

Briefly he told her. "The longer he hangs around with Stoddard and that crowd, the worse he's going to be. They're encouraging him. What do they care if he gets hurt, there's a chance he might get me."

"He's in terrible debt to them," Beth said, sipping at a cup of coffee. "I heard them talking—the Mexican, Santos and the one named Crabbe."

"How much?"

"Twenty thousand dollars."

"Christ. Does your father know?"

Beth shook her head. "I didn't tell him. Maybe he knows. I don't think he realizes how much it is."

"I'll talk to him later. Where's the colonel?"

"There." Beth pointed toward one of the wagons. Inside a lantern was burning. "He has a table and chair inside. He's dining on duck. All of his silver was brought from the train."

"Roughing it, is he?" Shell asked.

Beth smiled. "For him, I suppose it is. But I'll tell you this, Bill, there's still a lot of strength left in that man, if you ask me."

Shelter mulled that over. He tended to agree with her. But his thinking was colored by his own suspicions. It didn't seem quite right for Hart to come this far to assist an old friend. The colonel had his own scheme working, Morgan would have bet.

It was rapidly growing dark, the fire seemed bright against the sky, twisting red and orange flames writhing above the stone fire ring.

"We'd better have this out now," Shelter said. "It'll be seen for a long way." He nodded at the fire.

"They'll see us anyway, won't they?" Beth asked. "The *bandidos*, the Yaquis."

"Yes. If they're in the area, they'll see us. All we can do is hope they're not." He began kicking sand into the fire.

"I wish I had stayed in Santa Fe," Beth said.

"It's not too late."

"Yes, it is. I can't go back now. No," she said strongly, "I'll go on. We do have guns and men to shoot them."

"Yes," Morgan answered. But not enough guns, not enough men. Not to hold off Ramon Chavez and the Indians.

They saw Channing coming toward them and Beth rose hurriedly. "You said you wanted to talk with Father."

"Yes."

"I'll leave you alone." Then, breathily, "Maybe we'll have time to be alone later . . . and talk."

"We'll see. Go on now, get your rest. Tomorrow is going to be long and hot."

Beth scurried off and Shelter poured another cup of coffee. The fire was burning low now, nearly out. He waited for Bo Channing who was still unhappy.

"I think a small bone's broken. I can't tell. He's got it bound up. Did you have to do it, Sterling?"

"Yes, I had to do it." Morgan's eyes, in the deep shadow beneath his hat brim, were fire-bright. "He pulled a gun on me, Bo. What the hell did you want me to do? The only choices were to do what I did or start shooting myself."

"He's only a boy," Bo complained. He hooked the coffeepot to him and poured himself a cup. His anger was waning; by the dim glow of the fire he looked haggard, his face collected into deep furrows and ridges.

"He's a boy who needs some help right now if he's going to be any kind of a man."

"A kick in the butt?"

"That's it," Morgan agreed. "Do you know what he owes Stoddard?"

"Over them cards? I don't know. Hope it's no more than a few hundred."

"Twenty thousand."

Bo nearly choked on his coffee. "Twenty thousand!"

"Yeah. Harry's working on the premise that he's the son of a rich man. Like most people who never had to work for their money, he's good at spending it."

"We haven't got fifty dollars in our poke if the gold isn't there." Bo wiped his forehead with his folded handkerchief. "I mean, it should be there, but if it ain't, then what?"

"You'd have to ask Stoddard," Shell said with a cool shrug.

"I guess you don't think much of me, do you?" Bo asked surprisingly.

"What do you mean?"

"Bringing my children out here on this treasure hunt. Boy's not been brought up right. Beth, she's a good girl, but she's not strong. Shouldn't be here. Fifty bucks to my name—but that's it, Sterling, you see that, don't you? What the hell have I got to leave them kids when I'm gone? The gold's important. It'll give Beth a good life, education if she wants it—"

"And provide for Stoddard's future."

"Don't rub salt in, Sterling. I know Harry's made a big mistake. I don't know how to correct it."

"Keep him away from Stoddard, that's all you can do." Shell threw the dregs of his coffee against the embers and they hissed. "Listen, do yourself a favor and watch the colonel too, will you? Him and his Africans."

"The colonel's a good man, and already a wealthy one."

"Fine. Watch him anyway. If he's on the other side that leaves you alone with me."

"Are you with me?" Channing wanted to know.

"Yes. Why do you have to ask?"

Bo looked at him and with the stick he held in his hand he wrote a single word in the dirt at his feet: "Morgan." He looked at Shell and then toed it out.

"Well?" Channing asked.

"That's me. I can explain things—one word of advice first. Don't tell the colonel or anyone else about this."

"Hell, son—the colonel's the one that told me."

Shelter looked up sharply. Bo's face was craggy and shadowed in the faint light of the glowing embers. The letters he had scratched in the earth had been erased, but Morgan still seemed to see them there.

"The *colonel* told you?"

"That's right. Is this your right name?"

"It is."

"What happened to Sterling?"

"He was killed back in St. Jo."

"By you?"

"No." Morgan shook his head. "I don't know who did it. I took his place because I needed to get to Santa Fe quick."

"Not because you wanted to cut in on this treasure?" Bo asked craftily. "Because you maybe found my letter on Sterling's body?"

"No. If you've got to know the whole story, I'll tell it to you, but I'd rather just say that our trails came together and we happen to be going the same way. While I'm with you I'm on your side, Bo. Your side and Beth's. I won't leave you out here no matter what happens."

"Sure." Bo said it, but there wasn't much confidence in his voice. Morgan couldn't blame him a whole lot. He had been lied to. He had hired a gunfighter to protect him and his daughter; what he had gotten was a stranger, a liar, a man he knew nothing at all about. Obviously disgusted, Bo got up and walked away.

The thing that bothered Morgan was how the colonel had found out who he was. It was a puzzler. He could figure that everyone knew. Including Stoddard. So that part of the game was over. He had to explain it to Beth, that was all that remained.

And Andy Rice?

There didn't seem to be any point in exposing her now. She had already hooked on with the treasure party. No one was going to cut her loose and make her drift back to Santa Fe alone—likely if it came down to it, no one would take Morgan's word for it against the *señorita* Ramirez's anyway. Morgan was the one who had been proven a liar, not Andy.

Shell lifted his eyes to the dark horizon, seeing the stars blink on above the saw-tooth range to the south. Somewhere in those hills, or along the Yaqui River farther west, the Indians were waiting, watching. Somewhere to the south, the *bandidos* under Ramon Chavez waited. And somewhere out there a cache of gold lay hidden, waiting to be brought gleaming to the surface. The odds against coming out of this were so long as to be incalculable. It would have been nice to have a single ally, anyone Morgan could trust, but there wasn't anyone.

Well, maybe one. His eyes lifted to the wagon where Beth Channing waited and he started that way.

8.

Beth's wagon was empty and that worried Shelter although he figured there could be a number of reasons for her walking out onto the desert alone. By starlight he found a pair of small footprints leading east and he started off that way, letting the night close around him.

The stars were brilliant, huge against a purple velvet sky. The mountains far to the south still held a pale reddish glow at their tips. Somewhere to Shell's right a coyote howled mournfully.

He was into dunes now, white dunes which rolled in like a sea to meet the red sand of the flats. Shelter sunk in to his ankles as he climbed the low, wind-sculpted dune and halfslid down the far side. The world was suddenly empty, completely empty.

He could no longer see the wagons or the mountains. There were only the stars, blue-white and large, and the sand dunes silver in their light.

And the woman who stood there waiting, her dress thrown to one side, her naked body star-glossed, her eyes bright, her arms outstretched.

"Beth. How did you know I'd come?"

"I knew. I've been waiting."

"The waiting's over." Morgan took her in his arms, her body warm, competent, pressed against his. She bit at his neck, his chest with sharp, nipping teeth. Her hair tumbled free of its combs and made a silver-blond waterfall across her shoulders and slender bare back.

Her fingers had worked their way down his shirtfront and now attacked his belt buckle. Shelter cupped her breasts, toyed with the nipples which were beginning to stand taut, and kissed the top of her head, smelling the lavender soap she had used to wash her hair, her flawless body.

His fly was opened and her hands darted inside, reaching for him, encircling him. Shelter took off his shirt and tossed it near Beth's dress. He led her to this makeshift bed and sagged back, letting her tug his jeans down, feeling the slow caresses of her hands and tongue bring his shaft to rigid alertness.

She kissed his abdomen, her hand working diligently on his erection. She was in no mood for waiting on this night and neither was Morgan. She suddenly straddled him, facing his toes. Her ass was beautiful, round, smooth, white in the starlight. Beyond Beth the dunes loomed, tall and silver, delicately curved, and beyond them only limitless sky.

Shelter reached between her legs and spread her with his thumbs and she settled onto him, her inner muscles moving spasmodically, her body trickling warm fluid.

Beth sat upright, her head thrown back, and Shell sat up, to wrap his arms around her, his crossing hands squeezing the firm, resilient breasts, his lips working along her shoulder toward her neck as she trembled there. Her hands dropped between her legs and she touched herself where Shelter's big rod entered her, bringing herself to an incredibly quick climax which brought her body to jerky life.

She twisted and swayed, rocked back and forward, her breath coming in little effortful puffs. She turned, not losing him and came down to meet his kiss as her hips lifted high again and again, impaling herself on his swollen shaft.

"All right," she whispered in his ear. Her breath was moist and warm against his flesh. He felt her tongue follow the whorl of his ear. "Let it go," she said. Her body urged him on, her fingers, groping between her legs, found him again. "Please. Fill me up," she whispered and Shelter's loins, aching, throbbing, released their load as Beth, pressed against him, her breasts warm and near, her legs spread as she breathed small words into his ear, took it all in.

Shelter stroked her back, his finger trailing down her spine from her neck to the crack in her ass, Beth shuddering slightly as he reached bottom each time. She lay sated, full and ripe, completely, luxuriantly female. The night was warm. The softest breeze, too light to move the fine sand, moved among the dunes. Her scent was rich and earthy in his nostrils, her breathing gentle against his chest.

She had fallen asleep, and Morgan let her sleep as he lay looking at the stars, counting them, counting the minutes of his life, counting the dead and the yet to be born.

An hour on he shook her gently awake. "Come on. Your father's going to be worried."

"Be all right," she murmured sleepily.

"No, it won't. Get up, Beth." He kissed her once, but his hands were firm as he moved her away from him so that he could withdraw from her and stand to dress.

"Aww," she complained softly. "There's time for another."

"Plenty of time, but not tonight."

"What else is there to do?"

"We could try sleeping. Come on." He tugged her to her feet and indulged himself in one last long kiss, her naked body pressed to his, one of her knees lifted high, offering a second chance which Morgan had to refuse.

"You used to be such fun." She pouted.

"Dress," he commanded.

He stood looking at the stars, breathing in deeply, smelling sage in the distance, and somewhere scrub cedar. "I'd like to see the map," he said abruptly. Beth, who was tugging up a petticoat, stopped her motion and looked at him.

"What map?"

"The treasure map. I'd like to know where in hell we're going," he told her. They were just riding south as of now. If anyone besides Bo Channing knew where they were headed, Shelter hadn't been told.

"What did Father say?" Beth walked to him, straightening her clothes, patting at her hair.

"I didn't ask him. He wasn't in the mood."

"Oh?"

"Beth—everyone else seems to know. My name's not Sterling. I'm not the man your father hired for the job. I'm Shelter Morgan, and my business isn't gold hunting, it's man hunting."

"Man hunting? Who?"

"No one you'd know. It doesn't matter. I just wanted to tell you."

"Then why do you want to see the map?" Beth asked reasonably. "If you don't care about the gold, I mean."

"I'd like to know where we're headed, how near

we're going to the old rancho, how the land lies. I've ridden through here before, but farther south. I don't know where water is, where the playas or salt flats are, things like that. I want to know. If we have to make a run, I want to know which way to go."

"I see." She pressed a thumbnail to her front teeth. "You really need to see it?"

"Yes. I think so."

"In an hour—in my wagon," she said. "You be there—Mr. Morgan, is it?—and I'll show it to you."

"You can get your hands on it?"

"I think so. But you'll owe me." She moved to him again, her mouth meeting his, twisting against it as she made small satisfied sounds in her throat.

"I owe you," Shell agreed.

"Good!" She smiled and then went off across the dunes, holding her skirt up, her stride swinging, bouncy. Shell crouched down to wait.

An hour or so later he started toward the camp. It was dark and still. In the colonel's wagon a lamp or a candle burned low and there seemed to be a faint glimmer of light in Beth's wagon. The black man appeared from nowhere, directly in front of Shell as he strode toward the wagon.

"Evenin'," Morgan said. His body was alert, sensing something antagonistic.

"You kill Bambo," the uninflected, accented voice from out of the darkness said.

"Did I?" Morgan stepped back, wanting to be able to draw his Colt if need be. There was no need, not then. The African was gone, the darkness folding over him. Morgan stood perfectly still for a while, eyes alert, but nothing happened. He was gone. He had delivered his message—his warning—and then had gone.

He stepped up onto the tailgate of Beth's wagon

cautiously. The night was dark, but not everyone was asleep, tucked away in their beds. He had just had that demonstrated.

Ducking under the canvas flap he found Beth sitting on a crate of supplies, dressed as he had left her. Her striped hatbox was on her lap.

"Are you alone?" she asked.

"Of course." And who would he bring with him? Friends like Stoddard and Crabbe? Harry or one of the Africans?

The candle that burned in the wagon was well shielded. Only a minimum of light escaped. Shelter sat beside Beth and by that light she read his eyes.

"I guess you're still the same man, even with a new name," she said at last, and she lifted the lid to the hatbox she had carried since St. Jo. Her hand dipped in and came out with a big Walker Colt. Morgan's hand fended off the barrel pointing at his chest.

She smiled and put the gun down. "Father wants it in there. I don't think I could use it."

The map was in the hatbox, behind a false wall made simply by inserting a cylinder of cardboard inside the real side of the box. The map had been folded many times but now was flat. Where it had been folded it was torn. There were unidentifiable stains on the map. One corner was missing. It looked much older than Bo Channing had said it was.

Shelter spread the map on his lap, turned it once and then fell into concentration. He identified Isleta Sandia, or what he took to be that barren sand field and the Jicarilla Mountains. The scale of the map wasn't consistent, however; the draftsman had apparently belatedly realized he was running out of room. There was a sudden harsh line which was meant to represent the border, then a boxy formation of hills drawn with wavy lines, below that a small rectangle which was probably the Rancho Castillo y Cortes.

"Well," Beth asked, "what do you think?"

"I think the man was no cartographer, but it's a help. I have an idea where things are supposed to be. It's a long way, Beth. A hell of a long way yet. You talked about going back—maybe you should consider it again."

"No." This time she was definite. Shelter handed her back the map. "I won't do it, not now."

"That map," Morgan said, "there was no X, was there? No spot marking the treasure."

"You said you wanted to know where we were going, not where the treasure was. Do you want the treasure, Mr. Morgan?"

"No. Wipe that suspicion off your face, woman. I don't want it. I just wondered."

"The corner that is missing," she said. "That's where the treasure is marked. On the missing piece."

"And who has that?"

She smiled secretively. "If you don't care about the gold, then you don't need to know. Father doesn't want me to tell. I've already shown you more than I should, more than—"

They both heard it. The whisper of leather against sand outside the wagon. An insignificant sound, very loud in the night. Morgan had his pistol in hand and in two steps he was to the tailgate, leaping onto the ground.

He crouched there, peering into the darkness. There was no one, nothing moved. He slowly, warily, circled the wagon, noting that Beth had blown out the candle. Still he found no one, and the tracks in the sand were indistinct, much blurred by other footprints.

"Who was it?" Beth asked anxiously when Morgan returned to the tailgate.

"I don't know." He shook his head and bit at his

lower lip thoughtfully. It could have been anyone. Stoddard trying to find the map to the treasure, an African back to try revenging Bambo, Harry discovering that Shell and Beth had been intimate, that she was sharing the secret of the map with Morgan. It could have been anyone, and whoever it was, it was bad.

With daylight Shelter was up and riding. Sunrise was a pale red flush against the eastern sky, a flush which deepened and turned to crimson, casting the red sand desert into shadowed relief, the dunes to the east becoming a purple sea.

It was hot by eight o'clock. This was going to be their first full day on the desert, but by no means the last. Morgan rode with his eyes alert, his body leaking fluids which were whipped off by the dry wind. They were still far from the land of the Yaquis.

Only the Apache lived here. Nothing much to worry about. It was the home of the Chiricahua, but they were supposedly far south now, driven down into the Sierra Madres by General Crook. Maybe.

Maybe not.

Maybe the Yaquis were far to the west and south along the river which gave them their name. Maybe not. All Indians are nomadic, even the Pueblo and Navajo Indians who now lived in cliff dwellings or adobe *ciudads* had been nomadic. The Apache—his tongue was the same as the Algonquins in central Canada. He had traveled that far.

The rider behind Morgan had closed a lot of ground as he sat pondering their chances of running into Indian trouble. He reined up briefly and then disgustedly let the gray horse walk on.

She caught up anyway and Shelter turned aggressive blue eyes on Andy Rice.

"Howdy, cowboy? Lonesome?" she asked lightly.

"Not much."

"Sure you are. All cowboys are lonesome." She flipped her Spanish hat back and let it ride on the drawstring. Her hair was curled this morning, Morgan noticed.

"How about Spanish ladies? Are they lonesome too?"

"Sometimes. At night. That any problem to you, Morgan? Or do you maybe have someone to keep you company?"

"You have some reason for this chatter, Andy? Or did you just ride out to remind me what a nuisance you are?"

"Nuisance? The *señorita* Ramirez?" She pretended to be shocked. Shell didn't find it amusing.

They dipped down into a gully where much thorny mesquite grew. The ground was rough gravel, white and gleaming in the brilliant sunlight. They were temporarily out of sight of the wagon train.

"You're crazy to come along on this, Andy. You know that? What did you tell me the price was on Cord Levitt? Three hundred?"

"Three hundred then. You know what it is now? I asked the sheriff—just out of casual curiosity. Two thousand, Morgan! Two thousand dollars. They've got a lot hung on Cord now. Him and the Mex he runs with. Know what the price on this Ramon Chavez is? Five thousand. Five thousand." She shook her head. "That's a lot of loot, Morgan."

He didn't answer. They rode through the tall cactus, seeing a pair of desert rats scurry away before them. "Say," Andy Rice said finally, readjusting her hat, "who's crazy anyway, Morgan? Me taking the chance for seven thousand real American dollars or you taking it for nothing, for revenge?"

"I don't know," Shell answered honestly. "Maybe

the pair of us."

"Sure. You're right. We're a real pair to draw to, aren't we?" Andy smiled, but when Shelter failed to respond, her smile fell away as rapidly as it had appeared.

"Here comes boyfriend," Morgan said and Andy twisted in the saddle to see Harry Channing riding hard toward them, slapping his horse on the shoulders with his reins. "Going to run that pony into a lather for nothing."

"He's in love with me, Shell. Wants me to drop my drawers for him."

"You probably will."

"Probably." Her face was disgusted. "He smells of chocolate and sweat. Little boy smells. Probably ask me to marry him any time now."

"Why don't you do that too."

"Maybe—if he finds that gold."

"I don't doubt it. Money means a lot to you, doesn't it?"

"You know it does, Morgan. The difference between living and scrounging, being afraid that there's no food, that you might have to steal to survive—or kiss someone's big behind." Channing was nearly in range. "And so, *señor*, it ees my way, the way of the world, no?"

Harry was red in the face. He had come charging after her so rapidly that he'd lost his hat. "Maria, you shouldn't be out here alone!"

"I was with the *señor*, Harry."

"Yes, but . . ." Harry looked at Morgan as if he was something to be stepped over carefully. "I don't want you out here unless I can be there to watch you."

"I am sorry, Harry," Andy said, peering up shyly from beneath her long lashes. Shelter felt a little nausea rising.

Then Harry, careful to snub Morgan, took the reins to Andy's horse and turned it. There was time for Andy Rice to stick out her pink tongue at Shell before she resumed her polite Spanish lady pose for Harry.

Morgan grinned in spite of himself. He was uncomfortable having Andy around and he knew she would get in the way somehow before this was done. But she must have been pretty uncomfortable herself playing the lady. No whiskey, no Colt riding on her hip.

Shelter quit thinking about Andy and started thinking about something else. The tracks were obvious in the soft soil. The rider had beelined it south after approaching near to the road.

How long ago? Not long by Morgan's figuring. A few straggly blades of gramma grass had been bent over by the horse's hoofs and they hadn't yet sprung up. Within the last hour or so, say. That meant that the rider, whoever he was, had been watching for the wagons, had seen them and had ridden off to the south.

It didn't feel good.

The horse had been unshod. It was an Indian pony. The Apaches knew they were coming.

Morgan, scowling deeply, shifted in his saddle and strained his eyes looking southward. Although the land was flat and empty he still saw no sign of the horseman. He wasn't discouraged. He had the feeling he would be seeing him again, and soon.

9.

"Apaches?" Colonel Hart blinked rather uneasily. That was his total reaction. The round man sat on his bay horse, wearing a light gray suit and a gray hat. He squinted into the sun as if he might see a horde of Chiricahua riding toward them. "Are you sure, Morgan?"

"Sure as I need to be. I found the tracks of a scout."

"Maybe a white man," Stoddard said. Just to be saying something, Morgan guessed. It was a stupid remark.

"I thought the Apaches had all been driven south," Hart said.

"*Some* apparently have. Not all, it seems. Or it could be that the Mexican army is making a big push, chasing them back out of the Sierra Madres, chasing them north again."

"They couldn't be Yaquis?"

"I don't think so, this far north. It doesn't much matter if they are, does it? I figure Apaches, but you can bet your life—and we are—that they're hostiles.

What do you want to do, Colonel?"

"What can we do?"

"Turn back. Take the girl with you."

"Like hell," Stoddard said. He kneed his horse and drifted it over to come side by side with Shelter. Stoddard's face was still swollen from the last time he had argued with Morgan. "You want us to turn back—what about you? What kind of ideas have you got?"

"I've got the idea of going on. A lone man on horseback has a fair chance. Not worth attacking for one thing, for another I can move pretty fast compared to a wagon."

"And help yourself to the gold."

"I don't know where in the hell it is, Stoddard." Shelter was losing patience. "And if I did, I'm sure as hell not going to carry it out on a single horse."

"Then why—"

"Gentlemen," Colonel Hart said as if someone had raised a slight commotion at a railroad board meeting, "let us calm ourselves. I have heard Mr. Morgan's suggestion and I reluctantly refuse the option. One Indian is hardly reason to turn back."

"There'll be more reason," Shelter assured him.

"What is this?" Bo Channing, having seen the conference, had come forward, cradling a rifle in his arms. "Trouble?"

"Morgan has seen the tracks of a horse. He's convinced it's an Indian pony and wants us to turn back."

"I'm damned if I'll turn back," Channing said. "Not for a hundred Indians, not for Ramon Chavez."

"You see." Hart shrugged. "And what am I to do, Morgan? I can't go back and leave my friend Bo Channing out here. I have nine men with me, counting my Africans and Mr. Stoddard's crew. If I pull off, what kind of chance will Channing have then? You and the boy, two women?"

Morgan nodded, understanding. He had been half fooled by Hart earlier, but now the mocking tone, the light dancing in the colonel's eyes told him all he wanted to know. It was the gold the man wanted. If there had been the smallest doubt before, there was none now. Bo Channing didn't see it, but then he couldn't see anything but gold.

"I appreciate it, Colonel Hart," Channing said quite sincerely. "Why, without you, I wouldn't have a prayer of success."

"It's nothing, Bo," Hart said rather grandly and he even placed a fatherly hand on Channing's shoulder. Morgan didn't have the ammunition to counter that kind of bullshit and so he turned his horse away.

"Watch yourself, Morgan," Stoddard hooted. "Might be some Injuns out there." Morgan swallowed his answer. It wouldn't do any good to bandy words with the son of a bitch.

He rode the desert alone again. "You get yourself into some fixes, Morgan," he told himself. A hostile land, hostile Indians, hostile allies. There was no way to extricate himself from this that made any sense. The only way to do that would be to break off and ride south alone—leaving Beth behind. No, that wouldn't work. For the time being he was tied to this crew: Africans wanting revenge, Stoddard nursing his grudge, Harry angry and pouting, Hart waiting to snatch the gold. Shelter tugged his hat low and sat his gray horse as he peered into the hot sun, watching the land to the south, to the south where the Apaches and probably the Yaquis were, where Ramon Chavez plied his revolution, where Cord Levitt waited, safe, secure among his *bandido* brothers, living the life of a Spanish don in the old hacienda, now a fortress.

"I'll get you yet, you bastard," Morgan promised the empty land. "You think I won't, but I will. I'll live to see your bones bleaching on this desert, Cord Levitt."

And that was a promise.

The nights were cold and the days were white-bright furnaces through which they plodded. The eyes were scored by the saberlike rays of the merciless sun. The desert floor, shifting from red to limitless white as they moved southward, soaked up the sun and radiated it again upward, the temperature at the level of a man's boots, a horse's hoofs, soaring to near 150. There was no shade. There were bent saguaro cactus now, twisted ocotillo, plenty of cholla cactus. They provided shade for a mouse, for a desert badger, for the sidewinders which infested the country, but there wasn't enough shade anywhere for a man and his horse.

Their lips blistered and split, their faces, the backs of their hands and their necks grew raw and red. The sun seemed to shine for twenty hours a day and then just as the welcome relief of night settled, the bottom would drop out of the thermometer and they would be freezing cold. The cholla cactus, ghostly, silver, would be frosted in the morning, frosted with frozen dew which vanished like dust blown away as soon as the red rim of the morning sun nudged its way above the dark, solemn horizon.

The Apaches hadn't come. They had crossed the border into Mexico and still the Chiricahua had not come. The others liked to make a joke out of it. Morgan never made a joke about an Apache warrior.

"Where's the war party?" Stoddard asked, laughing his fool head off. "The man sees the tracks of a horse and loses his nerve! I always at least thought he had nerve."

Morgan didn't answer. What was the point? He continued to ride alone, well away from the wagon train, scouting the land, watching and listening, well aware that their party was visible for many miles. Besides, he didn't hunger for the company of Stoddard and Harry Channing, or the rest of their pals.

The second day south of the border Morgan found a little pool of water as big as a hat. He got down, tasted it and found it good; there was much calcium in it, but it was sweet. What had caused the minuscule spring to rise from the underground source which fed it, he didn't know. He watered his horse and watched to see how long the basin took to refill—far too long to do the rest of the party any good. He straightened up and was wiping his brow, hat in hand, watching the sundown sky go red when something glinted brightly to his right, near at hand.

He caught it from the corner of his eye and instinct caused Shelter to duck just as the Apache brave's steel hatchet sliced past. Shelter's horse reared and scampered away and Morgan let it go. He had more pressing matters to attend to.

The Apache had lifted his hatchet again, his broad face flooded with war-anger. Again he struck and Shelter had to drop flat on his back to escape the blow which would have severed his head cleanly.

The Apache spoke English. It was good to hear a familiar language. "I kill," was what he said. "Tear guts from your body."

Flat on his back, Morgan pawed for his Colt. It wasn't there. He grabbed the empty leather of his worn holster. The revolver had popped free. He managed to come up with his bowie, but that didn't even change the Apache's expression. Flat on his back with that knife the Chiricahua didn't figure Shell offered much of a threat. He was probably right.

The Apache circled as Morgan slowly got to his knees, his eyes on the Indian's feet, not on his hatchet. When he saw the foot move, Morgan rolled to one side. His legs scissored out, tripped the Apache and the man came down hard.

His hatchet was against the sand and Morgan, leaping to it, flattened it there with his foot. The Chiricahua left it and came to his feet, knife in hand. The rawhide-handled knife swept up in a menacing arc. If it had caught Morgan the way he wanted to, it would have "torn guts from his body" all right. What it got was shirt front.

Morgan leaped back, simultaneously kicking out with his boot. The heel of it caught the Chiricahua under the chin, slamming him back, leaving a piece of his tongue on the sand as his own teeth severed the tip of it.

Blood flowed from the Indian's mouth; blood was in his eyes, mad, angry blood. He was a man of medium height, stocky, thick through the shoulders and chest, wearing high Apache boots, white linen shirt and red headband. The knife was unspectacular. Both looked as if they were built for killing.

The Indian came in again, his knife slashing out. Morgan's bowie met his blade and steel rang. From beyond the sundown hills now Shelter could hear gunfire and his stomach tightened. The wagon train was ill-equipped to stand off a large number of Indians.

The Chiricahua slowly circled, trying to get the late sun in Shell's eyes perhaps. Morgan wasn't falling for that. He did some maneuvering himself.

His mouth was dry. Blood trickled from a razor-thin cut across his abdomen and ran into his pants. The Apache was patient, very patient, moving like a cat, softly, the knife loose in his hand.

"I kill you," he said again. He wasn't much of a conversationalist.

He leaped at Shell and again steel met steel as Morgan fended off the blow. He stepped back quickly as the Indian tried to strike again. Stepped back and kicked out savagely, trying for the Chiricahua's kneecap, missing, just as a volley of shots sounded from over the hill. Shelter's eyes lifted anxiously.

The Apache came in again. The knife slit the side of Shelter's shirt beneath his arm, but Morgan, moving in, managed to lock the Indian's arm under his own and they were frozen, face to face for a long moment, until Morgan's bowie lifted and was driven upward beneath the Chiricahua's ribs, the point of the knife catching lungs and heart muscle. The Indian struggled frantically in his arms, but there was no escape. It was just the automatic reaction of an organism trying to fight off mortality.

He was already dead. Shelter let him sag to the ground, yanking his bowie free. He picked up his Colt and started at a run toward his gray. Before he reached it he heard the approaching horses and he threw himself to the ground, filling his hand with the revolver.

He was behind a low shelf of dune and they never saw him. They must have seen the gray horse, but they were in too much of a hurry to stop and collect it. Six, seven horses raced past, one leaping directly over Shelter, spraying him with sand. And then the Apaches were gone, vanished again into the wasteland.

Morgan got to his feet and walked toward his horse, feeling a little stiff suddenly. He climbed aboard, slipping his Winchester from its boot, and started toward the wagons. Smoke was rising from the canvas top of one of the wagons, but it was rapidly diminishing. He could see an African to one side and then a group of people around a body.

Cursing, he urged his horse forward.

Beth was on the ground on her knees. Her face lifted, puffy, swollen, her eyes red. Bo Channing was dead, flat on his back, a nasty exit wound from a bullet in his chest. Shelter pulled the girl to her feet and growled, "Get a blanket and cover him up!"

"Yes, of course," a rather nervous Colonel Hart said. "Morgan, it's partly my fault, isn't it . . . three men dead. One of my men and Stoddard's friend, Baldy. If we had listened to your warning—"

"It doesn't do much good to hash it over now. Get a blanket." Morgan was still holding Beth, talking across her shoulder.

"I want to see—" she said, twisting away.

"There's nothing for you to see."

"But I have to." She pulled free and got to her knees again. Flies were walking across Bo Channing's face. His chin whiskers were smeared with blood. Beth yanked off his boot and reached inside, her face growing eager and then going blank.

"What is it?" Shell asked.

"Nothing." She stood, still holding the boot, her face blank as she walked to Morgan.

"What is it!" he demanded.

"The map. The corner of the map. The piece that had the location of the treasure on it. It was in Father's boot. Now it's gone." She dropped the boot and walked past Shell.

He watched her back for a moment then studied the faces around him, powder-blackened, set faces. Stoddard, Santos, Crabbe. The Africans, Harry. None of their expressions gave anything away. None of them had any. Shell might have been studying a row of stone monuments.

He waited until they had covered the body and started to dig a grave, then he walked away, past the partially burnt wagon. Andy Rice was behind it, leaning against the wheel, arms folded.

"I thought maybe the Apaches had gotten you," she said.

"Did you? I didn't hear any cheering."

"Shit, Shelter, you know I love you." She came away from the wheel and walked to him, her eyes dancing, moving across Morgan's face.

"Nice talk for a Spanish princess."

"Yeah. Well, I'm a little tired of being that. You don't carry a bottle with you, do you? God, I could use a drink after that. I got two of them, you know."

"You'll give yourself away with a gun."

"Nobody was looking. Drilled one dead center, another got a lovely nick in his arm."

"Terrific." Shelter was tired and bored. Andy confused him and he mistrusted her. He looked instead toward Beth's wagon.

"Like that?" she asked. Morgan didn't answer. "Say, before you go—you ought to know, Channing didn't get shot by no Apaches."

"He what?" Shell turned around sharply.

"Do I stutter, Morgan? I said he didn't take any bullet from an Apache. I know. He was near to me when it happened. I saw him get it. It was in the back—you saw that—and he was facing the charging Indians.

"Who. . . ?"

"I don't know. I never saw. You figure it out. Whoever shows up with that piece of treasure map, I guess."

"How did you know about that?"

"Keep my ears open. Hell, I never seen a bunch like this for spilling all their secrets. One thing I know, we won't be turning back on account of this. We'll just keep on going because they've got the map now. Only ones they'd have to worry about would be them that objected to the way things were being done. They'd have to be done away with, wouldn't they?"

Her voice was damn near impish. Was Andy enjoying all this? Would she enjoy seeing Morgan on the ground with a bullet in his back—because she was right about that, he would have to die now. The map had been taken and whoever showed it would be confessing to murder. No matter, everyone else would go along with it, likely even Harry, if only out of fear. Morgan wouldn't. They knew that.

"*Adios*, hombre," Andy said as she started away. He could have cuffed her. Or, strangely, kissed her.

Beth was in her wagon, sagged into a chair, hands clasped, dangling. She looked up almost disinterestedly as Shelter climbed up.

"The rest of the map." She nodded toward the hatbox.

"That figures."

"I suppose it wasn't a good idea. Carrying that hatbox around all the time. It just told them where it was, didn't it?"

"I'm afraid so," Morgan said, picking up the box with the false lining ripped out. He looked around for the big old Walker Colt, but it wasn't there. He wondered what kind of gun Channing had been shot with—too late to think of that now.

He sat down beside Beth on the packing crate and put his arm around her. After a minute she turned her head and burst into tears, burying her face against his chest, beating at his body with tiny, desperate fists.

Morgan slept well away from the wagons that night and with the dawn he rode out alone onto the flank.

No one had mentioned turning back. They just continued on, rolling away from the small cairn over Bo Channing's grave.

Morgan saw no sign of Apaches, although he didn't discount the possibility of their return. They had run into more guns than they had expected and beat a hasty retreat. There could very well be more Apaches out there, making up a larger force.

Then too they could fall to raiding, slipping in after dark, lifting a few trinkets, a horse or a scalp or two—whatever was handy. No, you didn't disregard the Apaches.

But the land they now travelled was enough to discourage anyone, even the Indians. An immense salt playa, flats with a dried salt crust, stretched out before them for mile upon mile. The playa was a dead inland sea where no fish had swum for eons. The sand had formed a skin on the sand below as the sea evaporated and now it sat shimmering, cracked and limitless before their wagons.

Nothing at all lived on the flats, and nothing grew there. The only sign of life was the constant hovering black forms of the searching buzzards. They were following the right party, Morgan decided. There was death riding with this bunch and plenty of it. It had struck and would strike again, and continue striking perhaps until all of them were nothing but carrion for the vultures.

And maybe it wouldn't be that long.

The line of riding men appeared on the heat-blurred horizon, dark, wavering, sketched against the sky. A long picket line of warriors riding directly at them.

10.

Shell stood in the stirrups and rode back toward the wagons at a gallop, his gray kicking up clouds of salt dust. He could see Hart pointing excitedly, see Stoddard riding a nervous pony beside him, see the stolid black face of the African driver, see Beth peering worriedly southward, Andy Rice coldly amused, her hand resting near the Winchester which rode in the wagon box between her and Harry Channing.

"Who are they? Apaches?" Hart was nearly shouting as Morgan rode up.

"I can't tell yet."

"There must be thirty, forty of 'em," Crabbe, who was riding beside his boss, put in.

At least. They watched tensely, the dust from the shifting of their horses' hoofs sifting over them. There was no breeze. The world was airless, white and hot.

"They're not Apaches," Morgan said. "Not Indians."

"Mexican army?"

"No uniforms."

"It's Chavez!" Hart cried out nearly with joy and

Morgan glanced sharply at the colonel. "We've made it."

"*Made* it?" Morgan said, his tones clipped.

"My dear fellow, you didn't think I came here for the ride, did you? No, you aren't that stupid. I came to deliver Channing and his map to an old friend of mine down here. That is, Ramon Chavez."

"Friend or business partner?"

Hart laughed. "It amounts to the same thing. Perceptive, aren't you?"

"Not perceptive enough. I should have searched the wagons. That's what you've got, isn't it? Guns. The guns Cord Levitt went east to buy. Maxwell was the middle man—you're the gun dealer."

"How clever of you," Hart said. "You're a little late in coming up with the proper solution, however. Stoddard, get his gun."

"With pleasure," Jake said. Morgan thought about drawing on Jake, but the others—Santos, Crabbe, the Africans—were around him. He wouldn't have a chance. "Give me the gun, boy," Jake Stoddard said, and as soon as he had the barrel of Shell's weapon in his hand, he backhanded Morgan viciously. Shell's head twisted around, blood filling his mouth. His head rang. Stoddard, laughing, hit him again, this time using the side of Shell's own gun. Morgan was knocked from his horse to lie against the blazing white playa.

"I said take his gun, nothing more," Hart said with authority, and Stoddard turned away with a little growl.

Shell was lying there watching Jake. He shook his head, rolled over and rose to lean against his horse, hearing the approaching hoofbeats now. When he glanced that way, the men began to take on clarity and definition. They wore sombreros or stetsons, carried rifles and at least two pistols each. They were dark, with here and there an American, some wearing crossed bandoliers on their chests. Every single one of them looked tough enough to bite nails.

Their leader was a man with a patch over his right eye. Chavez? Morgan didn't think so. He was burly, his stomach thrusting at the white shirt he wore, threatening to burst it. He wore a dark sombrero with gold-thread decorations. He had a long drooping mustache and a savage gleam in his good eye.

The bandits reined up in a cloud of dust, their horses rearing, nickering, the men cursing, laughing, crowding their animals in around Hart's party in a close circle.

"Welcome, gentlemen," Hart said, moving toward the man with the eye patch. "Glad to see you, we had a little run-in with the Indians. Señor Chavez could not come himself? Too bad."

The man with the patch stared at Hart coldly, turned his head and spat. "You got water for our horses?"

"We have a barrel of water left, but—"

"Water the ponies," the *bandido* told the man on his left.

"We will have to share what is left."

The man with the patch glared at Hart again and the colonel fell silent, perhaps privately planning his revenge. Surely Chavez wouldn't want his associate treated like this!

Shelter was leaning against his horse still, waiting, watching. The *bandido* was looking back now, staring, measuring.

"Is this one Morgan?" he asked.

"That's him," Hart said eagerly. "Shelter Morgan."

Patch turned his head. "Kill him."

"You'd better not," Shell said as hands grabbed for

him and held him.

"Why, hombre?" Patch spat again.

"I've got the treasure map," Shell announced. It was a weak bluff, but it was the only thing that popped into his mind just then. He waited for Hart or Stoddard to laugh and produce the missing map. Sweat trickled down from his sideburns, dripped into his eyes to sting them, soaked his shirt front. His mouth was filled with dust. Patch just stared at him.

"Search him," Patch commanded.

"I don't have it on me. I memorized it."

"Draw it!"

"Go to hell."

Why wasn't the one who stole the map, who took that vital piece of it from Bo Channing's body coming forward to punch holes in Shell's story? Hart looked befuddled, Stoddard darkly curious. No one moved. The hands maintained their grip on Shell. He could smell the strong odors of the *bandidos* who lived in a land where there was little water and took no advantage of it when there was some.

"All right." Patch didn't want to argue it. "Tie him, put him back on his horse. We let Chavez and Levitt figure what they want to do."

Still puzzled, Morgan was bound and put on the gray again, his hat jammed on his head by a narrow-faced Mexican who showed a gold tooth when he smiled.

"Hey, Patch, look!"

They found the women. Beth was being dragged by the arm to an accompanying chorus of boots, catcalls and whistles.

Hart stepped importantly forward. "Please, gentlemen. It's certainly not necessary to bother the ladies."

"Go to hell, old man!" someone jeered. Patch spoke to him rapidly in Spanish, and with a disparaging wave of his hand, the outlaw turned away. Beth was released.

Andy Rice, who had been dragged along behind, was examined closely. Patch moved to her, lifted her face and addressed a few words to her.

"Get away!" It was Harry Channing, showing more guts than Shell had given him credit for—and less sense. "Stay away from her!" His voice squeaked as he shouted. "Or I'll kill you!"

He never saw the blow coming. From behind a *bandido* on horseback slammed the butt of his rifle into Harry Channing's head and he went down like a pole-axed steer. Beth screamed, the colonel muttered a curse. Patch, bored apparently, turned away.

"Finish watering the horses. Then we ride."

In the meantime all of Hart's people were disarmed. Stoddard looked as if he might make a fight of it at that point, but Harry Channing, still holding his head, moaning, blood seeping from a deep scalp wound, was sitting in the dust nearby and Jake meekly handed his weapons over in the end. The Africans, Shelter thought, were ready to die over it, but Hart spoke quickly to them in their own tongue and they too handed their weapons over. Morgan was watching—nobody searched Andy Rice. That was their first mistake. He had never seen the bounty woman without a gun, and he would have bet that somewhere in the folds of that long dark skirt she was wearing, or under it, there was a Colt .44.

They set out southward, Patch and his *bandidos* silent, watching. Hart was fuming. He kept complaining that Chavez wouldn't like the way he was being treated. Patch managed to laugh once at that.

Morgan knew now why the guns had been paid for in advance, back in St. Jo. How the hell could anyone expect to get anything from Chavez and Levitt once they were down here in outlaw territory? No—Levitt had made that long trip to buy arms, had paid for them. James Maxwell had taken the money, passed it on to

Hart who was the brains of the operation, the man with the means of smuggling guns quickly, safely—in a private train. Now more Mexicans and border Americans could be slaughtered. New repeating rifles, hundreds of them, would allow Chavez to build up his army and remain a force in northern Mexico.

Beth was mounted on a horse. It was that or ride beside the outlaw with the gold tooth who was driving the wagon. She eased up beside Morgan.

"The map . . . when you told them that . . ."

"I don't have it," Shell assured her. "I never saw the missing corner."

"I thought . . ." She was all breathless again as her nerves played tricks on her. "Father . . ."

"I didn't shoot him. I wasn't even there, remember?"

She smiled weakly, almost gratefully.

"I was just trying to stay alive," he told Beth. "It's going to be a little difficult to do when I come face to face with Cord Levitt. It might," he considered, "be hard for any of us to stay alive."

"Colonel Hart brought them their guns."

"Yes. And now that that bargain's completed, what do they need him for?"

"But they haven't any reason to kill him!"

"I don't think," Shell said slowly, "men like Chavez need a reason."

"They'll find out soon enough you don't know where the gold is," Beth said.

"I suppose so. Especially if they search us all and find the missing map."

"Will they think of that?"

"Maybe." Morgan shrugged. "But then maybe whoever took it has done what I've claimed to do: memorize the map and toss it away."

"That would make sense."

"Especially now. Yes, it would make a lot of sense."

They rode on. The sun was going down but the heat was oppressive. Shelter's eyes burned. His hands had no circulation in them, tied as they were. The distances shimmered in a heat haze. The mountains, growing closer with each mile, were saw-toothed, barren, deep brown.

"How's your brother?" Shell asked after a time.

"He's all right, I think. They let Maria bandage him. Do you think she's in love with him?"

Morgan laughed out loud and Beth's wide green eyes got wider.

"No," Shelter said at length. "I don't think so."

"She's not Spanish, is she?"

"Why?"

"I saw her face when that man with the patch was talking to her. She didn't understand what he was saying."

"No, she's not Spanish."

"Then who is she?"

"You'd better ask her."

"Someone you know?" Beth asked a little anxiously.

"Someone I've met. A strange woman with a chip on her shoulder and a past I could only guess at. She's tough as boot leather, Beth."

"Her name?"

"She'll have to tell you."

"Because you don't want to betray her, because you care for her?" She was getting just a little frantic. Jealous?

"Because she wouldn't want me to. I don't care for her."

They rode in silence and after a while Beth turned back toward the wagons, to check on Harry, she said. Morgan watched her go. He wasn't the only one. The *bandidos* were showing a great deal of interest in her. A great deal.

To his right now Morgan saw a patch of green, so sudden and stark that it startled him, momentarily confusing his senses. He had been staring at white sand, at salt playa, mile upon mile of it and now—it was only a half acre or so of parched grass, but it showed signs of water, and that meant life. There was a series of low, sandy hills rising to their right now and as they followed them south and west they saw a cottonwood tree like something mysterious and otherworldly growing in the shade of the bluffs.

The tree and then the sparkling, narrow stream running down into a small, crescent shaped valley. That and the three riflemen on the bluff, lifting a hand to Patch and his men as they rolled past the checkpoint.

And just ahead was the end of the journey. The magnificent white villa which had belonged to the Castillo y Cortes family. Two stories tall, with red tile on the roof, balconies at nearly every window, the two arms of the U-shaped house stretching back to embrace a patio where a shimmering indicated a pond or fountain. To one side there was a stand of ancient oaks, beneath them a smith's shed, a stable—white though the paint was peeling now—a well and a tall white barn, also peeling.

As they rode nearer, Shelter could see that most of the place was in disrepair. Fences fallen down, glass broken, gardens overrun by thorny native stock, vines and creepers in a tangle of dried brown.

Beth was looking at it all with a little sadness. There was, Shelter considered, every chance that this place belonged to her and her brother. Apparently Bo had been his brother's only relative and the Spanish side of the family had played out long ago, according to Bo.

They rode now past a fenced field where dozens of

horses grazed—the horses were far from run-down. They were deeply muscled, finely molded, sleek animals built for running far and long. Bandits' horses, the best that could be stolen. A handful of dirty-looking men stood around a breaking corral, arguing—apparently over a bet—and they turned casual eyes to the passing wagon train and its escort.

Morgan didn't give them much more of a look-see. He had counted heads roughly, trying to gauge by what he saw the numbers of horses Chavez had, how many men he might have siding him. The answer was far too many. Maybe a hundred, maybe only half that.

It was an exercise in futility. Three were too many for Morgan—he wasn't going anywhere. He'd be lucky to live out the next few hours. All that had kept him alive this far was his thin tale about knowing where the treasure of the Castillo y Cortes family was.

The wagons drew up practically in front of the balustraded entranceway to the great house, rolling across what should have been lawn and planted garden.

Shelter was pulled down from his horse. He saw Beth and Andy Rice being brought forward, Hart and Stoddard pushed along to join them, all standing before the covered entranceway to the villa.

The door opened and Cord Levitt stepped out.

11.

Cord Levitt, former lieutenant, CSA. Looking the same but for a touch of gray at the temples, a little sagging of the flesh beneath the chin. His black eyes stared out at the gathering. Muscles tightened and then slackened again in his scooped cheeks. His knobby brow furrowed as if in deep thought, then those eyes opened wide.

"Morgan! Captain Shelter Morgan. Patch, what are you waiting for? I told you to kill this man when you found him."

"Sorry, Señor Levitt," Patch said smoothly, "but there is a complication."

"What complication?" Levitt demanded.

"He has the map," Patch said a little more coldly. They didn't seem to hit it off too well.

"Get it," Levitt snapped.

Patch tapped his temple significantly and Cord Levitt made a disgusted face. "Well," he said, "we can take that from him too. In fact it may be an enjoyable exercise."

"What will be enjoyable?" a softly accented, cultured voice asked. It was, had to be Ramon Chavez, but he was nothing like Morgan had expected. What he had thought they would find was a cigarillo smoking, mustached bandit in a big sombrero. The young, wavy haired man who emerged from the house was wearing vaquero's clothes, flared, slash-cuffed pants in black velvet with a gold thread stripe, a white shirt with ruffles at the cuffs and a tight, short jacket. He was carefully barbered and manicured. A young gentleman any father would be happy to have his daughter marry—if you didn't know about the hundred dead bodies in Chavez's wake. "What are you discussing, Cord? And why speak out here in the hot sun?"

"Señor Chavez! I'm Colonel Hart." The colonel pushed his way forward, shaking off his guards.

"Yes, so you must be," Chavez said.

"This is deplorable. These men holding me. Me! Why, I've come a long way to bring you your weapons."

"And the treasure map?" Chavez asked pleasantly.

"Why, yes. That is, I did have it, but . . ."

Levitt interrupted. "That's what we were discussing—Captain Morgan there has taken it and apparently memorized it."

"Yes?" Chavez's eyes shifted with haughty interest to Morgan. "So that is the one, is it? The one you fear, Cord."

"Fear him," Cord spluttered.

"The one who tracks down his enemies and finishes them. An interesting man, I think."

"He'd be more interesting dead. I've got a knife—let's find out what he knows and then be done with him."

"Can you make him talk with a knife?"

"I can make any man talk with a knife," Cord Levitt said coldly.

"Perhaps." Chavez was thoughtful. "Two charming young ladies as well," he said, his voice rising appreciatively as he looked at Andy Rice and Beth Channing. Chavez was wearing his very best manners. For a cutthroat he was exceptionally polite. Maybe living in the old villa had given him the idea that he was a cultured gentleman of leisure instead of a bloody, murdering bastard. Just then Morgan had to admit that he preferred Chavez's approach to that of Cord Levitt.

Chavez gestured. "Please, bring the two gentlemen and the ladies in."

"What about me?" Jake Stoddard asked. Chavez didn't even bother to answer him. His dark gaze flickered briefly to Stoddard, dismissed him, and darted away.

"My brother," Beth said breathily. "He's in the back of that wagon. Hurt."

Chavez looked Beth up and down, smiled widely, showing a lot of white teeth, and then spoke in rapid Spanish to some of his men. They nodded and went to the back of the wagon, hauling Harry Channing out. He didn't look so good with the blood all over his scalp and face, but he didn't strike Morgan as being so bad off as he pretended. The Mexicans carried him into the house, Chavez extended an arm in the direction of the door and Beth followed, Andy Rice on her heels, the colonel on hers.

"And Captain Morgan," Chavez said softly. "You must join our party."

"Sure." Shelter nodded and went up the steps, the pressure of a rifle muzzle against his spine prodding him on until Chavez spoke again and the rifle was removed.

"Also untie this man. Are we barbarians?" Chavez asked.

The correct answer was yes, but no one said it. Morgan's hands were cut free by Patch who still didn't smell very pretty. Shell rubbed at his wrists and went in, followed by Chavez and by Cord Levitt who was smoking at the ears.

"Everyone will want to clean up before dinner," Chavez said grandly. It was too much for Levitt.

"Are you going crazy, Ramon?" he cried. "What the hell is the point in feeding Morgan—he's going to die. What are you going to do—take the prisoners into your family?"

Chavez turned sharply, his eyes sparking for a brief moment, for long enough to show Shelter the big, killing cat that was hidden inside the "gentleman," Ramon Chavez. He cooled off quickly, through force of will.

"We must be civilized, Cord. There is nothing to be done which has to be done in such a hurry that we cannot dine. You intend to go on a treasure hunt tonight? In the darkness with an empty stomach? No—" he placed a hand briefly on Levitt's arm. "We shall eat, we shall talk. Everything will be made clear to Morgan. We shall proceed relaxed, fed, rested. See that the weapons are unloaded, will you? Please check to see that they are all as they were supposed to be, that the ammunition is the proper caliber."

Levitt didn't move for a moment. He didn't like to be placed in a subservient position apparently; but that seemed to be the way things were—Chavez was the boss. He owned the soldiers. Levitt clamped his jaw shut, spun on his heel and went off.

"Please—Eduardo, show the men their rooms." Chavez's hands clapped twice and a stout woman appeared from nowhere. "The women, Alicia, show them to their chambers please."

Morgan followed the man, Eduardo, quietly. What

else was there to do? Make an escape from that fortress with half a hundred men about it, across the hundred miles of desert alone, without even a gun? It was a time for being quiet, for taking it very slow.

The room was handsome but dusty, long unused. There was no linen on the big, canopied bed, only a spread which the man whipped off before bowing out, leading Hart and the men carrying Harry Channing down the hall.

Shelter waited until the door was closed then crossed to the French window which opened onto a balcony. Outside he looked down a rickety trellis overgrown by now-dead roses. Shifting his eyes slightly he could see two armed men in the trees not twenty feet from the foot of the trellis. They were looking right at him.

Morgan went back in time to see two young, frightened-looking men drag a zinc-plated tub into his room.

"Your bath, señor," they said. Well, it wasn't yet, but within fifteen minutes the hot water began to arrive, plenty of it. It must have been boiling all morning and into the afternoon—Chavez had planned ahead for his company. Or maybe they had been planning on soup.

Shelter undressed and stepped into the tub, finding it *muy caliente*. That would redden his little cheeks, he thought as he settled into the water with a sigh.

The water kept coming and a bar of scented soap, a backbrush and a huge, soft towel. Shell lay in the tub, his eyes barely open, thinking and watching, soaking some of the soreness away.

One of the little men came back with a clean shirt—black with black buttons—and a pair of socks. He placed these on the bed, and said, "Señor Chavez wishes to dine in ten minutes," and slid on out.

Chavez was falling prisoner to his fantasies, Morgan thought. He, who pretended to despise the wealthy landowners and wanted to lead a peasant revolt, was himself wealthy with stolen loot. He had a grand hacienda, maids and servants, an army to do his bidding. Now he was trying desperately to become a gentleman.

Shelter climbed out of the tub, walked naked across to the mirror on the wall and began to shave with the soap and razor that had been provided. Finished, he dried off before the window which was glossed with organge-gold at this hour from the dying sun. Dressing then, he went out of the room.

Two ugly-looking *bandidos* who had been playing cards at a half-moon table, looked up, fell in behind him, and escorted him to the dining room.

"Together again," Chavez cracked as Morgan entered the room.

Shell didn't answer. He saw the colonel, cheeks red from wine, sitting to one side in a smallish gray suit. He toasted Morgan silently.

In matching chairs flanking a window which was ceiling-height, framed by gold colored drapes, sat Andy Rice and Beth, both in white, both showing a handsome amount of youthful, smoothly sloping decolletage. Beth wore a crystal necklace to complete her costume; Andy Rice wore a disgusted expression. She must have felt trapped in her own disguise now. She wanted out of that dress, into some jeans and gunbelt.

Harry Channing looked pale. He had a bandage on his head, wore a green suit awkwardly. Chavez was sleek and polished, Cord Levitt in brown, angry as ever, and drinking hard apparently.

Dinner was a silent affair of roast beef and tortillas, wine and dove breasts.

It was Cord Levitt who went after Shell when the meal was over—presumably with Chavez's permission.

"I want you to come into the library with me and draw that treasure map, Captain Morgan."

"I don't think so," Shell said, sipping at his wine. Cord was across the table from him, his eyes bulging, his fists clenched.

"You will," Levitt said in a strangled hiss. "You will or you'll pay for it!"

"Maybe. I figure I'll pay a lot more if I draw the map."

"Mr. Morgan is perhaps afraid you will murder him," Colonel Hart said, trying to be jovial. "I'm sure if you will give him your word that nothing like that will happen, he would be happy to cooperate."

Nobody was in a hurry to promise anything. Chavez's face was dark and still. Levitt was rigid with anger.

"Let's go together," Morgan suggested finally.

"Do what?"

"I'll take you to it."

"What's that gain you?" Levitt asked.

"I don't know. You tell me. I'll take you to it if you'll let me keep riding after we find it."

"If we don't?"

"We will." Morgan was waiting. "What's your answer to my proposal?"

"Why should we make any bargain with you?" Levitt shouted. "I can cut the answers out of you."

"You can cut something out of me, but you'd never be sure it was the right map. Then if I was dead, you'd be out of luck for good and all, wouldn't you?"

Levitt started to rise from his chair, and at a look from Chavez sagged back. Beth was watching Shell anxiously. The candlelight glittered on her crystal necklace, shone in her eyes. Andy Rice was calmly sipping her wine. Everyone was waiting for an answer.

"All right," Cord said at last. "Why not."

Why not, Morgan can always be killed later. Shelter could read his eyes, his thoughts. No matter—he had gained a few days, a little time to try and find a way out of this death trap.

"We leave in the morning then," Chavez said as if they were going on a fishing expedition. He poured Hart a little more wine. "Which direction do we travel, Morgan?" he asked quietly.

"Into the hills." That much he was sure of from the map he had seen. Although finding the treasure wasn't his reason for wanting to go into those hills. If there was to be a prayer of escape it would be in rough country, not on the endless flats of the desert. "The women—they have to go along."

"Why?" Chavez asked calmly. Cord Levitt muttered, "Like hell."

"I won't leave them here with your *bandidos*, that's why. You think we could trust them not to bother the ladies?"

"Of course not," Chavez answered with a laugh. "Very well. What does it matter?"

"And I—" Hart began.

"We need you for nothing, Hart," Chavez said with surprising fierceness. His face smoothed out again and he smiled suavely. "I see no need for you to accompany us."

Morgan spoke up quickly. It could be that Hart was the one with the map. It could be that, blocked, he would say so and sign Morgan's death warrant.

"He surely can't hinder us. The colonel might be of considerable help. After we recover the treasure all of us—the Channings, the colonel, Miss Ramirez and me can head north and out of your life. You can remain here wealthier, better armed—"

"What do we get out of it?" Harry whined.

"What Mr. Morgan suggests," Chavez answered, "is that you win your lives in exchange for the gold." Harry swallowed hard as Chavez stared him down. "I think it is a fair exchange."

"Morgan don't get out alive," Cord Levitt said.

"I think so," Chavez answered. "What do you think? He is going to come back and hunt you down? Here?" An arm circled the room, taking in by extension the army outside the walls of the house, the desert beyond. "You have nothing to worry about. The gold, Cord, is worth more than this man's skin."

"I know him, he won't quit."

"He will quit. I give him his life once, and if he comes back then he dies. Very fair."

Very fair, also hardly likely. Chavez didn't give a damn if Cord Levitt killed Morgan or not. He was only trying to keep everything smooth and easy until the gold was recovered—and that was liable to take a long damn time if they were depending on Shelter to lead them to it.

Cord went away grumbling and Chavez fell into a discussion with Colonel Hart about Africa. Beth wandered the dining room and the reception hall beyond, looking at the faded wallpaper, the stained plaster, the tile floors, the solid, vast mantlepiece above the fireplace, perhaps wondering what it would have been like to live here in its days of glory.

Hart had shifted the conversation. He was half looped now, bragging to Chavez about one thing and another, mostly about his wealth. Morgan heard his name and he lifted his eyes to the colonel.

"It was amusing really. Cord had left word to look out for Captain Morgan. Well, Morgan had done everything to make himself visible and I knew where he was, but I didn't know how to take care of him. My first idea was to have Stoddard abduct him—all that got was a beating for Jake." The colonel chuckled. "Then lo and behold, Morgan presents himself at the station as this Sterling and begs a ride. Walked right into it. All I had to do was keep quiet and bring him along to Cord. I think I deserve a little something extra for delivering him, by the way."

"Certainly," Chavez purred. "Of course. I'll speak to Cord when he cools off. You know how he is, very hot-tempered."

Hart was being taken in by it all. He was great friends with Chavez now. He'd be lucky if they didn't slit his throat up in those hills, but he didn't realize it. Hart usually ran with a different kind of crook—those who would rob you blind and shake your hand gentlemanly as they left. Chavez was a different kind of customer. His life was based frankly on violence.

Maybe Hart was cleverer than Shell thought. Maybe he did have the map. To be used as an ace in the hole if things got tight, to hold onto if he could, to keep out of Chavez's hands. That was the one reason for keeping the map private that made sense—let Morgan be the one to fail, let Morgan be the one who got himself killed. Later, when time and the forces of the Mexican and U.S. governments had taken care of Chavez, then a wise man could come back, on the quiet, and take that gold out of the hills.

So it could be Hart. It could be any of them. Whoever it was was giving Shelter a few more days of life but little else. The noose was around Shell's neck and it was tightening. His string was very nearly played out.

Chavez rose. "Let us get some sleep. Tomorrow will be a long day, I'm sure. And the next?" He looked at Morgan who nodded agreement. "But not many more days after that, Mr. Morgan. You understand that? You have two days to find the treasure of the Castillo y

Cortes family. When the sun goes down on the second day I must have the treasure. Or you, I am sorry, will no longer be alive. That is very clear, I think," he said with brisk self-satisfaction.

Yes, it was very clear. Chavez put his wineglass down, summoned his servants and went out of the room. The Mexicans stood with their heads hanging docilely, waiting to show the guests to their rooms—and, Shelter guessed, to lock them in.

Shelter started out of the room. Andy Rice had sidled up beside him, a wineglass still in her hand. "When do we make the break, Morgan?" she asked with dark humor. "After we get the gold or before?"

He paused and looked into her eyes. Glancing at the patient servants he asked in a low voice, "You have a pistol, Andy?"

"What do you think?" she answered in her husky voice. "Think that's enough, do you?"

"It might be. When the time comes." Then he turned away again, walking through the door. The two *bandidos* who had followed him downstairs, followed him upstairs. Shell was placed in his room and locked in. Yanking off his coat and tie he walked again to the balcony and peered out. Still there. He could hear the guards below talking. He turned and looked up. There was a man on the roof. He could see his boots dangling.

Shelter slammed the doors shut as he went back in and stood in the darkness, feeling the noose drawing tighter.

12.

They rode out with the dawn, toward the reddish hills in the distance. Shelter Morgan, Chavez, Cord Levitt. Behind them were Beth and Andy Rice, both on horseback, then Jake Stoddard and his two remaining men. After that came the Africans, Harry Channing and the colonel. Behind them, leading the pack horses were twenty of Chavez's soldiers.

Twenty. The rest had remained at the villa.

Morgan figured he was already making progress. He only had half the enemies he had had yesterday. And thirty-six hours to live.

That is, unless he found that treasure, which didn't seem very likely. The hills sprawled out forever in all directions. Unless he stumbled over a lot of goldware and candelabra he wasn't apt to find anything.

He knew two things about its location—it was to the north in the direction the escaping American don had been riding and it was in the rugged hills. That being so the party leaving the villa would have had to ride along the bottom. There was no way through the hills for wagons or pack animals. The treasure itself must be near the trail—more accurately a dry streambed which angled northward.

Knowing that he knew nothing. They plodded on, the day growing hot, airless as they rode among the red hills where only stunted cedar and sage grew, manzanita in a twisted tangle. At times Morgan was beside Beth, then Cord Levitt, silent, red-eyed, would be there or Andy Rice.

"Got a good idea where you're going to lose us?" Andy asked once. She was still smiling, damn her.

"Not much. You have that item I was asking about, do you?"

"All six chambers of it and attached necessaries."

"Good."

Andy cracked, "Yeah, good. I've been trying to divide twenty into six and it won't go. Maybe we could get them to line up in a row for us."

"Could be. Who's got the map, Andy? You?"

"Me!" Andy laughed. "Not likely."

"Do you think we can find it?"

"Why? What's the difference?"

"It might make it easier to get out of this."

"I don't see how," Andy said. She looked casually around. No one was listening or watching very closely. They were strung out along a narrow streambed which twisted through the hills. A few gray cottonwoods overhung the trail.

"As long as we have it we live," Morgan said.

"Maybe."

"Chavez bluffs, but he's not that impatient—not impatient enough to kill us before he's gotten the gold."

"Maybe not." Andy shrugged. "I don't know where it is anyway."

"I'd like to search Hart one more time."

"Not likely now, is it?"

"No."

"How about Stoddard?"

"He's a possibility. Jake's only half dumb. He's possible. I just wish I knew."

He fell silent. Chavez was riding up on his left. The bandit leader lifted his hat to Andy Rice who pulled up, letting her horse fall back. Chavez laughed.

"She does not like me!"

"She wants to live. It's funny how you can hold a grudge against someone who wants to kill you or hold you prisoner."

"Yes." Chavez frowned. "Maybe so. What is it, Morgan—you think I will not keep my word?"

"No. I don't think so."

"You think I am a liar!"

"I don't think you'll keep your word," Shell said, avoiding the direct challenge. "If you wanted to, Cord wouldn't let it happen. He'll kill me if he can. It's more important to him than the gold, I think."

Chavez studied Morgan closely, the unblinking, ice-blue eyes, the solid line of jaw, the square shoulders. "Maybe you are right. I have heard him talk of you many times. There was fear in his words. Not in his tone, but in the way he expressed his own hate—fear was there. He must kill you."

"And you'll have to allow it."

Chavez shrugged. "What will be will be. You must first keep your end of this bargain. You must first find the gold—and do you know, Morgan, if I am a liar, perhaps I am not the only one here, eh? Perhaps you do not know where the treasure is."

"I know."

"I hope so, Morgan. I hope so very much. Because you have no idea the pain you will cause yourself and your friends if you are lying. If you think Cord Levitt is a cruel man, you have not seen Ramon Chavez when he is angry. What do you think of that, Shelter Morgan?"

"I think that *now* you are telling the truth," Morgan replied and Chavez threw back his head and laughed.

"We understand each other, Morgan. Now we understand each other."

It was a long day of dusty riding and airless heat, through long, winding canyons which seemed to lead nowhere. Sunset came early and they camped, Morgan knowing he was down to twenty-four hours now, having no idea how the hell he was going to get out of this.

It didn't help when they hobbled him with a short length of rope and tied his hands to a tree. A guard squatted down nearby, watching darkly. Chavez laughed again—he was developing quite a sense of humor. "Just so that you do not get any ideas, all right? I am *sorry* for the discomfort."

The sun went down, leaving the wall of bluffs opposite glowing a faint red yet. Faint red, purple in the hollows, black at the base of the bluffs where the shadows stretched out into the streambed.

Beth brought Morgan his dinner—beans and bacon—and she spooned it into his mouth.

"Are you all right?" she asked.

"So far."

"They're going to kill you," Beth said, and the hand that held the spoon trembled.

"If I don't find the treasure for them."

"And me? What happens to me?" she asked a little hysterically.

"You'll be all right."

"Will I! How am I going to be all right, Shelter? I am sorry—really. I am sorry, but I've got to do it for myself. I deserve to live too, don't I? If anyone deserves a share of that gold, it's me."

"What are you going on about?"

She was literally trembling from head to toe, her eyes starting out of her head, her mouth hung open. She dropped the bowl she had been feeding Shelter from and stepped away as if in fright.

"I'm sorry. It's you or us, isn't it?" Beth asked. "I've got to make my own deal while I can."

"What in the . . . you've got the map!"

"Harry does. He didn't kill father, but he got the map. He and I—we need something to live on. I'm sorry, Shelter!" She turned and started away, and stepped right into the arms of Ramon Chavez. The firelight beyond painted his face weirdly with moving shadows.

"What is this?" he asked smoothly. "A problem, Miss Channing? Is Mr. Morgan being bad?"

"No. It's not that." She looked at Shelter and then licked her dry lips. "He doesn't have the map. He never had it, not all of it. He couldn't have memorized it. Shell," she said again, maybe thinking that if she repeated it enough he'd believe it, "I'm sorry."

"So?" Chavez was smiling crookedly. His teeth were very white in his darkly shadowed face. "He never had it? He lied to stay alive, is that it?"

"Yes," Beth answered.

"Cord Levitt will be happy to hear this. Very happy. Who has the map then?"

"My brother and I. We have it."

"Show it to me."

"First—I have to know. We want to know, will you let us have a fair share?"

"Of course," Chavez said, his voice becoming positively oily. "I am a fair man, Miss Channing."

"Just a fair share," Beth rattled on. "That's all. We're not greedy, of course. Just enough to see us through for a few years, perhaps."

"Don't worry, Miss Channing," Ramon Chavez said, placing a hand on her shoulder. Beth's knees were wobbling furiously. Even then Morgan found it hard to hate her. Even though she had just handed him over to the executioner.

"Well, Mr. Morgan?" Chavez asked. "Is it all true?"

"The lady may have the map. I have it memorized," Shell lied.

"Yes? But I would rather have it written down than rely on your memory. You are of no use at all, are you?" he demanded.

There wasn't much Shelter could answer to that. There he sat, trussed, bound to the trees. Chavez sneered and walked away. "Call your brother, Miss Channing," Morgan heard him say as he led her toward the campfire. "Tell him we have reached an agreement."

"Certainly," Beth said. Her voice was just a little breathless. Morgan was rapidly finding that quality less appealing. He saw them walk to the fire, speak to those sitting there, saw someone—Cord Levitt, he thought—rise from the ground like a man with a spring under him. It didn't take much to figure out what he had on his mind. Chavez had just turned him loose. Now he was going to have himself a little fun with that knife. It was cold out; Shelter was dripping sweat.

Cord Levitt had started his way. He was still a long way off, but even from there Morgan could see the cold light in his eyes, the gleam of firelight on knife. Oh, yes. He was going to have himself a good time. Toes and fingers, ears and nose. Or maybe he wouldn't be able to hold himself back. Maybe he'd just slash the throat and leave Shelter there choking on his own blood.

"Well, Captain," Cord Levitt said as he walked up. "It's time. It's been a long wait. You've caused me a lot of sleepless nights. Now it's your turn to go down."

That was it then. The end of the long hard road. Well, he had always known it would come sometime. Still he hated to go down under the knife of scum like Cord Levitt.

"Untie me. Give me a chance," he said. Levitt just laughed.

"No, thanks. No chances. This is a sure thing, Morgan, you are going to die."

Shelter guessed he was. There was no way out, none at all. Cord crouched down and sat fingering his knife, anticipating, soaking it all up, enjoying each moment.

"I think an eye," he said and the sweat that was beading Shell's forehead streamed down his face coldly. It was fear, yes, cold fear. When a man has you bound and you know he's going to cut your eyes out, you're afraid. Cord Levitt managed to laugh. Shell pulled violently at the ropes which tied him, struggling, writhing, cursing, knowing all the while that there was no way he was going to get free.

"All right—that's enough fooling around," Cord said. The point of his knife was inches from Shelter's face, circling slowly as he zeroed in on Morgan's eye which studied the gleaming, sharp point of the knife automatically, studied its own end.

"Cord!" Ramon Chavez shouted out from across the camp, a little panic in his voice. "Don't do it!"

Cord spun around, cursing, coming to his feet. Chavez was running toward him, Beth on his heels, Harry standing awkwardly behind.

"What the hell's the matter?" Cord growled.

"You didn't . . ." Chavez peered at Morgan with relief. "*Madre de Dios!* The girl doesn't have the map. Her brother doesn't have the map. She is crazy."

"I don't know what happened to it," Harry shouted weakly.

Beth was nearer. "He told me he had it. He told me." Chavez turned and slapped her viciously across the face and she buried her face in her hands.

"Women," Chavez said bitterly, "crazy American women."

"Did you go through their belongings?"

"What do you think? There's nothing there. Morgan's the man of the hour again. You are alive again, Morgan," Chavez said, bending down. "How does it feel?"

"Dandy," Shell whispered. Chavez laughed and walked away. Cord Levitt hung around a minute longer.

"A short reprieve, Morgan, that's all. I'll have you yet."

"Your boss promised to let me ride out if I showed him where the treasure is."

"Yeah." Cord Levitt smiled nastily. "His promise isn't worth a lot. Mine is. Believe me."

Andy Rice had wandered over, a shawl around her shoulders. She looked at both men as with vague curiosity. Then she saw the bowl of food on the ground.

"Mind if I finish feeding him?" Andy asked.

"What the hell do I care," Levitt snarled. "It's a waste of time though, lady. It really is a waste of time."

Then he was gone and there was only Shelter and Andy and the Mexican guard who still squatted nearby, who had not spoken or blinked since Shell had been tied up.

Andy was looking for the spoon on the ground. She found it and wiped it off on her skirt. "Open up, big boy," she said to Morgan who had suddenly lost his appetite for cold beans. He took a mouthful anyway, his eyes boring holes in the back of Cord Levitt as he swaggered away, his naked knife still in his hand.

"A fun night, huh?" Andy said.

"You're not fooling anyone, tough guy. Your voice has got the shakes."

"Yeah—so's yours, Morgan."

"I've got the right."

"I guess so." Andy's voice softened just a little and what was almost a smile crept across her lips. She glanced around at the guard and then spoke down into the bowl, "Know anyone who'd like a used treasure map, Mr. Morgan?"

"You!" Shell shouted out before he could help himself. Now his voice dropped to a hoarse whisper. "You've got the map?"

"Sure. My man Harry had it. Harry loves his mommy. Harry is very careless. Now Mommy has the map."

"Well, damn you, Andy Rice, if you're not turning out to be worth something after all."

"Sure. I'm worth something. Worth exactly twenty-four hours to you. Take another bite of these beans, Pancho's watching."

Shell did so, chewing thoughtfully, slowly. When he had swallowed, he said, "Now what? The map doesn't do me much good really. Tomorrow at dusk I'm a goner anyway, gold or none."

"Maybe the bastard would keep his word—it's possible."

"Possible a rattler's got hind legs."

"I guess you're right—another bite." She practically forced it in his mouth. "How about this." The small metallic object dropped into Shell's lap. It lay there gleaming prettily. The blade was only four or five inches long, but it was plenty long enough to cut his ropes—or somebody's throat. And then what? The knife didn't appear to offer much more hope than the map. Where would he go, how?

"They'd run me down, Andy."

"It's a chance. You've got none here."

"What about you?"

"Me? I can count pretty high. I've an idea what that gold is worth, Morgan."

"You've got to be kidding. Chavez isn't going to share that gold with anyone, and you know it. What's the idea, Andy?"

"I don't know." She actually turned her face away. "I thought maybe if you were gone he wouldn't much give a damn so long as he had the treasure map. It's Cord Levitt that has the grudge, not Chavez. And these men are Chavez's. If you make a break Levitt will have to go after you alone and take a chance on losing his own cut of the gold—or let you go."

"Uh-huh. That sounds good, Andy—but I don't intend to take off and leave you here."

"Must be love."

"Or Beth Channing, if I can help it."

"After what she tried to do to you!" Andy stood bolt upright, mad as a wet hen. She slapped the bowl and spoon down.

"She was scared."

"Scared, hell, she was greedy. Morgan, you beat all—you can't tell when a woman's good for you and when she's not."

"You telling me something, Andy?"

"You? How the hell could I tell *you* anything? Do what you want. Throw your life away. Don't worry about me, though. I want to see that gold, Morgan. As much as Beth Channing. Chavez was worth five thousand to me. *That* was worth coming south for. You know what that treasure's supposed to be worth? Hart said half a million easy. You do what you want—I'm sticking with this outfit until I see what glitters and what don't. Andy Rice isn't some fainting society lady."

She stood there, still angry. "Get the hell out of here," she whispered. "Live. There's a loose horse down along the river, among the big cottonwoods. Use your sense."

And then she was gone and Morgan sat there watching the minutes pass, watching the Mexican guard, the dwindling fire, the long running sky.

13.

The knife was cool and solid in his hand. Shelter Morgan turned it and cut through the first strand of rope. His eyes never wavered from the guard's face. The man hadn't moved for an hour. He was either asleep or blessed with the patience of a stone. Shell knew he couldn't see the knife anyway, not from there. Getting free wasn't the problem. Moving after he was free was.

He had decided despite all he had said to get free and get out. Why? Simply because he couldn't do a damn thing to help anyone as long as he was held prisoner. What he could do against two dozen men even if he was free was another question.

The rope slid from his wrists. The rope around the tree was next. It fell away softly and still the guard did not move. Morgan couldn't see his eyes, hidden as they were in the shadow of his sombrero brim. Awake and playing it coy? Or asleep on his heels.

Shelter glanced toward the camp. It was still and quiet. If there were other guards out, Morgan couldn't see them. He had to chance it.

He coiled his muscles, ready to spring for the guard's throat if need be, although his chances wouldn't be too good, and rose, slowly, cautiously, his eyes alert. The guard didn't move.

He was asleep. Crouched there the bastard had fallen to sleep. Chavez was going to knock his ears off—Shelter was thinking ahead. That was no good. He hadn't got past the man yet, let alone away from the camp.

He backed away from the Mexican into the deeper shadows cast by the rising bluff behind him, then he circled toward the river. A horse, Andy had said, was waiting there. He might have been better off afoot in these hills, but if he needed to make a long run he would want a horse underneath and so he opted for the pony.

If he could find it. The shadows were deeper yet along the streambed where the dry cottonwoods straggled against the sky, making lacework among the stars.

The pony lifted its head and stared at Shell, ears pricked, eyes small gleaming points of light in the night. It was saddled and bridled, tied to the tree. It looked familiar and was—it was his own gray. How Andy had managed this, he didn't know, but then they wouldn't be watching her too closely. Why would they?

Shell led the horse upstream, the hoofs and his boots making no sound but a faint whisper against the sand. He walked for a quarter of a mile before he swung aboard. By that time the moon was rising, big and yellow against the dark sky.

He sat the horse on a small rise and looked at it for a time before shifting his gaze back to the streambed, the bluffs, the camp. What now?

There wasn't much doubt that the smartest thing to

do was to hightail it out of there—there wasn't much he could do to help the women out. Besides, Andy didn't want to come, she had said as much, and Beth—well, she had proven to have feet of clay. But she was frightened, and he really didn't hold it against her.

All of which was good rationalization but didn't hold water where obligation was concerned. The fact was two women were being held by a bunch of thugs. They needed help.

Morgan looked to the high ground and started up, choosing the difficult terrain when he could, the hard ground where he would leave no definite tracks, although he didn't anticipate anyone following. He just wasn't that important any longer. Except to Cord Levitt, maybe.

And Cord was still important to Shelter. Oh, yes. He was important.

Important enough to deserve killing.

Shelter surmounted the high bluff and swung down, watching as the rising moon drifted higher, shining like a torch into the deep gorge, illuminating the long valley. Nothing seemed to be moving below. It was possible they hadn't yet discovered that he was gone, although sooner or later the guard would have to wake up, or be awakened by a relief.

Morgan was free. Free and helpless. He didn't care for the feeling. What would Chavez's mood be on awakening to find that Shell was gone? Thin amusement, anger, rage? If he was angry, who would the axe fall on? The guard, Channing or Hart, the women?

Shelter didn't like this. He didn't like it a bit.

Dawn was a hot flush of red creeping into the eastern skies when he saw the first stirrings in the camp. Small, dark, antlike creatures waving furious legs. Even from that elevation and distance, the anger and frustration were discernible. A dozen men spread out along the river, riding south and north, searching for tracks. That didn't last long—although Shelter must have left tracks they could easily find, they gave it up and rode back into camp. Possibly Cord Levitt had ordered the search, Chavez calling it off. That was just a guess. At any rate the searchers gave it up and Morgan was left to ponder things as the sun rose higher and the desert heat invaded the canyon.

Andy had given them the map.

That was obvious. If not, Chavez would have spared no effort to recapture Morgan. Andy, bless her, was a clever one. She had sprung Shell and managed to keep him sprung.

After an hour or so the party moved out again, following the streambed for a little way before arriving at a feeder canyon and turning into it, following the sharp turn westward. Shelter smiled. They had the map all right.

They had it and they would all be smelling gold now: Chavez, Hart, Harry, Stoddard, Beth and even Andy Rice.

"This is it, Morgan, your chance to ride the hell out of this desert and forget the whole scheming bunch of them."

He wasn't built that way—he couldn't do it. Besides he saw something a few minutes later that turned his blood cold and made up his made for him.

Yaquis. They were following that treasure-hunting party, as silent as smoke, drifting up the hills, staying just out of sight, afoot, impervious to heat and hardship. Morgan estimated half a hundred of them.

What did they want? Scalps, horses, guns, women—especially women. Morgan ground his teeth together and slowly cursed. What the hell was he supposed to do? How could he warn Chavez? Why should he?

He started off toward the west, deeper into the red hills, on the heels of the Yaqui Indians.

The day grew rapidly hot, the sun branding his shoulders, neck and hands. Heat waves shimmered before his eyes. The gray horse moved heavily, trudging up the rock-strewn slopes, making far too much noise. Morgan wasn't inclined to leave the horse behind, however. He wouldn't have liked to be on foot out here with the Yaquis behind him.

Things took on an air of unreality. He could see nothing beyond the hillrise; there was no sign of the Yaquis, no sign of the Chavez party.

"If it weren't for the women," he thought. If it weren't for the women he would just turn and ride away, happily. Let the Yaquis have Chavez, let them lift Cord Levitt's scalp and Hart's. It would be tough for the kid, Harry, but he had asked for this, as had Stoddard and his people. Leeches, bloodsuckers.

The shots brought Morgan's head up. He heeled the gray into a run and wove his way up through the sage and manzanita toward the skyline.

By the time he reached it, the shots had increased. A moment later they ended again, but Morgan could see the puffs of smoke from the canyon below marking the battlefield. And battlefield it was. Morgan could see the Yaquis flitting over the broken ground, rushing the Chavez party. They would have a hell of a time rooting out Chavez, but the Yaquis had as long as it would take.

Morgan could see that Chavez's position wasn't good. The canyon had boxed out on them. That left one way out—eastward over the bodies of fifty Yaqui Indians. The weathered red bluffs rose up starkly all around. The land was red except for the dry grass on the rimrock, the few scraggly cedars pitched at odd angles here and there from the broken hills.

"If that map was right," Morgan thought, "then they have to be near the treasure." Near enough to spit and hit it. They were very likely at the same spot where the Castillo y Cortes massacre had taken place. The Yaquis should have a very good idea of how to go about this then.

Morgan, cursing himself for a fool, started forward. He had no weapon but a knife. He was alone and about as useless as tits on a boar hog. Nevertheless, he was going to try.

What he was going to try wasn't quite clear just then—but Beth and Andy Rice weren't going to be left to the savage Yaquis while he lived.

He rode the caprock of the bluff which was an ancient, time-eroded mesa cut through by running water and broken by shifting plates in the earth. Now and then shots sounded below. Once a man's cry echoed up the canyons. Shelter carried on.

He was walking the gray now, leading it along an eyebrow of a trail, a narrow, bootlace against the red canyon wall. He was far above the fighting, looking down into the sheer canyon through a stand of twisted cedar. The trail, ancient and narrow, was crumbling away beneath his feet as he led the horse onward, each shot from below lifting his pulse a little, reminding him that people were dying down there.

He came around a sharp bend in the path—and came face to face with a Yaqui Indian.

There was no way of telling who was more astonished. The Yaqui, a young warrior, had been posted way up here to watch the battle, to learn how to fight, perhaps in addition to see that no one escaped up the bluff from the canyon below.

The young warrior goggled at Shell, was momentarily frozen by indecision, and Morgan who had been a warrior more years than this brave had been alive, leaped at him, his small knife coming up toward the Yaqui's belly.

The Yaqui leaped away, crying out sharply. He was young, but he had Shelter far overmatched for weaponry. A hatchet rode at his belt, and a long knife. In his hand was a battered Henry repeater. He finally recalled he had that rifle and started to bring it up, but Morgan moved in sharply, getting inside the muzzle arc. The rifle exploded harmlessly. The gray horse backed up along the narrow trail, whickering its surprise. Below, the battle raged, and up on the trail, Shelter Morgan had his arms wrapped around the young Indian.

Young, but the kid was strong. They must have fed him on bear meat. He was thick through the chest, heavy in the thighs. He was a wrestler to boot. He tried to hip roll Morgan, was frustrated by Shell's boot hooking around in back of his knees. Shell ducked away as the Yaqui raked at his eyes with stiffened fingers.

Morgan's bootheel came down hard on the moccasined toes of the Yaqui and the brave throttled a yell of pain. He swung wildly at Shell's head with the rifle in his hands, missed as Shelter ducked, and hollered again.

The path was only two feet wide; below, the drop was steep. It wouldn't be certain death to fall, but anyone who went off was going to come up crippled, battered, broken. If he got up.

The Yaqui tried to knee Shell's groin. Morgan countered with a forearm to the windpipe. The Yaqui fell back, grabbing at his throat. Morgan back-heeled him and the warrior went down hard, flat on his back.

And then he was gone. He rolled over the rim and was gone, bouncing, tumbling, rolling to the bottom of the red canyon.

Shelter picked up the Yaqui's rifle and went on, leading the gray. The path rose, narrowed again and then flattened out as it met the rimrock far above the canyon below. A fierce blast of hot wind met Shell as he surmounted the last slope and stood, breathing shallowly, rapidly, atop the caprock.

He didn't stop to rest, but moved on to the edge of the crumbling mesa to look down into the camp below—camp or redoubt. He could see the insect-sized figures bunched together, up the canyon, see the Yaquis flitting from rock to rock.

It wasn't good, it just wasn't. The Yaquis had them sealed off.

Without food or water—and those would run out quickly—they would die there. This must be the way they did it the first time, when the Castillo y Cortes party was trapped in these red hills to perish.

Shelter could see the white river-bottom sand, see the sprawled figure against the earth. He couldn't be sure from that altitude, but the suit looked to be the one Colonel Hart had been wearing.

Shell crouched down against the hot red stone ledge and studied the layout of the land. He was staring at it and not seeing it until suddenly things came into focus.

There was a way out!

There was a way: a difficult, narrow trail winding up toward where Morgan now crouched. Up that trail, back along the narrow path Morgan had followed, and then out, leaving the Yaquis marooned on the far side of the canyon with no way up the steep slopes.

"For what?" Morgan grumbled to himself. To get

himself gunned down by Cord Levitt or Chavez, Stoddard or the Africans—he hadn't forgotten the grudge they bore him.

For what? For a little feather-headed blonde with great green eyes who spoke breathlessly as you spread her sleek thighs; for the gun-carrying bounty woman with the man's name and the sharp tongue? "Yeah. For them," he said, and calling himself a fistful of names, he started down the trail toward the besieged whites.

The gray he left picketed above. There was scarcely room for a horse on that trail. Morgan wasn't all that sure he could negotiate it. It was a tough path to follow, and from below, the foot of the trail was almost invisible and certainly didn't offer much promise of escape.

The Yaquis hadn't seen Shell yet, and after rounding a last tight bend that left him a hundred feet or so above the canyon floor, he decided to settle in and wait until nightfall. If the Yaquis knew they planned to try and escape that way they could cut it off. After dark it was a different story—they could make it up and out, on foot. No horse would make that trail at night.

Shell settled in, crouched against the hot bluff, seeing the occasional darting figure of a Yaqui, the sudden puff of smoke, hearing the following report of a rifle—and twice, the terrible screams of dying men.

Darkness came slowly. The canyon walls held the light of day, reflecting it back in red and violet hues. Shadows slowly crept out from the bases of the cliffs. The sun's fire slowly subsided to a last golden band of light.

Morgan waited. The chill of night came on quickly. The desert came surprisingly alive with sound. Coyotes, a dozen of them baying at nothing visible to human eyes, quail calling, cicadas singing, mosquitoes humming.

Below, there was no light, no movement. The Chavez party was dug in good. The Yaquis, reinforced the day long, sat watching, waiting up the dark canyons. Morning would bring them victory, or if not morning, the morning after. The Yaquis were a patient people.

Shelter Morgan rose stiffly. He didn't have a friend in the world, certainly not in that lone, dark canyon. He started down, tumbling to his fate.

14.

It was dark, too still, and there was the lingering scent of gunsmoke in Andy Rice's nostrils. Colonel Hart was dead. Crabbe was dead. An African was dead. And it was all up. They weren't going to get out of there alive and Andy knew it. She was only grateful for one thing—she had gotten Shelter Morgan out of there. Morgan, if he had any brains at all, was now riding for the border, intent on a hot bath, a cold beer and—damn him—probably a warm woman.

Andy still had her skirt on, but the damned thing was starting to chafe. It was too long, encumbering, unnatural! She meant to get back into jeans and boots soon.

She was carrying her Colt, but it was concealed in her petticoats. She hadn't fired a round all day, preferring to sit with Beth Channing and squeal girlishly rather than give herself away.

"We're stuck good," Andy said.

"We'll get out," Harry Channing said shakily.

"Why, you dumb ape, we haven't a chance."

"If there's a way."

"Someone would have to rub your nose in it."

"Maria!"

"What I'd give to have a man with us," Andy Rice said, turning away, folding her arms. Harry Channing stared mutely at her back, not understanding any of this.

"It's here!"

Heads turned. Jake Stoddard emerged from the shadows. In his hands was something bright and dully gleaming. "Gold," Harry said, leaping toward Stoddard.

"That's it, kid. Keep your hands off it."

"Why, it's partly mine."

"Yeah, who says? If it is, why, you owe me, don't you? Twenty thousand if I recollect."

"There's more than that to my share! It's my father's map, it's my uncle's treasure!"

"And what makes you think either of you will have an ounce of it?" Patch asked. There were three *bandidos* together, staring darkly at Stoddard and Harry Channing. "Where'd you find that, Stoddard?"

"Back . . ." Stoddard hesitated, saw that was not a promising tactic and rushed on. "Behind those pillars of stone. Where those slabs have folded down. There. Channing must have caved the stone in over the gold. I got to poking around and I dug this out."

"For all the good it will do us," Andy said coldly.

"What's the matter, little one," Patch said, "you don't like the gold so much anymore?" He moved nearer. His breath was rancid, his eyes hot. "You worry about a few stinkin' Indians? We finish them real soon. Then we go back, rich, huh?"

The arrow whizzed past Andy's ear, entered the right side of Patch's throat and emerged on the left. Blood gushed from his mouth as he grabbed at the shaft of the arrow with both hands, snapping it off before he toppled forward on his face. Guns erupted everywhere. To Andy's left and right, from behind. She got down fast, taking Beth Channing down with her.

Suddenly it was silent again. Incredibly silent. Beth was panting furiously; her eyes were wide with fear. Andy's mouth crimped unhappily.

"Come on, darling," Andy said, "you survived—this time. They fell back."

Cord Levitt, a pistol in each hand, his shirt torn open, rushed toward them, his eyes not missing the gold plate Jake Stoddard had found and dropped in his hurry to rush to the hastily built stone barricade the Yaquis had threatened.

"Anybody down?" Levitt asked.

"Patch."

"Son of a bitch! We lost one of our soldiers on the other side too."

"What's wrong?" Chavez demanded.

"Two more down. Patch and Miguel."

"Eight altogether."

"Bastards'll whittle us down," Cord said. "Damn it all, there's got to be a way out, even if it's right over them."

"Take it easy, Cord," Chavez said.

"Take it easy yourself, Ramon! We want to own this part of the world. For a hundred miles around people tremble when they hear your name or mine. And we can't even ride through these hills! The Yaquis won't be beat."

"They'll be beat," Chavez said. "Everyone will be beat."

"Then, goddamnit, you'd better come up with a way—quick."

That stopped Chavez. There was no way. Through

the canyon in the darkness? Not likely. Yet if they stayed here they were going to be slowly chipped away.

"What'll you give for a way out?" the voice from behind them asked and they turned sharply toward the shadows. Beth cried out, Andy Rice uttered a very unladylike curse.

"Morgan!"

"That's right. Leave that gun where it is, Cord. I've got a Henry repeater sighted on your chest."

Levitt didn't lose his composure. "Come on in and let's talk it over. You don't need a gun."

"No? That's not what you told me last time. Remember the knife?"

"Things were different then." Levitt's eyes were searching the shadows.

"Sure. Don't get any ideas, Cord. If you want to live, you'll deal with me. Chavez?"

"Yes?"

"What do you say? I know a way out of here. You deal with me or the Yaquis make carrion out of the bunch of you. What do you want to do?"

One of the Africans was singing a mournful, deep-voiced song, a song of suffering and death in a language no one understood. Chavez snapped, "Shut that black up!" Then he quieted. "Sure, Morgan. Sure, we're with you if you know a way out. What do you want for it? What's your price?"

"Same as before. The women and I get out of here alive. Us and the kid, Channing."

"Sure. I already told you that was OK."

"Before, you let Cord try to cut my eyes out."

"Well." Chavez shrugged. "That was then."

"And this is now. You agree to what I'm asking or stay here," Morgan said with some emotion.

"Sure, of course, Morgan!"

"Yeah? I want your word. You have a word that's worth anything, Chavez?"

"My word," Chavez said, biting off the syllables, "is always good, Morgan."

"Yes—what about Levitt?"

"Levitt does what I say."

"All right. All right." Morgan came forward, his rifle levelled. "I'll take you out of here. I have your word that I can go for the border with the women and Channing. That you'll leave us be."

"My word. I don't want you. I have the gold."

"Then that's that. Tell Cord how it is."

"Cord," Chavez said in that silky voice. "You have heard it all, the deal I've made. I have given my word. Do not try to stop Morgan, my friend, or I will have my people kill you. I am sorry, but that is the way things are now."

"For God's sake," Andy Rice said. "You men yapping and giving your word and promising and all—let's get the hell out of here before the Indians decide to come in again!"

"Yes," Chavez said. "The lady is right. How do we get out of here, Morgan?"

"By following me," Shelter said cautiously.

"All right. Whatever you say. Paco," the *bandido* snapped at one of his soldiers, "get that gold from under the rubble. Pack it in the canvas sacks we brought."

"Leave the damn gold," Shell said.

"No."

"You can't pack it where we're going!"

"I won't leave it. It's mine."

"You can come back."

"Not until every Yaqui in these hills is dead. They'll find it now. Or someone else—I'm not leaving it."

159

"Damn you, pack it then!" Shelter said.

There was humor in Chavez's voice. "I intend to, Mr. Morgan, I intend to."

Beth Channing was beside Shelter now, holding onto his arm. "My gold, my inheritance," she was saying. "Shelter, don't let them take it all from me."

Morgan ignored her. She was still not out of there alive. Anyone who would worry about gold at a time like this was beneath contempt.

"All right, tough guy," Andy Rice said. "You going to get us out?"

"I hope so."

"I hope so, too. I gave you your life once. I don't think I can do it again. Ready?"

"I am. What about you? Can you climb in that skirt?" Morgan still stood, back to the bluff, rifle in hands. He didn't have that much confidence in anyone's word.

"I can climb. But I'd like to change. We taking baby with us?" She nodded at Beth.

"Yes. She goes."

"Morgan, you're hard as mush."

"She hasn't done anything worth dying for." Beth's eyes met his again. Her mouth opened as if she would say something, but it got stuck in her throat, whatever it was. Stoddard, Channing, the *bandidos* and the Africans were all busy furiously filling sacks with the loot from beneath the rubble.

"If they hit us now," Shelter told Chavez, "we haven't got a chance. Your people got gold in their eyes."

"Yes. And you, Morgan?"

"One thing I haven't fallen prey to. Maybe I'm just not smart."

"Maybe very smart." Chavez's dark eyes shifted to the working men. "People die around gold."

"So I've heard. Listen, they can't take much longer at this—we've got to get the hell out if we're going."

"All right. How do we do it—you lead the way."

"I guess I have to, though I don't like having all those guns at my back." Chavez smiled a little. Shelter looked upslope into the darkness. "I don't think your people will make it with those bags of gold."

"Some will," Chavez said, almost with disinterest. "And maybe some won't."

"You'll have your share so it doesn't matter, is that it?"

"That's it. Yes." Chavez shrugged. Andy Rice had reappeared in jeans and boots, her blouse knotted at her waist. She had a gunbelt on. Chavez lifted an eyebrow. "Surprises all the time," he said.

Andy just looked back as if she could see all of those bounty dollars in his face. It must have made her trigger finger twitch a little.

"Don't get any ideas," Shelter told her.

"Me, never."

"Are we ready?" It was Harry Channing, dragging a bagful of gold behind him. Beth watched him nervously. The Yaquis, Shell was thinking, were too silent suddenly.

"Forget it, Harry," Morgan said. "You'll never make it with that sack. Just leave it."

"Leave it! I'll take half of it."

"Do what you want. You want to live, leave that here. The same goes for the rest of you."

Chavez intervened. "My men wish to take the chance."

They didn't argue with their leader, but they didn't look too eager either.

"All right," Morgan said. "This is how it's going to be. Me first, followed by the women. Chavez behind them, then Stoddard and Santos. Then the Africans." He turned his head. "Cord Levitt last."

"You think I'm going to shoot you on that slope?"

"You're not going to shoot me at all, remember? You gave me your promise. You're an honorable man, aren't you, Cord?"

"No more of that now," Chavez said irritably. "We climb."

"We climb," Morgan answered.

He needed a boost up to reach the ledge which overhung the little hollow. He swung a leg up and over and crouched there for a moment, looking toward the Yaquis. Nothing seemed to be moving.

Reaching down, he felt Andy's hand and he swung her up to lie beside him. "Damn," she said feelingly, "it's dark up here."

"Keep your voice down," Shell said. "Give me a hand."

"With the baby?" Andy reached down as well and they each took one of Beth Channing's hands, tugging her up onto the ledge.

Her skirts and petticoats were impossibly bulky. "Take off all but one skirt," Morgan told her, and she obeyed silently. Harry Channing was next. He was a load to get up. No wonder. He still had a sack of goldware across his shoulder. It was smaller but it still weighed like the devil, was bulky as sin and clattered like perdition.

"Muffle that junk. Here, use your sister's petticoat."

Harry obeyed. Chavez was next and then one of his soldiers with a sackful of loot to match Channing's. After that one was up Morgan moved on up the trail, Andy and Beth behind him, Chavez not far back. Harry and the *bandido* were helping the rest of the band up. From time to time Shelter could hear a silver candelabra and gold dishes clatter against each other and he winced. The Yaquis hadn't expected this move, but they were far from stupid. There might even be enough time for a band of them to rush to the head of the trail.

Right now Morgan wasn't sure he was going to find the head of the trail himself. It was dark, very dark. Looking up he could see stars shining beyond the rimrock, but their feeble glow didn't do much to illuminate the trail which was crumbling, narrow, steep.

They moved on, inching ahead now. Morgan had his back to the rising bluff. One hand held his rifle, the other Andy's hand. Below them was a seemingly bottomless chasm.

Shell could hear Andy's effortful breathing. Glancing toward her, he saw that her face was set grimly. There was nothing funny about this. Beth was only an indistinct pale smear beyond Andy Rice. He could see no one else. But he could hear them—damn them all, he could hear them! That gold was going to get them killed yet. The moon was starting to rise, he noticed with concern.

The rifle shot rang out and Shell leaped with the tension. They had been seen! The bullet struck the bluffs high and to the left of them. The second bullet the Yaquis sent after them struck flesh.

One of the Africans bellowed, shouting something in his native tongue and then pitched forward into the darkness. When he hit it was with a thump of dead flesh and the clatter of gold and silver. He had died a wealthy man.

The Yaqui guns opened up in earnest now and Shelter hurried on, stumbling over the rough ground, going down hard once. He paused and sighted in on the muzzle flashes from below and unleashed three quick rounds. At least let the Yaquis think about it. There was another yell from their own party and another man went down the ravine, bouncing and screaming as the Indians continued to fire.

Shell turned and started on, recklessly now. Andy had hold of his hand still and it was a good thing. She missed her step and one foot went over the edge of the trail.

"Shelter!" she called and he yanked her back up.

"Thanks," she said, and her tone was almost teasing. Shelter growled an answer and went on. The trail was familiar once again. They were nearly to the caprock. One more bend—and then another Yaqui appeared, looming out of the darkness, his body painted, his face illuminated by the flash of his gun as he spoke the language of death.

Shelter, the Winchester uncocked in his left hand, didn't have a chance. He was a goner and he knew it. But the blur of movement behind him, the answering stab of flame, blew the Yaqui into the gully below, a bloody mist painting the wall of the bluff.

Shelter looked behind him. "Thanks," he said.

"Even now," Andy Rice said. She winked and holstered her Colt.

And then they were up. Morgan tugged Andy up and over, onto the caprock. Then came Beth, breathing raggedly, Chavez and his men. Morgan had crossed to where his gray horse waited, roughly hobbled. He whipped off the rawhide hobbles and led the pony back to the head of the trail.

"Which way?" Chavez asked.

"This one, and we'd better do it quickly. The Yaquis will be here in force and damned soon."

"Lead out," Chavez said with a mocking bow.

"That gold's going to slow us."

"You worry a lot about the gold for a man who

says he doesn't care about it."

"I care about living. Gold cuts down our chances. Suit yourself. Andy—why don't you ride? Take Beth up with you."

"And have her arms around me?" Andy said with disgust. "No, thanks—you do it. I'll walk."

"Whatever we're going to do," Harry Channing said in a dry voice, "I suggest we do it now. That looks to me like the Yaquis coming up the slope."

15.

The Yaquis were coming again, all right. The *bandidos*, Shelter and Andy Rice laid down a barrage of gunfire which cooled the Yaquis a little to the idea.

They were silent and deadly people, the Yaquis. At the spate of gunfire they simply disappeared. They were swallowed up by the ground, covered over by blanketing shadows. Morgan couldn't see a single one moving, not a corpse—if they had produced any with their blind fire. It was eerie and not at all to his liking.

"Let's get," he whispered. No one argued.

They started back in the direction Shell had arrived from. He didn't know this area, and he didn't want to get himself trapped up some other box canyon, hung out on the end of a broken mesa or bogged in dunes. He knew the land to the north a little.

North they went.

"I'm sorry." Beth Channing was clinging to him, her cheek against his back. "I'm sorry for what I tried to do, Shelter."

"All right."

"You don't believe me," she wailed.

"Sure. I believe you—you're sorry." And that was the end of the conversation.

The sky brightened gradually and they moved on, Shelter and Beth on the horse, the others walking, plodding, staggering under the weight of the gold sacks they carried. Except for Chavez and Levitt. They carried nothing; they owned it all.

Twice the Yaquis sniped at them. Once someone was hit. Santos, Stoddard's friend. The bullet from an old musket-rifle went through the gold serving plate in Santos's sack and on into his heart. He died two minutes later babbling about Juarez, his home.

"I can't go on with this," Channing said. Harry was red-faced, beaten. The flaming sun was barely up. "I can't carry this gold." He threw the sack down and sagged beside it.

"Pick it up," Ramon Chavez said.

"I told you . . ." Chavez had produced a revolver and Harry gawked at it, his hands twitching nervously.

"You wanted to be rich, gringo. So—now you are rich. Carry that sack or I'll kill you."

"Shelter!" Beth pleaded, but Morgan only shook his head. Chavez smiled at the woman.

"Not over this. He will not die over this, Miss Channing."

The man was right. Shelter wasn't going to get involved. It was Harry's own greed that had produced this situation. His own greed that was liable to get him killed on this endless desert.

"All right," Harry said with a heavy exhalation. "I'll try it. I'll carry your booty. Let's go on."

It grew hotter. Shelter swung down from the horse and walked, leading it. Beth stayed on its back. She was chalk white now with tiny strawberries burned on her cheeks. Her emotions had given up the uneven battle. She was passive, accepting.

"Where are we going?" Cord Levitt demanded. "The villa is south of us."

"So are the Yaquis," Chavez reminded him.

"There's nothing ahead of us, though. No town, no water, nothing but sand."

"No." Chavez looked thoughtful. "I believe you are correct."

Jake Stoddard spoke up. "Look, nobody's asked me, but I'm with Levitt. This don't make good sense."

"What would you suggest, Mr. Stoddard?" Chavez asked with a great deal of sarcasm.

"Maybe find a place to hole up. Send a man back to the villa. On Morgan's horse."

"Sure," Harry Channing started to agree eagerly. Chavez cut him off.

"What happens then? The Yaquis catch up with us. Who says a man can get through to the villa past all these Indians? By the time he gets back it would be too late anyway."

"Then *what*?" Cord asked in frustration.

"We go on. Onto the flats. The Yaquis can see us for miles, but we will see them as well. We will have no water, but neither will they."

Shelter glanced at Chavez. "It's no good," he said. "Why?"

"If the Yaquis need water, they'll find it. Or they can do without it. They're that tough. We're not. They aren't carrying hundreds of pounds of gold either. These men will be walked into the sand the first day out. Without water, in that heat, they'll not make it ten miles."

"They'll make it," Chavez said, and it amounted to a threat. "If you have a better idea, Morgan, please give it to me."

Shell shook his head. No, he didn't have a better idea. They could play hide-and-seek in these hills, try to break through to the south, line out across the flats toward the border and white settlements where the Yaquis would be wary about following. Of the three Chavez's idea sounded the most logical until you considered that not one of the ideas offered a prayer of survival.

"You saved our hash," Andy Rice said, "but not for long, huh?"

"We'll make it."

"Yeah?" Her eyebrow lifted. "We're special?"

"We're not carrying any gold at least." He lifted his chin toward the poor bastards who were.

"And we've got the horse, huh? But it hasn't got any water either. And it would have to carry triple if we tried to make a break—because you wouldn't leave baby, would you, even now. Besides, you're not going to make a break until you see Cord Levitt dead, isn't that it?"

"That's it."

"Well, maybe I can fix that." She turned to look steadily at Levitt.

"Don't be a fool, Andy. You think these men would let you live after that? They don't care if you're a woman or not, this kind."

"All right." She wiped her hand across her brow. "I suppose you're right. You'd better come up with something else then, Shelter, because we're just not going to make it this way—no one is." She looked directly at Beth Channing. "Not even *baby*."

They trudged on. The sun rose higher and the sand underfoot became unbearably hot. Shelter walked on, not looking behind or ahead. Beth looked ready to fall from the horse. No one spoke. A Mexican dropped silently against the sand and stayed there. His sack was snatched up and they trudged on, leaving him.

The day was endless, white, searing. Shell's throat was dry and blistered. There was no water, not a hint of it, no moisture in the air.

The Yaquis rose up from out of the sand where they had been buried, lying, waiting.

Shelter threw himself to one side, feeling the gray rear up, seeing Beth thrown. His rifle was firing before he hit the ground. The Yaquis, dust-colored, primitive, spirits rising out of the earth, rushed toward them. Jake Stoddard went down, a bullet passing through his right eye and out the back of his head, blowing skull and gray matter from his body.

Morgan's Henry spoke twice and two Yaquis went down. One was shot through the groin, his face contorted with pained anguish. He clutched himself and sagged to the sand. The other man had been hit, but how hard Shell didn't know. He had simply vanished.

An Indian disappeared from before Andy Rice's sights as well. Going to her knee she fired twice and the rushing Yaqui, hatchet raised, lost his arm. It was blown from him to lie against the sand twitching. By the time the Yaqui reached Andy the blood had run out and he just folded up, dying practically at her feet.

Chavez shot one Yaqui and then his gun seemed to jam. He flung himself to the earth to lie behind another dead *bandido*. Cord Levitt was firing with either hand and Shelter saw him hit at least one Yaqui.

And then it was over. They were gone again, leaving only the dead.

Shelter moved ahead cautiously, peering across the

dunes.

"Where are they!" Chavez was at his shoulder. Morgan could only shrug. There was nothing moving out there, nothing at all.

They examined the pits dug into the sand where the Yaquis had lain for what must have been hours, waiting, and shook their heads in wonder.

Then they checked the damage. There was plenty of it. Chavez's people lay scattered across the sand, some dead, some dying. Stoddard was gone, another African—leaving only one—six *bandidos*.

But there was gold—oh, there was plenty of gold, scattered across the white sand to glitter and gleam and entice men to their deaths.

"All right," Chavez ordered his remaining eight men, "get the gold picked up. Everyone carries double."

"How?" one of them started to protest, but he fell silent when he felt glaring eyes on him. They silently picked up the gold.

"We got to use the horse," Cord Levitt said. "No way these boys are going to hold up under that load. Anyway, they can't fight with both hands full, and there's going to be some more fighting. I do have that feeling." He wiped his face with the back of his sleeved arm.

"You are right. I'm taking the horse, Morgan. The girl walks."

Beth looked incredulous. Just a sad, broken little doll. She should have stayed in the town. The seams had begun to show and then she had cracked wide open.

"Come on, girl," Andy Rice said, yanking Beth to her feet. "I'll help you along."

"All you'll accomplish is killing the horse," Morgan said as the Mexicans began tying the sacks together, throwing them across the gray's back. "It won't last long carrying that weight."

"Neither will our men."

"Then leave the gold!"

"Go to hell. We carry the gold as long as we can move!" Chavez insisted. And that was his final word.

"What about the wounded?" Morgan asked.

"I'm not a doctor. They were paid well to take chances. They took one that didn't work out!" Chavez was angry, sullen. Maybe a few seams were beginning to open up in him as well.

Harry Channing was sagged against the sand, his hands clasped. His face was an unhealthy chalk white. The eyes were unfocused.

"Come on," Morgan said.

"Can't."

"You'd better. They'll leave you."

"I don't care."

"You care. You care about living, everyone does."

"I'm a bastard, Morgan. I screwed this up."

"No, you didn't."

"Yes. I'm stupid. Hart killed my father. I saw him. I didn't do anything about it except take the map. Gold. You know."

"I know. Let's go though."

Harry shook his head but he let Morgan get him to his feet and point him in the right direction. Andy Rice, leading Beth around by the hand said, "Fine. Now we each got one."

"Yeah." Morgan was standing looking at the wounded. There was a man near him with part of his face shot away. One eye kept watching Shell. The lips moved and somehow that thing which had been a man managed to speak.

"*Agua, por favor.*" Shell couldn't do anything but walk away. "*Agua, por favor!*" But he didn't have water and he didn't have medicine or bandages or a blanket to make a pillow or shelter from the sun with. All they had was gold.

"Remind you of anything?" Morgan said to Cord Levitt. "No, that's right, it couldn't. You weren't there. Neither was I, but I heard about it. Men dying, pleading words on their lips. Blood everywhere. No medicine, no morphine to still the pain."

"What are you talking about?"

"Only then it wasn't white sand, it was snow. All those who had been waiting for blankets and medicine and food and ammunition just lying in the snow dying while their officers ran out on them—carrying gold, a lot of gold."

"What the hell did you want us to do? Win the war by ourselves?" Cord's hand was wrapped around his holstered Colt so tightly that his knuckles were as white as a skeleton's.

"I wanted you to be a man. To care about flesh and blood as much as you do about the goddamned gold! Well, this time the joke's on you, Cord. I won't have to kill you, no one will, because you're never going to get off this desert alive. Never, because you love that damned gold too much to put it down and live!"

Cord's gun started to come up but Chavez, who had been listening, drew his first. "No, Cord, put it down."

"I can't take any more of this bastard."

"Put it away. I gave my word."

"Your word! And when has that ever meant anything, Ramon!"

"Put it away," Chavez said, spacing his words out carefully. "If the Yaquis come back we need his gun."

Cord didn't answer. His anger was slowly ebbing, either that or he believed Chavez—believed the bandit chief would kill him if he shot Morgan. He jammed his gun into his holster and trudged on.

"You," Chavez said, "use sense. Keep your mouth shut."

"Sure," Shelter said. It hurt to speak. His blistered lips kept opening up. He took Harry Channing by the arm and started on, walking up the dunes, sinking to his knees in sand as the sun shone down, mocking them, beating them to insensibility.

There was nothing but sand, but the distances, the placing of one foot before the other, the dunes where you took two steps forward and slid back one. The sun. The stunning heat. The constant knowledge of impending death.

Eons later darkness came, staining the dunes to blue-violet, washing the sky to pink and gold, and they sagged against the sand to sit open-mouthed with exhaustion, staring at each other. No one spoke for a long while, they just stared and breathed, breathed as deeply as possible, inhaling the coolness of desert dusk.

Shelter's voice was hoarse, scarcely recognizable when he did speak. "Lookouts," he said. "Yaquis might try it."

They were sitting in a small hollow scooped out of the windward side of the dune. It rose around them to form a sort of barricade. Chavez looked up and around and then nodded.

"I'll take this side," Shelter said. And he started up the dune, every muscle stiff now that he had rested for a minute. He wanted to sleep, to close his red, abraded eyes and sleep through the delicious hours of coolness, but he didn't care to sleep and never wake up again. Someone had to stand watch. The Yaquis would be back. There was someone behind Shell and he looked back.

"Mind if I come along?" Andy asked.

"What for?"

"Don't like the company down there."

"Suit yourself. I'm not going to be much company myself."

"Haven't changed your mind, have you? We could make a run for it. Say around dawn when the horse was rested. Just you and me. No—I guess you haven't changed your mind. You'd still want to save baby's pretty pink hide. Plan on using it again, do you, Shelter?"

"What?" He seemed distracted.

"I say, could you sleep with her again after—"

"Quiet a minute. Do you hear something?"

"Like what?"

"I'm not sure," Shelter said, shrugging it off.

"We're not coming out of this with a damn thing, are we?" Andy asked, taking off that Spanish hat to prod at her hair with her fingers. "Me, I don't get any bounty money, no gold. You don't get to settle up with Cord Levitt. Stupid, I guess. Stupid to have come down here. The Yaquis'll—" She broke off and sat listening too, hearing something, a faint rustling, a shuffling sound they couldn't quite identify. "Now I'm hearing it. Banshees or boogers?"

"I think it's something a lot worse," Morgan said. "Altogether different and a whole hell of a lot worse."

They looked toward the horizon. Now, near the horizon, they could see no stars. The air was heavy. The breeze had picked up considerably.

"What is it?" Andy asked.

"What I thought. Something a lot worse than Yaquis. It's a sandstorm, Andy. The granddaddy of all sandstorms."

"Is that all?" Andy laughed. It was a bit dry, that laugh, but she managed to get it out. "What's a sandstorm mean? A little wind, a little sand. So what?"

Shelter didn't answer. He looked at Andy though and shook his head. They could hear it better now, see it. It howled and blustered, moving across the desert flats, reaching into the sky to blot out the stars.

What was it? Not much. A little sand, a little wind.

A hurricane is only a little wind.

The ocean is only a little water.

"Get yourself set," Shelter said. "Wake the others and hold on tight. It's going to be a night like you've never spent in your life."

16.

There was time, just a little time, before the sandstorm came in shrieking and ranting, filling the sky with enough sand to fill ears and nostrils, to blind a man or smother him.

There was time to slide down the dune and wake everyone up. While they sat peering skyward with bleary, sleep-encrusted eyes, their weary bodies reluctant to rise, there was time for a few other preparations.

Beth was in a daze when Morgan found her. The heat of the day had done its work. Awakened from a sleep she was as limp as a ragdoll when Shell sat her up.

"Beth!" He glanced to the sky apprehensively, then to Chavez who seemed to be watching him in the darkness. "Beth, wake up."

"What?" she asked in a small voice.

"Are you awake?" He shook her violently.

"What?"

It was no use. Morgan found Harry Channing, and speaking in an undertone, he told him what was happening. Channing was watching the approaching storm with wide eyes. His hair was blowing wildly as the wind rose and the sand came on like a huge roller waiting to break over them from out of a sea of sand.

"Do you understand me?"

"Yeah. Where's the rope?"

"Damnit, Harry, pay attention! By the saddle there. It's tied to the gray's neck. Can you see it?"

"Not in this light."

"Good. Don't look at the sand, look at me." Shell turned his face roughly toward him. "You're going to have to get Beth. It's up to you. If you don't cut it, she's going to die out here. Get me?"

"Yeah. Yeah, I get you."

"All right. Tie a scarf across your face and find something for Beth—the hem of her dress if she hasn't got anything else, but—"

"Morgan!" Chavez called.

"Yes."

"How long will this last?" he asked, nodding toward the storm.

"There's no way of telling. An hour? I once saw one go two days. That's rare. Tell your people to keep their heads down though, eyes closed. Mask across your faces. People have suffocated to death in a bad sandstorm. And I don't mean two or three people. I mean it happens. Often."

"Goddamn." Cord Levitt was standing looking northward, toward the storm. He had a scarf around his throat, ready to be pulled up, rifle in hand. "Looks like locusts. I seen locusts come once. Just like this."

"You haven't got long," Morgan called. They were having to shout to be heard. "Get your backs to it and hunch up."

Chavez turned toward Morgan as he started away. He opened his mouth as if to speak and then shut it again. He sat on the ground, tugging his scarf up, rifle across his lap.

"Well?" Andy was sitting on the sand, waiting anxiously. A white scarf masked the lower half of her face. "Everything set?"

"I don't know. I hope so. Neither of them's in good shape." Shelter asked, "You have it?"

"This you mean?" She showed him the end of a piece of lariat which ran to the gray's patient neck. Andy had the rope looped around her wrist.

"That I mean. If only they . . ." He looked across the camp to where Harry and Beth sat side by side, forlorn, small, childish.

"Hansel and Gretel," Andy said with a sigh. There wasn't time for much more conversation. The wind roared out of the north, gaining impetus, and the first few stinging grains of sand were flung against their cheeks, scant warning before the wash and fury of the dark sea flowed over them, burying them in an airless tide of sand.

The sky went abruptly dark. Morgan shut his eyes tightly. He hadn't forgotten the blind man in Las Cruces, the old one who had stayed in the sandstorm looking for his lost sheep. Too long he had stayed.

Morgan waited until the storm settled in good. It buffeted arms and legs, and bit at the face, neck, any exposed flesh with the force of lead pellets fired from a shotgun. The world was black, empty. Nothing lived outside of Morgan's brain casing. Nothing that could be touched, seen, tasted, felt, heard—nothing but the black and deadly sea of sand.

He lurched to his feet and was nearly blown over. He grabbed out, found Andy Rice's arm and drew her upright. She leaned against him briefly and then stood away, giving him a length of rope.

She started walking, fighting the deep sand underfoot, the waves of sand in the air. She walked on into the teeth of the storm, toward the north—or roughly north—with Morgan behind her, holding the rope, letting it slide through his hand until the gray came up even with him. He took the horse's bridle and led it on, checking the other rope which was taut now. Harry and Beth Channing should be back there, walking blindly after them, walking to safety—if the storm lasted, if Chavez or Levitt didn't realize what might be happening.

There didn't seem to be much chance of that happening. Shell peered out from between nearly closed eyelids. He may as well have been blind. There was nothing at all to see. The world had no reality. There was the sand, the wind, the horse's bridle. Nothing else.

They walked on and the storm roared, moving the dunes, stinging the flesh, clogging ears and nostrils. Despite the mask it was hard to breathe. Shell's mouth was filled with sand though he would have sworn he never opened it.

And was still walking—the line was taut. Harry and Beth were back there as well. At least one of them was. If Channing had left his sister . . . Shelter swallowed that angry thought and trudged on.

Hour after hour passed. Twice Morgan fell, twice climbed to his feet. He had no idea where they were. Maybe they weren't going anywhere at all. Maybe the wind had shifted and they were walking back toward the camp. That kind of thinking wasn't helpful.

He walked on. He had never done anything but walk through this sandstorm. The world was created of sand. Man was devised to stagger through it.

Then he opened his eyes and with a sort of shock realized that the darkness was paling. The sand seemed to be diminishing a little—and to his right the dawn was trying to burn through the clouds of sand.

"Andy!"

She had been walking on, head down, swaying on her feet. Now she stopped and turned, her mouth gaping.

"Shell? I thought this was all a nightmare—or a vision of hell. I didn't think—"

"Shut up, Andy," Morgan said, and as he walked to her he hugged her and she sagged in his arms.

The sand was still blowing, but they could see in varying distances in all directions. Sometimes things would close down and the visibility would be less than ten feet, but they could at least see the ground they walked over, and looking back two weary young people staggering after them. Harry and Beth wouldn't be treasure hunting again soon.

They waited now, panting, inhaling sand while they let the Channings, brother and sister, catch up.

"Are we stopping now?" Beth asked. "Are we going to rest here?"

"No. We have to go on," Morgan told her.

"I can't."

"Can you stick it out on the horse?"

She looked at the gray, the poor, weary, bedraggled gray which had been travelling without grass or water. "Yes," she said finally. "I can."

Harry spoke then. "Look, Morgan, I can't walk on either. I've just about had it myself."

Morgan saw something in Channing's hand then, something that tightened his mouth and brought the anger bubbling to the surface. "What's in the sack?"

"What?" Harry took a step backward, glancing down at his hand.

"What's in that damned sack! Gold?" Shelter's voice roared.

"Yes." Channing tried a smile. "Look, it's something my sister and I have coming to us."

Shelter stepped to the kid, knocked the sack out of his hand and stood with a trembling finger in his face. "If

181

you want that, you stay here with it. We'll not take it out of this desert."

There was no argument. Maybe Channing didn't have the strength. He certainly knew he wasn't going to win the argument. Morgan, still fuming, turned away.

"Will they come after us?" Beth asked. "Chavez and Cord Levitt, I mean?"

"No. They can't catch up. Not now." Or so he hoped.

"And the Yaquis?" she asked, her voice squeaking a little. "Will they come?"

"I don't know." Shelter turned toward the north. With the Yaquis you never know. Maybe they had had enough, maybe not. "Let's keep it moving anyway," he said.

They started on. In an hour the sandstorm had nearly died out. The fitful wind had the strength only occasionally to lift sand from the tops of the dunes like spume from a breaker. The great clouds of sand were gone. The heat was back.

The sun shined down, boring holes in their skulls, tearing at their flesh with fiery teeth. There wasn't enough moisture in Shell's mouth to swallow. They walked on. Northward. And how far was it? A hundred miles, a million?

The land ahead all looked the same, dunes on one side, playa on the other. They had come this way before but it looked different. The storm had shifted the sand, erased any helpful tracks they might have made on their way south.

Harry Channing went down and stayed down.

Morgan, panting, his face red, made his way to where Channing lay. Beth would have screamed, but she didn't have the strength. She put her fingers to her mouth instead.

"Dead?" she croaked as Morgan stood, dusting the sand from his hands.

"No. Sunstroke. He'll have to ride across the horse. That means you have to walk."

"Can't it, can't it carry?"

"No it can't carry double. It's a wonder it's staying on its feet itself. Get down, damnit, Beth. I haven't the strength to talk it out."

She slid from the gray's back, stumbling, falling to her knees. Andy and Shelter got Harry Channing up on the gray's back. He lay there inert, chalky, bloodless.

"Is he going to make it?" Andy asked.

"Maybe. Carrying that extra weight didn't help."

"Are *we*?"

"Maybe." Shell tugged Beth to her feet and looked northward. "It's a hell of a long way to the first settlement. If we could find some water . . ."

But that wasn't likely. They had carried their own water on the way south. Barrels full of the clear, cool water. Morgan's voice was dry, snappish.

"Let's get going. We'll never make it this way."

Each step took them farther from the Yaquis, from the *bandidos*. Each step took them nearer to exhaustion, to death. They walked on. The sun hung overhead and would not begin its downward flight. Shelter walked on, unthinking, his mind blurred by the heat. There was something nagging at his mind, something trying to get through, to make itself known, but it wouldn't come.

Beth kept falling. Half the time she leaned against Morgan, the rest of the time against the gray. If that gray went down they had all had it. Shelter couldn't carry Beth and Channing too.

Channing might have already been dead the way he bobbed and swayed on the horse's back like dead weight. Shelter didn't even check—there was nothing he could do for the kid anyway. Andy plodded forward, but her gait was slower, stiffer. Sometimes she veered to one side and then to the other. Her arms hung. Her ankles seemed loose, hinged the wrong way. The sun refused to go down.

"We're going to die," Beth said. No one argued. That about spelled it out. They watched the horizon, hoping for something, anything: a rider with a canteen, a settlement, the green of a tree. There was nothing. Only the endless dunes, the far-reaching salt playa, the distant, heat-veiled chocolate mountains.

Still something nagged at Shelter's mind, an unconscious knowledge. He couldn't clear his mind enough to focus on it. He thought only of placing his left foot, then his right. "A lot of good that does," he thought grimly. To die here or a mile on, what was the difference?

Andy went down to her knees. Then slowly she leaned forward onto her hands and stayed there, shaking her head.

"You all right?"

"What do you think, Morgan!"

"Get up."

"And if I can't?"

"You can, damn you, Andy!"

She looked up at him, at that face burned almost black, peppered with whiskers, the lips blistered and split.

"Sure," she said, and she got up.

She made it another ten steps. Then she went down, sat there, her head hanging, and said, "No more."

"You'll die."

"We're all dying anyway. Look at Channing. Look at baby. Hell, Morgan, look at you."

Shelter did. He slowly looked around him. The gray was on its last legs. Harry might already be gone. Beth was blind with exhaustion.

"Try, Andy. Get up and try."

"All right. One more mile. Walk the last mile." She was starting to rant. She got up but it was no good. Beth Channing keeled over and lay on her face in the scorching sand. Andy tried to tug her up and toppled forward herself and lay there, pawing at the scorching sand as she tried to right herself. Morgan lifted her and looked down into her sand-covered face. "Come on, tough guy," he said, brushing some of the sand away.

"You go on, Morg. Dump the kid. Take the horse and go on. You're tough, really tough. You'll find a way out."

"There is no way out." Suddenly the thought that had been trying to break into his consciousness made its way through and his head jerked up. "Andy—we've been through here! When the Apaches hit us. I know now. I saw the cairn that we built over Bo Channing's grave."

"Yeah." She lay there limp and frail, not knowing what he was saying. "You're right. I'm not so tough. You're tough, Morgan. Let me sleep. Nice and cool."

"Listen Andy! I'm going to leave you here alone for a while. Just a little while. But I'll be back."

"Nice and cool," she repeated and he laid her on the sand. Beth Channing was alive still, her heart fluttering wildly, but her breathing nearly peaceful. Harry was alive—but barely. Shell slid him from the horse's back and placed him with the women. The three of them looked like refugees from a graveyard. Lying in the sun like that wasn't going to help. He couldn't do anything about that.

"Come on." Morgan took the horse's bridle. "It's you and me, old-timer."

He started on across the dunes toward the playa, trying to find a landmark, trying to recall where he had seen the cairn. He was backtracking now, going south once more, cursing his mind for having played this trick on him. If he missed it now . . . and then he saw it. The cairn, marking the spot where Bo Channing had died. He remembered that day clearly, the Indian attack, the short battle, the Apache retreat.

Morgan walked due west. On the day of that battle he had had his own fight. A personal war with a single Apache warrior. It had happened right there, beyond the dunes . . . Shelter went to his knees, shook his head and came upright.

Right there. No, the sand had shifted in the storm. Over there. He got down to his knees again, this time on purpose, and started digging madly. The gray scented something and began pawing at the sand furiously, nickering wildly.

On the day of the battle Shelter had discovered a hat-sized, tiny spring, too small to help the stock of the Hart party, all of the people with the wagon train. But not too small now. It seeped up through the sand, staining it gray. Morgan put his face to the water, scooped some more sand out and watched the gray shove its muzzle into the spring, to drink greedily as Shell cleaned out the spring and clear, cool water came burbling up from beneath the sands.

It was slow to fill and refill, but Shelter drank all he could hold. He allowed the gray a quarter of what it would usually want, and no more that first trip.

Already, however, the horse looked more chipper. Shell, standing in the dry wind to wipe his eyes, felt alive once more. The perspiration cooled his body. His throat which had seemed clogged with sand for days was clear. He felt alive!

It was a long way to the border, but he thought maybe they could make it. Just maybe. There was at least a chance. He walked back to the spot where he had left the Channings and Andy Rice. He took the women first, loading them on the gray, trudging back through the hot sand to the spring. He placed them on the sand and scooped a little water in his hands.

"Andy?" He let a little water drip onto her mouth and she awoke instantly, her tongue darting out, seeking more precious moisture.

"Shell, is it real?"

He grinned. "Look over there. Fill up. Take care of Beth. I'll go back for the kid."

By the time he had returned with Channing, Andy was on her feet, Beth at least conscious and alert as she sat near the spring. Harry took a long time to come around, but gradually he came back. Nobody was going anywhere for a time though, and so they sat together as the sun finally, beautifully sank into night.

From time to time in the chilly, star-filled night, Morgan would get up and lead the gray to the spring, letting it drink again. The last time, an hour after midnight, he practically walked into the Yaqui.

Shelter had his rifle in his hands, and startled as he was, he was no more surprised than the Indian who had come looking for the waterhole.

The rifle blasted away the silence of the night and the Yaqui was hurled backwards to lie dead against the sand. Andy and Beth were on their feet. Andy had her Colt in hand.

"What in the hell happened?"

"A Yaqui." Shell was crouched over the body.

"Alone?"

"I don't know. Let's get up and get moving. Look back in there, Andy, he must have had a horse. Thought I saw one. Christ!" he said with disgust.

"What is it?"

Beth and Andy crept forward. Shelter had been searching the Indian's few belongings, wanting a waterskin if he had one, any food. He had found instead a sack which looked much like the ones Chavez had been using to carry his gold. When he opened it the head of Cord Levitt was looking back at him from within.

Beth turned her head away and was sick. Andy bit her lip. "They got 'em."

"It looks like it. If we don't want them to get us, let's see about getting out of here."

There was no telling if that Yaqui was alone or merely first to water. They found the Yaqui's horse—one of those abandoned by Chavez, and Morgan figured that with the border nearer, with them mounted and the Yaquis already victorious, there was a good chance that the Indians would give it up.

"Please," Beth was saying, "can't we hurry it up?"

"We're ready," Shell answered. "I wanted to fill the waterskin and let the other horses drink. Let's go. I'll ride double with Harry. All right?"

"Yes," Beth said, "but please let's hurry." Then with horror she saw Andy Rice pick up the sack with the head in it. She walked to the horse and mounted, beckoning to Beth.

"Let's go, baby."

"That—you can't take that with us!"

"Baby," Andy said, "that ain't a *that*. Not to me. That's proof Cord Levitt is dead. Baby," Andy said with a wink, "that is two thousand cash dollars!"

17.

"Well, not so tough after all, are you?" Andy Rice said as she entered the hotel room.

"It was a rough night," Shell grumbled.

"Rough hell, you haven't seen anything yet."

She banged the door shut and crossed the room to open the shades. Sunlight, hot, piercing, beamed into the Santa Fe, New Mexico hotel room.

"What're you doing up so early?" Shelter yawned.

"This is the day my money came in." She sat down and started tugging her boots off.

"They came through, did they?"

"What else could they do? I had the head. Two thousand. I took it in gold. Guess what else I saw?"

"I don't know." Shelter was sitting up in bed. Andy was unbuttoning her shirt and when she opened it, her round, full breasts came into view. She was smiling at him, damn her.

"Baby and Channing. Taking the morning train east."

"Good."

"How tired are you?" Andy asked as she cupped

her breasts and walked nearer to Shell.

"Not that tired now. You make a man work though, Andy."

"Do I? You love it." She slipped from her trousers. She had nothing on underneath. She placed one foot on the bed and guided Shell's searching hand to her warm, damp crotch. "Tired?" she murmured.

"Not at all."

"Then, damn you, get to it!" She laughed, whipping off the sheet. Morgan's erection was there, swollen, hot, ready, and Andy was on him in a moment, straddling him, leaning forward to flatten her breasts against his chest as her hips began to nudge him, to stroke and roll, encouraging Morgan's climax.

Shell lay with eyes closed, his hands roaming her strong body, hips and thighs, buttocks, breasts, throat, mouth, ears. Andy kissed his fingers in passing. Her body's rhythm was building, her pelvis thumped against his. Looking up, Morgan could see the concentration on her face. She bit her lower lip and looked toward the ceiling, beyond it, making small grateful noises as Shelter arched his back and bucked against her, burying his shaft to the hilt before he reached a sudden, hard, draining climax and Andy, grinding her body against his, touching Shell's pulsing erection with her own soft, open body, collapsed with a wet, quaking orgasm.

"Again," she panted. "Please. I don't have much time."

"You don't have much time?"

"No. Pat Dougherty."

"Who the hell is Pat Dougherty," Shelter asked, stroking her short dark hair as her inner muscles continued to work against him, to drain him. "Another lover?"

"There's just you, tough guy. Dougherty's a man with a price tag. Twenty-five hundred. He's supposed to be up in San Angelo."

"For Christ's sake, Andy," Shell said with some heat, "why don't you give this up! You've got the reward for Cord Levitt. Why don't you retire? Buy a dress shop."

"Sure. I will—if you'll retire, too, with me. You've got Cord Levitt crossed off *your* list. Why not quit?"

"You know I can't," he said and then there wasn't much more to say.

"They came when I was only thirteen, Shell," Andy said quietly. "They were Kansas raiders. They killed my mother and my father. They rode a horse over my little brother, crippling him. They took me into the barn and raped me then. They burned the barn when they were done—with me still inside. I crawled out through the smoke and I found my brother. I carried him away. The doctor, when I found one three days later, couldn't patch him right. He lives in a nursing home in St. Louis. A kid with crippled up arms and legs, with a face badly messed up. I need the money, Shell, to keep him. For the doctors and nurses. I need my revenge too—you understand that?"

Shelter just held her. He knew. He understood all about revenge.

He had dozed off somehow and when he awoke there was a note on the pillow next to his: "You slept past breakfast. I've gone out to get you some lunch. Back with it soon." It was signed, "Andy."

Shelter tossed the note aside and rolled over . . . and froze. The door to the hotel room had opened and without looking he somehow knew it wasn't Andy Rice. Slowly he shifted his eyes. He could see his Colt hanging in its holster across the chair on the other side of the room. Much too far away.

He heard the floorboards creak, saw a shadow touch the wall. Morgan sat up, lifting a defensive hand. The man in the room looked like a thing risen from a dark and horrible grave.

He was black, with patches of skin burned away, his nearly naked body clothed only in torn trousers, his flesh scabbed and bruised. His eyes were yellow, huge, crazed.

"I do not forget," the thing said. "You kill Bambo."

Then the African hurled himself at Shell and Morgan saw the butcher knife in his hand rise and begin its downward strike.

Everything happened at once. The African hit the bed, Shelter rolled, the knife flashed past his eyes and the big Colt spoke from the doorway.

The African lay still, his yellow, sun-maddened eyes twitching. Then the eyes stopped their movement and Shelter got to his feet to walk naked across the room to Andy Rice whose Colt still curled smoke.

"Damn," she said, "that one was for free."